CW00494645

The Anarchy: Slave To Fortune

Part 1

Reader discretion advised.

This is a story of the Middle Ages, a century before Magna Carta began to establish a legal code for the country and two centuries before the Black Death made working people more valued – and this only because sixty percent of them perished.
Human rights as a legal concept were not in existence.
Indeed, any example of simple fairness was appreciated, remembered and almost celebrated.
Peoples view of their world was utterly binary.
There was good and evil, rich and poor, the strong and the weak, the familiar and the strange – and strange meant dangerous to them.
Religious absolutes and superstition ruled much of their thinking.
All the discriminations that modern society decries, were the defaults in the Twelfth Century.

The year of Our Lord 1140 began with a blizzard; the following snows continued into March.

The winter's iron bleakness mirrored the conditions of the country's turbulent times; a civil war known as 'The Anarchy', with many factions fighting for the crown or position with any alliance that might win the conflict.

I myself had been a beneficiary of the troubles, though more by luck than by judgement...

As I gathered my cloak around me once more against the driving hail, I looked south to check my soldiers were not showing above the crest-line.

Satisfied with that, I turned my horse east to my future and my thoughts back over my past and of recent, almost unbelievable, change in my circumstances.

I, Walter de Marren, was born 21 years ago, to my mother, Elfleada and my master-blacksmith father, Guuste. He was of Norman extraction; my mother being a Saxon gentlelady with some land but no title. I was youngest of seven children, of whom only three survived into adulthood. Even as a youngster, I remember the harrowing grief that befell my parents as each loss occurred. My wonderful mother was perhaps changed forever by the death of the last one to go.

My grandfather had been in 'The Bastard's[1] cavalry when they came over in '66 and now my father was highly valued as armourer to Warwick castle; so, as an exceptional favour to him, I was appointed, aged 14, to be a squire to Roger de Beaumont, 2nd Earl of Warwick.
A tough six years followed; I grew taller and stronger, "looking more Norman each year" my father would say, with a touch of gruff pride.

The Earl Warwick broadly supported King Stephen but never burned bridges with other contenders and pretenders to the throne; in particular, he was rumoured to keep in constant communication with the Empress Matilda. But with Stephen's star currently in ascendant, I thus found myself with the other squires, guarding a dozen mostly piled-high wagons, somewhere in snow-covered Gloucestershire while a minor battle raged on the other side of our shallow valley. The knights told to do this duty with us had found it more compelling to ride to the sound of the trumpets; they abandoned us and the potentially vital supply wagons.
My instincts honed from many previous skirmishes and two battles, told me this was a dire position.
Left to be a juicy prize for enemy forces, or even supposedly friendly ones. As the senior, I ordered the twenty other squires to mount their horses, have helmets and lances in place (we had no shields) and then gestured for complete silence.

---

[1] William I aka 'The Conqueror'

A soft pounding of hooves and jingling of bridles could now be heard. The wind blew the sound away and then back, away and back again. Each return seemed louder, closer, seeming to come from the far edge of a wood to our north – the wrong direction for this to be our cavalry.

With hand signals, I had the squires form a line abreast facing the source of the sounds.

I stood up in my stirrups and checked behind us in case this was a diversion; seeing nothing, I committed to attack to our front. We had no advantage except surprise – and even to gain that required a gamble.

I listened intently to the noise of the approaching cavalry.

They seemed to be using the north edge of the wood as cover, where the trees were a little more spread out, about 400 yards away. This screened their movement to an extent but slowed them down somewhat.

Judging, or gambling, my moment, I signalled the direction to take and to have the horses begin a walk; signals followed to change our line to a vee, with myself at the point and to begin a canter with 200 yards to go.

As the first enemy became visible through the trees, I signalled the gallop.

The oncoming group of about sixty horsemen trotted out of the wood, to be met with a tight wedge of levelled lances at the full charge, voicing as much fighting fury as we could muster from our tender years.

My heart sank as I saw this was mainly a force of knights and not just mounted soldiers; now, as one, we all knew this had to be good or we all would die most painfully.

Caught unprepared, most of the knights wheeled their horses away to withdraw.

The nearer ones to me veered away, were caught sideways on and suffered accordingly from the lances on either side of me.

As the first few enemy cleared aside, I was suddenly facing the sight of a tall knight on a huge black destrier[2] - the most iconic image of awesome military might in our time. My arse contracted and my balls drew into my body. Time stood still, as I took in the shield with a single emblem, showing the highest rank of lord. This heraldic device was a black griffin on a scarlet background - symbol of William, Third Earl of Hereford, the most ruthless of any Marcher Lord, past or present.

As the distance closed, my world seemed to slow down, I saw everything, his shield ready to deflect my small lance, his bright sword raised high to cleave my head from my shoulders.
Death poised above me.
I shifted my aim as we closed and drove the point of my lance into the neck of his horse, immediately letting go of the butt, which swung down to the ground, widening the wound in the horse's neck. The animal reared to an enormous height, screaming in pain and terror. The rider snarled his fury, swung his sword as I passed but I was able to duck away from his now raised position. I wheeled my mount around to see his horse coming down from its rearing, my lance-butt had dropped to the ground, driving the tip clean through the poor animal's neck. Its instant death caused it to drop to the side with a thud, trapping the rider by the leg.

With my opponent down, I whirled my horse around to judge the state of my lads.
Their individual combats all now seemed resolved, one way or the other. We had three squires clearly dead on the ground, another couple nursing minor wounds. To my surprise we also had two likely dead knights and five unhorsed but alive, all moaning and groaning on the ground. This was in addition to 'mine', who was currently cursing us in Norman and French with a viciousness that seemed unwarranted, given his present condition of pinned-by-horse.

---

[2] a horse bred and trained for war

The squires were stopped, all looking frog-eyed at the knights.
I clapped my hands, my leather gloves amplifying the sound. They snapped their gaze in my direction; I signalled five to guard the knights and the others to circle our position.

The scouts quickly returned, reporting the enemy force had retreated. I posted four out to keep watch and turned my attention to our captives.

"Ask them all if they yield for ransom" I instructed my older squires.
The knights were stubbornly and sullenly silent, not wishing to surrender to mere squires.

The squires exchanged nervous glances.

"Show them steel like you mean it" I roared furiously.
Swords and daggers leapt at the throats of the various knights.
This produced an immediate and unanimous yielding.
I dismounted, had the knights stood up, gathered together and then I addressed them.

"You have asked for and been given pardon in the name of Earl Warwick".

"Break this pardon and you will die – we will ransom your bodies instead".

My mention of our lord's name and this very viable threat caused some gulping and a change of attitude amongst our captives.
My squires also seemed to gain something from this, a new confidence and in one or two, a pensive look across their faces.
To clarify for the slower ones and prevent arguments later I addressed the squires: "The loud one under the horse over there is mine, the others will be ransomed and the proceeds shared amongst you."

This further galvanised the outlook of the group, and in no time, the five live ones were on one supply wagon and the two dead knights on another - all ready to travel.

Lord William was still cursing and trying to free himself, just more slowly now as he tired. I walked over to him, stopped near and said loudly: "Sir Knight, do you yield?".

The man just grunted.

I wacked him on the helmet with the flat of my sword and repeated more loudly: "Sir Knight, do you yield?".

After a pause, an "I yield" came through gritted teeth.

I waved three squires over and indicated a very substantial fallen branch some yards away, at the edge of the wood. They fetched it back, drove it under the horse's body, just in front of the riders trapped leg. With a quick levering up, the hapless lord was able to squirm free and stand again, though clearly in some pain from fall. "I remind you sir; you are taken for ransom in the name of Earl Warwick". A curt nod was forthcoming. "Remove your helmet and coif[3] sir". He slowly complied, revealing a dark-skinned and scowling visage, with long jet-black hair, black eyebrows, beard and eyes. Those eyes, deep, dark, evil – projecting a malice beyond imagination. I remembered his alleged history and now understood that even the wildest stories could easily be true. I resolved to be on my guard at all times with this one, but on seeing his scabbard was empty I sheathed my sword. He turned to take in the wagon with the surrendered knights, who quailed under his gaze. "Cunts" he spat out and turned his back on them. "Are you the little shit that killed my horse?" he growled. "Yes," I said, "and that's 'big shit' to you sir!", we were much the same height after all. This bold response earned me a calculating glance... Godwin, one of the branch-wielding squires, squawked something, bent down into the long grass some yards away from us and picked up a sword. A very special sword; it had that silvery tone of the highest-grade steel some called 'Turkish'. Even my father was unable to produce anything like this – all our swords were a dull grey and liable to break after a few combats. The silvery ones were rumoured to be lighter, lasted better and would keep a finer edge. The cost and value of these was simply enormous. For just one second, I was transfixed by the sight of what must be Lord Williams sword, then from the side of my eye I caught a little shimmy in his arm nearest me. On full alert now, I pretended to be entranced by the sheen of that sword and beckoned Godwin to bring it to me, while easing one of my several daggers from its sheath on the right-side of my belt, the side away from William. I reached out my left hand, as if to accept the sword, then quickly used that arm to block the back-handed sweep of Williams knife, aimed at my neck.

---

[3] a coif is a chain mail hood

Acting on instinct I forced his right arm down and buried my dagger into his throat, till it stopped, lodged in some bone. He staggered back, clutching at his neck and making frantic gurgling noises. His eyes showed shock, then fury and finally fear before he fell flat on his back, shook in the body a few times and was still.

Not my first kill, but this certainly found me shaking afterwards…

One of the knights on the wagon stood and levelled an accusatory finger. I held up my hand to wave away his protest and shouted, "He yielded, twice, then tried to kill me". "Any trouble from you lot and the same fate awaits".

The knight sat back down and along with his companions, now seemed even more cowed by their experiences of the day.

Godwin was still standing there, holding the sword and rooted to the spot, looking open-mouthed at the very senior but very late Lord Hereford.

I took the sword from him with one hand and hugged him round the shoulder with the other, "Good job lad, well done!" I said.

He blinked and seemed to recover his wits.

I then noticed his scabbard was empty and gave him my (old) sword, for which he seemed very grateful.

"Now tell the others to search this place and scavenge saddles, weapons and anything of value, into another wagon".

He rushed away on his mission and I stood twirling my new shiny sword around.

Maybe an inch longer than my old one but still a little lighter, with the balance nearer the hilt, making it faster through the sweep and quicker on reversal.

What a find!

I relieved William of his fine leather belt and elegantly inlaid scabbard, finally sheathing my trophy sword on my side.

I waved the 'body wagon' over, to retrieve and carry that of William. While it was making its way, I recovered my dagger from its victim - very carefully and gently levering in the direction of the flat of the blade, so as not to bend or break the tip.

Once free, my dagger cut again and relieved him of the two heavy purses he carried.

A quick glance inside revealed many English silver coins in one and

French-looking gold ones in the other. Almost too much to take in, I was now wealthy beyond my dreams – except that another, better dream now occurred to me.

I called all the wagons together and brought in the look-outs. They reported much smoke from the direction of Gloucester, that implied Warwick's forces were victorious and likely they had forgotten about us, getting their supplies from that town instead. I weighed my options and decided to wait for nightfall.
If no word arrived from our last commander, we would journey the sixty miles home, taking the easterly route through Stow and Moreton as that region had more friends than foes. We couldn't risk waiting longer here, as our presence was known to some enemy forces at least.
At sunset, there was no word, so we set out as quickly as the wagons would allow. We made good progress by moonlight, the wheels rolling well on the shallow crisp snow.

The purses of the lesser knights bought us all a good meal of stew and bread from a farmhouse along the way. The horses too were all fed and watered.
We casually mentioned we were headed south to Salisbury but once out of sight, headed north-east towards Stow.
At midnight, I called a halt and we drove the wagons up a track into a dense copse. I risked a fire as we were very short of warm clothing and had half our small force on guard for an hour at a time before changing over.
None of us off-duty had any difficulty going straight to sleep.
The captive knights were watched but seemed resigned to their fate; the wagon bearing their erstwhile noble leader being a constant reminder to play by the rules.

After about four hours rest, I commanded a move out, I felt we really needed to be north of Moreton by next evening to be safer from possible pursuit.
There was some grumbling from my lads, but they stood to and got going in good order.
Luck was with us, the weather cold enough to keep most people

inside, with too much snow on the ground to allow any field-work but not enough to impede our horses and carts.

The low clouds thankfully held their contents all day and we made excellent progress.

Brief stops were made through the day for food, mulled wine and water.

A longer stop at a carpenter's cottage allowed the three carts that were carrying booty, bodies and noble prisoners to be converted into covered wagons; I wanted to hide our prizes from as many prying eyes as possible.

The tradesman was well paid and told to say, if asked, that we enquired on directions to "the London road". Our longest delay was at a small abbey. I bought three good coffins, had the bodies placed in them and bought preserving brandy, enough to submerge the corpses.

The abbot was requested (well, I paid him) to bless the departed and pray extensively for their souls through the coming weeks.

We had previously removed all tabards[4] and badges from the knights, whether dead or alive and hid all shields before we got there but... I had a feeling one of the assistant priests recognised William...

We made best speed through Moreton and on until just after dark.

The cloud thinned but lingered more this night, so the moon couldn't help us so much.

I found a track leading deep into the forest and directed all to go on as far into the trees as the track would allow.

With another squire helping, we used branches to sweep away the cart and hoof marks as best we could. Wouldn't fool a tracker or dogs but gallopers would miss it.

I was hoping the huge total worth of our prizes would cloud the judgement of any potential pursuers.

The wind was up and the night colder, so two fires were lit.

---

[4] a sleeveless jerkin, worn as an outer garment, usually displaying emblem and/or colours of the respective lord or sovereign

With having to stop earlier we got more rest this time, at least until the moon came out around four of the morning.

We packed up and pressed on all day, through a light dusting of snow to Warwick town.

As the castle became just visible in the gloomy distance, a squire was despatched to warn of our approach and also discreetly prepare for… guests.

I had no wish to cause an alarm at the castle and did prefer that a knight was there to receive our captives and further formalise their surrender.

After passing over the moat bridge and through the gatehouse, under both portcullis, we bore to our right, away from the main buildings visible across the huge expanse of the courtyard.

An army of masons and labourers were working hard on the curtain walls, all round the perimeter. This place never ceased to amaze me with its sheer size, even after years of living mostly there and seeing building works progressing. I dismounted, feeling very saddle-sore and awaited a party of knights, pages and minor ladies who rode over from the Great Hall.

I recognised the Warden amongst the riders - we exchanged a formal nod.

The riders parted and one emerged to the front.

To my utter surprise, there was Lord Roger himself, tall and broad, resplendent in black lacquered chain mail. Black hair cut short in the old Norman fashion completed his formidable appearance.

All the other squires immediately dismounted, the wagon drivers got down from their perches; thus we were correctly looking up at our feudal lord.

He addressed us with a firm, deep voice:

"Well battled squires, well done for protecting my supplies and acquiring such considerable prizes.", whilst waving an expansive arm in the general direction of the forlorn knights.

"You will take the deceased to the chapel, then escort your live… guests to eat with me in the Great Hall this evening – now tidy those wagons away" he continued.

This honour stunned all of us and as one we bowed, said "Thank you My Lord" and turned to take the carts over to the storesmen.

"Ah – not you Walter, you will join me in the Blue Room" said Lord Roger, while beckoning me to remount and join his group.

Though rather stunned by this turn of events, I managed to get on my horse without falling off and joined the rear of the group as they slowly rode their horses across the huge courtyard towards the Great Hall.

It was full dark by the time we reached the Hall.

Servants appeared from out of nowhere with reed torches lit to illuminate the steps. Stable-boys arrived to take all the horses away – including mine.

I managed to mumble something about my horse needing extra care, feed and water. The lad merely nodded while staring open-mouthed at the dirt and dried blood on the horse and then at much more of the same on me.

Following Lord Roger, we mounted the steps, went through the lobby and into the Hall itself. It looked like the evening meal was nearly ready as most of the tables were full of people sat waiting for service – that was until their lord appeared and they all sprung to their feet as one, the men bowing and ladies curtseying in his direction. He waved them all to be seated and all his party, bar myself, turned away to sit at their tables.

I followed him as he went across the Hall, through a doorway, turned right, went down a long corridor and waved a hand to stop me outside a blue door. I realised two guards had been following us and they took station either side of the doorway.

These were large and clearly very experienced soldiers, each wearing the Warwick emblem on their tabards with a visible pride. They both looked down their noses at me, as if to say "Who the fock are you, peasant" – even though I was stood there with the same, if very dirty and bloodied, tabard as them.

The devil in me made me smile, turn slightly to the right and with my left finger and thumb, casually lifted the silvery sword one inch out of my newly acquired and very ornate scabbard.

Two pairs of cynical, narrowed eyes suddenly opened wide.

A whispered gasp of "Fock!" came from them in unison – but before I could rag on them more, a commanding voice summoned me into the room.

I quickly unbuckled my sword belt and the more obvious dagger sheaths and went into the room.

I placed the weapons on a table just inside door.

You don't appear in front of a noble lord whilst equipped for war.

Stepping further into the room I saw it was not large but was very luxurious. A wood not stone floor, light blue tapestries that matched Warwick's shield lined the walls and a roaring log fire in the hearth opposite the door all made it feel very comfortable indeed.

Two bloodhounds lay at the sides of the hearth, briefly raised their heads to assess me, gave dog-sighs of disinterest and went back to sleep.

I took a deep breath and tried to align myself with this reality and away from the strains and jumbled images of the last few days.

Sitting in a high-backed chair to the left of the fire was Lord Roger, flanked by his two most senior knights, standing fully armed and armoured, either side of him. The lord regarded me with amused curiosity, meanwhile his hard-eyed companions were clearly reserving judgement.

I stepped in front of the chair (but not too close), bowed and said, "Squire Walter my lord".

Never one for casual conversation he said, "Young Walter, are you sure that's Hereford's blood you're wearing on my tabard?"

"Yes, my lord" I replied and gestured towards that sword on the table.

"By your leave sire?" I asked.

He waved permission and I retrieved the scabbard, being careful to hold it out flat, with my hand nowhere near the hilt.

Returning to my spot I knelt on one knee holding the item out and up for inspection.

One of the guardians stepped forward, partially drew the sword and paused for a long moment before (I thought) respectfully returning it home in the scabbard.

He silently nodded to Lord Roger and returned to his place by the chair.

I returned the sword to the table and went back again to my spot.

"If I may my lord, there was no doubt in his emblems, appearance and manner" I continued.

"So… you spoke to him before his… demise?"

"Indeed sire, he yielded twice, then tried to kill me"

The guardians gasped and looked at me now with frank amazement. Lord Roger merely chuckled and said "That does sound like bloody William."

"But how did you come to be… talking – about yielding? About anything?" he went on.

"I charged the squires at his cavalry force of sixty." I replied.

"I regret to say sire, our knights were… elsewhere" I said.

"That was indeed unfortunate" said Roger and exchanged a meaningful glance with one his knights, who nodded silently in response.

"But how did you… meet Lord William?" Roger continued.

"He appeared in front of my lance sire, in position and ready to kill me so… I killed his horse, it fell on him and I took his pardon – on your behalf my lord" I replied, bowing slightly.

Now all three looked at me with astonishment.

Lord Roger then thought for a minute or two, leaning forward, elbows on the armrests, fingers steepled as if in prayer but more likely calculating the politics and practicalities of the next moves that would be affecting us all.

I began to be a somewhat concerned; the convention at the time was that we squires had won our yielded knights, to do with as we wished – typically selling equipment unwanted by us, ransoming the bodies (dead or alive) and 'remembering' a better, more noble, death or capture story for those bodies (for a price). However, the legality of the situation was that we were in the sworn service of Earl Warwick, what we had was his…

I held my breath as my lord began his judgement…

"The squires will be rewarded as is customary" he said and I breathed out in relief.

"I know the liege lord of the five that survived and I'm guessing two of the dead." he went on.

"He will be reasonable, and the other squires will be well paid in silver" he said and then paused.

"Other squires?" I thought to myself, with doubts creeping back in.

"Your... prize is another matter entirely..." he continued.

"Do you have any plan for exchanging your... trophy?"

"I do my lord".

"Well it had better be a damn good one, else that black brood will surely kill you for the body and the making of the tale to wrap it in. Also, you can't be wearing my colours when you do this, it would be adding pitch to a fire..."

"Indeed sire".

"We," he resumed, indicating the three of them, "will view the bodies tomorrow before we break the fast – to confirm the identity that has... profound strategic implications".

"The squires will be summoned to the Hall later and my full announcement made – until then, not a word to anyone about this matter". I nodded respectfully.

One of the guardians bent down and whispered in Lord Rogers ear. He smiled and gently nodded.

"We are... curious to know... how much you will ask for the ransom?" he asked, clearly amused to hear a squire pluck some large number from the air.

"I was not thinking of mere coin my lord" I replied.

Lord Roger guffawed with laughter and the guardians looked again at me with surprise.

"By all that's Holy young Walter! You do your father and your Norman ancestors most proud! Such ambition, such awareness of custom and law," he said, looking at me now with narrowed eyes, searching my face and saying, "but yet... you don't feel... *bound* by any of it do you?".

That was not a question I wished to answer directly.

"I have given six years of, I hope, excellent service my lord. I have watched all, listened to most and learnt a great deal..." The Earl roared with more laughter even longer and louder this time, gasping for breath and wiping his eyes.

"By My Lady!" he gasped, "Walter, I hope we are never on opposing sides" he continued, after finally regaining his breath.

"But enough for tonight, join the others in the Hall and enjoy the meal. We will speak again in the morning".

"Thank you, my lord" I replied.

I bowed to Lord Roger, nodded respectfully to each guardian and walked backwards a few steps before turning, gathering my weaponry and exiting into the corridor.

I smiled and nodded at the door-guards, who now regarded me with clearly very mixed thoughts.

I made my way back to the Hall and this time the devil in me made me plant my boot-steps loudly and firmly on the stones of the corridor, at a very measured pace.

The trumpeter stood just inside the Hall, with his instrument poised at his lips, waiting to announce the Earl.

He drew breath as I arrived in the doorway and was just about to toot when he glanced sideways and saw...

That I was not Lord Roger.

He sharply whispered "Prick!" at me and relaxed to wait some more.

Many of the hungry diners were even less charitable, as they had seen the trumpeter prepare and had stood ready to greet their master – only to see a dirty and disheveled squire emerge from the doorway.

I merely smiled and waved them permission to go back to their seats, which caused more ribald comment and a few stale buns to be thrown at me.

I looked around for the squires and saw them sat at a table furthest from the dais[5], where the high table was laid out.

So it was true we were to eat with the Earl, just not at the same table.

Lord Roger arrived in due course, got his trumpeted entrance, took his place at the high table and servants rushed to present the first plates to all.

As squires, used to plain fare and not much of it, the meal seemed fabulous to us.

Several courses of meat dishes and two of sweet things.

And so much wine!

---

[5] A low stage or platform

We returned to our quarters and slept like logs – apparently no guard duty for us this night.

Next morning, after breakfast, the squires were summoned to the Great Hall.

The tables had all been cleared to the sides and we waited, standing awkwardly, facing the raised dais. This had the imposing, ornately carved, high back chair upon it.

Our weaponry removed and resting on a long table at the back of the Hall.

After some time, Lord Roger, his two senior knights, the Warden and some pages appeared from the wings of the low stage.

The Earl stood in front of his chair and addressed us formally.

"Squires, you have rendered me and my domains a great service this last battle".

"The ransoms will be paid to you in silver as soon as an exchange can be arranged".

There was much bowing and expressions of delight and "Thank you my lord" said in unison from the assembled squires.

"There is, however, one exception to this reward."

A gasp, again in near unison and nervous murmurings came from the young men. At a nod from Lord Roger, a very young page stepped forward and spoke out clearly.

"Squire Walter is called" and pointed to a spot on the stage, six feet in front of the Earl. After a moment of surprise, I willed my feet to carry me to the two steps up to the dais and forward to the place indicated. Just in time remembering to bow when I got there.

Seeing my thunderstruck face, Lord Roger smiled gently and spoke in a quiet voice, just so the group on stage could hear.

"Walter, we have viewed the departed – he was indeed William of Hereford" he said.

"I, or rather, we have thought long and hard on how to proceed – and we conclude that his kind will kill you at the slightest opportunity, if ransom is attempted" he continued.

"We have a scheme, which I trust will succeed."

"Very well my lord" I replied.

"Then listen most carefully young Walter"

I nodded and he waved the pages to the back of the stage; he continued, more quietly now, just so the senior knights and Warden could hear…

"Stratford-on-Avon is my most senior vacant title, when it is next granted, it will be for a period of one month and will not be sold, exchanged, given or passed by inheritance – do you hear my words?"

"Yes, my lord" I said, hearing of course, but not understanding a thing.

At some hidden signal, one of the knights gruffly commanded "Squire, you will kneel before your lord".

There was a gasp from the other squires looking on, as I dropped to one knee.

A bigger gasp went up as the other knight drew his sword, the metallic swishing sound magnified by the empty, echoing Hall.

The sword must have been passed to the Earl, as I felt a tap of the flat of a blade on each of my shoulders in turn.

I started shaking through my whole body…

Clearly and loudly, Lord Roger proclaimed "Arise, Sir Walter of Stratford."

I shakily rose to my feet and burst into tears of pride and relief and goodness knows what thoughts and feelings.

There was clapping and cheering behind me, a warm embrace from Lord Roger, also broad smiles from the previously dour companion knights and clear sign of water in their eyes too…

This wasn't an age that hid emotion; life was too sudden, brutal and often short to be too careful about anything. We deeply distrusted those who contained, concealed or rationed out their feelings.

In battle, we needed men alongside us who would commit to the death, without hesitation – it was often our only chance of life, and we knew it.

We couldn't take the risk on any half-measures at our side…

After much backslapping, congratulations and thanks exchanged, the Earl had the squires dismissed and invited me back to the Blue Room.

This time I went in with the Lord, winking at the door-guards as I did so, much to their consternation.

Goblets of wine were produced by servants and were drunk around the fire.

I sensed a very small feeling of camaraderie now existed between us men – but the dogs were still unimpressed by me, probably because I was still most scruffily and dirtily dressed.

After the wine-drinking, chairs were produced for all and the servants dismissed.
I was careful to sit down last.
Lord Roger was back to business.
"The squires..." he began, "how many will I lose when they become suddenly most solvent?"
"There are two who are really not best suited to the life my lord" I replied.
Then went on "The others all come from families who are struggling with debt, even if they have land – these troubled times have undone many people. So, they will be keen to stay in your service sire, knowing their families are secure."
Lord Roger nodded, then asked "And who should be my new senior squire?"
"Brooker is your man, sire" I replied.
"Is he not the er... short lad?"
"He is indeed the shortest of them all my lord, but he is also the bravest. An absolute lion in a fight." I replied and went on:
"He is also the most skilled in all weapons sir, except..." I hesitated...
"the longbow!" me and the Earl said, as one, laughingly.

Lord Roger dabbed his eyes from the laughter and gathered his thoughts.
"Now" he said, back to business, "the rest of the plan".
"After taking lunch, you will leave to take the body of William to Chester, where at least one of the dark-hearted clan will be in residence. To assist, I am giving you two dozen men-at-arms on horse and all will be in Stratford colours".
As I began to stutter my thanks, he held up his hand to continue.
"Do not be too grateful young sir, they will not be my best men and you will be paying them."
I merely nodded acknowledgement as his hand raised again, so he could continue.
"Additionally, I will assign you a Kings Herald - but for this journey

only"

I looked astonished, this was a huge and very real contribution. A herald was almost untouchable in our times, both by convention and in practice. They would wear the colours of the most senior member of the side they represented and be trusted messengers. Also, they acted as judges of fact and honest brokers between disputing factions, whether in war or peace.

So, I would be wearing 'my' colours of a senior lord, and alongside me would be a herald representing the King of England.

I dropped to one knee in front of Lord Roger, head down, arms extended, with hands together and sobbed – this man had given me both my future and a chance to survive it!

He stood, grasped my hands firmly between both of his for some moments.

"When you stand, remember you are squire no more - you are a lord, you should think as a lord and act as one, without fear or hesitation" he said.

Then, very quietly this time and with much emotion in his voice said "Now… arise Sir Walter".

I brushed my tears away and feeling quite… different now, I stood. I bowed low to the Earl and felt something or someone… new or maybe old, looking out of my eyes. My Norman ancestors? A spirit? I could not describe it, but it was there.

With this new gaze, I turned to each senior knight in turn and gave each a slow nod, as one peer to another. They returned my gaze and the slow nod.

I said "Good day my lords, I wish you well"

"God speed Lord Walter" they replied together.

I bowed again to Lord Roger, backed away a couple of paces and left the room.

On returning to the Hall I found a sergeant guarding my weapons. The only ones left on the long table.

I noticed his tabard was obviously new, with an emblem in blue, white, red and gold.

Two white swans divided by a blue wavy line were on the main shield of the badge.

I blinked as I remembered that Stratford was on a river and I guessed these were now my colours.

As I approached, he came to attention and said "Good morning my lord".

"Good morning sergeant" I replied.

"Your presence is requested in the armoury sir."

I nodded, gathered up my sword in its scabbard and the several sheathed daggers and we set off.

Once at the armoury, they requested I remove my very old and loose-fitting chainmail and leather under-coat.

Both had given me good service but were both desperately in need of repair.

Many missing links in the mail and tears in the leather meant these were not nearly as protective as used to be.

A linen shirt, a wool shirt, fine wool hose and a gambeson[6] appeared for me – all new. A screen was pointed out for me to change behind – another novelty to someone used to communal living.

With the new and expensive gambeson correctly laced and settled on me, the armourers sized me up by eye. They turned to some racks of chain-mail sets and picked one out. You just knew from the look and sound of it, it was expensively made. The links slithered smoothly over the arms and body of the gambeson and fitted very well first time. A coif was supplied, my first one. Also, a new helmet. Finally, a new tabard with my (loaned) Stratford emblem appeared for me to put on and a new black woollen cloak, with some sort of waxy coating on the outside – I guessed to keep the rain out.

I secured three daggers about my person and picked up my heavy leather sword belt (my purses being already discretely under my shirts).

The armourers' eyes were first drawn by the tooling on the belt, then they opened wide when they saw the embedded filigree on the scabbard.

Their jaws dropped when I slowly pulled the shiny sword from its sheath.

They quickly donned leather gloves and respectfully held their hands out to perhaps hold this rare and almost mythical item.

I allowed them to take turns to hold it, feel the balance and admire the finish.

They all muttered in breathless gratitude.

I then thanked them for their help, which seemed to surprise them.

In my new finery, I rescued the metal badge of senior squire from my old tabard and set off for lunch.

I went in the direction of the squires and senior servants canteen, until a discreet cough behind me from the sergeant redirected me to the Great Hall dining room for my soup and bread.

Afterwards, I had the squires summoned and paraded in the courtyard, facing away from the Hall.

I approached from behind them and they only saw it was me when I turned to face them. Their eyes popped and jaws dropped momentarily before they remembered their role.

"Squires" I said to them, "we have travelled far and fought bravely together. You have all done well. I move on now to other work and in my place as senior squire, Lord Roger calls..."

I made them wait...

"Brooker." I announced and stepped forward to pin the badge on his proud chest.

My last words to them were "Good luck and dismiss."

I sighed and turned away.

As if by magic, my horse was led up to me by a stable-lad.

It was saddled up, saddle-bags full of supplies for the journey and bedroll cinched to the back of the saddle. The animal looked calm and well rested as I stroked its nose. I mounted and walked the horse over to the Gatehouse.

Also, as if by a spell, there were my 24 men-at-arms, stood by their horses, all ready to go. One of them was obviously going to drive the two-horse covered wagon that was bearing the coffin, with his own horse hitched to the back of the wagon.

Another of the 24 was the sergeant, with one additional rider in splendid dress and mail, who was clearly the herald.

---

[6] A thin but heavy, quilted long jacket, densely packed with horsehair - think medieval 'Kevlar'

I was as impressed as ever by the organisation at Warwick.

This had all been quietly and efficiently arranged in not much time at all.

The men had been fed, as I could see one or two licking soup off their lips and beards.

At many other castles I had seen, there would be much shouting and running around, the plan would be hours behind schedule and every man would look like three pounds of shit in a two-pound bag. My men looked almost immaculate.

My men – what a change for me that was!

I nodded to them as I rode past, whether they made eye contact or not.

I reached the forward part of the formation.

"Good turnout thank you sergeant, we'll have half behind the wagon, half in front."

The sergeant seemed stunned by this small praise and managed a quick "My Lord" before moving to reposition the cart in the order of march.

I walked my horse on a little and introduced myself to the herald.

"Lord Walter of Stratford." I said.

He quickly mounted his horse and moved near enough to shake my hand.

"Percival, Kings Herald, in the service of Earl Warwick." he replied. Advanced in years with a white beard to show this, Percival nevertheless had a very firm handgrip. Wise grey eyes coolly met mine, assessing me no doubt.

Strictly speaking, I did, now, significantly out-rank him but the connections these heralds had were... difficult to ignore...

"Very glad to have you with us." I said, "Do you have a route in mind?"

"I do indeed" he replied, "North to Stafford, then on to Winsford and finally west to Chester. It's not quite direct but is much less risky than the shortest way. Probably five days with the wagon."

I gestured upwards with my arm, without looking behind to check if all had mounted – they better had.

I nodded to the guards on the gatehouse for the portcullis and gate to be open and we set off for Stafford.

Unbeknownst to me, my departure was witnessed from Caesars Tower.

Lord Roger and his senior knights quietly watched.

"He can certainly act the part sire – but can he see this through?"

"If he will listen to old Percival, I believe he can do it." replied the Earl.

Any independent observer of this scene would note the lack of any religious blessings from these hardened campaigners. We made good progress and the days passed quickly, the weather not too harsh.

I hired a veteran wagon-driver in Stafford, with no ties to the any region, he was just glad of a job. This freed up a horseman for a very low cost.

As Chester Castle came in sight, sitting proudly high on its hill, I sent two men ahead, to go into the castle and announce our arrival.

One man carrying a white flag with a black bar across the middle. Thus signalling our peaceful intentions and that we bore sombre news.

We drew near and the castle loomed darkly over us with storm-clouds overhead.

We paused before the bridge over the moat and waited for invitation from the gatehouse.

"Twenty-five with cart to enter." came from a strong voice.

We walked our horses across the bridge, under the portcullis and though two gates.

Turning slightly left, we halted between the well and the Great Hall. This meant we were still in the Outer Bailey[7], with the Inner Bailey closed off to us.

My men looked a little nervous, but I felt more curiosity than concern.

Percival had briefed me on the likely stages this would go through, so I felt ready.

My party dismounted but no one offered food or water, neither for us nor our horses. A page appeared, bowed and requested "The lords to please attend the Great Hall."

I had been advised to decline any invitations to tarry[8] for meals or divest of my arms, however charmingly these things were suggested.
So we entered the Hall with swords sheathed at our sides, my excitement increasing now.
The late Williams sword however, was temporarily on the hip of a very proud corporal, waiting with his horse outside. I thought it sensible to not wave that under the noses of potential mourners.

After shyly checking with us for our full names and titles, another young page announced our entrance.
A large man of around forty years was waiting for us in the middle of the Hall.
The page announced him to be Ranulf de Gernon, 4th Earl of Chester.
Dark of hair but greying there and in his beard.
Dressed expensively but not in a showy way.
His movement was a little awkward, probably from an old wound.
I instantly disliked and distrusted him, his eyes darted to mine and away – for a very powerful lord, he seemed very... furtive, certainly devious.

No handshake was offered by either party.
We exchanged no more than nods – this was clearly just going to be business.

---

[7] Aka courtyard

[8] To abide or stay in or at a place

His eyes flitted across my youthful face and proud (and rather senior) heraldry but made no comment.

He registered a slight reaction at seeing the Royal colours of Stephen on Percival's chest.

Little did we know how dangerous he would become to the King, starting in just a few short months.

He waved away the pages, leaving just the three of us in the middle of this huge empty space. This was a relief, as Percival had warned against confined places, or 'murder rooms' he called them.

"So..." began Ranulf, "you bring us William's remains?"

"I do sir." I confirmed with a grave nod and continued "He has been treated with honour befitting his station, correctly preserved and prayers for his soul made by the first abbot we..." stopping as Ranulf interrupted with

"Yes, yes – I'm sure you did him proud..."

Then with barely a pause said, "How much?"

I blinked once at this bluntness, but my face remained motionless, feigning near boredom, implying that this was a routine matter.

Without hesitation I said "I feel a man of Hereford's stature is nigh... impossible to value in mere coin..."

I was taking Percival's advice to use as few words as possible.

Ranulf rolled his eyes and gave a cynical smile "So a fief then?" he said.

I bowed my head very slightly to affirm this option.

"Hah! So be it." Ranulf responded, then turned his back on us without manners and bellowed "Gerald", very loudly.

After a few moments, an elderly clerk shuffled into view in the doorway.

"Fetch the roll of vacant title." Ranulf shouted and twice clapped his hands to underline his impatience.

"Yes my lord." said Gerald, in a shaky voice and shuffled out of sight.

Ranulf turned back to us and said "Deaf as a post and so bloody slow."

There followed a silent and uneasy couple of minutes as Ranulf was clearly no master of light conversation.

As Gerald reappeared, bearing a large scroll towards us, Ranulf clicked his fingers and said "Ah, I remember a waiting domain in Northumberland, huge place… "

Something made me glance past Ranulf at the slowly approaching Gerald.

He was subtly shaking his head…

I looked back at Ranulf as he continued his pitch, "…Yes simply huge, good place for sheep."

"How many serfs, sir, and does it have a market town?" I asked.

"Hmmm, not many peasants and no market town but it's very large.".

I did my best to look unimpressed, as if I had two like that already.

Gerald eventually shuffled past Ranulf and made as if he was going to read the list to us.

I beckoned him to merely unroll it and hold it out for me.

He unrolled it, reversed it and became as if a human lectern for me.

"You read Stratford?" said Ranulf in genuine surprise.

"I do." I said crisply, as if surprised at his surprise. In truth though, not many lords could read in any language and far fewer could write.

To be honest, I was not a great scholar, but my father had cuffed me until I agreed to take lessons from my mother. His reasoning being, as he had said, loudly and often:

"Your sword may win you three fortunes but the clerks, clerics and other men of letters will rob you of four!"

I started at the top, but my attention was soon drawn to Gerald's finger…

Tapping as it was, to one beginning with 'H' – his body screening this from Ranulf.

Our eyes met and he lowered his gaze twice, as if in affirmation.

I read the details, saw it was in Suffolk, far enough away from the centre of England to not be in the usual path of warring factions, yet not too isolated. It had a small market town, a modest castle and access to the sea through the river it was on – perfect!

I pretended to scan the rest and then rested my finger back on the 'H' one.

I confirmed with a glance at Gerald and he 'nodded' with just his eyes again.

"I will take Haverhill" I said with a conviction that my now excited and quivering body could barely manage.
"Haverhill?" said Ranulf, "Where the bloody hell is that?"
"In Suffolk my lord" replied Gerald as he rolled up the paper and bowed to his owner.
"It came to us in exchange for that..." he went on.
"Yes, yes I remember now, *I'm* not senile," said Ranulf, "why is it vacant?"
"The holder fell off the battlements while drunk sire, there were no heirs."
"I see..." said Ranulf, "hmmmm... that is far from any other holding we have, so I suppose I could let that go... now hurry along old man and get the deeds drawn up."

"My lords," he said, turning to us "you will give us an... accurate account of Williams demise?" more of a statement than a request.
Again I nodded in agreement.
Ranulf clapped again, called for chairs for us and a scribe to attend.

Once seated and the clerk ready at his tiny desk that had also been brought in, I began my (already practised) tale.
This was to be recorded in writing, signed or marked by those of rank present, with a wax stamp impressed with the Stratford seal ring supplied to me by Lord Roger and another (Royal) seal from Percival, as the witness to the now 'official' record.
All complete bollocks of course – just another example of the victors writing the history.
At least this time there was a huge prize for me, in exchange for the... improved account of the skirmish. And his family would have some solace from the telling.

I saw the clerks pen poised and began...
"The Earl of Hereford was in courageous defence of Gloucester town." I paused to allow this to be written.
"He seized a chance to counter-attack and led a noble charge

against greater numbers."

Pause.

"His proud destrier outpaced his companions."

"On reaching the enemy's line, he was surrounded by six knights."

"He slew four but six more arrived and the brave Sir William finally succumbed to his many wounds."

"He perished just as his forces swept the enemy from the field."

The formalities complete, we sat and waited quite a few more minutes, again in silence. Two copies of the Haverhill deed scrolls then appeared, one for me and one to eventually go to the Tower of London for Royal records of ownership – and consequent tax demands.

These now bore my name as title to that fief; I did my best to stop my knees shaking in excitement.

Ranulf, scribbled his mark on both documents, stamped the wax seal of each with his ring and stood.

Percival and I also rose, Ranulf handed me one copy of the deeds, we exchanged nods and we departed the Hall.

Business done.

I fought my urge to shout, scream, sing with delight!

Percival had drummed into me how routine this all had to appear.

I must play 'Stratford' to the finest degree, lest the brooding Ranulf realise he had given a valuable domain to a very recent squire.

This would have tested his black temper and may well have led to irrational actions.

The consequences would have been greatly disadvantageous to Ranulf in the long term but fatal to us in the short.

Well squire no more; I was now, in all truth, a titled lord and knight of the Realm.

All in exchange for a corpse and a good story!

Eight of Ranulf's men, all unarmed, came out to us.

I waved permission for them to take possession of the coffin of William.

They carefully removed it from the wagon, shouldered it high and slow-marched it with dignity, away to the Chapel.

Our sergeant had worked out the likely path they would take and had quietly called our men to line the route and remain dismounted.

We all stood to attention, helmets off, heads bowed until the coffin passed.

I cared not a jot for the black-hearted bastard but many people liked the formalities to be observed and seemed to gain some comfort from these customs.

With the coffin taken through the chapel door and on closure of that door, I signalled all to mount.

We walked our horses around the well and on towards the gatehouse.

Then I became aware of scuffling feet behind me. It was Gerald, his eye and the left side of his head now much bruised and slightly bleeding.

"My Lord Stratford" he called, his voice shaking.

I raised an eyebrow as my only reply, while continuing to walk my horse.

I was instantly on alert for a trick.

Puffing and blowing while rapidly shuffling to keep up.

"I am dismissed sire," he gasped, "I dropped some ink on Lord Ranulf's shoe."

"What do you bring me, man?" I asked.

He tapped his forehead and said "A reeve[9] for over twenty years sire, a vast heraldic knowledge of all England – and... who owes what to whom..." he panted out.

I considered that he could be a spy, but if so, I would wish to find out Ranulf's purpose before I... parted company with him.

I waved him away and merely said, "Join the wagon, we will talk later."

"Thank you, my lord" he said and waited, gasping some more, for the wagon to draw level, which he then managed to scramble on to.

---

[9] A warden or administrator for a small or medium size domain

We made our leisurely way through the gatehouse, turned east and continued at a slow pace until fully out of sight of even the highest watcher on the castle.

I halted at the next crossroads and made some quick adjustments.
I exchanged swords with the corporal again, much to his disappointment.

I had one of the wagon horses untacked from the yoke and beckoned Gerald to mount it. He looked puzzled, especially as there was clearly going to be no saddle but you do not quibble with a feudal lord.

I dismissed the driver and paid him off by gifting him the wagon and the remaining horse. His final task for me was to drive the cart to Winsford and then he was free to do as he wished. He was shocked - utterly shocked. In his mind, I had made him wealthy – with no understanding as to why. But again, no querying of a lord.

I mentioned that we were taking the road to Stafford and waved him on his way. I then waved for my troops to move out and on down the Stafford road to the south.

With the wagon well out of sight, I reversed our course back to the cross-roads.

I sent a rider back to scout down the Chester road to report any forces coming our way.

He returned and said none were seen.

By now, my soldiers were looking a little puzzled but yet again, no questions.

I could see a twinkle in Percival's eyes, he knew exactly what I was up to and why. Now that Ranulf had Williams body and the official 'death story', the deed in my possession was all I had as title – the ultimate bearer bond. Kill me, take the deed back and Ranulf is ahead of the game. My demise could always be blamed on renegades, bandits, etc.

With that in mind, I now waved them the opposite way from Stafford, heading for Northwich. Adding at least two days to our journey but hopefully much more to my life expectancy!

I galloped them for three miles, walked three, cantered for three more, then rode into some dense forest, away from the road, to hide in.

I sent men out to find water and a good stream was found a couple of hundred yards away. I moved our party to near the stream and set up camp, as we were losing the light now and all were hungry and becoming chilled.

I made a circle in the air for the sergeant, he nodded, sent lookouts to take the first watch and ordered others to get some fires going. We only had stream water to drink, warmed in a pot over a small fire, with our dried food to eat but all felt better for it.

My squire's habits hadn't completely left me, I woke three times in the night to check our dispositions, alertness and sentry rotation — which all stayed good throughout.

The men nodding to me silently while on watch, as is correct.

First light found us ready to travel and put some more good miles in before a hot breakfast at an inn on the main road.

Again we mentioned some more northerly destination, before heading east.

Avoiding any large towns before Stafford, we eventually made our way back to Warwick a few days later.

I said thanks and farewell to Percival, warmly shaking his hand.

He waved away my offer of payment, saying he had had some good entertainment and in any case, he was under retainer to Earl Warwick.

He watched us a while, before finally heading into Warwick's gatehouse as we set off for Stratford-on-Avon, my domain — well, for another couple of weeks or so.

I thought for a moment to visit my parents but a glance at the position of the sun meant there would only be time for a ride-past. Something my father would certainly enjoy but my mother would be upset if I couldn't stop for a while.

So sadly, time was against me and I had no wish to be caught on the road after dark in these dangerous days.

We arrived, having travelled the next ten miles, to one of the smallest castles in the land. A wooden palisade, visibly rotting in places, surrounded the bailey.

This view alone, confirmed to me that a senior title alone was no guarantee of great fortune; because land, revenue and wealth could be lost much more easily than acquired...

Central to the bailey was the mound, with its Keep rising from it. At least the original wooden structure of the Keep and been replaced with stone – but it was all so very... small compared to the hugeness of Warwick. The moat appeared in good order, deep and clear of obstruction but I was not impressed with the rest, it seemed to have fallen into disrepair, even since I last saw the place.

Our party looked to have doubled the strength of this small fort, in fact it was difficult to find stabling room for the horses and floor-space for the men.

Sunset was soon upon us and a quick glance at the gate showed me it was still open to the road. A quick gesture to my sergeant and some words of wisdom from him caused the rickety drawbridge to be raised and the gate closed, all in double-quick time.

The evening meal was a communal stew with some beer[10], so all were full and happy by bedtime.

I placed an extra sentry near my sleeping area, as I still had doubts concerning Gerald.

He did look utterly exhausted from the journey but still...

Again I checked through the night, that sentries were alert and relieved at the correct intervals and we survived until another dawn. Next morning, I announced a rest-day for my 24 men and then would be on our way again.

I didn't say where we were headed – and no one asked.

I took some men into the nearby village, bought some fresh supplies, particularly of river-caught fish and had them delivered. Morale improved and even Gerald began to regain some colour in his face.

So the following day and we're mounted up, ready to move out at dawn.

I had discussed our route with Gerald, as no extra risk accrued, he

---

[10] English beer in this period was made with herbs rather than hops

more than anyone knew my intended destination.

I was aware that Suffolk lay to the east but no knowledge as to which domains were currently loyal to Stephen and hence on Warwick's (and my) side.

Without Gerald, we would have had to go by back roads and forest tracks and that would have taken a month...

Gerald knew much about all the holdings of interest.

He enthusiastically spouted the list of Kings-men along a northerly route of main roads via Rockingham and Cambridge but warned me to avoid Huntingdon and its surrounds at all costs.

"How long to Haverhill?" I asked. "Six days my lord" he replied.

As we approached each sizeable town, I sent two riders ahead, without their tabards, to see which emblems and loyalties were evident.

We then waited in discreet hiding for their return.

After the first few, it was evident that Gerald's predictions were accurate. There remained the fact that he only needed to tell me wrong once, by accident or design but I decided now to only scout those domains with major castles.

For the villages and minor towns along the way, my plan was to make a show of force with colours on show, be robust if challenged and punch through any opposition if it emerged.

We were made very welcome in Rockingham for the night.

Then next day, travelled well, going ever eastwards, spending two more nights in dense forests.

Our progress slowed next morning however.

In carefully threading our way on lanes and tracks between a definitely hostile Huntingdon and an unknown St Neots, we lost half a day in marshy ground and finding a path between various lakes across our route.

But we made Cambridge just as the sun was setting.

The castle was not large but immaculately organised and maintained, with the drawbridge just about to go up for the night. Luckily the elderly and strict sergeant on duty recognised my colours, called me forward to ask some searching questions on our origin and purpose.

It helped greatly that Gerald had previously told me the fief-holders name and distant relationship to Lord Roger.

My party was allowed in four at a time, to then dismount and tie-up our horses.

I couldn't help noticing there were at least thirty archers on the battlements above us, arrows nocked and ready to draw.

The inherent risk of arriving at a fortified position near dark.

The sergeant noticed me, noticing the archers and we both smiled widely.

I shook his hand warmly and thanked him for taking the time and trouble to peruse us and not tell us to "Fock off till morning!".

He laughed loudly and said in his gravelly voice "You are welcome young sir, come and meet Lord Randall, he will be eager to hear stories of the war in the west."

Sir Randall Brereton was a very generous host.

We had a meal of three courses of various meats and one of something sweet.

Much beer was drunk, the log fire kept well supplied and tall tales told.

The men were being well looked after elsewhere, so I was relaxed and content.

Not so relaxed that I didn't notice how very... friendly the lord was becoming as the evening wore on, also that all the servants were young men...

"Ha" I thought to myself "at my castle, all the servants will be wenches!"

What an idea! 'My castle' – could it really come true?

The evening drew on and we all collapsed to sleep on the floor, my head resting on my cloak rolled into a pillow.

My sword was underneath me and sheathed daggers to hand.

The priceless deeds were in a small leather tube strapped under my tabard.

We awoke with the sun and blearily staggered out to the bailey.

A suggestion of breakfast was waved away by all, as we pointed our buzzing heads towards the stables.

Our horses looked well rested and fed but also sober.
So with waved thanks and farewells, we clumsily mounted and walked our horses through the gate, over the drawbridge and turned east once more.

I looked back at the men, a few had their helmets on backwards or their tabards inside out but all were present at least.
We had gone about forty yards when one had to quickly dismount and heave up his stomach on the bank of the moat.
This was a cue for much unsympathetic banter from the tower guards looking down from across the water.
"You can fockin clean that up!" and
"Don't you honk in our moat, you donkey" amongst others were heard.
The man remounted, groaning and we travelled slowly on.

I spotted a tack-shop on the outskirts of Cambridge and bought a simple saddle for Gerald's horse, as I believed this was the least I could do for him, as all his help had got us to this last leg of our journey.
He was delighted and effusively grateful, I think he'd been suffering somewhat.

We stopped for water, a lot of water, in the next village with a well.
I halted the column for a few more minutes for pissing, stretching, sorting the mens' dress and then moved on with more purpose.
We made reasonable progress on various tracks and lanes.
The signposts then became fewer, even milestones became rare as the width of the lanes narrowed.
In some places we guessed direction at forks in the road, aiming by the position of the weak sun that was trying to shine through the thin cloud...

By chance we came to a tiny inn, sometime well after midday. They supplied a remarkably good rabbit stew and a small ration of beer was allowed.

Most were by now able to eat something and of course the beer whistled down.

After more miles and with the sun now lowering behind us, we crested a small rise and saw a small town in front of us.

My sergeant spotted a rotted wooden sign that had fallen over into long grass.

"Haverhill, my lord" he announced.

I nodded and turned to the soldiers.

"Our destination men!" I shouted.

Cue some ragged cheers and muttered "Thank focks!"

We now sped up to a trot, into the town, all putting on a swagger – to not much result.

For the size of the place, there were remarkably few people about and many seemingly abandoned houses. Even those buildings around the market square looked gloomy.

I was all too soon to discover that the fallen name-sign and dismal appearance of the town were harbingers for my whole domain...

We slowed to a walk again, past the church on its small rise at the end of the main street. As an imposing Norman stone-built edifice, this church gave some feeling of importance to the town at least.

Then, the castle came into view, about a half-mile ahead.

Sitting on another, larger rise, with the river winding around behind it and the moat girding sides and front.

With the walls and Keep illuminated nicely by the low evening sun, you could see it was a good size and very well positioned.

To me, it looked magnificent – from this distance...

As we approached, my previous good impression faded more and more.

It was a complete and utter shithole.

But... it was, at least, my shithole.

The walls looked basically sound but had many clumps of grassy weeds growing and birds-nests sticking out.

Both these things revealed that chinks in the mortar were present and so the walls could potentially be climbed; typically with sharpened pegs being pushed into the large cracks, thus creating a form of ladder for more following-on soldiers to climb.

The moat was stagnant and choked with reeds, It looked to be only knee deep in places, if that.

The drawbridge was lowered but appeared rotten in part.

All the walls were un-manned, in spite of the approach of an armed party; the portcullis was raised, and the gates were open.

I signalled to spread the column out, in order to not overload the drawbridge.

Then we walked the horses over the moat and through the gates.

I closed the column up once we were in the middle of the bailey.

And

Still

No

Challenge!

My fury grew and grew.

Even a senior squire would have words to say about this, but I was now the feudal lord and I felt the temper of my Norman ancestors rise within me.

Some men with an appearance of soldiery were lounging around, leaning against the walls and chatting.

One or two waved to us!

This was too much for my sergeant, who raised a thunderous voice, stronger than I had heard him use before.

"Form a line and stand up straight you bunch of whores gets[11]".

---

[11] i.e. the off-spring of sex-workers

With much flustered trotting and tripping, a ragged apology for a line appeared where the sergeant had indicated.

Some of the twenty or so were swaying on the spot, clearly drunk. The sergeant dismounted, handed off his horse to one of our soldiers and proceeded to inspect the loose row of local men. "I've seen a dog piss in a straighter line that – check to your right". The soldiers turned their heads and adjusted their alignment – a bit. For one, the sudden head movement was too much, and he fell flat on his back, remaining there, snoring.

"Now then! Who am I?" boomed the sergeant.

"Don't know sir" said one, timidly.

"Sir? Sir? Do I *look* like a *fockin* sir?"

"Errrr no sir. Errr no I mean" stuttered the unfortunate one.

"Give me strength!" the sergeant went on and tried another approach.

"Who are... we? He yelled, using an expansive gesture to indicate myself and the column of mounted soldiers in their bailey.

"Dunno ssss... Dunno" said another.

"And WHY don't you FOCKIN know?" yelled the sergeant, having now found the resonance of the courtyard, he used it to amplify his volume to a truly shocking level.

No answer this time, from the line that was visibly shaking in its boots.

Suddenly, the sergeant started speaking in a normal voice, man-to-man, in a fatherly tone – this change being as much of a jolt as the volume that came before.

"You don't know, because no one was on guard and the gate was left open".

"Half of you are pissed and the rest might as well be".

Going slightly louder, he finished with "May I introduce your liege lord, Sir Walter of Haverhill" and bowed in my direction.

I acknowledged his bow with a gracious nod and a less gracious nod at the various bows from the ragged line, another of whom fell over and crawled away to be sick.

I dismounted, handed my horse off and looked around with disapproval and disappointment.

The place smelt as bad as it looked.

Four of my soldiers immediately dismounted to close up on me as I walked away from the column, past the line of locals and towards the Keep - hoping to find someone with some authority and hence responsibility for this farce.

As I reached the bottom of the wooden stairs to the Keep, another soldier stumbled down them.

He must have heard something from before as he smiled a stupid smile, slurred "Welcome, welcome your lordy-ship" and went to throw his arms around my neck.

He also, then fell to the ground.

The difference was, this one was dead, the hilt of my dagger visibly protruding from under his chin.

A gasp went up from the courtyard.

I sensed the soldiers from Warwick now sat or stood up straighter, looked sterner, looked more alert.

If they had any lingering doubts at all, concerning my apparent youth, my character, or recent elevation, they now knew *exactly* who they were serving.

I was told later that two of the locals pissed themselves at the sight.

I stepped over the late, late-comer and went up the stairs.

Pausing at the top of the steps, I turned, looked at my sergeant, looked at the gate, then the battlements and back to the sergeant.

To the puzzlement of the locals, he simply nodded, said "Yes my lord" and raised his voice again.

"Right you shower of shit. SECURE THE CASTLE – MOOOVE!"

The locals rushed around like chickens trying to escape a fox but slowly began to raise the drawbridge, drop the portcullis and finally get the bloody gates closed.

Meanwhile, two of my 'Warwicks' went looking for stabling, two more for water and food and the remainder manned the battlements.

They knew by instinct that my party would search the Keep, it was a routine we'd all done several times for Lord Roger, in different places. I drew my sword and my soldiers followed suit.

With the light fading outside, it was very gloomy through the door of the Keep.

Just down the corridor, a door on the left opened. My men spread apart as far as the confined space allowed, with one watching to our rear. A woman came out through the doorway, accompanied by a strong smell of vomit and worse.

She was startled when she saw us, my drawn steel shining quite evidently, even in the dim light.

"Do not be alarmed... miss" I said.

"We are not here to sack the castle, merely take ownership!" I laughed.

"I am Lord Walter of Haverhill; I have taken possession of this fief as granted by Lord Ranulf of Chester" I continued.

She quickly regained her composure, realising that she wasn't going to be cut down – well, not immediately anyway.

"Good evening, my lord" she replied, as she bobbed a slightly unsteady curtsey.

"I am Lady Eede de Brus of Lochmaben." She went on:

"I'm afraid you catch us... unprepared – for almost anything."

"I regret that the late Lord Hugo was not... careful with his domain".

Then she hiccupped, burped and swayed a little.

From her dress and manner, she was clearly all of a lady – but also rather inebriated.

"My lady" I asked, "it is early in the evening but seems everyone is... drunk?".

She hiccupped again and giggled before answering.

"So true my lord" and giggled again.

"You see, there is no water; the well collapsed last week and no stone-mason will attend to repair – there are many, so many bills out... out... to be paid." And burped again.

"But thanks to Hugo, there is LOTS of beer!" she finished, smiling wide.

"I understand my lady but who is in charge here?" I said.

"Ahhh... no one at present my lord – the warden and both sergeants lie sick abed", she waved at the doorway to indicate where they were.

I had to check, so I gently moved her aside, took and held a breath, then kicked the door open.

A wave of stench greeted me, as I surveyed the small room, floor to ceiling with my sword ready.

Lit by a couple of small candles, the three sufferers lay on rough beds, one groaning, two lying still.

I closed the door and said quietly "Will they live?".

"God willing", she replied "but I have no more water or honey for them now...".

I nodded grimly.

"Stay here till I return" I instructed.

I turned and said "Light torches" to my men.

"None seen my lord" they replied.

In exasperation I turned to Lady Eede.

"The reed-man also left some time ago..." she sighed.

My men shuffled down the corridor into the darkness.

"Two part-torches here my lord", said one, "A half-one here sir" another said.

Flint and steel sparked in the blackness.

One reed torch sprang to light and would have to do for the moment.

We trotted down the first stairs we found, down two floors to the dungeons and cellars.

The cellars were quickly searched.

Many a counterattack has been launched from the depths of a Keep or tower.

We could not leave this duty to chance, in spite of the unlikeliness of it here.

The door to the dungeon was kicked open and a tall and rather portly jailer seen, carving a wooden religious item by candle-light.

He sprang to his feet at our entry and was quickly searched for arms by a soldier.

"Good evening jailer, I am your Lord Walter – do you have any... guests?"

"Good evening my lord, I am Milo" he replied, "and the cells are empty".

My men checked and confirmed.

I was about to leave when a thought struck me.

"Milo" I said, and he drew himself up straighter.

"Yes my lord?"

"You are... not drunk"

"Errr... thank you my lord."

"Why are you not drunk?"

He was silent with his eyes darting from side to side.

"Well?" I said, much louder, slapping the flat of my sword on my bootleg in frustration.

"It's a secret my lord." he whispered.

"Bloody hell man, you can tell me, I own this bloody place!"

"Lord Hugo made me promise not to tell, on pain of death".

I whipped my sword, up and round to cut his neck just under his ear.

"Then die to protect the secret!" I snarled.

"Nooo! Wait!" shrieked Milo in terror and locked his eyes on a large cupboard, that was let into the wall of the dungeon.

I tipped my head that way for a soldier to investigate.

The cupboard door opened to reveal in the flickering torchlight...

A windlass with handle, with its rope and bucket in good order, poised over a well. Possibly the only thing in this godforsaken place that looked capable of functioning!

With the main, much larger well out in the bailey, a second well in the Keep was not unusual if it could be dug successfully. The aim was to have a last-ditch ability to withstand siege in the Keep, until help arrived.

I just sighed, partly in relief and partly in puzzlement.

As a besieger, I would always assume there was a well available unless I knew otherwise; no real need for secrecy at all.

I began to wonder at the sanity of the late Hugo...

"There will be visitors to the well Milo, and you will assist the Lady Eede in any matter she requests unless you have prisoners to look after."

"Very well my lord" said Milo, still shaking and bowing as we left.

We searched the next basement floor up – two empty storerooms, one full of sacks of grain, another full of beer barrels; many of them with corks removed and empty.

I returned to Eede, gave her the precious news about the well and with my men, continued to search that floor and the three above.

All the rooms were empty and abandoned, dusty and cob-webby, as if the inhabitants had suddenly been spirited away one night.

We emerged wearily on to the battlements, just as the last torch sputtered out.

The door to the fresh air initially stuck fast; so obviously had not seen recent use.

We sheathed our swords and looked down on the bailey

We could see the castle was now properly locked up, with men on watch atop the small towers of the curtain wall.

I shouted down to the small figure of my sergeant "Keep is secure".

"Yes sir" he shouted back.

I pointed to two of the soldiers and to two of the corners of the Keep.

They nodded and moved to take guard duty.

"I'll send up your cloaks and food soon, relief in two hours " I said, then chuckled and added "and there'll be some water as well".

"Thank you, my lord" they replied with smiles.

No one had eaten since lunch and that was beginning to feel like a very, very long time ago...

We found some more bits of torch and I ambled downstairs to see Eede with a servant girl who had suddenly appeared from goodness knows where.

The girl had a pair of milk-maid buckets and they were just setting off for the dungeon, lit by a candle that Eede was carefully nursing.

We exchanged nods and I told her that the jailer was to assist her as required. She nodded again, in appreciation.

I walked out into the less-fresh air at ground-level and sat on the steps of the Keep, suddenly rather tired.

I waved my two remaining guards to sit as well.

My sergeant came over and reported.

"Castle secure sire; stables in good order, feed for the horses adequate and the trough has enough water for tonight – but only just."

"Bad news about water my lord" he continued, "the well is fock.. er sorry sir, the well is badly stove-in and unusable; no food found, other than in our packs sir."

"Thank you sergeant" I said, "Luckily, there is a another well in the dungeon."

I went on: "Send some food and water up to the top-guards."

"Oh, and their cloaks too."

"Change all guards every two hours and let the corporal give you a rest in turn"

"Yes my lord" he replied.

I paused for thought, took a glove off and rubbed my forehead.

"Orders for tomorrow," I went on:

"At first light, send four Warwicks and a local to the town and come back with a baker."

"We have plenty of grain here but tell him to bring any other... bits with him"

"Tell him we have coin to pay him and if he is any good, he can stay here"

"If he's busy, well, just convince him" and we exchanged a look.

"Also first thing, send a hunting party to the forest – if we can eat it, they bring it back."

"Finally, have an escort of six Warwicks ready to leave for Cambridge after breakfast"

"Purpose is to take Mister Gerald there, return the next day"

"Understood my lord but that leaves us a bit thin..."

"Agreed", I sighed, "but we must have some artisans here, and soon."

"Very well my lord" he said, nodded, turned and set off to delegate my instructions.

I saw Gerald out in the bailey, the elderly chap slumped in his saddle, looking almost asleep.

I waved and he didn't see me.

A passing soldier helpfully slapped Gerald's leg as he went by.

Poor old Gerald jolted upright and nearly out of the saddle, looking around with alarm.

I beckoned him over and he walked his horse over to the Keep, stopping near the bottom of the steps, looking down on me as I sat on a step...

I heard my guards behind me tutting at Gerald and felt the wind of their gestures for Gerald to dismount.

He finally grasped their meaning, got down off the horse and then wobbled down on one knee, saying "Sorry my lord".

"You may stand Gerald" I said.

"Tomorrow you will go to Cambridge with an escort."

"See me after breakfast for instructions"

"For tonight, look after your horse, eat from your saddle bags, water will be available soon – then get some rest".

"Yes my lord" he said with a very tired voice and turned away.

He turned back to me and, with more conviction said "Thank you for my... position sire and good night"

"Good night Gerald" I said.

I walked across the bailey, still with the two guards attending.

I checked in the stables, to see my horse was taken care of, then unstrapped my bedroll and saddlebags.

I looked back across to the Keep, now all dark and foreboding except for some flickering candlelight occasionally visible when anyone fetching water opened the door.

I decided to bed-down with the men, it would be easier if there was an alarm in the night and would keep our sword-power closer together.

Question was, where were they?

I took a guess, based on where I would have chosen and headed for the largest of the buildings that adjoined the curtain wall.

Yes, there they were, well those off duty anyway, bedded down on the floor of the Hall.

Actually, this place looked to be in fair condition – and didn't smell too bad either.

I grabbed a straw mattress from a pile by the door, picked a spot on the small raised dais or stage thing and sat down cross-legged.

My guards stood close but not too close as I ate some bread and hard cheese from my saddlebags. I drank the last of my water from my goatskin carrier and lay down to rest.

What a day! My thoughts a jumble for a few moments and then blissful sleep.

I woke sometime after midnight, as is our custom in these times; found and used the midden[12] near the kitchen, then returned to my bed for a second sleep.

I next woke some two hours after dawn – just as well I was the lord around here.

The smell of fresh bread drew me from my bed.

A makeshift table had been set up near the kitchen door and my soldiers were taking turns to get big chunks of warm bread and what looked like a dollop of butter.

I went to get my share and the lads gave way to my outstretched hand.

We shared "damn this is good" smiles and nods.

I swallowed the last of my bread and saw the sergeant standing nearby, looking my way.

I waved him over and we both sat on the edge of the small stage.

"A quiet night my lord, no incidents" he began, "We have found some mixed stores in various places."

I gestured for him to go on, still savouring the last of my bread that was stuck in my teeth.

"We have at least eight dozen Haverhill tabards, most in good condition – looks like this place once had a full complement..."

"There are thousands of longbow arrows, they appear to be like new – but no bows, neither long nor short, not one, anywhere!"

I slapped my forehead at that. Longbows were rare, expensive and hard to find archers who could use them.

"Anything else?" I asked.

---

[12] Medieval toilet and/or refuse chute

"There were twenty-one local soldiers here when we arrived, you dealt with one sire, there were four others unfit for your service and have been discharged."

"So... we have an able strength of forty..."

We exchanged a look, both knowing that was very light for a place this size, especially with no archers – or bows.

I raised my eyebrows to question if there was more.

"There is a fine wood store sir, plenty of pitch, huge quantity of rope – in all sizes and a large stack of candles was found under some old grain sacks".

"But no horses apart from ours, no tack, salt, sugar, no fresh food, no preserved food".

"The only weapons found were some lances, all in fair condition, various weights and lengths."

"The hunting party has left sir; they may have trouble without bows but they know there's no lunch if they come back empty-handed."

"And the escort is fed and set to go when Mister Gerald is ready."

"Thank you sergeant" I said "tell Gerald to meet me in the Keep. The room opposite the sick-room."

"Yes sir" he said and left on his errand.

I walked across the bailey, followed by my two guards, our breath all misty in the crisp morning air.

I noticed the place was beginning to smell... well, less badly.

Up the steps and into the Keep, I entered the first room on the right, indicating the guards should stay outside.

It was as I remembered it from the previous night; completely bare, no tables, chairs, shelves, nothing.

Footprints in the dust from our search the previous night but that was it.

I closed and barred the door, checked that there was only an arrow slit for light and dug under my clothes for my two purses.

I took four gold pieces from one and six silver coins from the other.

I tucked away the purses, both still reassuringly heavy in spite of the withdrawal.

I put the gold in the palm of one glove, the silver in another.

There was a knock on the door.

I unbarred it and waved Gerald into the room, closing the door behind him.

He shuffled to the middle of the room, turned, bowed and said, "Good morning my lord, you called me to attend".

I nodded back and replied, "Good morning Gerald".

"Your tasks for the trip to Cambridge are several but I regret I have no paper to list them".

"I will manage my lord; my mind is in better shape than my body."

"Very well" I said.

"First task is to change one or more of these…" and pulled the glove off the hand holding the four gold pieces.

Gerald's eyes popped and he gasped.

"My lord that's… oh my lord that's so much!",

"Indeed it is, so you will only show one at a time, travel swiftly between money changers[13], to get each their best price in silver coin, so they will not have time to conspire against you. Also try the Jews if there are any. If you are getting good prices, change as many as you can to silver. Then change half of that elsewhere to smaller coin.

Remember the Jews will haggle but give a fair price, the others are devious bastards and can rob you blind."

"They will tell you these are French and are worth nothing. In fact, these are the purest I've seen. The weight and softness of the metal tells all."

"I will be on my guard my lord." said Gerald, "I have a good chance at this, after my twenty years of lessons in the devious…"

"Good" I responded.

"Other tasks…" I went on and gave him a long list of tradesmen and supplies we needed. He nodded his understanding of each item.

"Any questions?"

"No, my lord" said Gerald.

I gave him the four gold pieces, two of the silver and wished him a safe journey.

---

[13] Usually goldsmiths but not always

With the discovery of the candles, I decided to now make my quarters in the Keep.

I climbed the stairs of the Keep, to the third of the four floors above ground level and opened the door to what seemed to have been Hugo's chamber.

I walked in and the guards remained in the corridor.

The large room did not smell too bad, though there was clearly a midden nearby.

Weak morning daylight came through the arrow slits, I thought that would improve in the afternoon as that wall faced westerly.

There was a large bed, table, desk and a couple of chairs.

A great many empty wine bottles lined the floor near the walls...

Suddenly the animal skins on the bed lifted and rippled – some beast we had missed last night, no doubt. A dog? Wolf?

I drew my sword and called for the guards.

They burst in, swords ready.

We all stared at the bed as the movements divided – and two tousled female heads appeared. Both blinking in the light.

I sheathed my sword and waved the guards back to the corridor. I think they smirked as they left.

The girls in their night-gowns got down from the bed, suddenly seeming smaller and younger now.

In unison, they said "Good morning my lord" in quiet, tired voices, then with no preamble at all, whisked their nightgowns off and moved closer to me, reaching out to unbuckle and undress me.

I backed away in horror as their nakedness now revealed their all too evident youth, more children than women.

Their limbs so thin, faces drawn, cheeks hollow, mouths immobile and eyes... eyes so... dead.

I gently commanded them to stop whatever they intended and to get dressed.

Their clothes were heaped on the far side of the bed and they dressed with slow, wooden movements, then picked up their night-gowns.

I ushered them carefully out of the room, down the stairs and over the yard to the kitchen table.

I called the sergeant to detail one man to be on guard of these two at all times and be sure to get them some bread and water.

I left them chewing disinterestedly on the tasty new bread while thinking what depravity had Hugo descended to, before his unlamented passing...

In going back to the Keep, I met Lady Eede – she looked very concerned.
We exchanged greetings and then she said, "The sick are very weak my lord, we have water for them now but without honey and salt, I'm afraid it passes straight through."
"We used to buy honey from the priest, as he has many hives, but we owe too much now".
I gave her the silver colins remaining in my glove and told her to get some honey. Then into the town for salt, spices and anything else she thought we could use.
"Do you ride my lady" I asked, and she nodded.
"Then see the sergeant for an escort of four"
She curtseyed low and went away on her errand.

I pressed on back up to Hugo's, or rather my room, to check every cupboard and crevice for more surprises - none emerged.
I then went up to the battlements and enjoyed the view in the strengthening sunlight. My domain!
I spent some time at each of the walls, soaking in the details of all I could see.
Then returned to ground-level, grabbed a horse and toured the outer walls with my guards. This took some time but was mildly reassuring in that nowhere seemed in any danger of collapse and the most deteriorated wall was the south side, that I had seen on our arrival. The sun-exposed parts of a wall were usually the first to decline in condition.

With excellent if fortunate timing, Eede returned with her supplies – just as the hunting party returned from the forest, they being cheered by the other soldiers at their obvious success.
Some rabbits had been snared and a massive boar had been ridden down with lances.
You could see the effort spent on the pig-hunt when you looked in their faces...

Blooded and bruised from tree-branch strikes and their eyes bright from the excitement when the boar turned on them.

We managed a soldier's stew-of-rabbit for lunch and I sent a party to the town to 'borrow' a cook for the evening meal of spit-roasted boar.

Lady Eede reported that the Warden was partly recovered, had been moved to another room and wished to speak with me.

I went to see him and learned that, as I now expected, the castle coffers were indeed empty.

Outstanding bills totalled over £1000, a simply huge amount that took my breath away.

However, uncollected taxes were estimated to be at least £2000. There was no certainty on either figure because bloody Hugo had destroyed so many records as if to make his problems disappear. He was also too lazy or nervous to press the more important merchants and so no one ended up paying their taxes.

I asked for the names of the largest debtors and he was able to name the three millers in the domain and their owings, before he fell faint again and Eede intervened, insisting that I let him rest.

I sent for an escort of twelve to be made ready, as Eede used a stick to draw me a rough map of my parish, in the dust of an empty room.

It was fairly simple to grasp, just follow the river for the first one and go up each of two tributaries for the other mills. The last one would require use of a ford that might require some care this time of year.

I walked briskly out to the bailey, jumped on my horse and I waved my men forward; all of us now wearing tabards of my title.

Through the gate as it opened for us and over the drawbridge we rode.

As we travelled along the riverbank, I reflected that you never saw a poor miller. Like goldsmiths, they always had a way of 'tipping the scales' their way.

They charged for their services, but you often did not end up with quite as much grain as you expected – even if you stood and watched the noisy, dusty process…

The biggest watermill, the one directly on the river itself, was my first target.

We rode up in some style and a man, looking like the owner, came out front to meet us.

"Miller" I said, "I am Lord Walter of Haverhill, you owe £300 in taxes."

He replied in heavily accented Saxon "I am Adelaert, I am from Holland, I owe you no taxes lord." And crossed his arms defiantly.

I stood in my stirrups and made a show of looking for Holland.

"I see your mill, it stands on English soil, MY SOIL and uses MY WATER!" I said with a cold fury and unblinking gaze that made him step back a bit.

The noise attracted four young men from the depths of the mill. All were large and looked strong; all bearing some resemblance to Adelaert.

They brandished clubs and knives in a foolish attempt to be menacing – I guessed this may have worked with Hugo and his smaller or lesser party.

My men, all of them trained and battle tested, just laughed at them. So, the miller's lads, used to facing down mere yokels-in-uniform, suddenly all looked very disconcerted.

"Your sons?" I said, Adelaert nodded.

"Pick one" I said, and he began to look nervous.

"What for" he said.

"WHAT FOR MY LORD" I roared to correct him.

"What for my lord" he said, his voice shaking.

"So he can be my... guest for as long as you take to pay."

"You can't do..." he began but I chopped my hand forward and four of my men surrounded Adelaert with their horses; four more surrounded the nearest son and hustled him away from the others by neatly sidestepping their mounts.

The breaking point for Adelaert, was the appearance of a length of rope to bind and lead the unfortunate one back to the castle.

"I pay, I pay, I pay" he sobbed, holding his head in his hands.

My men squashed him more with their horses and he looked at me in mortal terror.

I had my hand cocked by my ear.

"I pay... my lord" he gasped and fell to the ground as if praying to me. I gestured with my chin to let him up.

He and the three sons not in custody, trotted into the mill.

After some minutes and much thumping of doors and other woodwork, they started coming out with bags of coin.

They placed them in the men's saddle bags as I directed.

Then more money bags came out. Then more.

I feigned an air of bored indifference, but this was going much better than expected.

Thinking I'd have to take at least some payment in grain, to be sent on later, I had not thought what £300 in pennies might look like. Or weigh!

I just hoped at least some of it would be in shillings or even pounds and in any case, that we had enough room in our saddle bags.

Eventually they seemed to be finished.

I beckoned to Adelaert and he approached with great timidity.

"If you are short, we will be back" I snarled.

"Yes my lord" he said and bowed and bowed until we were out of sight.

Once round the next bend, I halted the column and turned my horse around.

I looked at the men and nodded in appreciation - they nodded back.

"You know what this means men?" I said.

"No, my lord" they replied as one.

"Tomorrow... is... payday". They cheered!

On our return to the castle, I had the empty strong-boxes moved up to the third floor from their idiotic place on the first.

This made it harder for casual theft and easier to guard the whole level, as men would be posted on my room anyway.

Two of my soldiers claimed ability to sum adequately and the dear and ever helpful Lady Eede was able to supervise the counting and storage of the money we'd acquired.

The counting took some time and the sun setting by the time she returned to me.

She held out a pair of 'split tally'[14] sticks that indicated the amount – 308 pounds, 3 shillings and 9 pence.
I took one half of the stick and gave her the other. She looked surprised at this sign of trust.
"I very much appreciate your help my lady."
"Until the Warden is recovered, I fear I may ask too much of you…"
"You must do what is needed my lord." she replied.
I could smell the roasting meat in the kitchen, so we adjourned to the Hall for supper and a discussion of the day's events.
All my subjects within the castle were able to stuff themselves with perfectly cooked boar and a ration of beer.
We hired the cook, who turned out to be a relative of Milo the jailer.
So, with the castle secure, guard details set and everyone fed I adjourned to my room for a well-earned sleep.

After breakfast the next day, I held a pay parade.
The local soldiers that were left did ask about back-pay owed but I deferred that until the Warden recovered and could confirm amounts.

I led a tax-gathering force out in the morning, to other, smaller mills.
Splashing across the ford to get to one.
It seemed word had gone around because they had their payments bagged and ready.
Over £500 between the two debtors. Another good day.
Good enough to give me a chance to take time and hunt in the afternoon.
Mine was not a Royal forest, so we bagged a deer by using a makeshift rope and lance method.
Sad news on the day was that one of the sergeants had succumbed to his illness.
The following morning, I awoke to the sound of voices in the courtyard.

---

[14] A means of keeping matching copies of accounts

Many voices, too many voices, a babble of voices and donkeys braying?

I glanced out of one of my rooms arrow slits and saw a mass of people packing my field of view.

"The castle is lost" I thought.

Furious with myself, and furious with my men.

I grabbed my sword and rushed out of my room and down the stairs, pursued by my guards.

I burst out of the Keep door and paused at the top of the steps, looking for someone to kill.

Hundreds of people it seemed were there, packed together.

But none of them armed or armoured.

The whole bailey was a sea of men, women, children and carts.

Those carts had produce piled high with the cries of traders looking to sell their wares echoing all around.

I watched my sergeant force his way through the crowd with a concerned look on his face.

He stayed at the bottom of the steps, staying well out of reach of my sword.

"What in the name of all that is Holy?" I shouted.

"It's Wednesday my lord" he said - as if that explained it!

Seeing a fury building in me, he tried more words.

"That is market day here, sir"

Lost for anything bar swearing, I speechlessly indicated the direction to the town.

"Lord Hugo moved it sire, seems he charged a shilling to the traders to come in and two shillings to let them leave."

"They started coming in at first light sir."

"Said they were supposed to pay to come in."

"Didn't seem to be very many at first but..." he finished and looked nervous.

I guessed that was a very easy way to raise revenue. God damn Hugo.

I noticed that all exits from the bailey were guarded, so nothing belonging to the castle could be stolen. Everything seemed peaceful and I just could not help laughing.

Partly in relief and partly at the ridiculous scene.

Looking slightly relieved the sergeant said, "Orders sir?"

"Have three horses brought over and if cook or Lady Eede want to do some buying here, make sure they have an escort".

"I will my lord" he said and turned to use his sword pommel to force a way through the masses to the stables.

I went back to my room, dressed myself fully in mail, coif and helmet. More for show than any expectation of threat.

I made sure my tabard was clean, showing my Haverhill colours to their best and went down with my two guards to mount our horses and tour the 'market' that my castle had become. There were some occasional cries of welcome or greetings from the populace but mostly a sullen indifference.

We arrived eventually at the Hall and enjoyed a late breakfast.

By the end of the day, the only good news was that the Warden was continuing his recovery and that we had taken £9 in tradesman fees from the market.

Gerald and his escort returned at sunset the next day and we met up the following morning.

His quests had gone better than I expected, with most things on my list either with him or on its way. The four archers that arrived were immediately tested on a target at 40 yards range. They used their own weapons, one of them a longbow. It immediately became apparent that three archers were excellent, and one was a fraud, who was promptly taken out of the gate and thrown in the moat. Gerald started to apologise for his poor choice, but I told him to not worry, these things happen.

The three archers who were staying, got down to the task of bedding in the single longbow and dozen short-bows that Gerald had purchased, along with 500 short-arrows.

The newly arrived fletcher[15] took some time to look through the existing store of arrows, then reported back to me with a long face.

"They are very well made, my lord – I'd say all by the same hand or his apprentice..."

"But..." I said.

"They are all broad-head, no bodkins[16] and very... pretty, all with white flights, set for a fast spin..."

I clapped my palm to my forehead – yet again dismayed at Hugo's choices.

He had gone for show, for appearance - with no thought to military realities.

Being white feathered, they could be seen from a long way off and so potentially ducked or shielded against at the longer ranges.

With all flights coloured the same, it was slower to align the nock[17], especially in the dark.

Some did say that a spin would help accuracy but at Warwick we found little difference, except that the more spin, the slower the arrow and the shorter its range.

"We must have better..." I said.

"Begin changing them to black or dark grey, as you find the geese to match in markets around here. Set the flights to not spin. Have the cock feathers[18] marked with lime white and the nocks dipped in the brightest ochre we can get."

"Yes my lord," he said, nodding in appreciation. I handed him two silver coins and he left to begin his very lengthy task.

The newly hired torch-and-candle maker went off to gather reeds from the moat, while grumbling at length about "Spring being the wrong season for this..." but he had made some good suggestions for use of the animal fats from recent cooking of game and quickly made up some lamps for use in the Keep.

---

[15] Arrow maker and repairer for the shafts and flights (feathers)

[16] Sharp nosed, heavy, conical tip for piercing mail, helmets, etc

[17] Notch in the base of the arrow that engages the bowstring

[18] The feather away from the bow that would immediately align nock to string

The ever-busy Gerald was commanded to write notices for display in the town. One declaring that the market will permanently return to the town and be free for all tradesman. The other announced the opening of 'Manor Court', to be held at the castle on market day. Any citizen of my domain could bring his claim or allegation to me for judgement. Court would start after the prayer time of Terce[19] was rung on the church bells.

This was something of a challenge for an all-too recently ex-squire, but I had seen the importance of these courts in other fiefs and I was determined to strengthen my holding by this service to my subjects. Gerald found two residents who could read and had strong voices to act as bellmen[20] each day – for a very modest fee.

The notices would be read out after the Sext (noon) and Nones (3pm) church bells.

Some good news on the day was the improvements in the health of the warden and the surviving sergeant.

Another challenge to grasp was rebuilding the relationship between church and state - at our strictly local level.

The fact that the priest had not come to visit by now, meant that he had given up on the castle as part of his parish, no doubt thanks to the unspeakable Hugo... Worse, if the castle or title had been condemned in spiritual terms, I would need that reversing, for many reasons.

I had watched Lord Roger balance and use the influence and wealth of Holy Church with great care. Money was power and the Church as an institution had a great deal of wealth. The richer the parishioner, the more he usually donated to save his soul.

And at my level, there was much the priest would know that I might benefit from...

So, at the first opportunity, I rode out to visit with the priest.

I aimed to arrive between prayer times one morning and, leaving my escort at a distance, managed to find him in the church garden, tending to his beehives.

---

[19] So would start around 09:30 in modern time

[20] Aka town criers

I exchanged greetings with Father Aldous and we quietly considered each other's apparent qualities. We accepted each other as equals, he as head of the spiritual aspects of the parish, me as head of temporal matters. I saw an average size man, around thirty years of age, maybe a little stout, wearing the typical black gown and having the severe haircut of the time. He had a calm and wise demeanour, not someone to be rushed – or forced into anything.

We shared some brief words about my predecessor, not much else to add on either side. He then solved my problem of the two waifs I'd found in Hugo's room; they would be adopted by a loving couple in the town, where Aldous could keep an eye on them for me.

I said "Father, I can see what's needed at the castle but why have so many people left the town?" He stroked his chin, made no immediate answer but beckoned me to follow him out of the garden back gate and into the cemetery. He stood to one side and waved a gentle hand towards the nearest rows of graves and markers. I walked slowly along the long lines, reading the clearly legible inscriptions. The names and ages thus revealed: child, child, mother and child, child, mother and child, child, child, child, mother. The seeming endless rows of little headstones broke my heart, I felt my mother's grief again, even at this span of distance and time. I fell to my knees and wept, my shoulders shaking, tears streaming.

After leaving me some time to settle, Father Aldous gripped me by the shoulders and suggested a sit inside. We went inside to some anteroom at the back of the church and he poured us out some wine. He mentioned that before his time and before Hugo, he believed that expectant mothers went to the castle to give birth and stay a while after.

This explained another mystery, the obviously once pristine, if now rather dusty 'white room' beyond the kitchens at the castle. Lime-white walls, floor and ceiling and... empty.

"I will send word when that can happen again" I said.

Aldous nodded and said, "Will we be seeing you in church this Sunday Lord Walter?"

"Perhaps...." I replied and he chuckled. I think we understood each other.

Feeling calmer now, I looked around and saw a small twig fall past me on to the floor.

Looking up I saw a hole in the roof and tree foliage beyond that.

"Father, do you know you have a hole in your roof?"

He nodded ruefully and said "Indeed – and it's worse over the nave"

"I'm afraid I fell out with the Bishop some time ago and church funds all just seem to go... one... way."

It was my turn to nod in acknowledgement. I took my glove off and placed two gold pieces I'd hidden within, on to the table between us. I kept my finger on the coins and said, "For this parish, only, Father..."

"Accepted - and thank you my son." said Aldous, looking rather stunned! We shook hands warmly; I went back to my men and we returned to the castle for lunch. I felt very good about using some of William's gold for such a purpose.

That evening I discussed the 'white room' with Eede. She had heard rumours that a nun or nuns used to be at the castle, in residence, as midwives and thus served women from this parish and others further afield. I asked her to write to the nearest convent and see if one or two could be spared. She should have it delivered by rider and he would wait for any reply. In my heart, I could feel that my parents would be deeply pleased by this and with my calculating feudal lords' hat on, I knew I needed to stop the exodus of my subjects, my taxpayers, and - keep them from dying unnecessarily.

After a few days, a letter came in reply from the convent.

It stated they would be happy to send a nun and a novice to us, indeed they had been praying for this to happen for many years.

They included a long list of items to be present in the room, with medicines and treatments also.

I just gave the list and a gold piece to Gerald to get on with, saying "I hope there's some change out of that."

The poor chap will be soon be sick of going to Cambridge I thought with a chuckle.

The next day, a carpenter and apprentice arrived and were hired.

They made repairs to the drawbridge and improvements to the gates.

Then started to fashion shelves, beds, stools for the midwives' room that were on the long list from the convent.

Now somehow, word of these preparations must have... circulated and I had a visitor from the town requesting an audience – most unusual. I was told it was Rhoslyn, the midwife from the town...

I decided to use this to try our arrangements for the forthcoming court session, next market day. I now had a high-backed chair, set centrally on the wide dais in the Hall, all tables cleared away. Rich dark-red velvet curtains had been found all crumpled and dirty in a cellar but now hung cleaned and very regal, either side of and at the front of the low stage. The whole arrangement looked most imposing.

I took my seat, with my guards standing just behind my chair and I signalled for the subject to be allowed in.

My sergeant escorted in the short, middle-aged woman and showed her where to stand, a few feet back from the steps to the stage. She turned to face me and bobbed a curtsey in her plain brown dress. Her manner was... odd. The smile was there but seemed... forced and something about her made the hairs go up on the back of my neck. The mild Spring warmth in the Hall, seemed to chill and I felt in the presence of... evil. She was sallow of skin, unkempt, dirty of face and hands with long, grubby fingernails. My mind flashed back to my mother's birth-helpers, Miss Rose and Miss Daisy. They had been the image of pink cheerfulness, with small, pink, clean hands with trimmed nails. All the births had been successful, regardless of the offsprings' fate in later years. This... in front of me could have ploughed a field with those... paws.

"My Lord" she began "I hear you are building a place for birthing." I nodded slowly.

"I am Rhoslyn, midwife to this parish for many years and I wish to offer my services".

"They will not be required, madam" I replied, hearing Percival, the herald, in my head saying "...use the smallest number of words...". Her smile slipped, just a little... "But my lord, I..."

"DO NOT 'BUT' YOUR LORD" I thundered.

The smiling mask had gone now, her face contorted with fury.

"I need to make my living" she snarled.

"And I need to stop my subjects dying." I replied.

"You are banned from my domain and are never to return".

She uttered a demonic howl and seemed to fly from her spot towards me. I barely had time to begin to draw my dagger.

Her outstretched fingernails were now no more than three feet from me when a loud 'THWACK THWACK' was heard. A pair of broad-head arrows each drove through her ribs from one side to the other, ending up poking well out of her body. She fell at my feet, pushed slightly to one side by the arrows force. A gurgling was heard, and a pulse of blood seen coming from her mouth as she shuddered away the last moment of life.

With my dagger now in hand and my guards having their swords out, we backed away from whatever *that* was. As one my guards and the now arrived sergeant stepped forwards and drove their swords through the back of this thing; then pulled the blades out, wiped them on the now departed's dress and sheathed their weapons.

I sheathed my dagger, turned to my two archers, hidden behind the curtain to my right, and hugged them like family. My sergeant and guards joined in the hugging and we swore, wept and exalted at what had happened.

The sergeant turned back to the corpse, did a check for life with his boot and called for some more men.

While we briefly waited, my archers recovered their arrows, by using their knives to carefully slice away the flights, then pushing and pulling the shafts clear though the corpse. Our fletcher would put the valuable pieces back together.

The soldiers arrived with a large cloth, wrapped the body in it and carried it away.

Later that afternoon, the thing was dumped deep in the forest for the foxes and wolves to dispose of – there was no place for that in consecrated ground.

We resolved to make some changes before the first Manor Court. But first, I called for a table for us all and we had a great deal of beer through the rest of that day!

There were many more long and busy days guiding the restoration of the castle, its finances, basic food supplies and so on. My... firm handling of the millers had started a wave of voluntary payment of back-taxes, particularly from the larger debtors. The castle thus became solvent, more fully staffed and began to have a 'sound' about it. The sound of constructive activity. I knew from experience that silence meant inaction - through slacking, lack of oversight or a shortage in supplies. Warwick Castle hummed like a wasp's nest, from first light to last and I began to sense that here now at Haverhill.

So, with the fief beginning to run itself each day, I began to feel more and achingly more in need of... companionship. Many a lord would simply grab the nearest servant, willing or not – there would be no reckoning or justice for him to face this side of eternity. Some of my comelier serving wenches were always bright and cheerful in their curtsied greetings to me, often smiling and giggling on their way to their duties and leaving me with lustful thoughts.
However, I had seen the effects of this usage from the other side, when away from Warwick; the lord would steadily lose respect from all his minions, especially as it was often accompanied by forgotten pay, awful food (for the employed) and so forth.
The castle staff would begin to very quietly drift away to other fiefs and any that remained could not be relied on when needed.
The late and unlamented Hugo, ex-Lord of Haverhill and his Lady Eede had been married - just not to each other. Their respective spouses had succumbed to various diseases, and the union of widow and widower of rank was one of convenience and not convention. Hence Haverhill became vacant as no title could transfer to the Lady Eede.

With the passing of Hugo, Eede was rendered destitute, in spite of her noble Scottish blood, as many branches of her family had been lost to plague, murder or battle.
She was a dignified and compassionate woman, so unlike the drunken and perverted animal that Hugo had become.
She had been extremely influential in the financial recovery of my holding, spending days touring my land with the, now recovered,

Warden - to assist him in the collection of the remaining back taxes. Her local knowledge being crucial as Hugo had lost or destroyed so many of the castle's documents, including the original Domesday scrolls for the parish and the later revisions. She also tutored new spinners and weavers for the castle to begin selling wool clothing that was much in demand in the bitter winters of the last few years. I was happy to allow her to stay in a room in the west corner of the Keep, providing her with a very modest retinue of a chambermaid and a guard. She also ate as well (or badly) as I did.

I felt unsure of my course, as my conversations with Eede had always been purely about the business of the fief and its subjects – but now, my blood was up.
The sun had just set when I dispatched a maid to the kitchen to warm some mulled wine. She returned to my room with the bottle wrapped in a cloth against its heat.
So equipped, I left my quarters and headed for Lady Eede's room, my two guards falling in step with me, no command required.
On arrival at her door, I nodded at her guard to stand aside and knocked firmly. No need to announce myself, no one else would have passed the guard and be knocking on a lady's door.

She unbarred and opened the door, welcoming me in most warmly, as if I was expected, and secured the door behind me.
On seeing the bottle I carried, she took two silver cups down from a shelf, smiled and gently indicated I should sit at her small table.
We sat facing each other, the candlelight illuminating her amused smile and sparkling eyes. I noticed the room was very warm from the log fire and the number of tapestries hanging against each wall, almost covering them. I poured some wine for us, saying "I hope all is well with My Lady".
"Indeed it is, My Lord Walter, thank you for asking."
We sipped our wine and found it extremely good; smiling and nodding together at our shared discovery. We sipped again.
"You could trust Hugo to have certain things that were most important to him!" laughed Eede.

We chatted for some considerable time about the state of my castle, the town, the market and my staff.

I thanked her for her help with the fief and she thanked me for the protection of herself and her dignity.

I eventually felt a very pressing need to piss and looked around for the midden.

"There's a door behind the green tapestry" said Eede with a smile.

Indeed there was, a small door opening to a very small space let into the wall.

With the door closed behind me, the bare walls were very cold, but I sat on the wooden seat and let my bladder empty blissfully into the void below.

In her turn, Eede went behind the green cloth as I resumed my seat at table to sip more of the excellent wine.

When she reappeared, she did not return to her seat but instead walked past me, resting a gentle hand on my shoulder as she did so.

I turned to watch her as she put more logs on the fire and stirred the embers.

She warmed her hands on the new flames and I joined her to do the same.

Standing upright again, she turned to me and said

"Can I be of any other service to you Lord Walter?".

I glanced at her in some puzzlement.

Her hands disappeared briefly behind her head and then quickly behind her back.

She shook her head and then her shoulders. Her glossy auburn hair cascaded down her back and her richly embroidered gown cascaded down her front, leaving her stood naked in the firelight!

"Of any service at all?" she said, smiling even wider now at my frog-eyed expression and open mouth.

Ten years older than me at least and plain of face but by god she had a beautiful body. Slender but wondrously curving, flawless creamy skin that was warmly highlighted by the fire.

I gasped at her loveliness, then gasped again at the discomfort of my surging cock that made me bend forward slightly, constrained as I was in gambeson and chain mail!

She chuckled warmly at what she guessed was my predicament.

"As you can see, I am unarmed my lord, so perhaps we can dispense with your armour?"

"You are indeed most beautifully unarmed my lady!" I replied.

She stepped away from her crumpled clothes and with practiced hands she had my mail and gambeson undone and pulled over my head in short order. This left me in my shirt and hose[21].

I threw my shirt on the heap of clothes, leaving me standing with a very obvious bulge in said hose.

Eede reached for the draw-cord and pulled.

I stepped out of my boots and hose, then took her hand to lead her nearer the fire. "I see you brought your lance Lord Walter," she said, giggling. "will you joust with it this night?" she continued.

"I intend to my lady!" I replied and crushed her soft body to mine. "Oh good!" she chuckled. We shared a deep and passionate kiss, tongues writhing over each other. We drew back, both panting heavily, looked deep into each other's eager eyes then kissed again. This time she reached a hand down, wrapped her delicate feminine fingers round my stiff cock, gently squeezed and stroked. All reason left me. I threw her down onto the bearskin rug in front of the fire. She laughed, got up onto her hands and knees, looked back at me over her shoulder and purred "Time to ride my lord!", offering her long hair back and up towards me as 'reins'.

With an animal snarl, I knelt behind her, roughly gripped the offered hair with one hand and guided my cock to her heat with the other. After some clumsy fumbling, I found her entrance and we shared a gasp of joy as I pushed inside.

She was so warm in there, luscious and small.

So small, I had to firmly push to make my way in full length, urged on by Eede until our union was complete. I forced her head around so we could kiss again but I think she had other plans. I felt her fingers on my firmly bulging balls. "Oh, my lord, your purses are SO FULL!" she said. "Time to spend EVERYTHING!" she cried and squeezed.

---

[21] hose, aka breeches or trousers

Again, reason left me, I grabbed her shoulders and began my thrusting of her fabulous body. I could not believe how much force I was using on her, driven on by the exquisite sensations, with our bodies slapping hard together. Any moment I expected her to cry in pain but the only sound she was making was a long drawn out "uhhhhhhhmmmmmmmmMMM".

Then that sound stopped, and she turned her head and said "That's a good canter my lord but it's time to gallop now!"

More strength surged through me than I knew I had, my speed and force increased and I realised I was on an unstoppable ride.

My whole body exploded like a bottle of Greek Fire[22] and I roared like the lion I'd heard of in stories!

Then I fell across Eede, with shaking arms and legs, while she giggled at my sudden weakness.

She held me by the fire for a little while, then led me to the bed for a blissful sleep.

We awoke around midnight and took turns with the midden.

When she got back under the coverings, I realised again the deliciousness of holding a naked woman in my arms.

Eede was similarly delighted but this time she guided me to please her – I learned a great deal.

Though at one point I thought I'd killed her as she howled, shuddered in her whole body and lay very still, as if taken by a seizure.

With much relief, I saw she still breathed and after some minutes had passed, gradually came to her senses – though slightly incoherently...

We slept till well after dawn – most unusual for either of us.

The mutual welcome we shared on waking, saw me quickly into her arms and between her legs.

Though this time we shushed each other and giggled at our efforts to keep our noise down now that the castle was awake for everyone.

---

[22] An inflammable/explosive used in castle defence

Then we giggled more when our memories came back, of our furious swiving[23] the previous night and exchanged a wide-eyed look when we realised that our passions must have echoed across the bailey!

I think we shared an unspoken concern on how our staff would react to... events.
But we agreed that I should leave first, as if nothing was unusual and Eede would go out a little later to begin her duties.
At least for both of us, we were the ones people waited on. I finished dressing, paused to gather my thoughts, firmly unbarred the door and marched out to get breakfast – my guards following without word or hesitation. After my meal, I was still feeling very, very relaxed.
All seemed normal enough in my world but as the day went on, as I toured the castle, checking all was in order and all works progressing, I noticed the men standing to attention a bit smarter and a shade more respectful - something was different.
Then I noticed the maids and other servant girls were curtseying lower, not giggling now but blushing when I caught their eyes...
Well!
As spring turned to summer, Eede continued to... look after me.
The castle gained a very good blacksmith and a capable stonemason with apprentice.
The idiot lord at St Neots had neglected to pay them for half a year, so they came with their families to Haverhill.
The masons first job was to put up some more accommodation for tradesmen. Their second and much longer job was to fix up the mortar of the curtain wall.
The blacksmith had an immediate job of making us some bodkin arrow heads.

---

[23] Saxon for fornication

For the summer fair in the town, I offered large money prizes for an archery competition. This attracted men and boys from far around and enabled us to recruit more good bowmen, including a few with longbows.

The next day though, brought a letter to Eede that caused me mixed feelings. It was an offer of marriage from Brian Fitz-Count, to the Lady Eede. Brian held the lordships of Wallingford and Abergavenny, was very powerful and extremely well connected. His wife had died, so there was an opportunity for him, in his forties, to propose to a titled lady. Distant family connections raised the idea and thus the letter arrived in her hand. She clearly had to accept; this Brian had the wherewithal to support Eede to her proper status.

This did mean we had to curtail our swiving as it would be... impolitic for her, a widow of many years, to appear with child at first meeting with her new prospective husband!

She had expressed concern at the absence of off-spring from previous couplings but nothing is certain in that area so I sadly concurred that we had to abstain.

I believe I ruled the next few Manor Court sessions with a rod of iron and my quickening temper was noted by most!

I still conversed at length with Eede, the only true confidante I had. We would usually talk in my room after the evening meal.

One night, Eede arrived with her chambermaid, a pretty, young Saxon woman called Ella, very shy and quiet.

I thought it a little odd but raised no objection.

After some light conversation about the events of the day, I poured two goblets of wine.

Eede smiled gently, squeezed my hand and said she had to go but that Ella had asked to stay...

All I could manage to say was... "Oh!" I stood and Ella curtseyed to Eede, as her mistress left the room.

I'm suddenly tongue-tied!

Ella asked very quietly if she could sit and I stammered that she could.

I nodded at the goblet that I'd poured for Eede and she shyly picked it up, then I reached out to clink her drink with mine and I said "Waes Hael[24]!"

She giggled, repeated that and drank too deeply – making herself cough a little but she recovered well.

We talked very gently on this and that, she said she was very much enjoying the horse riding she and Eede had done, whenever an escort could be spared. I excused myself to the midden and she went after me. I was looking out to check the weather when she returned, standing very close to me but noticeably shaking.

"Is my lord ready for bed?" she asked in a quavering voice.

Having made up my mind as to my path, I said clearly "Yes I am, will you join me Ella?" In the candlelight, I could see her blush like a beetroot, and she nodded without speaking. I blew out the candles, so only moonlight through the arrow ports illuminated the room. I sat on one side of the bed, she sat on the other. We undressed in the dark and met together under the coverings.

She was shaking and shivering so much that I just held her close and stroked her shiny hair. She felt thinner than Eede but still had that womanly, rich, creamy smoothness of skin that is so intoxicating to caress. I gently kissed her hair, her lips, her throat, her shoulders and everything all the way to her feet – and then back up again. She seemed surprised by all this and calmed somewhat.

Then she returned the favour by kissing all my parts from head to toe, though with some considerable hesitation around my middle bits. I showed her how to give me some... relief, but I could not, or rather would not mount this delicate creature – well not this night anyway...

As letters went back and forth between Lady Eede and her fiancé, me and Ella became more... familiar.

---

[24] Saxon for Good Health or Cheers

She was with Eede during the day and with me each night.
She seemed convinced it would happen the way animals mated in the farmyard, which was very acceptable to me! Thus, after a few bedtimes of gentle exploration, we achieved a mutually satisfactory union.
She became a different woman overnight, now so calm and confident.
The next morning at breakfast, Eede looked at Ella waiting contentedly in the corner, looked at me and smiled widely, I could only smile back and try not to blush. Just as the August harvesting began, Eede had to take her leave.
Wallingford sent an impressive escort of thirty men and two carts, for her and her possessions. However, Eede preferred to ride, using her lady-saddle[25].
Her favourite horse in our stables was a fine bay mare and she was delighted when I gifted that to her as a parting present. The whole castle turned out to cheer her on her way and wish her well, a most emotional event for all.
I felt more than lost, a large gap was there in my life.
Luckily, I had the Warden and Gerald to run the day-to-day matters of the estate but even so, her wise insights on business and myself were sorely missed.

The summer had been hot and dry but as September came around, there was an early chill on some days.
The serfs laboured even harder to get the harvest in and all was done by the rains arriving mid-month. Also done was my service from Ella! She asked to move back with her parents in the town, as she had met a young suitor at church on the Harvest Festival. The young man was son of a new tenant farmer, recently arrived from Norwich. I believe my temper slowly began to worsen again...

---

[25] Side-saddle in modern terms

In consolation, I turned to the now plentiful supply of apple and pear ciders that seemed a pleasant alternative to beer.

We exported much of this, often in exchange for excellent yew staves[26] from Flanders and beyond but I insisted on a regular check of the quality. The pear drink especially, was truly a way to forget all your problems in a very short time.

One morning, later that chilly and damp September, I was riding out with my escort, chasing payment of some overdue tax money. We came back through the town around noon, seeing how much brighter and livelier the place was, compared to when we arrived. We walked our horses to the market square and were struck by the large crowd gathered there. I could see the auctioneer's wagon was back in town, looking like slaves were the lots of the day. I could see a dark-skinned young man waiting on the cart, and of much more interest, a dusky-skinned woman was next for sale – so I rode a little closer. Then - across the heaving, odious and noisy crowd of townsfolk, our eyes locked together. Curiosity in my gaze, contempt in hers!

Being seated on my horse, I could see above the masses, as could she, standing in the auctioneer's cart – although she was slave-for-sale and not vendor. Dressed in a very faded and tattered pale purple gown, veil and head-dress, she held her head high and gazed around her with serene assurance radiating from her dark eyes – seeming untroubled and remarkably immune from her truly very lowly condition. The auctioneer's assistant was pointing to her features, making curving movements with his hands to excite the crowd. "Show us the face" roared some near the front of the unruly mass. The assistant reached for the veil and was met with a back-handed blow of her knuckles catching him under the nose. He staggered back from the unexpected shock, while clutching his face. With one final step, he met fresh air beyond the end of the cart and toppled over towards the nearest laughing onlookers – who promptly stepped aside to allow him unrestricted access to the muddy ground and there he fell in a groaning, hurting heap.

---

[26] The uncut wood from which to shape a bow

The auctioneer carried on his pitch, trying to ignore the distraction caused by his assistant's sudden departure.

He touted loudly on the youth, health and 'good nature' of the property for sale. At this last, there was much loud laughter, hooting and heckling from the unwashed. He continued his promotion by stating the item had been well looked after by the previous owner after her capture in the Holy Land. Said owner being a neighbouring and very elderly Templar lord, relatively unlikely to have... overused the item.

Now that Eede and then Ella had departed, I was in considerable need of a 'bed warmer', or two!

So, having one vacancy at least and after a quick calculation, I nodded to my trumpeter.

Following three sharp notes from him, the crowd immediately quietened and turned my way – as well they should, this was my town, along with its surrounding lands, I owned all their lives, if not all their property.

"Four pounds" I stated clearly for the auctioneer.

He duly bowed his head, acknowledging the very fair offer as a concluding price – I wasn't going to short-change a fellow liege-lord.

The crowd nodded in sage agreement – until a voice called out "Four pounds, two shillings".

The audience gasped as one in shock, anyone bidding against their lord must be of higher rank or very stupid.

The people edged away from what then become discernible as a merchant, plump and richly dressed.

My sergeant quietly nudged his horse up to mine, leant over and whispered in my ear.

"Rumoured to be in the wool trade my lord - from London and very wealthy".

The auctioneer was clearly in a panic – his wide eyes darted a look in my direction, with an unspoken plea for guidance.

I gave an almost imperceptible nod.

The relief on his face was obvious and he confirmed in a slightly nervous voice "Four pounds, two shillings is bid", while looking round the square as if yet more bidders would be found.

"Four pounds, four shillings" I said, and the auctioneer bowed again, while visibly shaking in dread of another bid.

"Four…" was heard from the merchant, followed by a small shriek. With his voice trembling, the auctioneer said, "Four pounds, four shillings is bid – any advance".

"I yield to the lord" said the fat merchant in a querulous voice. "Ahhhh" sighed the crowd, realising the show was over for the day and began to quickly disperse as a chill rain began to fall. The people thus failed to notice the dark figure standing behind the merchant. One of my corporals had quickly dismounted, removed his helmet and tabard, and quietly walked around behind the fat fool and dissuaded him from further interference; with the point of his dagger resting against the base of the merchants spine, while whispering words of wisdom in his ear.

The auctioneer bowed low to me, I acknowledged with a nod and turned my horse away.

He knew he would immediately deliver the goods to the castle and then see my Warden for payment.

This might be in coin, silver or promissory note, depending on the state of my coffers on the day.

After a long discussion with my Warden on finances and a late meal, I eagerly made my way to my chamber. Keen for a warmer bed than of late… I went in, closed the door and pushed the locking beam across – no interruptions this night.

The slave was sat by the small table and so was keeping warm near the hearth with its log fire on this unseasonably cold night. She stood as I came in and clearly now looked unsure of herself. I wasted no words; the Warden had mentioned that she spoke neither Norman nor Saxon. I smiled, warmly I hoped, then waved her to take her place on or in the bed, I didn't care which. Her eyes now twinkling, with perhaps a smile behind that veil? She acknowledged acceptance of my instruction with a gentle nod of her head and gestured graciously with her hand that I should take 'my place' on the bearskin rug in front of the fire.

I could not help myself but roar with laughter at the cheekiness of this young wench!

She too seemed highly amused, as I wiped the tears from my eyes. I regained my breath and decided a clearer message was in order, as I'm sure we'd be able to find her a replacement dress in the morning…

At that very moment, there came four quick knocks on the door.
What bloody timing I thought...
Four knocks meant I was urgently requested at the top of the Keep.
I picked up a cloak, grabbed the slave's hand and pulled her with me
as I and my guards trotted up the stairs to the battlements, I didn't
want her running off, or barring me from my own room.

As we emerged on to the walkway, the sergeant of the guard
indicated the problem.
Some forest-bandits had stolen a wagon and kidnapped a girl,
probably snatched from one of the peasant houses at the edge of
the town.
Apparently, this had happened four weeks before – and that girl's
body had never been found.
I looked at the glowing orb of the full moon and shared a glance
with the sergeant.
We both now knew this insanity was probably related to the lunar
cycle and we silently resolved to stop this affront to my status and
power. But for now, we had the bandits parading their captive in
the wagon, up and down the road just beyond our moat. They
taunted my soldiers on the outer wall, who studiously ignored them.
"I've checked the gate is secure my lord, also the guards are all
watching their sections".
I nodded my thanks for the report. Always good to know the simple
matters were being handled correctly, despite distractions.
Wouldn't have been the first castle to accidently leave the gate
open as night fell, on occasion leading to the loss of the castle and
all within it. Back beyond the moat, the screaming girl made a break
for freedom but was clubbed around the head and tied to the back
of the driver's seat. Only her upper half was visible to us – but we
could clearly hear her sobs.
"Can we reach out there?" I asked the sergeant. I knew there wasn't
time to get the right men over to the top of the gatehouse.
"I believe our Rolfe could do it my lord" he replied.
I nodded to confirm my wish.
The sergeant turned to give the instruction to the young giant of a
longbow-man stood nearby.

His bow was taller and arrows longer than his fellow archers, thus giving me hope he could range that far.

It was a long and very tricky shot, passing over the bailey, over the curtain wall and then the moat.

At least 120 yards, this was too far for a heavy arrow and would have to be the light but fast one.

The sergeant was almost whispering the final part of the shoot order.

Rolfe had an arrow nocked and ready, smoothly drew back, sighted and loosed.

The arrow flew with a cracking noise, dipping just enough as it crossed the moat to arc down into the wagon.

A thwack and gasp were heard, then silence from the girl, as we saw her head drop forward.

The bandits had dived for cover when they heard the arrow pass by. It took them a few moments to realise what its target had been. Then with howls of rage, they rode their stolen horses away as fast as they could, to get away from any possible follow-up volley from the castle. Sadly, they also drove away with the wagon but at least the girl's soul was safe from any further devastation, even if her body was not.

Meanwhile the sergeant had gripped Rolfe in a bear hug, thanked him quietly and led him away – no doubt for a beer or several. As they passed, I squeezed his shoulder, not in triumph but in understanding.

There were tears in the big lad's eyes. Deep in thought, I turned towards the stairs, beckoned the slave to follow me and heard her footfall behind me. As I reached the doorway, I realised her soft footsteps had been… receding. I whirled round to see her standing in a gap in the parapet, teetering near the edge. She began a low, soft chant with her head thrown back and her arms outstretched. "DEAR GOD NO!" I shouted.

The guards' heads whipped round, saw I was in no danger and immediately turned back to watch to their fronts. No problem to them if a slave wanted to step into the hereafter somewhat early.

At the sound of my cry, she slowly turned her head around, to look at me with wild, wide eyes - her breathing deep and fast.

Something in my voice had caught her, perhaps my desperation, my sincerity?

Both were in those three words, driven unbidden from me by instinct.

From my time with my mother and sisters, I knew I was a natural protector of women – in spite of occasional... lapses.

I slowly reached out to her with my hands, palms up.

My eyes locked with hers as I tried, with thought alone, to convince her to step back.

I tried to show her what was in my soul – and I could not explain, even to myself, why I felt I had to do that, why I must do that.

Still breathing like a racing horse and also trembling now, she slowly turned away from the edge. I slowly reached for her and lifted her slight, shivering body by the waist and gently lowered her to the walkway. She was wracked with shakings and gaspings. I threw my cloak around her and gripped her across the shoulders to guide her to the stairs. I ordered one of my guards to roust out the duty chambermaid, have her find an empty room, make it ready and fetch water, milk, wine, bread, cheese – anything I could think of.

A small room in the south wall of the Keep was found to be usable, if a bit musty. I took her in and sat her down on a rickety chair. Checking around, I made sure there was nothing more than an arrow slit that would let air in but not a person out...

Moonlight poured through into the room and made her previously dusky skin look even paler. While the maid brought in a new straw mattress and a couple of old plain blankets, I tried her with the wine, which she declined. The maid left but had the sense to send up the log-man, who quickly got a roaring fire going in the small hearth and was gone before I saw him. Meanwhile, I watched as the slave had sipped some milk and nibbled some bread and cheese. Then she suddenly looked utterly exhausted.

I guessed she'd been up at dawn to be taken to the market and it was now around midnight. I knelt beside her and held her delicate and unresisting hand, until eventually her shivering passed.

With the room now warm, I stood and gently tried to indicate that

the bed was ready for her and her alone.
Still wearing my cloak around her, she bowed her head in reply,
partly I thought from tiredness but also, I thought, in thanks.

I went along the corridor to my room, instructed the door guards to
allow no one into or out of the slave's room and closed my door on
a long and tiring day.

As I started to fall asleep, my head was thinking "Well that was four
pounds bloody wasted" but my soul was saying "There is something
special, something precious about her... and anyone who can make
me laugh that much is beyond price.".
My last thought was to realise how much her honour meant to her,
thus reminding me to consider, how much mine should mean to
me...

The next day, I told the head chambermaid to look after the slave;
make sure she was fed and watered, show her round the castle –
and keep her away from any long drops.
Her language, that I assumed was Arabic, was a considerable
problem for us. Difficult to make use of her when she understood
nothing...
I guessed her previous owner had enough Arabic from his time in
the Holy Land.
I asked the Warden and senior sergeant but we had no Arab-
speakers at the castle.
The bellman was summoned from the town and dispatched back to
issue calls for anyone with that language to report to me
immediately.

One man was found but the Warden had to send a cart to fetch him.
So it was nearly dark when the ragged, smelly, hobbling creature
was brought to me.
He was clearly a beggar of some sort, leaning on a crutch that
supported him when standing. His left leg being visibly bent awry,
probably broken and never set well.
But when he saw me, he straightened up as best he could and
looked me right in the eyes, a pride and confidence there that

belied his appearance.

"Your name, man? Where are you from and how do you know Arabic?" I asked.

"I am Luther my lord, born and raised in Haverhill as a merchant and trader. I was a pilgrim to the Holy Land, years ago. I joined with the Templars out there, stayed some time - until I was trampled by Turkish cavalry in a skirmish near Antioch." he replied.

"I see" I said, "and how good is your speech in that foreign tongue?".

"I had a gift for it sire – but I may be a little slow with it now, it's been a while."

"Very well," I said "the Warden will find you quarters and your work begins tomorrow morning. You will translate when needed and assist my Warden at other times"

"Thank you, my lord" he said, doing his best to bow without falling over. I waved him away and looked forward to my evening meal, such as it was.

The next morning, I finished breakfast and settled in the parlour room next to the Hall.

All of these later constructions were built against the outer (curtain) wall.

I had my high-back chair brought from the hall and a good fire was made ready on the grate. Then two smaller chairs were brought in and the slave and translator summonsed.

Luther arrived first, I waved him to a chair.

He looked transformed from the day before, in clean clothes, washed and trimmed of beard and hair. Even his wooden crutch had a new coat of varnish.

The maid soon arrived with the slave, sat her down and left us to get on with her other duties.

"Let's get a name from her and where she's from," I instructed Luther. "Also, what job or skill she has that we can use round the castle." Luther nodded and they began to talk in that strange harsh-sounding language. A sentence from him, a sentence or two from her; then Luther rocked back in his chair. There followed what sounded like a repetition of all this from him and her, though this time she spoke more slowly. Luther gently held up his hand to stop her for the moment and turned to me.

Clearly now a little nervous and hesitant, he cleared his throat and began:

"My lord, may I introduce Amira Azizah al-Din Husayn, Princess of Nishapor, daughter of Shah Izz al-Din Husayn, King of the Ghurid lands".

He went on as my eyebrows went up and up some more.

"The...ah... Princess is Persian by birth but has some Arabic as a second language."

"She was captured by what she calls Turkmen when they raided her country."

"The Templar Knights later defeated her captors in a battle, took her to be Turkish and so to Spain as a slave and hence to England."

I was quiet for a moment then asked, "So where is this Nish-nish place", trying to remember anything from the barrage of long-winded names and countries. Luther translated, received her reply and said, "One hundred and thirty days ride beyond Jerusalem my lord". Now it was my turn to feel pushed back in my chair.

That amount of distance was almost unthinkable – I had heard it said that the Holy Land was six months to ride to, if you had multiple horses to relay each other. I glanced at whatever-her-name-was and thought I saw a tear in the corner of one eye, above the veil.

I paused for some time, thinking of the possible significance of this sudden and most unexpected news.

I spoke gently and carefully, so she could hear my tone if nothing else.

"Explain to her that we live in very troubled times in our country."

"Warn her most clearly that any hint or mention that she is, or even was, a princess regardless of country, would be very dangerous for her – and for us."

This was all translated, twice I thought, with her nodding at each sentence.

"Can she pick one name we should use?" I asked.

Without needing to ask, Luther replied "Azizah is her first name my lord".

"Does Azizah realise that she came here as a slave, that some job of work has to be done by us all and that the only title around here that matters is mine?" I asked.

After some back and forth between them, Luther answered on her behalf:

"She does accept all that my lord and thanks you for her safety".

"What a clever answer" I thought to myself.

Luther went on "She claims some skill with food my lord - there are other things, but we don't have enough words between us to understand."

"No matter," I said with a smile "our kitchen needs major improvement, so tell her that." and Luther did.

They both now looked at me to see if there was anything more and I asked, "What is the purpose of her face covering?".

Again, Luther could answer, this time from his knowledge of her religion "Sir, the veil is, together with her head-dress, to maintain her modesty from anyone except her immediate family or guardian".

I thought for a moment, "Would she consider me as her guardian?". Luther turned to Azizah and translated. I looked in her eyes and she gently nodded and looked back into mine, then glanced meaningfully at Luther.

"Wait outside Luther" I said. "Certainly sir" he replied and hobbled out of the room, closing the door behind him.

"So, now..." I wondered to myself, "is the covering truly an article of her faith, or is it to cover some deformity?"

I gestured to Azizah to remove her veil.

She pushed her shawl back from her head and slowly removed her veil.

My

Jaw

Dropped

Long shiny black hair framed an oval face of perfect symmetry, with a delicate chin and elegant neck.

The darkest brown eyes, with long thick lashes, held mine with a steady gaze. They were almond-shaped, slanting slightly up at the outer edges.

Her skin a dusky light brown, purple-pink lips, full-shaped like two bows against each other. The line of her mouth between them being straight and not wavy. I'd noticed in others that this straightness of mouth seemed to go with the firmer, more resolute characters, so I considered myself forewarned. Her nose quite large, curved and noble - all in such perfect harmony. She now seemed much younger than her manner and bearing suggested, not even my age I would say. So, nineteen or perhaps twenty? No matter.

I blinked, quickly shut my mouth, tried to appear unaffected - and utterly failed! She smiled gently at my obvious distraction and unspoken compliment. I smiled too, as much at myself as to her. I gestured to her to replace her veil and shawl, then beckoned her to follow me. We collected Luther and walked across the hall and through the corridor to the kitchens. Past the bread ovens, now cooling from their early morning work and into the main kitchen. The cook stood quickly to attention, the kitchen and scullery maids curtseyed, and all chorused a "Good morning my lord".
"Good morning to you all" I replied.
I went on "This is Azizah" indicating the exotic-looking but also rather shabbily dressed young lady. "She is to help in the kitchen and Luther here will translate".
Turning to Luther I said, "Teach her Norman words if possible, otherwise Saxon".
"Yes, my lord" he replied.
Cook didn't look too happy but that was no concern of mine.
I then went on a tour of the outer wall with the senior sergeant. I finished my rounds of the castle around noon and adjourned to the Hall for lunch. In between audiences and court sessions, I kept a dining table on the dais for myself and any senior staff I invited to discuss matters of my estate.
The Warden was at table with me this day and our soup and bread arrived. Used to little more than hot water with chunks of tasteless chicken in it we glanced twice at this very different content. There were clearly many ingredients, a much thicker constituency and a divine smell.
We exchanged glances and raised eyebrows before ceasing our conversation dead and reaching for our spoons.

As the other tables around the Hall were served by the kitchen maids, a chorus of "Oooos" and "Ahhhs" went up.

Someone asked for more, but I banged my spoon on the table to get my bowl refilled first!

Having finished a double helping of our usually good bread and most unusually good soup, we continued to debate the advisability of more accommodation within the bailey but then... chaos erupted from the kitchens, echoing down the corridor. A shriek of a woman's anger, followed by incredibly loud and fast female shouting in a foreign tongue. Some male voice arguing back in Saxon and the verbal duel went on and bloody on. I raised my chin to the corporal I saw nearest the kitchen corridor and he went to investigate.

Moments later the cook scurried into the Hall and stopped at the stairs to the dais, all the while wringing his hands.

He bowed and waited for me to acknowledge his presence.

"I'm sorry my lord, but I cannot work with that... that... woman!".

"She will not do what I tell her and keeps telling me what to do – and she is just a slave!".

Meanwhile, Luther had hobbled into the Hall, lightly supported by Azizah. I waved the cook aside and indicated that Azizah should take his place. She did a nodding sort of bow to me and waited for Luther to explain.

"My lord" he began "the p... I mean Azizah is used to... leading in... her...her... work".

I looked at Luther sternly and he realised his blunder in nearly using the 'princess' word. I pondered a moment and then asked the group "Who made the soup this lunch?"

The cook answered "It was me and the kitchen maids sire, all doing what this woman said to do – she did nothing except keep telling us what to do – she's very persistent my lord..." he said, wringing his hands some more.

"I cannot work this way my lord, I am the man, the head of the kitchen..." he went on, and sunk himself in the process.

I had to suppress a smile when I heard Percival in my head again "...say as little as possible..."

"Cook," I said in serious voice, "if the Empress Matilda calls here to visit – will you tell her she cannot rule because she is... a woman?"

"I... I... suppose not my lord" he stuttered.

"Very wise" I continued, "as a sudden death might result."

"So... cook... you were appointed as cook, not head of kitchen."
"You will be advised by this woman and produce more excellent meals – or leave us."
"Very well my lord" he said meekly and hung his head.
Meanwhile Luther had been whispering translations in Azizah's ear, and I could see her eyes widen in surprise.
I turned to Luther and said "Tell her to be more... gentle in her... leading of the kitchen"
He translated for her and she acknowledged me with another nodding bow, turned to the cook and gave him a small bow of apology – making the cook blush, smile with embarrassment and do a clumsy bow back.
I waved them all away but called to Luther as he started to hop off "Do have the maids show Azizah how to curtsey".
"Certainly sire" he replied.
I rubbed my forehead to try and relieve a sudden headache, turned to my table companion and said, "Come Warden, let's go to the forest and kill something!"

That evening, the hall was packed with tables and all off-duty staff.
Word had gone around after lunch and it was a full house.
The evening meal did not disappoint.
Thin slices of juicy venison with crisp bacon slices between them, covered in some sort of dark red, nearly sweet fruity sauce. The buttered leek with parsnip and other vegetables were also delicious.
A sweet that followed was a flat tart of apple and cinnamon, with cream in a jug if wanted. We did want.
Afterwards, I had to shake my head in wonderment, this was all our produce, just as before – but ohhhh so much better in this meal.
With the maids having cleared the plates, I called for all kitchen staff to come into the Hall.
They appeared, all looking a little apprehensive – apart from Azizah.
I just called out "Excellent, thank you!" and clapped them.
The happy diners raised the roof with a cheer.

The morale around the castle further improved, with even our breakfast porridge made better with honey and fruits of the season.
We had new recruits from far and wide, queueing up to be taken

on; discipline and efficiency improved even more as the soldiers and other staff became determined not to be let go.

I thought long and hard about Azizah – in so many ways!

The least I could do was release her from slavery. As a freewoman, she could earn money and own property - even leave if she wished. But I hoped, very much, that she would stay.

So, I held a ceremony in the Hall, one morning before Manor Court. She received a scroll signifying her freedom, with a copy going to the castle records and another to the church. With her remarkable and rapidly increasing grasp of Saxon, she was able to say "Thank you my lord" while performing a fair curtsey. The sweet, accented sound of her voice, saying those words, left me with many a sleepless night.

With the kitchens now well organised and supplied, I would often take Azizah with us around my domain. Point out the purpose of the various buildings, answer her questions. She was good company – once she had managed to curb her instinct to head the column and learnt to ride behind me. Clearly, she had found the much more widely used Saxon language easier to pick up. Thus, she had used such words to train her usual horse to kneel, so making it easier for her to mount, as she preferred and was determined to use a normal saddle. This lowering of the horse also stopped the 'accidental' walking by of the men trying to view her legs if she was swinging herself up on the stirrup.

She still had her purple gown but its badly fraying condition caused the maids to 'find' some material that I imagine I paid for. They made a replacement for her, a new white linen gown with large purple sections let into it and a purple shawl to cover her hair, with a new purple veil to match of course... She wore it with pride and style, indeed from any distance, she now looked more the lady of the castle than servant...

The Warden was due to go to London and pay the Royal taxation owing on the fief. He was to go with an escort of twenty, signifying the importance of the mission. I told him to wait while the money was recorded, check the amount on the receipt and to buy the senior clerk an expensive meal out, all as insurance for anyone claiming it hadn't been paid. Ohhhh the things I had learned in Warwick's service! Also, after much thought, I gave him the task of finding a couple of very unusual items to bring back.

Although a couple of days longer on the trip than planned, the Warden reported that all had gone well. The tax receipt was then duly filed, in the now improving castle records.
Once we were in private, he produced the two items both nicely wrapped in some dark green shiny cloth.
"These things were not expensive after all, sire, but my goodness they were hard to find."
I nodded my thanks and unwrapped the weightier of the two.
This was a large book, with a much faded red and gold cover, its spine had split but you could hold the parts together adequately.
The long strokes and tight squiggles of the writing was beyond any understanding for me.
"Is this Arabic?" I asked.
"The book-seller swore it was Persian sir" he replied.
"Very well" I said, "I imagine either will do.".
The other item was a Persian dagger - very unlike my Norman one.
It was broader in the blade at the hilt, curving to its point, with a white handle, shaped for good grip and possibly made from bone?
"Tusk of elephant, the vendor said sire", and we shared a "whatever an elephant is" look between us.
It had a cloth sheath, attached to a broad belt, made in the softest leather.
"The blade is supposed to be 'Turkish' sir" he said.
I wiped the blade with a clean cloth and with the dust and light grime removed, you could see it had the same silvery finish that my sword possessed.
"THIS was NOT expensive?" I asked in considerable surprise.
"Seems no one wanted the curved blade my lord, it had been in the shop for years"
I tested the blade with a piece of wood – it was wickedly sharp.

Some days later, after the evening meal, I had Azizah fetched to my room.
She entered, curtseyed briefly and stood looking a little unsettled.

I smiled in genuine happiness at seeing her and I think she relaxed, well, maybe a little.

On my table were the two cloth-wrapped items.

I picked up the larger one with some ceremony and with it born in my two hands, stretched out to present it to her.

She reached out to accept it, slightly puzzled by the size and weight. Then she carefully began to unwrap it, seeming to guess it was a book and feeling a small wobble in it as the spine shifted, she went even more cautiously.

As the end of the green cloth was lifted and the red and gold cover was revealed, she seemed to recognise something in the pattern and the deepest gasp I had ever heard from anyone, came from her. She started to shake in her whole body, her hands quivering as she traced the outlines of the gold decoration. She fell to her knees, and still shaking, opened the cover with great gentleness. Her fingers floated above the lettering and she let out the loudest wailing cry. If the highest joy and the deepest grief could be in one sound, then this was it. It felt like a call to her homeland, the place that was so unimaginably far away.

The wailing ended. She slowly closed the book, hugged it to her chest and sobbed and sobbed and sobbed.

I knew not what to do. I'm sure Eede would have known but I had no idea. So I reached down, gently but awkwardly squeezed her shoulder. Then I went down to the Hall for a beer or two with the Warden and sent a couple of maids to look after Azizah.

As my second beer was going down, I saw Azizah walk slowly into the Hall and stop at the steps to the dais. I beckoned her to approach. She walked up the small steps, stopped and gave the deepest and most gracious curtsey I had EVER seen, her long gown fanned out wide against the floor.

I was stunned!

She stood up slowly and with tears still in her eyes said, "Thank you my lord, thank you my lord". Then she bobbed the smallest and fastest curtsey I'd ever seen, hitched up her skirts and ran sobbing from building.

I turned to the Warden who had been caught mid-drink by this display. He swallowed, turned to me and said, "Women eh my Lord, women!"

"Indeed Warden" was all I could manage in reply.

We clinked our tankards and got back to the beer.

The following week on a Tuesday, the day broke fresh but very sunny. Thinking this could be the last pleasant day before the next threatening bitter winter, I called for Azizah and an escort of twelve and went for a ride up the river. As a courtesy call, we stopped at the mill of Adelaert. He was always nervous to see me, even though up to date with his taxes.

As we rode away, Azizah spurred her horse alongside and asked, "Do you joke him lord?". I had to laugh!

"Yes, I'm afraid I was joking" I admitted.

She gently wagged a finger at me and said "Bad lord, bad lord" while giggling.

I just grandly waved her back to 'her position' behind me.

We stopped for a sit on the riverbank, just as the sun reached its warmest for the day. Our escort fanned out in a half-circle and gave me some space.

I had an old blanket hitched to my saddle, so we sat on that and watched one of the last trading boats of the season make its way upstream, being towed by a couple of horses on the far bank.

I thought for a moment, then gestured her to stay sitting and went back to my horse's saddlebags.

I pulled out the other green-wrapped package, took it back to her and sat down next to her again.

Glancing at my soldiers to check if they were still all facing out and away from us, I put the item on the grass and pulled away the cloth. She gasped deeply at this present, though with less fervour and reaction than for her religious book, thank goodness.

I pushed it towards her and gestured that it was to be hers. She gasped again at the implication of the gift. I was giving her the power of instant life or death. The ultimate last resort protection against... me, the world or almost anything was now in her hands. She drew the dagger slightly out of its sheath and made a purring sound at the shine of the blade. She used some word in her tongue

to describe it, but she sounded impressed. I did notice that, although the dagger hilt was a bit small for me, it seemed to fit her little hand perfectly. I had no idea if she would have this as a keepsake in her room, or was something she would carry, some or all of the time but I was soon to get an answer. She stood up and looked around to see that the boat was gone out of sight now.
She looked along our soldiers and saw all were on guard still, facing away. I stood up puzzled for a moment at her actions.
Then she looked me boldly in the eyes and said, "Lord no see."
"See what?" I thought, then she raised her eyebrows as if to say "and you're still looking!" I finally saw her meaning, said "Ahhhh." and she teasingly rolled her eyes. I turned my back to her and spread my cloak out with my arms, to further give her some privacy. I heard some swishing and rustling of fabric, some quiet little intakes of breath, more rustling, then silence.
"Thank you my lord" she said beautifully.
I turned around and in bowing to me, she reached out and kissed my hand. I smiled wide, nodded gently to her and gestured that we should go. I noticed the dagger and sheath had disappeared, somewhere, and she had kept hold of the green cloth, carefully folded. I reflected, as we rode our horses back home, that it was not unusual for ladies of the time to have a little something tucked away just in case... but it was HIGHLY unusual to arm your servants.
But being honest with myself, I could not regard her as a servant any more...

Azizah was very quiet on the way back, lost in thought, very subdued; so much so that even the escort noticed.
When we returned our horses to the stables, Azizah curtseyed to me and wordlessly departed for the kitchens.
"Lady alright sir?" asked the corporal.
"Women eh corporal, women!" I replied.
"Amen to that sir." he said and turned back to begin looking after his horse.
I handed my mount off to a stable-boy and smiled to myself, because even to the rough, tough soldiers, Azizah radiated quality; a Lady indeed – if only they knew.
Amira Azizah, Princess of Nishapor – if only they knew!

The Anarchy:
Slave To Fortune

Part 2

Monday 4th November 1140, Haverhill Castle

This day brought in a chill wind and letter of some concern.

I, Sir Walter De Marren, Lord of Haverhill was required to attend the Kings Parliament, this being confirmed with a Royal Seal.

As a very minor fief-holder compared to most in the realm, I had assumed that such a call would almost never arise.

On further reading, I found I was to represent Aubrey de Vere, Count of Guines in Normandy and holder of many English lands and titles. The letter stated that Aubrey was 'too ill to attend' and I was to step in. When I discussed this with Gerald, his eyes grew wide at the possible implications; seems Aubrey held most of his domains abroad from the Empress Matilda, rather than her enemy, our present King Stephen. After much discussion, we decided I would act as the simple messenger-boy, while taking as strong an escort as could be spared.

The date of attendance allowed little time to prepare, particularly as I would first need to visit Aubrey, at Hedingham Castle, to gather his instructions. I would be gone up to two weeks and would have to leave my fief in the care of my Warden, the two senior sergeants and Azizah. Her ability to speak Saxon had improved significantly, even coping with the many Norman words that were now being mixed in by everyone. As things now were, she only occasionally needed Luther to translate.

It was a wrench to leave my castle, my land and... Azizah. Her delightful presence around all parts of the fief cheered everyone, especially me. However, duty called, so I reluctantly set off to Hedingham and thence to London, accompanied by 24 soldiers.

I visited Count Aubrey without issue, he appeared in good health and it seemed that Gerald's estimation of 'diplomatic illness' was correct. Indeed, Aubrey seemed more interested in the finishing touches to his new castle than matters of state.

The parliamentary session was relatively brief, by the standards of these things, so the trip only took ten days and passed without incident.

Indeed, the only surprise came at the very end...

We arrived back in mid-afternoon, paused 200 yards from the castle to allow us to be recognised. The drawbridge was lowered for us and we entered the bailey.

Now came the shock.

I saw Azizah, walking from the Keep across to the Hall and smiled to myself – briefly. As she passed each maid, the servant would bob a small curtsey, and as she passed each man-at-arms, he would briefly stand to attention and nod. Azizah would acknowledge each of these signs with a gracious nod of her head!

I walked my horse towards the Keep as the Warden and senior sergeant walked quickly from the Keep to greet me, as I stopped and dismounted.

"Welcome back, my..." they both began.

I held up my hand and pointed at Azizah, just as she was going into the kitchen door – past an 'honour guard' of three soldiers who had just come to attention. With a mixture of puzzlement and growing irritation I said with increasing volume,

"Seems my servant is promoted... **chatelaine**!" using a very Norman word for a lady who runs a castle or large house.

My Saxon sergeant may not have known the exact word, but he certainly knew what I meant.

"Much has happened, my Lord..." he started.

"So I bloody see!" I said with some feeling.

I took a breath and looked at the two men - they looked concerned at my temper but not worried about anything they might have done wrong. I trusted these two, had trusted them, with everything I had. Maybe I'd been hasty, perhaps tired and sore from the journey. I turned, waved dismissal to my escort and turned back.

"Time for a beer" I said.

"Yes, Sire!" they said as one and we adjourned to the Hall.

It took the first pint to catchup on the matters of my domain. The Warden confirmed our tax-collecting was going well, while supplies and stores were slowly improving in quantity and quality. Work on the walls had gone well until more frequent rains slowed the progress.

The sergeant stated manning strengths and described progress on training the less experienced men. He informed us that at least half of the original stock of broad-head arrows had been improved and we now had 400 new bodkin[27] arrows.

At that point Azizah appeared, waiting at the steps to the dais where I had my dining table. I paused the conversation and beckoned her to approach. She gave me a truly graceful curtsey and said:

"Welcome, my lord, journey London good?" - all in quite understandable Saxon but with her exotic accent giving it a very special sound. I almost forgot to reply as I was captivated by her lovely eyes, showing above her veil. Blinking myself back to reality, I said "Thank you Azizah, the trip went very well."

All the while thinking "God, I've missed the sight of you, the sound of you..."

Her eyes sparkled at me as she smiled behind her veil.

"We think venison dinner, my lord, is good?" she asked.

"That would be very good, thank you Azizah" I replied.

She nodded, curtseyed wonderfully again and went back to the kitchens.

"You could tell her to take that mask off, my lord, she might look the better for it" the Warden said.

"I could - but I will not," I replied, "the veil is to do with her religion and that's that."

"Ah" he said and stayed quiet.

The beer jug then arrived to break the awkward silence.

After a few sips, I said "So, who wants to explain the apparent... elevation of my servant?". It was the sergeant's turn to say "Ah!" and I gave him my undivided attention.

As the sergeant told it, it all started with a routine trip to the town market the previous Wednesday...

---

[27] Slim, needle-nosed arrow heads for piercing chain mail and wooden shields; so **not** the bigger, heavier, tin-opener type used in later centuries against thicker plate armour

A corporal and six men were escort to the supply cart for the weekly supplies. The cook was due to accompany the cart-driver but fell unwell the previous night. So Azizah offered to come, to help chose produce and, as it turned out, to be a ferocious haggler with the traders, getting us top quality and best prices on most things.

All was fine until they left the town around Sext (noon) and immediately, the cart had a wheel collapse. They were too far from the castle to signal for a replacement cart and by the time the wheelwright was rousted out of an inn, fetched his tools and carried out a lengthy repair, the light was beginning to fade.

Torn between staying the night in town, with no money left (after paying for supplies and wheel repair) and heading briskly for home – the corporal decided to push on to the castle.

It was only a half-mile...

Mid-way between town and castle, bandits pounced from the forest. Fifteen or sixteen of the villains, on about twelve horses. The solo riders attacked our soldiers and the two-up horses dropped a man each at the wagon and went on to engage the escorts.

Three of the brigands thus landed on the back of the cart and made straight for Azizah. All three died there and then.

"Seems she must have grabbed one of their weapons and turned it on them!" said the sergeant.

One attacker had been carrying a short-bow and a quiver of arrows. Azizah grabbed the bow, hid behind the cart and sent arrows into the backs of the bandits that were beginning to push the remaining soldiers further away from the cart.

A couple of our men were dead on the ground at that point.

It wasn't known how many she pegged with her shafts, as some screamed and rode away bleeding. But four were unhorsed and met their end under the swords of our remaining men. We had two dead soldiers and three with wounds too severe to ride.

The wounded were laid in the cart, on straw between the supplies and Azizah commanded the driver to drive like his life depended on it. Apparently, the sight of a fighting-mad Azizah, covered from head to toe in bandit blood would have motivated the Pope to do her will!

A hasty relief force galloped from the castle to prevent a further attack and recover the two bodies of ours.

A hundred yards from the castle, the newly repaired wheel broke again, with all the spokes now coming off the hub. The cart promptly slanted to the ground on one side. The horses felt the increased load and stopped in their tracks. Azizah was now tending to the wounded in the back of the cart, using torn strips of her dress to staunch the bleeding. Her forceful, kitchen-slang-Saxon orders to the driver were heard at the top the keep. He whipped the horses till they dragged the lop-sided cart to and over the drawbridge and into the bailey. Azizah commanded the wounded be gently carried held flat, into the 'White Room', to be placed on the beds in there. With the rooms torches all lit, Azizah went from one casualty to the next. The corporal of the escort, who had survived with minor wounds, looked into the room and said final prayers for all three, they were bleeding so much. Azizah turned to the birthing room supplies, clinked through the small potion bottles and found one that was promising and sniffed it cautiously. She poured the contents of the little bottle into the mouth of the screaming man with a sword-thrust wound to his stomach. Moving to the chest-wounded man, she whirled round, tore a strip off the bottom of a nearby maid's dress and mimed for her to tie it tight around the body and to "Make tight he not breathe."

The last casualty had a deep wound in his thigh, that was pulsing his blood away.

She thought for a second and called for the blacksmith to bring his tools. At this point, no one was going to question this blood-soaked apparition. The blacksmith arrived, panting, with his box of favourite tools. Azizah picked the tongs from the box, looked round and saw a spectating soldier with his first beer of the evening.

Grabbing the tankard, she plunged the tongs all the way in then turned back to the leg-wound man, put a cloth in his mouth, plunged the tongs into his wound, gripped something in there and hung on. The man screamed into the cloth and fainted. Azizah then asked the blacksmith to come and hold the tongs and to keep gripping with them.

Moving back to the stomach-wounded, who was writhing in pain and groaning, Azizah stroked his forehead, held his hand and crooned words in her own language.

He became quiet and still for a few minutes, then died.

"Have no worry," she said quietly, but to everyone in the room "I send him your god, not mine." The gentle caring she'd shown and the visible tears in her eyes moved the watching men and women to tears themselves.

After some time, she asked the blacksmith to slowly release the tongs and the chest bandage to be untied. The leg seemed not to be bleeding nearly so much but the chest had to be tightly bandaged again. Azizah struggled for Saxon words at this point, with everyone trying to help – to no avail. The call went up to "Fetch Luther", who soon arrived from the Wardens office. After a few sentences of Arabic between them, Luther announced "We need the strongest drink there is", the rest was drowned out by a vocal response of "Don't we all!" and "Large one for me!" and "Waes Hael!" from the onlookers. "No, you sodden bastards," cried Luther in frustration "it's for cleaning er... things"

"Ohhhh" went the crowd, disappointed now.

"Lord Walter has some strong wine locked away" said someone.

"You mean brandy, you old scobberlotcher" said another.

"Bran-dy? What is? Where?" asked Azizah getting louder again and moving towards the watchers.

The crowd shrunk away, and many headed out the door.

Quite soon the Warden arrived – then fetched some of the brandy. Meanwhile, Azizah had asked for needle, thread and honey.

Again no one questioned this and maids trotted away to fetch the items. Azizah poured the brandy into a bowl, then washed her hands with soap and water in another bowl. She placed the needle and lengths of thread into the brandy, along with a small spoon from the kitchen. Then she rested her fingers in the brandy for a few minutes before shaking off the drops and turning to the leg-wound in the still unconscious man.

She poured a tiny amount of brandy into the deep wound then squeezed the fluid back out and onto the floor.

The onlookers groaned at the waste and Azizah hissed at them to keep quiet – which they did.

She spooned a generous amount of honey into the wound and reached for the needle and a thread. She proceeded to close the wound with a broad stitching, ignoring two of the crowd who fainted at her first pull tight. Finally, she turned to the man with the chest wound and did much the same for him.

The remaining watchers now nodding to each other, as instant 'experts', as each step was followed. The sergeant finished his telling, looked in his empty tankard and sighed.

I waved for more beer.

I was speechless, as was the Warden – who, before now, had only heard a small part of the whole story. Our tankards were refilled from a large jug and we sipped in silence for a minute, letting that all sink in.

"So, you see sir, we lost three men, but it could have been eight, and lost the lady – and the wagon with supplies…"

He went on "The two she treated are healing well but won't be back on duty for a while, especially Roberts with the leg."

"The lady cleaned herself in a laundry tub, err… so we heard sir."

"And the maids were up all night, cleaning and fixing the lady's gown."

"So, with the Lady Eede gone, I think the castle-folk have… taken to a new lady, adopted her like…" and his voice trailed off in thought, wondering if he'd said too much.

"And you Warden, how do you see things?" I said.

"Well sire," he said with the frankness of two large beers in him "I think the lady has brought nothing but good things to us all."

They both sipped in silence, waiting for my reaction.

"Thank you both for your words, I will consider all," I said and suddenly felt the need for some solitude.

"Join me after breakfast tomorrow, there are many changes we must make, and a plan must be laid to put an end to those bandit bastards." I stood, as did they. I walked away as they bowed, and I went to my chamber in the Keep to ponder much.

I could smile at the fact that no one had realised that Azizah's dagger had no doubt been in play against the bandits.

I could frown that this precious person had been at such terrible risk.

And I could fury at the insult to my authority the forest thieves had thrown at me.

Once in my room, I scribbled a list of things to add or change at the castle and went back down to the Hall for a much-needed dinner of venison.

After the meal, Azizah came to my table to ask if I had enjoyed everything. I thanked her for the marvellous meal and waved her to the chair where the Warden had been sitting earlier. She sat, looking a little curious and I had to smile wide at the sheer joy and relief of her survival and smile more at my delight in her gentle presence. Then I remembered her actions that fateful day and felt my face change to admiration for this small, feminine person who could also fight with fury and protect those around her.

She saw the expressions cross my face and seemed to want to know the thoughts. "What troubles you lord?" she asked.

"We nearly lost you Azizah" I replied and felt my face reflect the despair I felt at this thought.

"Your gift saved me Lord Walter – but I think no people see I have khanjar[28].", her eyes smiled.

"Even so," I went on "from now on, if you leave the castle, you must have an escort of 24."

She thought for a few moments to work the number from Saxon to Arabic and then Persian – and gasped.

"That is most you take lord – I not be so... good."

"You have become so good, so... important to everyone here"

"Him... poor... tent? I... I... not know?" she asked.

I stopped her with a gentle hand gesture and looked round for Luther. He was just finishing his meal and I waved him over.

"My lord?" he said with a bow. "Luther, what would be her word for 'important'?" I asked. He replied "*muhimun*, sir" and Azizah gasped a little. "Thank you, Luther, dismissed."

"Yes my lord" he replied, bowed and limped away.

I turned back to Azizah and said

"You first won our stomachs, now you have won our heads and our hearts." while patting over those parts of myself.

"Tomorrow I will make you Stewardess, the important lady who commands all the ladies of the castle and some of the men."

---

[28] Arabic for 'dagger with curved blade'

She sat back while she processed the new words and her eyes widened in shock at what she thought they meant.

"Slave I was for two years. I here as slave – now important lady!" she said, and I thought she was going to cry.

I grabbed her nearest hand and squeezed it until she blinked her tears away.

The next morning, as was customary before Manor Court in the Hall, I gave out the latest news and announcements to all castle staff who were not on duty. I let them know that the nuns had arrived to help with illnesses and births of the domain. The sisters were to be protected and assisted as needed. Also, that some people had earned more pay for doing excellent work and others were to move to new ranks. The senior sergeant was promoted to be 'Marshal of the Castle' and Azizah was to become 'Stewardess of the Castle'.

The murmurs of approval that greeted the earlier announcements became claps and cheers when Azizah was mentioned.

My final item related to my plan for eliminating the forest bandits. I announced a short-bow contest, to be held the next morning. Anyone wanting to enter should be able to ride and shoot at the same time.

That produced a very mixed reaction – until I indicated there was a cash prize for the best shot.

The next morning dawned bright but cold.

Three straw-figure targets were placed in a line about 20 yards apart, down the middle of the Bailey.

Each rider to pass both ways in front of the targets, while staying at least 20 yards away from them.

I watched with the Warden from the doorway of the Keep, as man after man tried and mostly failed to hit anything. One fell off his horse in the attempt, one dropped his bow, and another sent an arrow over the curtain wall towards town. Meanwhile our professional longbowmen just stood well back and shook their heads at the show.

One of the younger new soldiers did best - with one target solidly hit on his first pass and clipping one on the run back.

Then... Azizah slowly rode her small horse from the stables. She held a short-bow that I guess she'd kept from the skirmish, also a quiver of arrows was on her back.

She stopped opposite us and bowed her head, as if asking permission. I had no idea what this little lady would be able to do but with everything she'd shown us up to now, I was curious to find out. So, I nodded back and waved her on to do her worst. The men who had been watching in the courtyard, rather ungenerously, ran for cover.

Azizah turned her horse away from the targets, giving herself a long run-up, certainly compared to what we'd seen before. She turned back, gave the horse a good urging with her heels and started a trilling kind of war-cry that froze us all in open-mouthed surprise. On reaching full gallop, she loosed three arrows for three hits. After the last target, she stopped and turned the horse, all with her knees. Galloping back, she managed a hit on the first two targets – and two arrows into the last one.

She stopped her horse, made it kneel and gracefully stepped to the ground – and she hadn't touched the reins since the start. She bowed with a flourish to me and then bowed with even more flourish to the rest of the courtyard – the men broke into claps, cheers and whistles.

Even the guards on the battlements had turned around to watch the second run – and were promptly shouted at by their corporals.

I beckoned her over and she walked gracefully to just below us. She bowed, I nodded back and dropped her down the small purse for her winnings. She was thrilled, she'd clearly never had any money before – well not since Nishapor anyway.

That evening, the men from the skirmish with the bandits, found their beers had been paid for the next week – by Azizah.

Next day, I asked Azizah if she could train some men to ride and shoot. She accepted the task, going on to exercise the selected soldiers for a couple of hours each day for three weeks.

Considering how... firm she could be on occasions, she was very patient and encouraging with the men – and they hung on her every word.

The results were very worthwhile indeed, with a squad of ten, all eventually able to nearly match Azizah's example.

It was about this time that some of our soldiers were off-duty and in town for a change of ale.

A cattle-drover was at the same inn and after several pints, chose to bad-mouth our new Stewardess...

He warmed up by poking fun at our soldiers for only being part of a (relatively) small castle, owned by a very minor lord (fair comment) but my men ignored him. But then he got as far as saying "I wouldn't eat no food done by that dirty Arab slu..." before dying in the ensuing melee of cattle-folk and soldiers.

A week later, the drover's widow arrived at Manor Court claiming Wergild[29] in the sum of a very optimistic three pounds because her 'wonderful husband' had 'never done anyone wrong'.

I asked her to wait until the afternoon session and the kitchen provided lunch for her.

The innkeeper was summonsed, along with four of the soldiers that we knew had been there at the relevant time. All these witnesses (and possible defendants) requested Azizah be asked to leave before they would speak. Once she had left the Hall, the witnesses all told a similar tale of some drink and a great deal of provocation, with the worst of it impugning our lady's virtue. Even the innkeeper stated the cattle-folk were first to draw steel. I scrutinised my men as they stood in front of me; they seemed direct, truthful and clearly still feeling the insult to Azizah. Having heard the witnesses, I believe the widow recognised the weakness of her allegation and likely already knew her late spouse had been a drunken slob.

I dismissed her claim.

My toughest challenge to date at Haverhill was now upon me.

The forest bandits must be dealt with; the leaves were off the trees, but the worst of the weather was yet to come – the time was now.

I had bribed, threatened and blackmailed as necessary, any and all woodcutters, poachers and field workers from the plots near the woods; all to find out where the thieves' den was not.

---

[29] A punishment for murder. This was a fine paid to the victim's family and seen as compensation for the loss of life. The fine payable was decided by social status - your class judged how much your life was worth

This did, however, reduce my area of unknown to about a third of the extensive forest to the south of my castle. I set a pattern of sending out strong 'hunting parties' across that part, to bring back fresh game - and also look for signs of robbers. Their reports meant that I now had one swath of the central woodland that hadn't been swept. It was roughly square in shape, bounded by foresters' trails to the east and west. A good stream was known to run through that part of the forest, so my guess was they were mid-way between the tracks and on or near that stream.

I had three 'hunting parties' chosen that afternoon, 48 men in total, the most I could risk. I sent them up to the walkways on the northern curtain wall, all looking back, into the bailey. All were very puzzled, especially as this meant they were all looking down on their lord. With the help of the sergeants, some hoes, rakes and long ropes of different colours, I mapped out the forest that they could see in the distance over our southern wall.

The routes the groups would take was demonstrated and the need for silent approach made extremely clear. I explained it as two hammers hitting a piece of steel on an anvil, which seemed to register with even the slowest soldiers.

At the end I looked up at their stern faces and they all seemed to have got the idea. And they were greatly cheered when they realised there was no guard duty for them that night. The castle was now closed-up early, no one in or out, in case gossip spread.

Our 'hunters' left at first light, each party taking a different route. Two parties swept east, one on each side of the stream, came across the bandit camp and drove the bastards straight into the third party waiting on the trail. Luckily, we had the mounted archers in the force, as the bandits numbered more than sixty, with a few more that were sick or injured. The bowmen used their new skills to greatly thin out the numbers reaching the blocking party. As I had ordered, only three of the surrendered were brought back to the castle. All others were left to feed the foxes and wolves. As my hunters returned, I sent another force with extra saddlebags and rope to carry or drag back anything of use from the robber camp. They came back loaded with various weaponry, clothing, pots, metal candlesticks and other church items. Also, well over £300 in gold, silver and pennies – and they recovered as many arrows as possible.

The three survivors arrived with hoods over their heads, including the so-called 'leader' of this iniquitous band. All were put in the dungeon cells until next Manor Court.

I would give them a fair trial before finding them guilty and executing them.

Come the next court day and the three malevolent individuals were presented in front of me in the Hall. All rope-tied by hand and foot. I had as many of my men as we could spare, line the walls, with spears at their side. We had far more spectators in the building than usual and I would not tolerate any disruption. I dealt with theft first, asking them to state how they had lawfully acquired the money, church property and other items that were laid out on the stage. They could not account for any of it, so I confiscated all and ordered the return of the church's belongings. Then I moved on to more serious matters - the four dresses retrieved from the forest camp. The families of the missing girls were allowed to view these on the stage and two pairs of parents broke down sobbing, when their daughters clothing was put in front of them.

I asked the brigands if they could show me where these two girls now lived, thus reducing the charges to 'merely' abduction.

They were silent and hung their heads.

I sensed a mood of justifiable rage was growing in the Hall.

Many townsfolk were becoming loud and unruly, ready to pass their own sentence – which I would not allow against my authority.

Some force drove me to my feet and I felt that Norman fury inside me burst out.

I thundered for silence – which was immediate.

I briefly and clearly reminded them that this was my fief, my court and my judgement.

Then I made them all wait, while I scanned the Hall for any dissenting thought, let alone voice – you could have heard a pin drop as all avoided my gaze. Tales of my temper having been well told throughout the domain.

I addressed the accused by name, stated that the charges of theft, abduction and murder were all proven.

They would be returned to the dungeons while gallows were built in town and their execution would then take place.

The packed crowd erupted with a growling, howling cheer and the sobbing villains were led away. I commanded the Hall to be cleared and we adjourned for lunch. I did then notice the steadiness and pride in the faces of my soldiers, pleased to have been part of this closure to a trying time for the people of my land.

The afternoon court session was tame by comparison.
We now had a new bar across in front of the stage, so plaintiffs, defendants and witnesses had to step to this bar to speak. This seemed to add more solemnity to the occasion – and act as a barrier to any more flying witches.
The families of the murdered girls asked for some Wergild, which I granted at a relatively high amount of £10 each – as the claims of virginity seemed genuine as, of course, was their understandable grief.
Later on, I had some water rights to decide, petty theft, strip ownership, plough damage to neighbor's land and so on. Another novelty was that Azizah had asked to view the proceedings, a request which intrigued me. I called for a chair for her to sit on the stage, behind the curtain, next to the longbowmen standing guard with arrows nocked. A moth-hole in the curtain, not yet repaired, gave her sight of the people at the bar.
By late afternoon, I had had enough with dispensing justice for the day and closed the session. I called for cloaks for Azizah and myself and asked her to walk with me, as I needed to stretch my legs after an unusually long and intense court day.
She was clearly lost in thought for a while as we toured the bailey, checking on progress of the building works and dropping in on the various tradesmen, to make sure they were being productive.

She eventually broke her silence.
"I saw you hear all people lord," she began "man and woman are same…"
"Important?" I suggested.
"Yes lord, same important. If man say a thing and woman say other thing, how choose you?"
"If that is all there is, I have to watch very carefully for truth…"
"Your law same same for woman and man?" she asked.

"We have no written law, just customs and rules passed down from King Arthur many years ago". I'd learned this from lessons with my mother and watching the Steward of Warwick hold court in Lord Roger's usual absence. I went on "Women have the same... voice in law although fewer property rights, but... they do not get punished as badly as men". "I... think I know lord, thank you. It very... different my land" I walked her back to the kitchens as full dark fell.

The reedman was doing the rounds replacing torches and still grumbling, this time about the coldness of his work – much of it in the waters of the moat and river. As the nearest new torch took to flame, I could see Azizah's sparkling eyes and thought she smiled behind her veil; I know I was smiling like the village idiot, just delighted with her company.

She curtseyed her farewell and I bowed in reply to my Stewardess.

We had two bright and sunny days but then, as in life, especially in our times, storm clouds rolled in. The number of letters arriving for all of us suddenly increased from the infrequent to the daily. The Warden was receiving from other wardens and reeves, Gerald had his own connections across the country. My own increased both in number and the darkness of tone.

We'd had a visit from one of Lord Roger's senior knights, one of the hard-eyed pair I had met at Warwick when I was knighted. I'm sure he didn't come all this way just for us; no doubt he had first seen Count Aubrey. When we were alone after an evening meal and sat by the fire in my private parlour room next the Hall, he gave me a scroll of instructions. Details on how to validate and interpret future letters, how to write and send replies...

He complimented me on the good state of the castle, soldiers and food. Also, he mentioned how useful it was that I could read and write, to avoid sharing anything with clerks or scribes – thanks again to my parents I thought. He'd seen that we still flew the Royal Standard over our Haverhill colours on the Keep flagstaff. He gently suggested that the royal colours should be taken down "for a lengthy clean and repair..." I nodded slowly with much thought and some shock; dark clouds certainly were looming.

Two days later, my first letters arrived from Lord Roger. One gave me news of King Stephen's 'difficulties' in the North, largely caused by that Lord Ranulf de Gernon of Chester. Ranulf was the evil one, from whom I had secured my fief in exchange for the body of the slain William of Hereford. The other letters advised me to do certain things in one letter and warn me not to do those things in the other – in complete contradiction.

The difference was that one contained the secret letters and numbers to tell which to act upon.

In summary, this all pointed to a shift away from backing our current King and towards the Empress Matilda. In my region, that meant at least being civil to Geoffrey[30] of Huntingdon and his spider-web of subject lords – quite a change in position.

The very next morning, shouts from the Keep lookouts announced sight of a large armed force, three miles to the southeast.

Trumpets sounded, all soldiers reported to the battlements, archers made ready, drawbridge raised, portcullis down and gates closed – all in a very few minutes. After half an hour or so, the Keep reported red and gold colours seen – Matilda!

From my place atop the gatehouse, I glanced up to ensure our Kings colours had been removed from the high flagpole. Then I commanded the drawbridge to be lowered and the portcullis raised, leaving the gates closed. The sergeants and corporals briefly queried their hearing of the order but quickly complied, while looking very puzzled indeed. After another few minutes, the mounted force came into view. Five hundred light cavalry, all smartly turned out, headed by a lady on a magnificent bay horse. As she drew nearer, we could see her flaming red hair and pale skin, common in her family. She wore a gold coronet over a white silk shawl, with a rich red gown.

I called the men on the battlements to attention and bowed as she passed. She gently nodded acknowledgement and I think smiled slightly at the message I was sending. With the gates shut, I was clearly not inviting her in, but I was allowing her to come over the drawbridge and knock, if she so wished.

---

[30] Geoffrey de Mandeville II, 1st Earl of Essex

"Important lady?" Azizah asked from over my shoulder, getting to give good use to her new word. "Indeed," I said, "very important..." I just hoped they weren't hungry, else my town might be somewhat pressed as the force passed through. I turned away from the parapet and saw Gerald looking off in the distance – and audibly sighing. I think he had been impressed by the Empress before – as he would have previously seen her several times at Chester. Azizah lifted her gown a little, to go down the open steps from the battlements, so I gently held her arm to keep her safe from a stumble. We reached the bailey floor; she twinkled her eyes at me, bowed a little and I watched as she walked away towards the Hall to chase up our delayed lunch. Halfway there, she stopped, turned around and saw me looking still. She bowed again, to which I responded, and we went on with our day.

As the sun was setting, a solitary figure was seen, hobbling along and using a staff to keep him upright.
He claimed to be a pilgrim and was looking for his son, who lived in this county.
The guards allowed in this very elderly man, before shutting the castle for the night. The sons name was Gwilym, who proved to be our fletcher – with the old man being his grandfather, Morfran. I was told of the arrival and I ordered that he be given a meal if he wanted and bed-space for the night. Next morning saw me on my rounds of the tradesmen when I came across these two in intense but incomprehensible discussion in Welsh. I shook Morfran's hand and complimented him on having such a fine grandson - they both blushed with pride. The old boy looked very ill though, with frequent coughing whenever the cold wind blew. When he got his breath, he said he had 'some experience' as an archer but had been unable to draw a war-bow for many a long year. He also used to work in bow-making back in his native Wales. I remembered that 'bows in Wales' meant the longbow that had greeted the first Norman expeditions into that country. Even 'The Conquerors' army

had decided not to push against that and left it to the Marcher Lords[31] to invade for their profit, at their risk. He had inspected our arrow stocks and suggested we remove the varnish from the shafts; his reasons being that it saved a little weight, took less time to make and the rougher surface rode the air better than the polished. I pointed out that this would make them more vulnerable to rain but Morfran sharply told me to always keep them protected. He did at least say "my lord" at the end of his firm recommendation! I instructed our longbowmen to test this change as soon as possible. They reported back later that day; they couldn't measure the weight that was saved but the unvarnished did fly five to ten yards further when shot to pass through a barrel hoop eighty yards away. During the afternoon, Morfran talked with the bowyer and passed on some advice on finishing yew staves into longbows. Our man had been struggling to get the draw weights matching the height of the bows for different sized archers. All this contribution meant that granddad was treated to another good meal and some beer that night. Next morning, he said his farewells and resumed his quest to visit the shrine at Fornham All Saints.

Shortly after his departure, the Keep lookouts reported a body on the track to the east. Morfran had collapsed and was brought back to the castle and into the White Room. The nuns only had time to give him his last rites before he expired. Gwilym was deeply upset, indeed the old chap seemed to have made a connection to all who had met him. After a moment's thought, I instructed a coffin and cart to be made ready, with an escort of four soldiers. I told Gwilym to take his grandfather to the shrine, have his soul blessed and return for burial in Haverhill. The young man broke down and sobbed at my feet, he seemed particularly moved that his grandfather would be having an escort. I just patted his head, mouthed some platitudes and thought to myself that the protection was really for my fletcher, who would be hard to replace.

---

[31] i.e. the lords of lands on the borders

When all was ready, I gave the senior soldier a small purse for food along the way and the blessing, then waved them on their way. Come the last week of November, we were visited by a vassal[32] of Count Aubrey's. This was Lord Clément Devereux of Saffron Walden and other fiefs. Not someone I would have offered to host prior to the recent shifting in the political sands. He had ferret-like features, was slippery by nature and was as Norman as his name implies. He disparaged anything Saxon and insulted Azizah when she visited our table to simply ask if we had enjoyed the meal. He took one look at her veil and dusky skin and cried "Ah ha! So, this is the famous Arab har…" I raised my hand to silence him, just as the guards nearest us growled through gritted teeth and Azizah swept away back to the kitchen. "Ho! Haverhill!" he cried, "you should keep your dogs on a shorter leash", gesturing to the mainly Saxon soldiers around the room. I said loudly, slowly and clearly "The lady is Stewardess of the Castle and is Persian by birth. Persians have fought the Arabs for centuries." Clearly an utterly shameless bastard, Clément was unrepentant, saying, "Well that's as maybe but you can't tell me you haven't tupped that?" Now that freed my inner demons. I felt a change in my face, felt my ancestors looking through my eyes – he saw them too. With his face paled he said, "Perhaps I was over… hasty to judge". I nodded twice, very, very slightly.

I crisply requested Azizah to be asked to return up to our table and stood up. Clément suddenly grasped that he should stand too. She did return, but this time her smiling eyes were gone, replaced with what I had come to know as her 'princess eyes'; serenely and effortlessly confident, shrewd and commanding by her very presence. Our guest saw something there too and looked genuinely, if briefly, contrite. "Lord Devereux, "I said, "may I introduce The Lady Azizah, Stewardess of Castle Haverhill." Clément was so unsettled, he almost bowed first but just caught himself as Azizah gave a half-curtsey, with her unblinking gaze never leaving his. He gave a formal bow and said, "Very pleased to meet you… my lady," and stuttered, "thank you for the excellent meal."

---

[32] a holder of land and/or title by feudal tenure on conditions of homage and allegiance

"You are very welcome lords" she replied. Turning slightly to me, she gave me a glorious full curtsey and went back to the kitchens. "Well fock me Walter, that put me in my place!" he gasped quietly and seemingly without rancour. We resumed our seats and I waved for some wine – from Normandy of course. Adjourning to my room next the Hall, we continued our discussions late into the evening - or rather, he talked a lot about his holdings and very little about the purpose, if any, of his visit. He shared some news about the progress Matilda was making in the northeast, which combined with her already firm positions in the southwest and Welsh Marches, was beginning to make King Stephen look weaker with each passing day. We both doubted much more would happen before winter had run its course. Seems no one wanted a repeat of the blizzard battles that were experienced the previous year.

I had two large rooms on the first floor of the Keep allocated to him and his men. With a significant number of my soldiers already quietly positioned on the second floor. Also, I had allocated two guards to be with Azizah at all times, just while Devereux was at Haverhill. This did all leave us a bit thin on the outer wall, but on this night, I judged the most danger was from within.
Morning came without further incident, Devereux and his men departed after breakfast.

More letters arrived for all in the next two days. Mine from Lord Roger urged any bridge-building that could be done to 'stabilise' Huntingdonshire, Suffolk and Essex. He meant 'prepare for military alliance'. This coincided with an invitation from Lord Devereux to have a return visit with him, view his just-completed castle at Walden and to 'bring Lady Azizah to organise his new kitchen staff'. I deeply, deeply distrusted this man but felt obligated to attend.
I sent letters to Lord Roger in Warwick and Sir Randall Brereton in Cambridge, to let them know my intentions and destination. We set off on a cold, grey morning that matched my mood.
I took an escort of 24 and Azizah, making sure all had cloaks against the winds. Azizah had added a plain woollen shawl to go over her usual white and purple one.
Luckily, it was only about 15 miles, so we were there well before

dark. On arrival at Walden, Azizah was shown to the kitchens and I was guided to the Hall for a drink before dinner. It was quite obvious that Clément had made a head start on the wine. We talked for a couple of hours, about matters of state and practicalities of fiefs but nothing of great consequence. The meal arrived and was quite good. Azizah had obviously done what she could, and it was again more than enough to impress Devereux... Suddenly, emboldened by yet more wine, he gauchely said "So, Walter, how much for the woman?" "Lady Azizah is a free woman and therefore is not property to be bought" I said with increasing volume. "Yes, yes," he said, ignoring my rising temper, "but if you don't want to bounce it then at least pass it on to someone who does." I stood and left the table without any acknowledgment to him. I was making for the kitchen to fetch Azizah and get to the horses.
But...
Too late.
There must have been some secret signal, because each of my men suddenly faced three of Devereaux's men. My hand went to my sword and I felt two men each grab an arm, and another show a sword to my throat. My weapons were taken from me, including all four daggers. Next, I see Azizah being brought into the Hall, dragged by the arm, by a huge soldier, who then threw her on the floor – she was making quiet whimpering noises. I forced my captors to turn so I could face Clément, "YOU DARE DO THIS?" I thundered. "I do Walter," he replied, "too bad this lesson in strategy came too late for you."
"Take those two to the dungeons" he ordered. It took six men to carry me away and one to guide Azizah, who seemed to have given up, making quiet sobbing sounds while she obediently walked. We were taken through the dark night, across the bailey and down into the lowest, dungeon level of the Keep. I just hoped this was all a bluff and my men would not be murdered. There'd been no discussion of terms, so Devereux was either too drunk, too mad or too stupid to realise the implications of his actions – which made me begin to be concerned for Azizah and myself. At least they have a decent reedman here I thought. Plenty of torchlight and lamps, even down here. We were thrown into separate cells and the wooden beams rammed across to lock the doors. My cell had straw

on the floor, a wooden bench and a bucket as the total contents. I turned my back on the door and pissed a goodly amount into the bucket. I thought I heard a similar action in the next cell, followed by quiet sobbing and whimpering. "Don't worry Azizah," I whispered, "we'll get out of here." But all I heard was more sobbing.

A few minutes later, a couple of jailers appeared at the barred window let into the cell door. They both seemed to enjoy inspecting their new prizes. "Well Odo," said one, "we've got a right pair here, a lordy and a sort-of lady..." "So Jeffers, "said the other "which one do you think our master will want to play with?" "You are a mutt, Odo – he'll want the dusky maiden there." "Mmmmm – does seem a waste, I mean, is he going to want every bit do you think?" "What are you thinking friend?"
"Well, we could have a piece and leave the rest...?"
"Ahhhhh I see – yes, and we must have a look at all the goods at least, make sure they're fit for his lordship!"
I heard the bar pushed across on her cell and the door creak open.
"Oh look, " said Jeffers, "she's trying to hide in the corner, bless."
"Come here girly-girl, we won't hurt you" said Odo, sniggering.
I heard soft, slow, straw-moving sounds.
"Here she comes, that's a good girly, come to your daddies" chuckled Jeffers.
"Oh, Oh, listen!" said Odo, sounding fit to burst at his own impending wit.
"We've got Lord Have-her-hill in one cell and Lady Have-her-ho..."
There came two rapid swishing, slicing sounds, like you'd hear at a busy butcher's stall on market day. Then choking, gurgling, gasping, bubbling noises, two thuds and straw threshing sounds; then silence.
After a few moments, I heard my cell being unbarred and the door opened.
A still-veiled Azizah stood there with her eyes sparkling.
I came out to her, gripped her arms and looked her over for injury.
"Are you alright Azizah?" I asked with greatest concern.
"I have blood on my dress again lord." she sighed.
I'm stunned by her calmness.
Clearly the weeping and wailing was a trick to make these abusers

of women dismiss her all the more – and not search her! I willed myself away from her beautiful eyes, went into the other cell and dragged one body to a far corner. Then dragged the other body to a corner of my cell.

We ran up the stairs to the storerooms, glancing quickly in each for weapons or anything like... pitch! I spotted, or rather smelt the small barrels. I threw one down the stairs to the dungeon floor, where it easily splintered and threw the black contents all over the floor and into the cells. I smashed another on the stairs below us, one more in the 'pitch room' and took one more with me. Azizah needed no instructions, she took a couple of torches from the wall and threw them down into the dungeon area. Tall flames immediately sprang up and began spreading. She tossed a lamp into the pitch store and we quietly scampered up the stairs to the first floor, where the exit door would be.

With no weapons found so far, I knelt a couple of steps down from the top of the stairs and slowly put an eye around the corner at floor level. I saw two guards and an archer between us and the door. I slowly drew back and held up three fingers.

Azizah nodded calmly and pressed a hand down on my shoulder, meaning I should stay there and she would go forward!

She magicked her khanjar from wherever it was hiding, then hitched her skirts up enough so the drop of the material hid the dagger behind the flow of the dress.

There may also have been a part in her plan to distract the men with a display of her slender ankles and a hint of shapely, smooth-skinned calves. Well, that sight certainly distracted me!

The first smoke now billowed up the stairwell, giving her a perfect signal. She trotted around the corner with tiny steps, with her head down; suddenly coughing, sobbing and, in a high voice, crying a pitiful "Help me, help me" in Saxon.

She killed the first guard easily, scratched the second and mortally wounded the archer.

I was right behind her, grabbed up the first guard's dropped battle-axe and went for the now fully alert and fighting man. He was young and huge – his height had saved him thus far, as his vulnerable area was just too much of a reach for Azizah. We traded blows, his long sword against my axe. He drove me back away from the door, with me mostly defending as, without armour, I could not afford a single mistake. His mistake was to have chosen too long a sword, even for his height. This common error meant his recovery-to-on-guard was slow and feints were sluggish. I double-bluffed with the axe and used the stairwell to flank him, getting past him and nicking his leg with the spearpoint on the top-end of the axe-shaft. This enraged him, causing him to lose control and hence lose technique.

It was my turn to push him back a yard or two before he regained his senses and I felt him reclaim the advantage until...

Something... made him flicker his eyes past me, over my shoulder. That was his undoing, because that was all the opening I needed to bury the spearpoint below his helmet for a fatal wound.

I glanced down to be sure he was out of the fight, then turned back to Azizah near the door.

She was now... smoothing her dress down and I think was blushing, though that was hard to tell in our veiled and dusky damsel?

Puzzled but with no time to discuss, I ran to the top of the stairs and smashed the last pitch barrel on the corridor floor. We gathered what weapons we could, threw down the torches from the walls behind us as we scurried out the door and closed it behind us – not wanting the alarm to be raised immediately.

We ran as fast as we could to the stable block, found all was locked away, bar one horse tied to a rail outside – which was odd, especially as it had no saddle, just a bridle. I unhitched the animal and set a course across the bailey that would lead us near the gate but not straight to it as we were walking and hiding as best possible behind the horse.

Two heavily armoured guards stood by the gate and were alert enough to challenge us with a "Halt, who goes..."

And that was all he spoke, as the fire in the Keep reached the grain storeroom and exploded the dust, which blew out the Keep door and lit the bailey with a tongue of flame.

Never one to miss an opportunity, our fighting princess leaned . around the horse's arse and used the very recently borrowed bow to skewer the first guard through his gawping mouth. She drew back at the second guard with full and obvious intent. He held his hands

up, drew the bolts and opened the gates just wide enough for us.
"Follow" commanded Azizah - he did.
"Close" she said, and he pulled the gate to.
"Kneel" she said, as we walked over the drawbridge and the man
knelt while shaking fit to burst. We neared the end of the
drawbridge, relieved there was no gate-tower guard – this would
never happen at Warwick, or even Haverhill.
As we stepped onto the road, the guard judged himself safe enough
and drew breath to shout the alarm – and died for his lord. Azizah
tutted herself that the shaft went through the side of his throat,
rather than the middle...
I had a sudden thought of "Thank god she's on my side!" I mounted
the horse and held my arm out and down for Azizah to swing herself
up behind me. So good to feel her warmth and womanliness
pressed against me. We walked the horse a few yards, then gently
trotted, then cantered – all the while balancing distance against
noise.
The road north or the road east could be used to get to Haverhill.
So, I headed south, planning to cut east later. I thought pursuit
would be unlikely to follow away from our obvious destination.
I just prayed, harder than ever before, that my men still lived. We
held our breath as we passed three inns full of Devereux soldiery –
they must have felt full of confidence in their premature
celebrations.
We cleared the last houses of the village south of the castle and
made reasonable progress down the narrow country lane.
I steered the horse to take the third easterly turning we came to
and tried to speed it up. It slowed down - and began to wheeze -
badly. The reason for its isolation was now apparent, it was very
sick. It managed another mile before starting to cough and shake.
I guided it to the grass verge, we stopped and dismounted. The poor
animal's legs started to shake even worse and it was clearly in great
difficulty. After a minute or two of clearly struggling for a single
breath, it fell over and obligingly disappeared into the deep ditch
adjacent to the verge – and expired.
We looked at each other and saw between us we had: her dagger, a
bow, a few arrows, a battle-axe and a dagger that was now in my
boot. No water, food or weather protection. Azizah in her long

dress, shawl, veil and leather slippers, me in shirt, hose and boots –
with storm-clouds rapidly building from the south-west.

It was going to get cold in the early hours – bloody cold.

Between the drifting clouds, I pointed out the North star to Azizah.
Then used the tips of the crescent moon to find south on the far
horizon. I explained we were to head North-East, for twelve miles,
between four and five hours if we kept to the lanes. Back for a late
breakfast. She simply nodded and started walking – what a girl!

Distant sounds of many dogs barking, and trumpets blaring caused
us to look for a way across the wide, deep roadside ditch and into
the forest. We found a make-shift bridge, made from a couple of
half-logs and crossed using that. This led to a woodcutters and
poachers trail that did at least point in our preferred direction.
Annoyingly, the dog howls were clearly not all together, there were
at least two groups of hounds, maybe three - they were splitting up.
The bugger Devereux had unfortunately started to think. We walked
briskly down the forest trail and stopped where a stream ran across
our path. I listened and quietly cursed when I realised that some of
the dogs were on our side of the village.

I looked at Azizah and saw she heard this too. I grasped her hand
with both of mine and looked in her eyes. She held my gaze and
nodded silently; she knew as well as I did that this was going to get
tougher. I led her into the stream, which was wide, shallow and
very, very cold. Luckily the streambed was gravel not clay and we
made good progress. My boots started to leak almost immediately,
and I made a memory for myself to get a proper leather-man for the
castle. Poor Azizah's feet would have been soaked from the start
but she was careful to keep her bow and arrows dry.

After 200 yards in the stream, we left it, then rejoined further up,
left it again then rejoined further up – and repeated this, many
times. Then we left it, went downstream, went back into the water
and pressed on upstream for another 100 yards before I could take
no more of the cold water and we left on the far bank.

We moved on another couple of hundred yards before I called a halt
and we sat on a small log, behind a large bush. Azizah had started to
lag and although she made no complaint or protest, I was
concerned for her condition. I looked around and found some dry
moss on the trunk of a nearby tree, the branches above thankfully

keeping the rain off this part. I used my dagger to cut out big chunks of moss and went back to her. I knelt before her, gently eased her slippers off and patted her feet dry with the moss as best I could – noticing in the faint moonlight, just how small, soft and… well… pretty her feet were. I then found some more moss to rest both under and over her feet while I worked to drain and dry her slippers, with yet more moss, to best possible.

I glanced up at her, to try and gauge how she was doing. Difficult to see in the darkness… but she had a new look on her. Definitely not her 'princess eyes' but a new and very gentle gaze.

I stood and listened anew to sounds of pursuit. One dog seemed to be on the lane well to the north of us, another was fading away to the south. Strange they should have missed the very turn we took whilst on the horse? What would I be doing if I was in command of those men?

The answer came to me and my heart sank. Azizah saw my frown and stood up, placed a hand on my chest, with a question in her eyes. I leaned down to her and whispered, "Do you know the word 'instinct'?" She shook her head. "A… feeling?" I whispered. I tapped my head and shook it. Tapped over my heart and nodded. Tapped my stomach and nodded. She twinkled her eyes, nodded and patted her stomach. Whispering again I said, "I have a feeling that trouble comes our way." For once, she looked concerned and whispered, "Trust your… feeling lord, it has served us well." Still whispering I said, "We will move half a mile more, then must stop for quite a while." She nodded, and we set off along the trail – with me checking the direction from occasional glimpses of the Moon.

The weather was worsening by the minute, a light rain had started but we had to keep going. At last I saw the place I needed, a big and long clump of bushes on one side of the track, just before trail curved. We walked on another 80 yards or so, then moved right, off the track, going well into the forest, then doubled-back, to arrive behind the wide clump of bushes and undergrowth. I gestured we were to wait here and Azizah nodded. Next, I saw her scooping handfuls of damp earth and smearing much on the white parts of her dress and some on the purple parts. Then she nipped some leaves and twigs with her fingernails, tied them in her hair and onto her dress. Lastly smearing some earth on the shinier parts of the bow. Not for the first time I wondered to myself "Who **is** this woman?" I copied her in smearing my hands, face and the shiny parts of the axe with damp earth. I thought my dark brown hose was adequate but Azizah flicked her chin at my top half, to get me to muddy the lighter brown of my shirt. Once complete in my… decoration, I made a gesture meant to indicate 'no more movement'. She just blinked at me to acknowledge.

We waited, peering through the bushes.

And we waited some more.

The rain fell harder.

We still waited.

I was prepared to give this a couple of hours but…

After only about an hour, I thought I heard a panting coming from our left, the direction we had come along. Moving at a very brisk walk was a party of three men, led by a wolfhound the size of a small horse! The hairs went up on the back of my neck. They passed us, with the dog's nose to the ground, still tracking well in spite of the fresh rain – bastard thing. We rose and eased silently but swiftly through the bushes, a task made less risky by the dampness underfoot and the ever-increasing rain. I glanced right to make sure they had gone around the curve, I looked carefully left to check for a second force – there was none. We tiptoed quickly round the curve, going after the dog-people, weapons ready. Luckily the track was grassy rather than stony, thank god.

We tip-toed quickly a few yards nearer and I moved to the left of the track to give Azizah a clear shot from the right side. I immediately threw my battle-axe, aiming at the head of the nearest man but unsure how it would fly. It actually plunged straight but low, inflicting a terrible wound in the area of his arse and causing him to scream and fall forward. While the axe was in the air, Azizah had loosed an arrow into the back of the next nearest man and he fell as if shot through the heart – which he had been. But now we had a problem, the dog had obviously heard the action and had whirled around. The owner pulled the thick lead rope from around its neck and shouted "Get!". The huge and snarling hound sped towards us, hate and fury in its eyes, getting terrifyingly close. I had my dagger out of my boot and was preparing to attack this devil-dog when it opened its jaws wide, and Azizah put an arrow down its throat. The body continued without aid of the legs and its speed alone took it between us as it ploughed into the ground. I stabbed it twice through its lungs and cut both rear hamstrings, just to make sure it wasn't coming back into the fight. The axe victim had fainted after his initial scream but was showing signs of coming round, until my dagger went in between skull and spine. I recovered my axe from the body, pleased the spearpoint hadn't bent.

And now, as one, we turned to the dog-man who was standing still, in shock at the carnage before him. He knelt before us, begging for his life. I ordered him to undress the corpses, which he did. Unfortunately, that meant he had to break the arrow that was deeply embedded in the back of one. I watched him in this task while Azizah faded into the bushes on the outside of the curve to watch for following forces. I told the still-living one to undress himself, which he did, finishing standing naked and shivering in the rain that was now turning to sleet. I pointed in the direction of Haverhill and said "Go". He set off saying "Thank you sir, thank..." and died with my axe blade buried in the join between his neck and shoulder.

"I've got to get me one of these!" I thought, weighing the axe in my hands after levering it out of the body. Maybe this one was a tad heavy for me, but it was a wicked piece of equipment. I turned to the piles of clothing and picked the large, thin-leather cape and the larger wool shirt and a leather cap. I looked back down the track and could not see Azizah at all.

My attempt at an owl's hoot got her to pop her head out of a bush and I waved her back to me. I took turn on lookout and gestured to the pile of clothes to help herself. She added a wool shirt, wool cloak and fur hat - rejecting any of the hose, which was understandable given how soiled and rank it was. There was a pair of big leather boots with furry tops that Azizah could put her foot in with her slipper on. I sliced the arms off one of the shirts we weren't going to wear, knelt in front of her again and gestured to Azizah to remove one foot at time from her 'new' boots, while she balanced herself with a hand on my shoulder. I took her slipper off, slid a shirtsleeve over her foot and up her lower leg, under her dress. "Dear god!" I thought "that leg feels so smooth, firm and delicious!" and put her slipper back on and the boot over that, so she was warmer, and the boot wouldn't wobble nearly so much when she walked. I checked down the track for enemy again, then repeated for the other leg – which felt every bit as good! We also gained a goatskin of water and a leather bag of dried bread.

So, we left the scene much better equipped, leaving the bodies where they fell - as a message that might be interpreted as there being a larger force out here than just us…

We steadily pressed on along the trail for another couple of hours but with worsening sleet and cold, I had to admit I was exhausted and poor Azizah was really struggling, though still not complaining. In my past, I had seen men die of cold, even though placed in front of a fire – seems they just went to a point of no return. I was never going to risk that with our dear lady.

I stopped and leant my head near her ear and said, "We look for shelter now." And she nodded.

We walked on for a few more minutes, while I looked for a clump of the oldest and biggest trees I could find. On spotting a likely set, we did our trail masking again, even though it had done sod-all for us last time, we did it anyway… We then moved off the path and across muddy, leafy earth under the smaller younger growth until reaching the bigger older ones. To our great good fortune, there was one huge oak that had been felled by lightning many decades ago. The enormous hollow trunk was resting on the ground, a natural home-from-home. I could hardly see in the darkness, but I thought it was open at each end. A swift hurl of the battle-axe proved it was open both ends and had no furry denizens lurking to surprise us. We placed the weapons and bags in one end of the trunk and together we turned away to look for vegetation to block the ends. I discovered a grassy patch nearby, cut turves with my dagger and carried them to quickly plug one end of the trunk. Azizah had used her dagger to cut some clumps of dense foliage that we could pull in after us. Now, we were ready to get in the shelter, and not a moment too soon.

The cold had worsened noticeably, and the hail increased in size so that it hurt my head even through the hat. I could hear Azizah's teeth chattering and was desperate to get her warm. I put my cape around her shoulders and slid into the hollow trunk, lying on my side as I called her in. She edged along, keeping her cape and cloak

close round her, her dress down and pulling the foliage in behind her. In process of maneuvering along to be level with me, she managed to get a dainty knee in my nuts. I gasped and she giggled, saying "So sorry lord, I not mean step your kindler!" using the Saxon word for a thin piece of wood used for fire and lamp-lighting.
"Just don't do it again!" I said.
"I promise lord" she replied and giggled some more between teeth chattering. There was no need to whisper, the hail drumming on the trunk was astonishingly loud.
"We must warm both of us" I said and grasped the edges of cloak and cape to draw her shivering body to mine. I got my arms around her and with some mutual wriggling, she guided the cloak and cape as far around us both as possible. Then she put her head on my shoulder and her hands together against my chest. I thought that in other circumstances, this would be magical, as it was – this was still magical! I held her close, deeply concerned for her.
"Is far tomorrow?" she asked.
I lied and said, "We're halfway there."
"Ahhhh" she said.
Thank god, we both warmed up nicely. Her teeth chattering stopped, her shivering gradually reduced to nothing and quite soon after, she went to sleep, and I had finally found out where she hid her khanjar, just above and behind her right hip, with a hidden opening for her hand to reach it.

The hail eased a little and then some faint moonlight made it through between the scudding clouds and the leaves at our entrance. In that pale light, I could just see her hair under the shawl and the part of her face above the now slightly tilted veil. I was very, very moved at this sight of her and whispered my thoughts.
"Amira Azizah, my princess – even though you smell like an utter swamp-donkey, I absolutely adore you, in every way."
I sighed and knew nothing else till morning.

A loud cough, from very close by, awoke us - sometime after dawn. The bright sunny morning meant we could see well enough to share the alarm in our eyes.
Then another massive, deep cough came.

Then a grunt and some chewing noises.

It was my turn to smile and giggle, while Azizah looked puzzled. I moved a hand from around her and mimed antlers for her. She chuckled at my play and nodded, looking relieved. I closed my eyes and listened for all the forest noises; all were in place. The birdsong, wood-pecker noises and deer all painted a picture in my head – a picture without people.

I smiled and noticed Azizah's veil had slipped all the way down. My eyes tried to drink in her beauty, no man could ever get tired of looking!

She patted a hand on my chest and asked, "Should we go lord?"

I pretended offence and replied, "Do you not like my new manor?"

"I admit it is small," I went on, "but I have big plans for it!"

She laughed saying, "Warm and dry is lord - no room my horse!"

We slowly pushed the foliage out the end of the tree trunk; cautiously wriggled our heads out to look around and then pushed our way out to ease our aching joints. By mutual thought, we turned our backs on each other and pissed on the forest floor.

I waited for her to touch me on the shoulder before turning back to her. I didn't have to wait very long at all – which made me puzzle again. Her speed in relieving herself implied she had no undergarments. Not at all unusual as most of the girls and ladies I'd bottom-grabbed did not either. In deepest winter, many would wear linen draws or hose, but at other times, not. So... that would explain her not wanting the soiled breeches next her skin!

But did this also explain the fatal distraction of the giant guard I was fighting in the Devereux Keep last night.

Would she...? Did she...? Lift her skirt and win me the victory? What a little minx!

I looked at her with admiration, nodded slowly in appreciation and smiled widely - she smiled back with her eyes, looking slightly puzzled.

Thinking now done, I used a branch to dig the turf from the other end and we picked up our weapons, food and water. I offered Azizah some of the water, which she drank. I had a few gulps too. She declined the hard bread, saying "Save later lord." We then paused, looking at each other in the daylight – and laughed. With our mismatched and ugly clothing, dirt patches everywhere and bits of greenery springing randomly from our persons, we looked like a couple of pirates who had been shipwrecked up a river!

Laughter over, she restrung her bow with effortless technique, made sure her five remaining arrows were neatly arranged in her hand and looked to me to lead on. We started walking but I had to ask before we got back on the quietness of the trail…

"Your skills – Azizah, are they given to all important ladies in your homeland?"

"No lord," she replied, "just me."

"I two brothers same age, they learn… trade of warrior - I want same – this very not like by many."

"My father give in, I very strong do this – I ask, ask, ask."

"So, you are triplets? Three babies, same time?"

"No lord," she laughed, "my father four wives, my brothers one month, three months more than me"

"Four wives…" I said in some surprise and then we came to the trail and had to proceed quietly. I was leading, Azizah checking behind us. We walked in silence for a couple of hours, maybe covering another four or five miles as the forest trails meandered and narrowed, sometimes partially overgrown. It seemed the further east we went, the denser the forest and the poorer the paths.

Dear Azizah seemed to be coping well in her boots, but time was marching on faster than us and I urgently needed to get back to Haverhill. So, at the next fork in the path I went north, to hit a lane or road and grab some transport of some sort. That would be a risk, but delaying our return added risk also. The forest began to thin, and the trail to widen, so we slowed down. A sudden church bell ring made us both jump; it sounded close, to our right, maybe 100 yards or so. Five more rings made it Sext (noon) already! We slowly emerged from the forest and turned left down the verge of a well-used lane – and waited. I sat on the grassy verge, Azizah stayed hidden behind a tree, with all our weapons. After a few minutes, a cart appeared from our left, and so going our way.

I would have preferred a horse or two but would take anything to speed our progress homewards. At least the slow cart could use the main lanes and roads… As the cart and its single horse drew near, I stood to engage the drayman, noting the beer kegs on the back of the cart. He eased the cart to a stop and gave me a very sceptical looking over.

"Good day sir" I began, "could I hire you to go to Haverhill?" – no sense beating around the bush! "Well zir," he replied in a strong local accent "don't know if I'm going that way…"

"I am Lord Walter of Haverhill, I will see you are suitable rewarded." He looked at me up and down, very pensively.

"Well zir, if you are Lord Walter, I'm the Archbishop of Canterbury!"

"Well Archbishop," I said louder now, "you may not recognise me but…" and I gestured to the forest, "she does!"

Azizah stepped from behind cover, arrow nocked, bow drawn. The shock on the man's face was complete.

Losing my temper now I said "Sir, clearly you still live, but only at my pleasure – now - do you drive, or do we?

"Well *that* sounded like a Norman lord alright" said the drayman, hanging his head and sighing. I waved Azizah to bring our possessions and get on the back of the cart. I checked the driver knew the way and got on the back myself, making a small bed of empty grain sacks for Azizah to lie on, cradling her bow and arrows, and another two to cover her with. Our other weapons were hidden under the last sack. I would look like a drayman's assistant, but it would be very unusual to have a woman on such a cart. That might attract the wrong sort of interest. I joined the driver on the wide seat up front and indicated to set off, with him still casting a wary eye over me.

We soon came to the church we'd heard earlier; clearly now I could see this was the tiny village of Castle Camps. Trundling through the crossroads in the middle of this little place, we soon came to a rundown wooden castle – one of the first built after the Conquest. I had a memory that Gerald had said this belonged to Count Aubrey but clearly it was not a priority to him. It was in very poor condition with an understrength and disinterested garrison. What a problem to have! So many fiefs that you don't feel the need to care for them all! A single bored guard on the gatehouse, idly watched us pass. No doubt wishfully thinking to get at the contents of the kegs on our cart! After a couple of hours, we rolled through Haverhill town, no one recognised me of course, and shortly after, we arrived at the castle. The drawbridge was down but the gates closed and portcullis down. The numbers of my soldiers on the battlements seemed to indicate the sergeants were concerned that the party that had left for Walden were not yet back.

"Ho! Drayman, what business do you have here?" was the challenge from a corporal over the gate. Indicating me, our driver replied "I bring you Lord Walter…"

Much hysterical laughter greeted this utterance.

"If he's Lord Walter, then call me The Pope!" shouted the corporal. I stood up, removed my ghastly leather cap and thundered "Your Holiness, open the bloody gate for your Lord!"

Muffled "focks" and a shouted "Yes my lord" were heard from the parapets; the portcullis creaked upwards and the gates swung open. We trundled into the Baily and I directed the drayman to the base of the Keep.

We stopped by the Keep with a crowd of off-duty soldiers, servants and other staff around us. I stepped down from the cart, went to the back and uncovered Azizah who blinked in the light – I guess she'd been asleep. She stood, and the crowd gasped at her total dirty disarray and obvious fatigue. There was much muttering and growing concern from the onlookers. I reached out with my hands to lift her down, she still clutching her bow and arrows.

Once standing safe on our ground, she looked up at me and smiled her eyes, before bobbing a one-handed curtsy and walked slowly away in her boots, heading, I guessed, for the laundry room! A young and obviously very new soldier offered to help her by taking the weapon, but quickly stepped back when she hissed at him! Seeing the Warden, I said "Pay the driver a pound and send him on his way." Then I climbed the steps to the door of the Keep, turned outwards and rested my hands on the wooden rail.

Pausing for some late-comers to join us and checking my senior staff were all present, I began.

"We were betrayed by Devereux at Walden."

Gasps and growls from the crowd.

"Myself and our Lady Stewardess were imprisoned."

Now furious shouts and swearing from the crowd.

"Our men are lost from us; we know not their fate."

A shocked silence in the crowd, not a murmur.

The enormity of that hit me and I stood there and sobbed for a moment, with many of the crowd also in tears.

Most of the escort were my original 'Warwicks'. I was distraught and pounded the rail with my fist.

My Marshal climbed the steps and gave me a big bear hug and we sobbed together. The crowd waited quietly, respectfully. Gathering my composure, I drew breath to continue.

"While escaping, we did much damage to his Keep!" the crowd cheered.

"Several of their men got in front of Our Lady's bow" more cheers and some laughter.

"And I learned a new weapon."

Cries of "Ooooo".

I pointed down to the cart and gestured to lift up the sacks. The ones who could see went "Ahhhh" at the sight of the battle-axe. It was brought up to me by a corporal. I held it over my head, so all could see – the blood still on the spearpoint and blade. A cheer went up.

I went on "We must prepare for an attack on our castle, not one that we caused, but they will seek to justify their own black-hearted deeds". More growls.

At that moment a cry from the Keep lookouts came down.

"Scarecrows running from the west"

Everyone looked at each other and said, "What the...?"

"Say again" yelled the sergeants together.

"Scarecrows running from the west"

"How many?"

After a very long pause the shout was "Twenty-four."

I exalted to hear that number, that could be the men of our escort. But as we were now in some danger, I ordered all short-bow archers to the south wall and all battlements to be manned. The drayman was not going to get home tonight and he seemed to realise this. I did shout to him as I passed on my way to the gatehouse "Kitchen, food" and pointed. "Thank you, my lord!" he replied brightly, with the new zest for life his pound had given him.

We had one half of the gate open, with a wedge of spearmen ready to push back any would-be invaders. As the first 'scarecrow' drew near, he was identified as one of our corporals, purely by voice, as his attire was just a sack stuffed with straw, breeches and boots. He shouted "Twenty-four on foot to come in, enemy cavalry seen" as he ran across the drawbridge, gasping for breath. The last one came in a few minutes later with clearly hostile mounted troops in pursuit.

"Archers - horseman to your front - watch and shoot" came the stern command from the sergeant now on the gatehouse.

The enemy halted a good sixty yards from the nearest part of the castle. Then proceeded to shout insults, to which my men replied in good voice. This gang from Walden were clearly ignorant of our longbows and I wished to maintain that ignorance... They believed that their estimated sixty yards was safe enough from short-bows, however, just as the wind dropped, an arrow left our parapet, from the nearest point to them. It started seemingly a bit too high but arced gracefully down, caught the nearest horseman high on his chest and knocked him off his horse. His companions turned tail and retreated, and his horse bolted – all to raucous catcalling from our men. The party of spearmen dashed out and dragged the sorry individual back into the castle. He would be treated and then questioned. As he was being dragged to the White Room, he was roundly harangued for "being shot by a lady." And calls like "Our Lady wants her arrow back you twat!" Of course, I should have known it would be her to take on that target.

Excitement over for the moment, I met with Azizah as she came down to the battlement steps to the bailey, still clumping in her boots. Her eyes showed her triumph at the successful shot.

"I keep bow – is good" she said.

I glanced at it and noticed for the first time that it was an expensive-looking item, made with horn and wood.

"But need clean me now" she went on, gesturing to her dirty and disheveled state.

"I let you know lord" she finished with.

"Know what Azizah?"

"When tub clean you."

"I think I will just change my clothes" I said.

She turned to me, rested a hand on my chest and wrinkled her nose through her veil.

"Lord Walter," she said sternly "you smell like swamp-donkey!"

I roared with laughter - what an odd word for the kitchen staff to have taught Azizah!

Then in my head I suddenly thought "What?", "Wait?", "Last night?", "Could she?", "Did she?", "Was she still awake - when I spoke those words?"

My face must have shown my confusion, as she giggled and turned away, dancing a little and singing softly "Swamp-donkey, swamp-donkey, big smell, ring bell, swamp-donkey, swamp-donkey!". I turned away, shaking my head in sympathy, for her brothers – and her father. Life cannot have been easy or peaceful with this one around!

My sergeants and the escorts corporal appeared and gave their reports. Seems our 'scarecrows' had been surrounded at Walden castle, then stripped of weapons, armour and some clothing while we were being captured. They were then herded out of the gate, some without boots.

Their judgement was to stick to the main roads to the north, as the pursuit they heard develop seemed to be always to their south. Facing the same or even worse difficulties with the weather, they had borrowed sacks, straw from farms and tattered clothes from actual scarecrows. During the worst of the storm, they sheltered in some empty chicken coops. They made best progress they could after daylight, with scouts moving ahead of the main body.

Many times they dived into the forest when horsemen where seen or heard but thankfully all made it back. Though some had foot injuries and some slight 'cold burn'.

I waved Gerald over and discussed Devereux's likely strategy from the accounting and political points of view. We agreed his most likely course would be to attack Haverhill for gain under pretext that we had 'attacked' his Keep first. We estimated his strength at nearly three times ours, so he would feel optimistic of success if he struck quickly. I felt he would also greatly undervalue our mostly Saxon soldiers against his mainly Norman crew.

As the light began to fade, I moved back to my senior soldiers. I ordered a great many preparations to begin, with the expectation of an attack the next day, anytime from dawn onwards. I advised them not to work everyone through the night and make sure meals of some sort were taken by all. I emphasised that our plan was to appear small in numbers and to act in apparently disorganised ways. They nodded grimly, repeated the instructions back to me, then broke away to delegate all tasks. I visited the tradesmen and gave them a long list of jobs, which would see them working through the night, but at least they would not be fighting on the morrow, well, not unless things went very badly wrong...

So after some time, and with all preparations now in hand, I turned to go to my room, suddenly very tired indeed.

Then from out of the darkness, a Saxon maid from the kitchen appeared in front of me.

She curtseyed, saying "Your hot water is ready my lord."

I groaned, sighed and walked reluctantly towards the kitchens and then along the corridor to the clean-smelling laundry room.

The laundry had no door but was now divided by a curtain from wall to wall, two big wick-lamps providing light. The maid, who had followed me, indicated I should go behind the curtain.

There was a very large and very new-looking laundry tub – something else I guess I paid for. In the tub was clean water that steamed with heat. Slowly, I peeled off my dirty and rank layers of mismatched clothing. Stepping into the hot water was a shock – this didn't seem natural, though I did recall tales of 'steam baths' in Spain and the Holy Land. I carefully eased my bits and my backside into the water, then leaned back against the side of the big round tub. This, was really, rather good I thought and closed my eyes.

Well, closed them for a short while, until I sensed someone nearby. The fair-haired Saxon maid was standing there, along with another, brun[33]-haired maid. Both had a hand over their mouths, trying not to giggle but their shoulders were shaking with mirth. Their eyes were all over me and I drew breath to ask their purpose here.

But before I could speak, the brun-girl announced "Lady Azizah told us to make sure you used lots of soap my lord."

"Oh did she?" I responded, "I am not a great soap user..."

"Seems not my lord!" they chortled as one. With yet more giggling, they each knelt by the side of tub, gently but firmly grabbed an arm each and started applying blocks of soap.

---

[33] Norman word for Brown

"What are you doing?" I said, more in surprise than concern.

"Following our instructions Lord" they said again as one.

I began to sense a plot was afoot... But not an evil one. In fact, this being soaped idea could be growing on me, I thought and as the soaping reached my chest, that wasn't all that was growing on me... There was no hiding the natural effects of the relaxing hot water and the gentle touch of feminine hands on my naked body!

The flaxen-haired maid noticed, squealed in fright and ran out of the room. Brun-hair was clearly made of sterner stuff, as she said in a husky voice, "Don't worry lord, I can manage."

"Good" was all I could say, as my eyes closed with enjoyment of her washing and rinsing my hair.

She then moved round and did my feet and legs – god that was good too!

"Well my lord," she said "I've washed down as far as possible – and up as far as possible. Do you want me to wash... 'possible'?"

"Please do" I whispered. She got some soap on both hands, reached into the water and gently soaped my rigid cock and balls.

This was too much!

I opened my eyes and locked my gaze to hers.

She seemed flushed of face, also her chest above her bodice.

I reached for the shoulders of her dress, gripped and started to pull. She put her hands above her head and backed away, leaving her dress behind. I tossed the garment aside and looked her up and down – every inch of her full body naked, creamy-white and curving; her dark nipples poking out like chapel hat-pegs, as she took her slippers off and stepped into the tub. She knelt over my middle, our gaze locked again and then our lips. She reached down for my 'sword' and guided it into her hot, moist 'sheath', then pushed herself slowly down the 'blade'. We both sighed loudly when she reached the 'hilt'. We kissed deeply again as she gripped my shoulders and started to ride my hips like she was breaking in a new horse! Her eyes closed as I braced my feet and back against the tub. This seemed to give her the firmer saddle she was needing. She began to moan and sped up her action a little, with the water now splashing the sides of the tub. The moaning got louder and louder – and louder. Her riding got more and more energetic until, she peaked with a crescendo of Saxon swearing!

She hung on to my shoulders panting and grinning at me. Then she collapsed on my chest and I held her close, enjoying her full breasts against my skin. After a few minutes of rest, she raised her head, hair now in complete disarray, eyes looking somewhat misty. I kissed her again, then her neck and wonderful breasts. I stroked her hair some, then got hold of a good handful. Guiding her by the hair, I moved her up, around and down – to end up with her kneeling in front of me. I forced my knees between hers, gripped her hips and took her forcefully – my turn to ride! She held on to the sides of the tub and moaned incoherently as I battered her glorious behind until my desire was spent inside her. I collapsed over her, shaking and breathless and rested for a minute or two. It was only then I realised that the other maid had returned and had been peeking past the curtain, probably for the whole time – mouth and eyes wide open! I turned to our spectator and said, "Is there something to dry us? "Yes my Lord," she stammered and fetched us some linen towels that she placed over a nearby chair. "Now fetch clothes, boots and a cloak from my room" I instructed.

"Yes my Lord" she replied and quickly departed. I stood up in the tub and gently helped my brun-maid to her feet. We paused and frankly enjoyed the remarkable differences in our bodies. This again produced a natural effect and she cupped my balls in one hand and my rejuvenated cock in the other. "My lord is very strong" she whispered and proceeded to kneel and ease my stiffness with her lovely mouth. After that, I certainly needed to use the chair to sit for a minute - wrapping one towel around me while she used the other and then slipped her dress back on. She kissed me briefly, curtseyed with a big smile and went back to her duties.

As I stood to finish drying off, the fair-haired one returned and placed my clothing and boots on and beside the chair. I 'accidently' dropped the towel and her hands flew to cover her mouth, not knowing what to do with herself but still getting a good look! However, she seemed very uncertain as to her thoughts and, as I had been very well… looked after by her friend, I wasn't going to tempt her too much! I stood there and thanked her for arranging the bath and fetching my clothes; while standing naked with my hands on my hips. She then did a mumbling, blushing, bowing, curtsey thing as she stumbled out of the room.

I smiled as I dressed, thinking I could get used to this bathing!

My stomach then reminded me that there'd been no food in it this day. Delicious smells were now wafting from the kitchens, so I went in search of dinner.

After a huge amount of chicken and ham pie and a large apple pastry, I was full. I pushed back in my chair and pondered - beer or cider...?

At that moment, Azizah appeared from the kitchen and I waved her to sit next to me.

"Have you had food?" I asked.

"Yes Lord, chicken pie for me" she replied.

"No pork?" I asked. She made a gesture of opening a book, that I guessed meant 'her book' and so a religious matter. I nodded gently, then looked at her closely and asked how she was feeling.

"Me tired my Lord – but feel we…" and ran out of Saxon words.

No sign of Luther, so we were stuck this time. I borrowed a coin from one of the guards. I pointed to 'heads' and then her, to 'tails' and then me. I tossed the coin and it fell as heads. Pointing to her I said, "You lucky" and then to me and said, "Not lucky."

"Ahhhhh," she said, "this day feel we lucky."

I smiled, nodded and tossed the coin back to the guard, who looked relieved!

She leaned closer to me, so I leaned closer to her.

She sniffed, then giggled.

"My Lord not smell – bath good?" she said with no trace of mischief or inuendo.

"Bath good," I replied "I may have another one next year." She thought that through, then laughed, gently wagged a finger at me and whispered, "You like be swamp-donkey?" and giggled some more as I shook my head and smiled at her. Then a thought came to her and her eyes clouded, and she was quiet.

"You know we may fight tomorrow?" I asked, while miming bow-shooting and swordplay. She nodded silently, suddenly looking very small and very concerned for me.

"Where I be?" she asked.

"The Keep" I replied, while miming with my fingers her walking up one flight of stairs – I wanted her on the second floor

"Have no shoot from there" she said firmly.

"If things go badly for us, I need you there to guard the money and you will have much to shoot at – the soldiers will fall back to the Keep if we lose the wall – and I will come to you" I finished quickly as more concern showed in her eyes. I gripped her hand and said, "But if I am hurt, the men will fight for you." She nodded, visibly saddened at the thought. I patted her hand, stood and reached down to touch her veiled cheek as we shared a long look. I sighed and went to my room for a few hours' sleep.

As I drifted off, I could hear the digging noises from near the gate, the clanging and hammering from the blacksmith and the chiseling and tapping from the carpenter.

At first light, our little wasps' nest of Haverhill came buzzing into life. I dressed in my second-best gambeson, mail and helmet, cursing when I found I had no spare coif[34]. All my best equipment was stolen at Walden. Including to my enormous regret, that hugely valuable sword of William, that I had won in battle. I stomped downstairs, with a common grey sword on my hip, though cheered a little by the heft of my newly acquired battle-axe, and so began my day.

Two messengers rode out to take copies, of several letters, by different routes. Because, however the day went, I needed my certain allies in Cambridge, Rockingham and, most of all, Warwick to be aware of our situation and the causes.

Right after the messengers left, the youngest men and boys ran out the gate and spread around the castle. All without armour, to hasten their return. Each clutching some wooden pegs with white lime just on one side; these were used to pace out and mark ranges from each tower in our walls.

Following on next, I made my biggest wager; I sent out my best ten mounted archers, with food and water for the day. They were to hide deep in the forest and would attack on hearing a certain trumpet call. Their task was to disrupt the enemy commanders, invariably marked by pennants or flags. If they could pass very close, they would shoot for the knights themselves, otherwise, they would

---

[34] a coif is a chain mail hood

shoot for the horses and disrupt their coherence as a fighting group. Under no circumstances were they to stop, slow or divert for any reason but to sweep ahead and gallop for the drawbridge that would be lowered for them.

Just as these archers disappeared into the trees, a shout from the lookout announced "Soldiers coming from the west. Many wagons and cavalry."

"Dear god that was fast" I thought.

We continued our preparations with renewed urgency. The new 'gate' was hurriedly wedged into place, it's varnish and other coating not even dry yet. The real gates were left open, the portcullis up and the drawbridge left half-raised.

All this certainly raised eyebrows amongst the men – but we needed to show apparent weakness, including a faulty or broken drawbridge. Wooden tubs were carried to the gatehouse, including my bathtub I saw! These were filled by buckets passed up from a wagon that fetched them from the long-since rebuilt well in the Bailey. Next up were small, delicate barrels placed at intervals along the battlements. These had a wick at the top, containing pitch and other minerals that were Luther's best knowledge on the ingredients for 'Greek Fire'[35]. All tradesmen, including the drayman, had contributed to the making of these.

The digging in the Bailey was finished and carts made ready with horses near the Keep.

Time to review the enemy – and most impressive they were. They formed rows of foot-soldiers behind shields, with large numbers of cavalry to their rear and flanks. All drawn up to our front, beyond the road and in front of the forest.

I joined my Marshal on the gate-tower, and he reported.

"About 180 cavalry and a few knights my lord – all armoured, 100 men-at-arms with long shields. About 30 archers – no long-bows seen."

"They brought the foot-soldiers on wagons, but I think some of the wagons have another purpose" and pointed out the three with what looked like grey roofs.

---

[35] Medieval napalm

"I think they will try for the moat with those, sir."

"I agree" I said but saw no need to change our plan.

As was the custom, they sent a herald to announce their 'just cause' and 'reasons why we should surrender' – all of which was greeted with rude ripostes from the men we chose to show at the battlements. Fully a third of our soldiers and half our archers were kept hidden. The rather young herald retreated, looking a bit surprised at the firmness of the rejection!

With no more ado, the enemy foot soldiers closed up and formed a shield wall. Behind this crouched their archers and all advanced to near the road across from our moat. Then their archers began pot-shots at our men on the battlements and a few of our short-bow archers took a few careful shots back. In the Bailey, the boys of the castle, carrying small shields, fetched the spent enemy arrows to our fletcher for checking and potential return whence they came. Meanwhile, the roofed-wagons of the enemy were drawn near our moat by horses. These were then unhitched, then soldiers pushed them nearer the water while sheltering under what we could see were metal roofs – then they stopped, clearly waiting for something.

Part of the shield-wall edged forward, with smoke visible, whisping from behind it. Our archers were prepared and took aimed shots at their bowman that had loosed fire-arrows at our 'gate'. Difficult to miss that target and we pretended we had no water to throw on it – much panic was acted-out on the gate-tower.

This was, after all, merely the pretend item we had just put up that morning. This new 'gate' lacked the fire-taming, weed-sap coating of our real gates and also its 'varnish' was mixed with pitch – so caught alight quite easily. The enemy cheered at the sight and began to edge the armoured wagons into the moat, because that way they could bypass the drawbridge and gain entry with the gate destroyed. The bastards had guessed correctly that the moat was not fully recovered from Hugos legacy. Almost all of the reeds had been removed but only the shallows had been dug a little deeper, just lack of time and manpower. The main part of the moat was still silted and not as deep as it should have been. From behind a parapet, I could see the wheels of these 'bridging' wagons were three times thicker than normal, and so would not cut into mud and

bog down so easily. Bloody Clément had been thinking alright. The first one entered the water and was further pushed across the moat by long poles. We waited for all three to be positioned and soldiers began to cross, somewhat crouched, underneath the metal roofs. The nearest sergeant gave the signal to light and launch three little barrels of our Greek Fire. The first one burst perfectly at the exit of the wagon nearly touching our side of the moat. The flaming fluid splashing the attacking soldiers and causing real panic and a wish to return to the far side. The second barrel missed low and fell in the water but still managed to burn for many seconds which I found very impressive. Third one was a good hit on the roof of the far wagon, with the burning liquid dripping down the gaps of the crude construction and setting clothing, spear-handles, almost anything alight. This effectively ended the probing attack via the moat.
In the meantime, our 'gate' was burning up like a storm. The tall flames and impressively dense black clouds of smoke would have been visible to any within a mile or two of our castle. Within a few more minutes, the wood was completely charred, and some chunks fell away, revealing the daylight through from our Bailey. Following my plan, the top wedges of one side of our 'gate' were then knocked away by poles poked through the 'murder holes' in the ceiling of the gateway. The 'gate' then sagged and collapsed on that side, showing a partial but clear view of our Bailey. The enemy cheered again, and we staged another panic in trying to raise our drawbridge – but each time we raised it a little, it was allowed to drop more. We repeated this charade until the drawbridge had fallen all the way down.
The opposing knights, mounted soldiers and many foot-soldiers began to funnel towards the now open door to the castle. Twenty of my foot-soldiers appeared in the gateway, as if determined to make a bold stand but melted away when the few knights, many mounted soldiers and running attackers poured across the drawbridge. All in full voice, convinced of victory.
With a steady eye, our Marshal gauged when as many of our enemy had crossed the bridge as we could cope with and signalled to drop the portcullis. It fell with a grumbling and a thud, followed by the screams of the three soldiers trapped underneath its spikes. Meanwhile the leading knights had pulled up short at the barrier of

carts, wagons and rope that formed a large box based at the gatehouse. Four of the wagons to their front had a longbowman and an assistant standing on them and immediately, knights and cavalry were pitched dead or dying from their mounts.

At this range, no mail or helmet would stop a longbow shaft with a bodkin head. Their shields were only partial protection as a trick from old Morfran meant our longbow assistants would stick a wax ball on tip of the bodkin, when called to by their archer. Somehow this wax gave our arrows three or four times the penetration against even the best of the knights' metal-and-wood shields. But shields were no protection at all against the two longbows in action on the right side of the mounted enemy. The mounted men fell thick and fast, with temporary survivors being penned in by the press of foot-soldiers coming on behind them. A couple of the cavalry tried to go left by jumping the ropes, but their horses' hooves broke through the disguising wooden covers of the pits that had been dug last night and they were then down and out of the fight.

One bold and determined knight, with proud high-ranked colours on his tabard[36], charged forwards and forced his way between two archers' wagons. Having broken through, he turned his horse, to attack the archers from the rear. Well... he intended to but... he was too close to the Keep at that point. An arrow from Azizah shot his mount in the rear flank. The horse reared and threw him. The fall dislodged his helmet and Azizah's second arrow dislodged part of his brain.

As this sideshow played out, the last act of our play began.

All of our short-bow archers on the battlements now engaged the foot-soldiers down in the Bailey. A sleeting of shafts swept the soldiers. The sheer number of shots and the closeness of the range meant that the poorer armour of these men was no lasting defence and within minutes, little moved on the killing ground. There were sounds - of moans and groans but nothing bar the odd struggling horse was moving.

---

[36] The highest status families would typically have the fewest badges or sections on their heraldry, e.g. the single lion of Warwick

I gave a nod for the trumpet signal that would cause our 'forest fighters' to attack. To further distract the remaining enemy still to our front, I roused our men to shout, and curse them – not difficult as the triumph they felt was running through their veins. We all roared together at the devious Devereux.

Looking across the ground between moat and forest, I could see their commanders had moved nearer in erroneous anticipation of the castle falling. They remained about 200 yards away, and hence 100 yards from the trees, from which our mounted archers were now galloping. I prayed that Clément was there and would catch an arrow in his evil face.

My column of horsemen swept past the high-ranking targets. Two of the six were seen to fall from their horses and the rest scattered along with their pages and squires. The archers swung away from the remaining enemy horse and on towards their second target, any enemy archers they could catch without great deviation from the route to our gate. My men did lengthen their route a little, god bless them, by following a wide 'S' shape that took them across the rear of the enemy line, who were fully engaged at shooting at our battlements, where we taunted them over the failed assaults.

A belated tooting from their rear made one or two glance around but too late. Every archer in that enemy line was killed or severely wounded, their role meriting no armour at all...

My men thundered over the drawbridge, to a roaring cheer from our men. I called for the gates to be closed and the drawbridge be raised. Looking over the ground to our front, we saw the remaining foot soldiers walking away, with their shields on their backs against possible arrows and the mounted soldiers just milled around about 150 yards away.

Two of their commanders and a standard bearer came forward, coming at a very gentle trot.

"Was this Clément," I thought "and... where would he stop?"

"Rolfe to the gate tower" I shouted, and the call "Rolfe to the gate tower", was relayed all-round the Bailey.

Our young giant of a longbowman, came running up the steps to the battlement and then up a few more stairs to the tower top.

"Yes, my lord" he panted.

"Nobody point" I said loudly. Then quietly to Rolfe as I faced him,

"Do you see over my shoulder, the party of three on horses?"

"Seen my lord" he said.

"When will they be in range?"

"Hmmmm..." he murmured, "they all be wearing fine mail."

"Have to be a bodkin..." he mused, "so with the wind as is and maybe only one shot, I'd want them at 100 yards or less m'lord."

"Let's see where they stop then" I said.

The three horsemen trotted on, straight towards our gate. Trotted on past the small white stick that marked 100 yards and stopped halfway to the 80-yard marker, well back from the line of bodies that were once his archers. I could now make out the colours and emblem of the evil Clément, the leader in this trio. This was confirmed when his voice drifted to us on the wind. "You were lucky this day, Haverhill" he shouted. Our men instantly roared back "Fock you!" "Ha," he went on, "when I return, you will all suffer - and I will roast on my spit that Arab whore" and made crude thrusting gestures in his saddle. Another louder, deeper roar of "Fock you in hell!" from all.

I noticed Rolfe was furious at the insults to our Lady.

"Steady man, steady," I said, "shoot the loudmouth, loose when ready" and stepped away to give him room.

Rolfe took a couple of slow, deep breaths and nocked his arrow. Another slow, deep breath, a glance at the distant trees and nearby grass for gauging the wind. He waited for the latest gust on his face to subside, then smoothly drew back, paused for aim and loosed. Clément caught a very late sight of the dark-coloured arrow, as with rat-like reflexes, he managed to get his shield up just enough. But the bodkin tip must have punched through, enough to pierce his arm; making him yelp and try to shake the shield off, as if to rid himself of the pain. But the pain did not last long, as Rolfe had now got a perfect gauge of the wind and his second bodkin punched through Clément's mail, through his gambeson and deep into the centre of his chest. All of us could see the ochre paint on the nock of that arrow, dead centre of its target.

All on the battlements held their breath, until the suddenly stiffened body keeled back and over the horse's rump, hitting the ground headfirst. The loudest roaring cheer went up from all of us.

Two men tried to lift Rolfe in triumph but failed – he was a big lad!

My Marshal then roared for silence and shouted the Keep lookouts for enemy dispositions.

"Foot-soldiers and cavalry retreating to the west," came the cry, "no other forces seen." Each tower was asked in turn to report; having checked both ways on the state of their walls, they all declared no enemy hiding close-in.

I instructed that Clément's body should be brought in, but others left in place. Any horses, equipment and purses outside the castle that could be swept up quickly were to be fetched in. The drawbridge went down, all archers stood guard on the walls, as parties of spearmen and some carts rushed out and recovered as much as possible. Some mounted men galloped out and brought in a couple of dozen stray horses, some of them very fine thoroughbred animals.

The mess in the Baily could wait until morning. If anyone at Walden was going to do the decent thing, they would send wagons for the dead on the morrow. I would have to check with Gerald on which of the departed might be worth a ransom – but not today.

With the field of battle swept of most of its value and all back in the castle, I glanced at the sun through the white clouds – amazed to find it was well into the afternoon. What seemed like an hour or maybe two had taken over six hours.

I sent word to the kitchens to start an early dinner and walked to the Keep and up the stairs to its door. I turned outwards and stood on the spot where yesterday I had announced the forthcoming battle. All men not on lookout gathered around, as they had yesterday. Knowing most of the men were both religious and superstitious, I began with "Thank the Lord and our Saints that we have won this battle!" An enormous cheer went up from assembled men. Thumping my chest, I said, "I, also give thanks to our tradesmen" and waved an arm in the direction of the workshops, where those men were sitting on benches, leaning against each other in a state of exhaustion. The crowd turned to them, waved and cheered – all knowing the items made through last night had been the main difference to this action. The tradesmen and Luther stood, looking bashful and managed a sort of bow to acknowledge the acclaim.

I went on "I thank my archers" - another rousing cheer.

"Our horsemen" – more cheering.

"And my humble thanks to all who were with me on the walls this day."

I spread my arms wide to encompass all present and bowed deeply and sincerely. Thunderous cheering ensued, with a chant of "Walter, Walter, Lor-ord Walter" repeated for some time. So, I bowed again.

Another cheer went up, for no obvious reason, so I just smiled and started to bow once more, but the chant changed to "Zee-zah, Zee-zah, Lay-dee Zee-zah". I glanced around and saw that Azizah had just emerged from the Keep and waved to the crowd.

She still had a quiver on her back and carried her bow, so she curtseyed to me one-handed and walked down the stairs. She turned towards the middle of the Bailey and the crowd parted in front of her, as the sea did in the Moses bible story we had heard as children. She walked towards the fallen knight, lying there with an arrow sticking out of his head. She rested her bow across the body, planted a dainty foot on the corpses shoulder, put her hands on her hips and tipped her chin up in gesture of victory. The crowd excelled itself with a new roar and more cries of "Zee-zah, Zee-zah, Lay-dee Zee-zah". She put her foot back on the ground and bowed deeply to them, three times. I knew then, beyond any doubt, that all of Haverhill would fight and, if called to, would die for Our Lady.

She bobbed a little curtsey in my direction then picked up her bow and walked over to the White Room to help attend to our wounded. Most of these had caught arrows to the upper body while on the battlements.

I found out later that the nuns, unsurprisingly, had no knowledge in this area but Azizah knew a trick of using two quill pens with the sharp ends cut off. The stiff hollow stalks were used to cover the barbs on the embedded broadhead arrows and allow removal with much less pain, minimum additional damage and reduced bleeding. But now, as I finished watching her disappear from view, my Marshal trotted up the stairs bearing a sword in its sheath, holding it crossways in two hands. Near the top step, he knelt and presented me with a sword, my sword, Williams sword, recovered from Clément's body.

A sumptuous meal for all followed that night; each had just a single beer provided as we knew not what the morning would reveal.

First light saw us all ready on the battlements, with two groups of mounted archers already hidden in the forest. The day was cold and overcast but visibility clear for the Keep lookouts and all appeared peaceful. By Terce[37], there was no sign of enemy forces, so we began the cleaning-up. The attack-wagons, still smouldering in the moat were dragged out by horse-teams and thence to the workshops for repair or breaking-up for parts. The bodies beyond the moat were searched more thoroughly, then with my archers back in, the castle was closed up.

We turned silently, sombrely, to the swathe of bodies in the courtyard, all long-since stiffened up. Firstly, the corporals used tally-sticks to count the grim totals. We had seven knights of various degree, including Devereux. Also, 39 cavalry and 21 foot-soldiers. I left the knights for Gerald to identify where possible and assess any worth for ransom. The others had all their purses, weaponry, armour and any quality clothing or boots removed and placed in piles.

The Warden came and took the purses to be counted into the coffers in the Keep. Then I waved the Marshal to take his pick of any item that he needed to enhance or replace anything that he owned. I turned away and went to the Hall to confer with Gerald, knowing that all the men would now take turns, by seniority, to select from the piles. Whatever was left would go into the castle stores.

Once in the Hall, I sat at my dining table with Gerald opposite. We had some warm mead[38] in front of us, the first we'd had in the castle. After a few sips to warm us up, Gerald began to read from his scroll. "We have five landless knights my lord, all were simple, rough follows - merely followers of Devereux; there will be no one to pay ransom or maybe even claim their bodies.

---

[37] 9 a.m.

[38] Alcoholic beverage fermented from honey and water

There is one young knight, of proud and ancient title, who should be worth something to someone."

"Where was he from?" I asked.

"Not far away sire, if my memory serves, only a few miles."

"Very well," I said, "have a coffin made, add some preserving brandy if the town has any and deliver him tomorrow – take an escort of six, see the Warden for a travel purse."

"Yes, my lord," he replied, "that just leaves… Devereux."

"Indeed, that Clément…" I said.

"Politically, at the moment, we are on the same side," I went on, "so I do not think it wise… to ask his liege[39] for ransom and a 'good death' story" and we both chuckled.

"I think I will ask for £100 and the return of all my armour and weapons" I said.

"That should be acceptable to them, my lord" said Gerald, nodding, and we resumed the sipping of our mead.

Sometime after Sext[40], many empty wagons were reported, coming slowly from the west. We manned the walls and put on a show of force. The very nervous-looking Warden of Walden slowly rode until opposite our gatehouse. We had met briefly on our unhappy visit to that castle. His assistant rode behind him with a white flag, but the pair still looked fearful as I stood at the parapet, helmet on, with my arms folded.

"I am Warden Nash, Lord Walter, m..m..m.. may we have permission to recover the d..d..d.. dead" he stuttered, barely audible across the moat.

"You may" I said loudly, looking steadily and unblinkingly into his eyes. He visibly gulped and went on "And those inside?" he asked, timidly.

"There will be terms" I said, and he hung his head in resignation, clearly not surprised.

---

[39] Aubrey de Vere, Count of Guines

[40] Noon

"You alone may enter and five wagons, with one driver each" I went on. "Thank you, my lord" he said. I nodded to my Marshal – he shouted the Keep lookouts to check for an "All clear."

Then he shouted down to the gates and drawbridge. "Five wagons and one wally on a horse to enter." The cry was repeated by those manning the gatehouse, the drawbridge was lowered, and the gates opened. The Warden rode into the Bailey - followed by the wagons, that went on to stop by the rows of Walden bodies. The wagon drivers got down and, working in pairs now, began to swing the corpses onto the backs of the wagons. Our men turned away in disgust at the lack of respect shown.

Nash dismounted and led his horse to follow me, as I walked across to the Keep. My escort of two soldiers staying with me. I pointed for him to wait near the bottom of the Keep steps and went to call for my Warden and Gerald. The quickly appeared and we gathered at the top of the steps.

We looked down at the timorous Warden Nash and I noticed a hand was moving nervously under his cloak.

I made a guess as to his action and asked, "How much is in your purse there?"

"I have £200 lord" he replied.

"Very well," I said firmly "these are my terms."

"The young knight…" I paused gesturing for Gerald to prompt me.

"De Meri, sire" he whispered.

"The body of the young knight De Meri," I went on "will be ransomed back to his family."

"For the rest, Walden will pay £100 for this egregious breach of the Kings peace and another £100 for the insults to the honour of our Lady Stewardess."

"And any of my property remaining at Walden will be returned to me tomorrow."

"Notice that I have recovered my sword" as I tapped it on my hip.

"Do not make me bring it to Walden again" I finished.

"No, no sir, this will be taken care of" he stuttered and reached for his purse. I directed one of my soldiers to bring me that purse up the steps and turned to my Warden, whispering, "Put half of this into the coffers and give the rest in the purse to the Lady Azizah."

"Immediately, sir" he said, gave me a quick bow and departed.

I turned back and looked down at the Walden man.

"You are dismissed Nash," I said, "go and make sure they take only the agreed bodies" and lifted my chin in the direction of the wagons.

"Yes, lord, thank you" he said, then bowed and led his horse across to the remaining corpses. My sergeants were standing guard over the bodies of the knights, knowing they had possible value. I watched as Nash explained which he could take, and the senior sergeant turned to look over to me for confirmation. I pointed and gestured to keep the one and sweep away the others. He bowed quickly in acknowledgement and waved the wagon-drivers to complete their grim task.

"Some more mead and a letter I think, Gerald," I said, "join me in the Hall with scroll and pen."

"Yes lord" he replied.

I walked across the Bailey and noticed that a coffin had appeared alongside the visibly very young but now very late De Meri.

Four of my men, gently lifted and placed the body in the coffin. Then two more appeared, to carry the coffin to a trestle in the tiny chapel, next to the White Room.

Our nuns would then bless the soul and add preserving brandy when it arrived from town.

I settled at my table in the Hall, the warm mead arrived, followed by Gerald. We sipped a bit and then I began to dictate a letter, to Count Aubrey. In it, I stated the events and the outcomes. No apologies and no explanations. Devereux had clearly committed grievous wrongs against a fellow lord and ally. I scanned the letter through, asked Gerald if I should add anything.

"No sire" he said.

I signed and sealed it and called for a rider to gallop this to Count Aubrey, at Hedingham Castle. I thought the rider should make it before last light.

The next day dawned bright and cold, with considerable surprise in store. After breakfast, Gerald and his escort left with the coffin on a wagon, to return the body to the De Meri at Great Thurlow. Then my coif, gambeson, daggers and other minor items were delivered back from Walden. Nothing unusual there...

The unexpected occurred just after Terce, as I was walking with Azizah, around the walls. Our rider returned from Count Aubrey, bearing a letter in reply to mine. I was immediately curious as to the contents and I adjourned to the parlour off the Hall, asking for my Stewardess to be called to me.

With a small fire going in the grate, we sat in the warmth and I began to read the letter, stopping where needed to explain any new words to Azizah. In the scroll, Count Aubrey regretted the poor behaviour of the departed Devereux – and offered me the titles of Walden and Castle Camps - I was stunned!

It was well established that although acquiring your first fief was a challenge, the second one was a higher mountain to climb. The more risk you took to gain a second fief, the more likely to lose your first – and end up a landless, penniless knight. Politically though, this would mean I had a foot in both the main camps.

Haverhill paid its taxes and 'owed spears'[41], direct to the Crown, King Stephen at present. For Walden, I would owe rent and soldiery to Count Aubrey – and hence, probably, to Empress Matilda...

I had no idea about little Castle Camps – I would have to ask Gerald on his return.

Then it struck me – Walden was a brand-new castle, admittedly a trifle damaged but nevertheless, there was a great deal of land with it and Castle Camps abutted Haverhill, so I would own a modest but continuous swathe of Suffolk and part of Essex! The greatest advantage was the tax and revenue potential of all this land, assuming it was well managed. I knew Walden had an abbey that no doubt took a big bite of the pie but even so, the prospects were stunning. I had no idea how I would staff or manage this large expansion but that was secondary to the size of the opportunity. As Gerald was away, I called for linen-paper, quill and ink and carefully wrote my own reply, accepting the offer. It took me a long time, with Azizah giggling at my tongue's contortions as I concentrated so hard, but my mother would have been proud of me.

---

[41] A liability to provide a certain number of men when war was declared

I signed and sealed the paper and called for the duty messenger; the same poor chap as had gone overnight appeared, looking a bit tired. He held out his leather bag, into which I put the letter, then put four shillings in his hand for expenses and a consideration.

"Get a fresh horse," I commanded "and place this in Count Aubrey's hand today."

"Likely there will be a reply."

"Yes, my lord" he said, cheered somewhat by the extra coin.

Aubrey's response arrived just before we closed up the castle for the night. It contained the two scrolls-of-title and also included a summary of taxes owing on the two fiefs, nothing much of concern there – which was quite a relief. It made me wonder though, if the building of the new castle had been fully paid. After dinner, I sat in the parlour with Azizah and marvelled at my good fortune. More letters to send would be needed for tomorrow but enough for today and we enjoyed the fire and our warm drinks.

Next morning, I wrote and despatched letters to Cambridge, Rockingham and Warwick. I briefly described recent events and the fact that I now held two more titles. With an escort of forty, including ten mounted archers, I rode the 5 miles to Castle Camps. From an abundance of caution, I insisted that Azizah stay behind – because we had no firm idea of the number or disposition of the remaining Devereux forces.

I needed to assess the condition of the wooden castle, because my brief view of it when I passed on the drayman's wagon, just the other day, was that the place was in poor condition. We arrived mid-morning, to find the gate ajar and much decay in the wooden piles of the outer wall. A corporal bobbed his head through the gap and reported nobody seen. We advanced through the gate and into the overgrown bailey. With my archers arrayed to handle any possible threat from the Keep, my other men searched the out-buildings, including a tiny hall. A corporal and four men went to search the Keep. All was eerily quiet as I rode around the base of the motte[42] with my escort. What we found on the far side made the gaping front gate an irrelevance. A well-worn path led from the outbuildings to the fence and through the gap where three pilings had rotted through at their base, had fallen over and been rolled out of the way. The path then continued to the edge of the forest, which was not that far away. Seventy years of neglect had seen this place turn into a tidemark of history. My guess was that some of the eastern Saxons had put up some resistance to William The First's initial push for control in this area - and this place had been the temporary frontier of Norman conquest. Haverhill and then Walden had both constructed much more recently. Indeed, Walden was only just completed.

I rode back towards the gate but stopped when I saw some scruffy soldiers being herded by my men. "Found them twelve in the stables, my lord," reported the sergeant, "seems their day hadn't started yet." I looked over this dirty dozen. At least they didn't seem drunk, and they stood with a degree of pride – as far as their clearly worn-out clothing and equipment allowed.

"Thank you, sergeant," I replied, "post lookouts as best possible, don't mind the gate, the palisade is broken down at the far side. Everyone else can stand down."

"Yes sir" he answered and went about his orders. I dismounted and looked around for somewhere to sit. Before I could find a spot, the corporal's party scrambled down the rough, stony steps of the motte. All were breathless and wide-eyed, glancing back at the Keep.

"Take a minute, lads" I said, seeing their struggles to catch breath, and waved everyone to sit on the ground. On recovering his composure, the corporal began his report.

"The structure is rotten from the ground to at least halfway up, my lord, and the walkway at the top is mostly crumbling" he began. "Looks to be abandoned and completely bare."

"I did find some documents in an alcove, but nothing else."

"Any cellars, dungeons...?" I asked.

"One large open cellar, my lord," replied another soldier, "I used my flint and steel to see if there was more but not even mice, sir."

---

[42] A flat-topped mound of earth, often made artificially, on which was built a wooden or stone defensive tower, usually called a keep

"I'm sure it sagged a bit when we got near the top, sire," said the corporal "we felt the whole thing move to one side." And they all nodded vigorously at this description.

"Well that's not dally here then" I said, glancing a wary eye up at the Keep. I mounted my horse and walked it towards the gate, then signalled to my sergeant to bring everyone in and form a column outside. While my men obeyed, I beckoned the senior-looking resident soldier.

"I am Sir Walter De Marren, Lord of Haverhill, Walden and… Castle Camps" I began. I could see the surprise and the question on his face, so I continued

"Lord Devereux is deceased."

"How long have you been in service here?" I asked.

"Six years, my lord."

"How long since you've been paid?"

"More than half a year, sir"

"How many of you have skirmish or battle experience?"

"All of us sir, the youngsters all gave up and went to work in other places, other trades."

I nodded slowly, while thinking.

I patted myself down, found a purse that wasn't too obstructed and handed down twelve silver pounds.

"This is the backpay I'm offering." I said, "Any who are willing to continue in my service should report to Warden Nash at Walden Castle. Keep in mind, all skills claimed will be tested in due course. As for this place - leave it to finish falling down."

"Yes, sir, thank you sir, of course sir" he replied while attempting to salute and bow at the same time.

I walked my horse out the gate, as I checked my calculations.

To put this castle back in service would cost a huge amount. The forest would need clearing back, with the Keep and palisade to be removed and rebuilt. I would then have a tiny old-style castle with no moat – and no source to fill one, even if it was dug. Also, with the stone castles of Haverhill and Walden only five miles away in either direction, and the village of no strategic importance… this place was redundant.

I assumed the head of my column and led them off and into the village.

Apart from the surprisingly large church, visible at the end of the street, there was an inn, some hovels and a few cottages. I waved to stop at the inn and heard an anticipatory murmur from the men. I turned to the sergeant and asked him to roust out the keeper. On his appearance, I introduced myself and told him to send word around that any taxes due from this parish, should be submitted to Haverhill within the week. If I had to come and fetch them, I would not be pleased. I also mentioned that Manor Court would be open to the people of Castle Camps on a Wednesday, the Haverhill market day. The surprisingly young host of the inn took all this quite well and accepted his new roles of 'town crier' and 'lords assistant' – not that he had much choice. I was getting better at organising and delegating.

With some regret evident in the men, I turned our backs to the village, and its inn, to return to my proper castle.

The following day saw some nervous taxpayers appear from Castle Camps. Then the wagons from Haverhill and further away began arriving with the replenishment of wood, pitch and other items consumed in our defence against Devereux.

There was no sign of Gerald and party, nor on the next day – which was a concern. It was less than two hours away, even with a wagon – maybe the River Stour was in flood...

Gerald with escort but without wagon finally appeared very late in the following day. I managed to reserve judgement, for once, and waited to hear his report. He looked exhausted, most unwell.

He managed to murmur "Good afternoon my lord" before I gestured him to silence and called for men to carry him to the Hall to be fed and then to the nuns in the White Room. The corporal of the escort sought me out to give his account.

"Was nothing to trouble us, my lord," he said, meaning the soldiers. "It's just the talking went on and on and poor Mister Gerald was looking dog-rough the last day or so."

"Seems the purse ran out and there wasn't much to eat there sir, even the cats were starving..." he finished on a slight hint I thought. I chuckled at that – god knows this had happened to me, more than a few times.

"Horses away and fed, then tell the kitchen to feed your men early"

I said with a smile. Then with a frown "Lose a wagon, did we?"
"Not exactly sir, seems it was part of the... arrangements Mister Gerald was making."
"Oh well," I said, "no doubt all will be clear tomorrow – away with you now corporal."
"Yes sir, thank you sir" he replied with enthusiasm.
I took a walk around the Bailey, as ever with two guards in close attendance. Briefly, I wondered what talks could have taken so long, but nothing came to mind and I dismissed the problem for the moment and went to inspect the tradesmens' workshops.

Next morning at breakfast, Azizah came and sat with me. She seemed concerned about Gerald and told me that she and the nuns agreed that he had a galloping of the heart[43] and a bloating of the blood[44] - all giving him headaches, dizziness and tiredness. They recommended two to three days in bed, a good leeching and some special herbs. I nodded and asked her to let the Warden know of anything we needed to buy and to source everything with urgency. She nodded, smiled, curtseyed and went about her duties.
"Yes," I thought, "she still veils her face, but I can still see her eyes smiling and that makes my heart sing."
I just hoped I didn't catch old Gerald's galloping heart...
Fortunately, the senior nun volunteered to locate both the right leeches and the correct herb – apparently, it would be a good lesson for the novice nun to go too.
So, an escort was arranged, and they left mid-morning, to search the wetlands and copses on the north side of our river. Meanwhile, I was still wondering about 'right leeches' – my experience pointed to them all being wrong!
They arrived back mid-afternoon and Azizah set to making the potion from the roots of the valerian herb. Gerald was still in the White Room when the leeches arrived and were put immediately to work – poor chap.

---

[43] Tachycardia in modern terms

[44] High blood pressure

I suddenly realised, I had no idea where Gerald's room was, so I called for the Warden. He told me that Gerald had simply taken a corner of a storeroom in the basement of the Keep; apparently that was what he had at Chester for many years and thought that suitable. I was disappointed in myself for not checking where everyone had settled – those early days here were such a whirlwind that I'd missed doing that. Gerald had been crucial to me picking Haverhill, vital to me getting here as quickly and safely as possible; also, he was someone I relied on most days to assist in making difficult decisions.

"Have his things moved to the second floor, the one underneath Lady Azizah's room" I said.

"Make sure the maids clean it first and the log-man gets a fire ready to light."

"At once, my lord" said the Warden and left to carry out my instructions.

Thinking ahead, I had the carpenter summoned and tasked him with making some litters[45]; we were long overdue to have some around the place. I preferred ones with legs on, because they could serve duty as beds in emergencies and from experience, they were a damn sight easier to pick up.

After dinner that night, Azizah joined me in the parlour next to the Hall and we talked about each other's news of that day. She told me Gerald had greatly improved already, from both the leeching and the herb, which was excellent news. He had wanted to resume his duties, but the ladies had used my name, quoting my orders, to ensure he stayed resting in the White Room, where there was always someone to keep an eye on him. Luckily, we could leave him there for a while, as no births were due for a few weeks - that we knew of, anyway. As ever, I delighted in the sight and sound of Azizah sitting next to me in the warmth of the room.

After another day of rest, Gerald was allowed out of the ladies' care and was taken by litter across and up to his new room. Seems he was astonished 'to be so promoted' as he put it.

---

[45] A simple wooden stretcher

A further couple of days rest followed, with a maid always with him to ensure compliance with the lady's instruction to allow himself time to recover. The next day, he was allowed to walk slowly to the Hall for lunch, with a maid in close attendance, just in case. I invited him to sit with me for the meal and he looked quite transformed, so much better. He began to apologise for his 'failings' but I waved this aside and said everyone was very relieved he was feeling better. He also started to thank me effusively for the new room, but I apologised to him, saying I thought he was in that place from the start. This extremely rare apology from a feudal lord seemed to shock him so much that I was concerned his heart would start galloping again...

After lunch, we adjourned to the parlour and had some very leisurely beer with our talk - the maid being asked to wait outside. Gerald sipped reflectively on his drink.

"It is quite a story, my lord" he began.

"Tell all," I said, "there's no rush."

"Well, we arrived without a problem, it really isn't far – but then could not find anyone."

"Great Thurlow is a huge demesne[46], yet never was granted a castle – it has a fortified manor house, and not much else."

"With the wagon needing watching and only six soldiers, we couldn't search far – so we waited hours, and then the owners returned from working the fields."

I blinked in surprise, and he nodded to confirm what he had just said.

"Lord and Lady De Meri are, as I thought, an offshoot of the Norman De Meri's – but they are not from the rich and powerful de Bohun branch of the tree."

"God," I thought "even I know that name." "Soooo," Gerald went on "as times have been harsh on these gentlefolk, they are now in dire circumstances. They had one disease take all their sheep, another did for their pigs and a blight took their orchards."

---

[46] A piece of land attached to a manor and retained by the owner for their own use

"They started again, twice, but each time, the forest bandits took or destroyed everything – Hugo did nothing about them, and they never had a garrison... Their serfs drifted away over time, unpaid and with no work to do anyway..."

"Ah – but I'm getting a little ahead, my lord."

I gestured for him to take a sip and catch his breath. Thus refreshed, Gerald resumed.

"As to our main task – it was harrowing, sire, to break the news to the parents of the loss of their only surviving child."

I hung my head at that thought for quite a few moments. We both took a sip before Gerald went on.

"Rémin was their pride and joy, he was their last one and their best hope for sustaining their land."

"They had signed him up through Devereux to be squire to Count Aubrey – or so they thought."

"I saw the document, it indentured Rémin to Devereux and only promises 'introduction' to Count Aubrey. The De Meris don't read, except just enough to recognise Aubrey's name on the scroll..."

"I also think the Devereux faked Aubrey's seal..."

I just shook my head, in despair at the depths of sin that bastard had reached.

"Burn in hell" was my fervent wish for Clément. My mind also sent grateful thanks, yet again, to my father for making me learn to read and write with my mother.

"Soooo, my lord, no ransom, in fact... ", he paused to fidget and cough, "you paid for the blessings and the funeral, sire. We left the wagon, so they could take the coffin to the church – they had no other means..."

"Quite right, Gerald," I said firmly "a good and proper decision."

"There is more, my lord, I did... take a modest liberty..."

I raised my eyebrows and encouraged him to complete the rest of the confession.

"They are rich with land, sire, but through age and ill-health, cannot work it effectively – they are out of coin and near starvation."

"So... I... offered to buy their land, on your behalf lord" he finished and blushed with confusion at his own boldness.

No wonder his blood became bloated on this trip I thought.

I roared with laughter at his, or was it 'our', audacity.

"They would keep title to the manor house, we would have the land, that is nearly as big as the Haverhill holdings. In exchange for putting in a lane from the main road and... well... their asking price was... £1000."

"Good god" I thought "that's about what Haverhill castle would have cost to build."

Gerald quickly added "but I think we could win it for half that if we guaranteed to put in tradesmen to fix the poor old manor house."

"Hmmmm," I pondered, "is there any heraldic title to go with this?"

"No, my lord, just the land – but it does butt against our northern boundary, which is a main reason I, err... we were interested."

"Oh well," I said, "never mind, I have enough titles to be going on with" and broke out into a huge smile and a chuckle at Gerald's expression.

"My lord? Titles?" he said, in a constricted voice.

"Mmmm, yes" I said, trying to sound casual, "Count Aubrey granted me... Castle Camps... and... Walden!"

Gerald's face was a picture and I wondered if I should have kept this news until another day.

"We'll talk more tomorrow, Gerald, go and rest for today."

I called the maid in and instructed her to help Gerald back to his room. As they left, Azizah knocked on the door and I called her in. She looked quite disapproving but still did a little curtsey before saying "You talk much time, my lord, our Gerald... need much rest." I stood up, held my hands up and agreed with her. I thanked her for looking after him so well and asked her to thank the nuns for their work. She looked boldly into my eyes and said, "My lord can do that." I sighed, opened the door for her and followed her to the White Room. Dear Azizah, her dresses were never styled as tight as many and were made to cover up to her neck but if you watched closely, you could sense her hips swaying as she walked gracefully down the corridors.

We arrived in the White Room and I gave a good little speech of thanks to the nuns. They seemed appreciative of the recognition but that didn't stop the rather imperious senior sister asking for more and better supplies for the birthing service they were providing.

"How many have we helped now?" I asked.

"Nine, so far Sir Walter" she said, never using my other title, as in her eyes, her Lord appeared to out-rank me…

"How many… lost?" I asked very quietly.

"None so far, sir" she replied, a trifle more gently now, sensing something from me.

"Good, good," I said, trying to cover my utter relief with some jollity "see the Warden for what you need."

I turned away to hide my emotion and walked quickly past Azizah and out the door. We shared a glance, she with her 'gentle eyes' now, and I knew she had seen something in me that she hadn't known before. I stomped away down the corridor, pondering my inner contradictions; I could use sword or axe to take a life in battle and not think twice, but a mother or child in danger would break me.

That evening, I ordered preparations for my visit to Walden the next day. I needed to see the accounts and which of the staff could be kept and which to let go. I planned to spend only a few hours there and return the same day, so we left after an early breakfast – taking basic supplies in case.

My escort of forty was about the most I could spare from the castle, with ten of those being my mounted archers. These bowmen having shown their worth in our recent battle. I was in no doubt that Count Aubrey would have notified Walden of their new lord, but I had no certainty that all Devereux deviousness would cease with his demise.

Therefore, we branched off the main road, after passing the church of Castle Camps. We rode through the forest, using the trails and paths, recently walked so uncomfortably by myself and Azizah. The dog-men bodies were where we had left them, well, parts of them were still there, the forest animals having helped themselves. My men commented loudly on the size of the dead hound.

The route took us south of the village and castle, so at least we arrived from an unexpected direction if any ambush was lying in wait. As we rode up towards the moat, ten of my cavalry with their heavy shields spread left and right, then the ten archers formed behind them, arrows nocked but not showing the bows above the shields – yet.

We saw the drawbridge was raised and gates closed. Helmeted heads and spears were visible above the battlements, but no bows were to be seen. I rode through my line of mounted soldiers, wearing my coif and helmet that had been returned to me.

Not the most careful of moves but often a show of confidence would tip the balance.

"Warden Nash," I thundered "open for your Lord Walter De Marren."

After only a moment's hesitation, the drawbridge clanked down, and the gates creaked open. As previously ordered, shield-bearers and archers rode in as pairs, forming two columns in the Bailey, facing outwards. At a nod from the corporal, I crossed the drawbridge, rode between the columns and into the Bailey, with my four personal guards in close attendance. I looked around with imperious and critical gaze. In assessing the manner of the Walden soldiers and staff, they looked to be a beaten force all right – but I felt there was more amiss here than that alone.

I nodded to the Warden, who'd come out to meet me in the Bailey. Then I called for all the Walden soldiery be drawn up for inspection, leaving the minimum on lookout duty.

Myself and my sergeant then walked along the four ranks, but somehow, we were expecting more bodies on parade...? All were well equipped and looked healthy but clearly demoralised, almost none being able to look me in the eye.

I asked to see the wounded and was taken to the Hall.

Here we had the explanation for some the shortage outside, but this was still a puzzle to us.

We believed we'd killed most of their casualties, by various means, mostly by arrow. Where had this number of injured come from and how were so many suffering from obvious sword and lance wounds? Also, on many, the blood seemed not that old. I raised an eyebrow at the very nervous-looking Nash and inclined my head for him to meet me outside.

"What occurred?" I asked, nodding in the direction of the Hall and its casualties.

"Well sire, on the return from battle, the two knights that survived had assumed command. They held no title, but we had no instructions left by Lord Clément nor from Count Aubrey at that time. So…" he stammered.

"They seized the castle" I finished for him.

"Indeed, my lord. There was much… indiscipline that followed. Feasting, drinking and… women."

"And then, Count Aubrey's instruction arrived, and much consternation ensued."

"The knights and their drinking friends wanted to hold the castle against… well… you and Count Aubrey." I roared with laughter. The domain of Walden was large and should be very profitable. The two optimists could have taken Castle Camps and never been bothered by anyone – but to unlawfully seize somewhere like Walden was to sign for your own execution.

I gestured for the Nash to continue.

"Most of the soldiers now did not want to follow the knights – and a skirmish broke out inside the castle. The two ring-leaders tried to steal from the coffers, but I had hidden myself away with the keys."

"The knights then took to their horses and escaped, along with some uninjured supporters."

"I see," I said, musing on all of this "what help for the wounded is there here?"

"None at all, my lord. We used to have a couple of ladies with skills, but they were… mistreated by Lord Clément and left suddenly – months ago now."

I nodded, asking "What wagons are there?"

"A large number in the village sire, we keep ten in the castle and two carriages[47].

"Really, carriages? What are they for?"

"Lord Clément liked to use them to fetch… er… the ladies in from nearby towns. Seems more would visit if the trip was not so rough there - and back…" Nash faltered with embarrassment.

"So how many turncoats[48] are in with the injured? I asked.

---

[47] Looks like a 4-wheel wagon but has the flat-bed suspended from the axles by leather straps. They still lurched on rough roads but were much less jarring

[48] Betrayers

"Only three remain now sir, one had died, and a couple of others left yesterday."

"Those three took up arms against me," I said, very sternly "they remove themselves immediately or I will end their troubles for them."

"For the rest of the wounded," I went on "send any that can travel to Haverhill, in the carriages."

"Yes, my lord" he replied and turned as if to leave.

I gestured for him to wait "Is there no Marshal or sergeant to hand?"

"No my lord, first and Second Sergeants left with the knights, third one was injured and didn't survive."

"So they all had turned on me?" I asked.

"Yes, my lord."

"Well, good riddance, saves me killing them. Any corporals I can use?

"I will send them over, sir" he said and scurried off to delegate my orders.

I shared a look with my sergeant, we both rolled our eyes at this shambles of a military establishment.

The two corporals ran over and stood to attention - both looking very young.

One looked at the ground and shuffled nervously, the other looked me in the eye and introduced himself,

"Corporal Jacot, my lord" he said, clearly and confidently stating his very Norman first name.

"Corporal Jacot," I said, "you are now Sergeant Jacot."

"Thank you, sir," he said, somewhat surprised.

"Don't thank me yet, sergeant, you will have a high standard to achieve and maintain."

"Yes sir."

"What are you going to do next with this... shower?" inclining my head at the paraded men. "Get them to check the horses are groomed, fed and watered for the day. Then... weapons cleaning and inspection, lunch and appoint a guard rota for the week. Sir."

I stood up straight and said loudly, "Carry on with your tasks, Sergeant Jacot."

"Yes sir" he responded, then bowed and trotted away, with the other corporal trailing.

I shared another look with my sergeant that said, "Maybe not all here is complete dross."

Warden Nash returned and we adjourned to his room in the Keep. I left my sergeant to manage the Haverhills and placed my four guards down the corridor. I noticed how the place still reeked of smoke and burnt pitch.

I requested the current balance of taxes owed and owing.

The figure for owing was small and matched Count Aubrey's.

The amount owed was trivial and was obviously being well managed. I turned to the two large chests, taking up the width of the far end of the room. He unlocked the first, which was half full of pennies, the second one was nearly full - of shillings and pounds!

I managed to keep my face in check but only just.

"How much is here?" I asked

He referred to some tally sticks on his desk and replied, "Two thousand, three hundred and fifty-four pounds and... fourteen shillings my lord."

I was stunned but tried not to show it.

"How much in unpaid bills for the building – and elsewhere?"

"Just over nine hundred pounds on the castle sir, and around two hundred pounds on provisions, other tradesman and so on"

I was shocked. "So, that sounds as if very little is paid off on the castle? How is that possible?"

"Lord Clément kept delaying and delaying, then taking on new tradesmen from further away, which is why it took so long to finish. The stone was all paid for on delivery but foundation work for the gatehouse was greatly underestimated – hence the large amount still remaining."

"I'm surprised anyone will supply anything to this place!" I said.

"That indeed has been a problem these last few months, my lord."

"You have records for all this?

"I do sir."

"Pay it – all of it."

"Yes sir" he replied, with some surprise in his voice.

"I will return in a few days. Other tasks for you Warden, look for some nursing help, make sure the kitchen staff are up to strength and announce Manor Court to be held here first Monday of each month, starting after New Year."

"Yes sir, and when will you be back?"

"When I appear at my gate Warden" I replied.

"Of course sir" he said, bowing as I left the room.

I rejoined my guards and we went down to the bailey.

I gave silent signals for all my men to mount up, form up and move out of the gate. This was done quickly, quietly and with some swagger – really putting on a show to the Walden soldiery. We took the direct road to Haverhill, pushing a couple of scouts out in front, just in case. I waved my sergeant up to talk.

"Well?" I said.

"The wounded have set off sir, we may pass them in a bit. Water supply seems good – but there's only one well - in the bailey. They seem to be about out of food, so just as well we weren't stopping for lunch. Horses seem well looked after. Wood, pitch, rope and general stores almost all gone. There are workshops like ours, but no tradesmen seen."

"I see..." I said, "not unexpected... We'll have our bread and cheese in a while, when we stop at the inn at Castle Camps."

"Yes sir" he said with enthusiasm and pulled back to pass the word.

We stopped in the village on our way back, dispersing our men around the green. The horses had their drink from the communal troughs. I had the innkeeper send out wenches with the beers on trays, all very popular with the soldiers. We even had some faint sunshine break through the overcast for the duration of our brief stop, but this changed quickly, with the temperature dropping and darker heavier clouds appearing that hinted at another harsh winter to come. Indeed, after we arrived back at Haverhill, a few snowflakes fell as the light faded on this December day.

I returned to Walden a few days later, this time casting a critical eye over the structures. I could now see there were many unfinished parts, especially the Keep battlements - unsurprising in the circumstances of unpaid bills. I smiled grimly at the long queue of creditors that waited at the stairs of the Keep.

A soldier would call them in, one at a time, to see the Warden and get paid if their accounts tallied.

Many of the waiting ones doffed their caps and said "Thank you, Lord Walter" as I rode past – I nodded in reply.

This time, I left my Marshal here, with twelve of our best soldiers. I'd become wary of leaving all that coin in hands that might change their allegiance...

Before leaving though, I held a brief parade for the Walden soldiery, to introduce my Marshal and emphasise that when they heard his voice, they should hear it as mine.

Back at Haverhill, I had another, much shorter talk with Gerald. I wanted him to think about someone who could act as his assistant, do most of the travelling and so on. He said he believed there were a couple of possible candidates and would write to their fathers.

We also wrote to the De Meri's, saying we would, in due course, make an offer to buy their land and included twenty pounds in silver coin to tide them over into the New Year.

There followed a few days of extremely heavy snow, clearly no one would be rushing to campaign through this winter, the long bitterly cold conflicts of last year not having faded from memory.

Azizah used this time of relative quietness around my domain to suggest I had another bath. I protested that I'd had one only a few weeks previously - to no effect. At each mealtime, or just after, whenever it was just us together, she would start sniffing the air through her veil. She'd make a show of following an odour around the room – and always ending up at me. Then she'd say something with fake surprise, like, "Oh, it is Lord Walter – I thought swamp-donkey in castle!"

I gave up after three days of this gentle harassment and ordered a tub to be filled.

Having no idea who was on laundry duties that day, I was pleasantly surprised to see the same two maids there – for a moment. They immediately started an unseemly catfight over who was going to 'help' me. Indeed, by the time I'd quickly disrobed in the chilly room and got into the blissful hot water, the pushing and shoving had escalated to fingernails-out and hissing!

I firmly commanded them both to cease – and get in the tub with me.

It was a tight squeeze but such a delicious one, with much all-round kissing and all-over soaping. Feeling much cleaner now but also rather… strong, I was very rough with brun-hair, then most gentle with flaxen-hair and much enjoyment was had by all. The next day, I ordered a fireplace, chimney and water-heating frame be built into the laundry. Then after more thought, I commissioned a much bigger tub from our carpenter – for improved defence against fire on our gates of course!

The following days brought their longer winter evenings, with many that were memorable for me. After dinner, I would sit by the fire with Azizah, in my parlour, and we'd talk about our early lives, our families, the politics of our respective lands or anything that came to mind.

The castle settled in for winter. Letters between fiefs, ceased to arrive. The snow-covered land was hushed for miles around. Extra woollen shirts were issued to the guards from the stores, much holly was brought in from the forest to decorate the whole castle and a very large quantity of mince pies[49] was prepared for the twelve days of Christes Maesse[50].
In each of the days before the 25th, carol singers would gather in the Bailey before dinner. They would sing us into the meal, all standing warmly wrapped, holding candles and sounding rather fine.
Apart from her kitchen and supply management duties, Azizah was seen very little during the festivities, spending much time in her room in the Keep. I would drop by from time to time to see how she was, but never felt it appropriate to tarry[51].

---

[49] Made rectangular in this era, to represent a crib. Made with shredded meat, cinnamon, cloves and nutmeg.

[50] Christmas

[51] To abide or stay in or at a place

Father Aldous held a Midnight Mass in the town church of Saint Mary's, on the 24th. It was a crystal clear, starlit night with a bright moon shining off the blanket of snow that covered the land. For once, I allowed the castle to be very short-handed indeed. I was left on the gate-tower with four of my longbowmen and three soldiers, with just two guards up on the Keep, freezing their bollocks off in double-cloaks and woollen cowls under their helmets. You could hear their feet stamping from down where we were. I resolved to put a brazier up there, and one on each of the wall-towers – for use when the weather was this bloody cold. I looked up at the heavens and thought that the roof of our world, where those star-lamps would be, must be a very, very high ceiling to draw away so much warmth from the ground...

Against my better judgement, I'd allowed all the wagons out and as many horses as needed to take my castle-folk to the Mass. My proviso being that a small guard at least was maintained on the very valuable transport. The Marshal ensured a discreet rotation of soldiers on duty, changing every twenty minutes or so. By happy coincidence, the wide-wheeled wagons we'd won from Walden were much easier to pull along the snowy lanes than our usual ones, which got us thinking. Much of my northern and eastern land could flood or become boggy from the Stour, so this change of wheel design could be a help. Anyway, everyone had returned before the two rings of Vigil[52] rang out from the church and I and the other frozen guardians of the castle could hobble to the Hall for mulled wine or mead.

The twelfth day after Christes Maesse saw in the celebration of the Epiphany[53]. The weather then eased for a few days and much hunting was done, to replenish food-stocks and get some air into our lungs after our recent inaction. It truly felt like a New Year and high time to get back to the business of being a feudal lord.

---

[52] 2 a.m.

[53] Celebration of the visit from the three kings or wise men, the Magi, to the baby Jesus bearing gifts of gold, frankincense and myrrh

The first arrival of the year was Jeannot, second son of the Warden of Rockingham. Gerald had written to his father with an offer of a clerk's job at Haverhill. The real responsibilities, however, were going to be much more than the abilities to read and write. After two days of preparation with Gerald, this Jeannot set off to Great Thurlow with an escort to see the De Meris and make an offer of £500, with the added promise to fix the roof of their manor house. After several trips, there and back, a price of £720, a tax waiver for life, with repairs to roof and walls of the manor house was agreed. The ex-De Meri demesne doubled the size of my Haverhill domain but presented the challenge of management. There were no taxpaying residents or tenants so far, just swathes of unruly pasture, failed orchards and unkempt copses.

After consultation with Gerald, my Warden and this sensible but still very young Jeannot, we formed a plan to pay our visiting Dutch and Flemish merchants to announce the availability of good land to rent, at half-price in the first year, to Saxon-speaking people from abroad. It would not be wise to poach tenants from other lords... This should give us income from the plots near the lanes; for the rest, we would clear the worst of the overgrowth by putting out many horses and goats in the first year then throwing it over to sheep.

The orchards would be replanted, wherever simple pruning couldn't save the trees.

Other matters continued at the castle. The original Haverhill sergeant died from the lingering effects of the stomach illness he'd had when we arrived, combined with a drinking habit that far too often led him to be stupidly drunk when off duty. There were also many stories of his long-suffering wife looking bruised and cut about the face, after he visited her in town. The funeral was held the next day and we sent an honour party from the castle. This was led by our Marshal, who'd returned from Walden leading the guards of a very large shipment of my coin.

As an insight to our times, the long-standing widower Marshal proposed to the new widow at the graveside – and was accepted. Thus, he pre-empted the queue of would-be suitors at the cemetery gate!

She, Blaedswith[54], was a rather tall but very comely woman, who'd born her previous troubles with dignity. She had no land or title but kept a clean house and was rumoured to have the finest legs! From her point of view, as a single woman with no male relative as protector, she would be vulnerable to many types of predation – so with our Marshal, she would be safe – well, as safe as he allowed. Proven rape in our time was generally punished merely by fines or compensation. In many of our families recently come in from southern Germany, this type of assault was seen as a form of forced, pre-marriage arrangement.

As a senior man at the castle, the Marshal had his own room in the Keep and after they married, much swiving[55] was heard through the nights. Seems the lady had suffered a dire lack of... attention from the late husband. On my way back to my room, I would often share looks and raised eyebrows with my guards when their growls, howls, shouts and cries echoed through the corridors! Made me realise just how well sound travelled along these stone walls...

The new couple were totally besotted and would usually take meals together. Blaedswith showed some very useful skills in spinning and making woollen garments, so quickly became a very welcome addition to our fief.

However, a darker episode was soon to follow...

After another blanket of snow, the weather eased again, which allowed me to visit Walden to check on their condition. While I was away, the temporary opening of the roads allowed the first potential new recruits of the year, to appear at our castle. One of these was an extremely large and very experienced soldier from the west. He claimed prior service as a sergeant but had fallen out with his lord and so had moved away to seek new employment. The Marshal talked to him and the soldier went on to pass basic tests with different weapons.

---

[54] An old Saxon name meaning splendid and strong

[55] Fornicating

He was taken on as an acting corporal until he could be assessed further. At some point he'd caught sight of Azizah walking across to the Hall and asked a passing soldier about her. He was told that that was the Lady Azizah, Stewardess of the Castle. His reaction as a stranger was not unusual when he said, "A darky eh?" before going on with his duties. After lunch he was seen to casually go into the kitchen when, in fact, he must have been following Azizah. Unbeknownst to all but a couple of maids, Azizah was then on her way to the laundry, for what was now her regular weekly bath. The soldier followed her into the laundry and was confronted by the maids, who tried to push him out of the room. He responded by punching each girl in the face with his chain-mail-gloved hands. They both collapsed, silent and bleeding on the floor. He then tore the curtain aside to see Azizah backed into a corner with just a towel wrapped around her – too far from her dress – and her khanjar… He roared in delight at the prospect that seemed to be in front of him, took a step towards her and felt Luther's crutch thud and break on the back of his head. Luther had been taking lunch in the Hall when this huge stranger seemed to be going in an odd direction, and certainly wasn't going to the midden. So, Luther had followed, at his best hobbling pace. The soldier grunted at the interruption, turned, brushed aside Luther's follow-up attack using what was left of the crutch and threw him against the wall, breaking his arm. Meanwhile, one of the maids had regained some of her senses and screamed. This brought soldiers running from their lunches in the Hall. The huge brute was disabled by sword cuts through his boots, damaging or cutting the tendons of both ankles. With his helmet knocked off, multiple sword pommels were used to batter him down enough to get him subdued and then he was hog-tied. At the moment of Luther's intervention, Azizah had grabbed another towel and made a shawl of it, thus covering her hair and face but had stayed out of the way of this armoured monster.
A litter was fetched, and he was quickly tied down to that, while sealing his fate with his own words,
"Lads, lads, I just wanted a go with the darky. You've all had a go, right?"
If there was ever, ever a wrong thing to say around Haverhill, he managed it at first attempt. The eight men now carrying the litter

changed course as one, in one instant. They had been heading for the Keep and hence to the dungeon, but now the low growl of these men and all the off-duty soldiers that had rushed to the sound of fighting was the sound of implacable fury. They changed in that moment, from disciplined soldiers in my service, to the Berserkers[56] of their far-distant ancestors. Their destination now was the south wall – they almost ran up the steps, despite the size of the load. The man's stupidity continued, with him saying "All right lads, maybe I should have asked. Waited my turn. No need to take a joke too far", as maybe now a sense of uncertainty crossed his small mind. With not a word spoken, the foot of the litter was braced on the parapet, two nooses were thrown around his neck and tied off around merlons[57]. With a massive effort and the use of spears to give enough reach, the head of litter was raised.

He shrieked, "What, Wait, No... I'm one of you... You can't do this... I'm..."

The ropes securing him to the litter were cut with daggers and his body shot over the edge, for a short drop with a very sudden stop. He'd wrenched his arms free of the bindings but now his bulky chainmail gloves blocked him from gaining any grip on the ropes around his neck. His frantic gasping, sobbing, gurgling and pounding of feet on the wall could be heard as men took it in turns to stand in the embrasures, lift their mail and leather undercoats and piss on him. The outcome wasn't quick by any means, but ironically, the brute size that had enabled him to bully his way through life, hastened his death.

After a moment or two of silent satisfaction, the Berserkers blinked at each other and as one said, "Our Lady". They became Haverhills once more, and rushed back to the kitchens, thence to the laundry. Azizah was not there, but after a moment of confusion they found her by following the cries of the wounded - all had been moved to the White Room.

---

[56] Ancient Norse warriors, who fought with wild or uncontrolled ferocity

[57] Solid raised part of a crenelated parapet between two embrasures (gaps)

Now properly attired, Azizah was helping the nuns assess the injuries. She heard the urgent footsteps and sharply turned, to see a corridor full of soldiers on their knees, all giving thanks for her preservation. Puzzled for a moment, Azizah then relaxed, took her hand away from near the hilt of her hidden khanjar and rushed to quickly reassure the men, some of whom were sobbing their apologies for not getting to her sooner.

She soothed their worries away with gentle words and urged them to go to the Hall and finish their meals. Most did do this, but by another unspoken consent, two remained on guard; on guard of Azizah that is. From that moment on, Azizah would have the same size guard detail as I did – all day, all night, no exceptions.

When the Marshal pointed out this hadn't been approved as a duty, the men gently but firmly stated that "this was going to be done, sir, whether by off-duty men or 'on'".

Back in the White Room, Azizah had decided the order of treatment. The ever-useful poppy-juice was given to Luther and the flaxen-haired maid, who was still screaming from the image she had seen of herself in a mirror. Her pretty nose had been smashed sideways across her face and she was inconsolable, unreachable by any words or actions. When the poppies had made both wounded drowsy and quiet, the nuns carefully aligned the bone ends in Luther's upper arm and gently bandaged the broken pieces of his crutch to the arm, to act as a splint. Azizah was now coo-ing words to the sleepy maid as she gently manipulated the nose back to its rightful place. All the ladies now turned to the brun-haired maid, cleaned her up, decided the cuts needed no stitches but did need sealing with honey. Also, they made up a herb poultice, to sooth the pain and bruising that was across half of her face.

The injured were to remain in the White Room for that night and Azizah requested the carpenter make a new crutch for Luther. Another representation of soldiers to the Marshal, brought about another order for the busy carpenter and the mason. A very substantial door, with locking bar, was put on the laundry by the time I returned.

When I came back from Walden, the very large figure suspended from the battlements was difficult to miss.

Not an unusual sight at some fiefs, but it was... unexpected at Haverhill. I rode into the Bailey, dismounted and waved away my escort. Tipping my head towards the south wall, I said, "Time for a beer?" to my Marshal as he approached me. "Indeed sire" he smiled grimly, and we walked to the Hall.

I saw Azizah crossing from the Hall to the Keep, accompanied by two guards, keeping in step with her and looking as smart and as proud as could be. Turning to my Marshal, I raised an eyebrow and he said, "All part of the same story sir".

Over a couple of pints, he told me everything.

Next day, all the wounded were out and about. Luther hobbled into the Hall for breakfast on his new crutch and was cheered by all present. Word had spread that he had been first to tackle 'The Beast'. The injured maids adopted veils, like Azizah's, while their terribly discoloured and swollen faces healed. This strengthened the assumption, made by almost all at Haverhill, that Azizah's veil hid some deformity, probably they thought, the one that afflicted some children from birth, where the mouth runs up to the nose. The very few who knew her veil was for religious reasons, assumed everyone else knew and never mentioned it.

Meanwhile, there was furious competition to be on the Stewardess's guard rota. I approved the extra manning but had to be firm in my instruction, that her detail could be equivalent to mine but not larger or more senior.

With the roads being open more often from late January, letters began to flow again as the pulse of the realm began to speed up from its winter torpor.

A most unexpected scroll arrived for me, a proposal of marriage into a substantial family of Norfolk. The offered spouse was the Lady Janine Bigod, a cousin of the powerful Earls of Norfolk and also linked to the equally impressive d'Aubigny family. She was thought to be around 24 years of age and would bring a couple of substantial manor houses, each with a large demesne, and of course, connections - so certainly something to consider. After consultation with Gerald, we thought that, if this was the result of a political chess-move by Lord Roger, it seemed to indicate a leaning back towards King Stephen – all so complicated...

I wrote back, to invite her to visit Haverhill, at her earliest convenience; at which time I hoped, more details of her dowry would be forthcoming. A bitter, icy three weeks of driving snow and howling wind ensued with all activity ceasing except eating, drinking, sleeping and for the fortunate few, swiving. Finally, as the last drips of snow went down into the streams and the spring flowers began to come out, a letter arrived to say that Lady Janine was on her way.

The castle hummed into action, with cleaning and tidying a priority. In this game, I believed my hand was stronger, as I had two stone-built castles and a very substantial tax-base. Demesnes could be useful but were not financial or political powerhouses.

Four days later, she duly arrived around Sext[58], with an escort of twenty. As she stepped down from her horse, I could see she was... average in all respects. As if to confirm my previous judgement, she curtseyed to me and I bowed to her. Clearly and correctly, she felt her titles were secondary to mine. But she did, nevertheless, manage to project a very superior manner...

We walked towards the Hall for lunch and my senior staff were introduced along the way; my Warden, Marshal, Marshal's wife and... Stewardess.

Warden and Marshal bowed and were acknowledged with nods. Blaedswith curtseyed deeply, while casting her eyes down, and was acknowledged with a nod. Azizah made a small curtsey but effortlessly held unblinking gaze with Janine, using her 'princess eyes' to full effect. Janine did her very best to stare down Azizah as she passed - but utterly failed, instead stumbling on a piece of uneven Bailey. I caught her arm to prevent any chance of her falling and glanced back at Azizah, to see her eyes sparkling over her veil. We had a superb lunch in the Hall, though with Lady Janine clearly unsettled once she realised that our Stewardess also ran the kitchens...

---

[58] Noon

Azizah had visited our high table after the meal, to ask if we enjoyed everything. Her full and graceful curtsey to us, well mostly me, was wonderful to see.

The Lady and her more senior staff adjourned to rooms that had been prepared for them in the Keep, to rest after their several days of travel from the north of Norfolk. We squeezed her soldiers into our stables and barrack rooms; they didn't mind as this was still better than their lot often was and clearly the food here had been a treat.

We all rejoined in the Hall for dinner and another splendid meal was served, remarkable in view of the earliness in the year for both game and other supplies. After the meal, the real business began. I invited Lady Janine into my parlour, next to the Hall, along with Gerald, Jeannot and two of the Lady's advisers. Scrolls of title and summaries of accounts were produced by her people and verbal descriptions of my titles and holdings read out by Gerald. Seems there was some possibility of a place for us at the hugely impressive fortifications currently being built at Castle Rising in Norfolk, but glances between me and Gerald confirmed that we thought this was a remote hope and of no weight on the balance sheet. Another carrot dangled for me was mention of a sizeable fief that could be mine on marriage but again, this was less than a confirmed offer. By now, much wine had been drunk by all and we agreed to retire early and meet in the Bailey, at Terce[59] the next day, for a tour around my domain.

The following morning, we left the castle after breakfast. Her escort of twenty and mine of twenty-four made a fine sight as we trotted along the riverbank. I waved to Miller Adelaert and smiled at his panic at the sight of so many soldiers. We crossed the river and toured my land to the north. Finding a piece of rising ground, I led the party to the top and was very pleased to note that the very distant Keep of Walden castle was just visible in the pale sunlight to the west.

---

[59] 9 a.m.

One could also see the northern extent of my demesne and the high forest around Castle Camps in the opposite direction. We travelled back through Haverhill town, putting on a good show for the humble folk and then back to the castle for lunch.

I attended to domain matters in the afternoon and we reconvened over another excellent dinner. More wine in the parlour followed, but this time it was just me and Lady Janine. I'm afraid the drink did nothing to reduce her haughtiness. She was quite plain of face and figure, though this mattered not in my calculations, but her manner would undoubtedly grate after a short while. Even so, if this would've been a smart match for me, I could have closed my eyes, thought of the titles and fiefs and done duty to extend the bloodline that she and her family wished to continue. After all, I wouldn't be seeing her very much, certainly not living with her all year, or even part thereof. Except that – after some more wine, she let slip that her expectations included me being with her at least half the year, or more if I wasn't campaigning. Well, if I had still been thinking of taking this offer, the thought would've died there and then. I was though, intrigued with her mention of campaigns. I wondered if she'd heard anything about this year's plans – she was, after all, very well connected socially...

After breakfast the next morning, we staged a formal farewell for her, my soldiers on parade and flags flying on the battlements - my senior staff were also in attendance. Lady Janine's horse was brought for her, then as I was holding her hand, ready for her to use a stool to help her mount, she leaned closer to me and said "Of course, Lord Walter, if we are to join our houses, then *that* will have to go." On the word 'that', she tipped her head back in the direction of our Stewardess. Azizah, though twenty paces away, still caught that action, guessed its meaning and began to silently laugh behind her veil, I could see her shoulders shaking. Azizah then turned her back to us and mimicked the head move, laughing more and more. I fought to keep a straight face and murmured something about how good a Stewardess she was, but Janine remained unimpressed and blithely unaware that she had now reached far beyond her position in the scheme of things.

The marriage of the holder of even a minor title was a shrewdly calculated business. Sometimes care, or consideration, or even love on rare occasions may have developed but primarily this was business, with clearly defined roles. If a Lord wished to keep staff for any... purpose, he would do so. One would employ a degree of discretion if keeping a mistress or two but there was no scandal attached, that's how things were done.

I waited only for her to clear the drawbridge, then immediately turned to Gerald and his assistant, Jeannot and headed for the warmth of the parlour. Not too much to discuss, we had all come to the same conclusion – this was not a worthwhile trade. If she had been an absolutely stunning and gracious beauty, then Gerald might've been faced with a different challenge – where he had to talk sense into me. As things were though, this was purely a matter of shaping the letter to decline the proposal. Nothing too difficult, anything other than a suggested wedding date meant a refusal. So, we began with some waffle about how nice it was to meet the Lady, whatever her name was, and that my ambitions were leaning towards owning more castles rather than increasing my farmland. Leaving Jeannot to pen a draft, I took an early lunch and went hunting with the Marshal.

Following dinner that night, I invited Azizah to the warm parlour. I thanked her sincerely, for organising such excellent meals for everyone. Once again, I was amazed by the ease I felt in her presence, the way I could confide any matter for an honest opinion in return – if she thought I was wrong about something, she would say so and give her reasoning. But this night, she simply made me roar with laughter when she asked me how I had liked 'Lady-Jane Snooty-Boots'! Apparently, the kitchen staff had given her that name, based on the impression they had gained from their very brief contact with her ladyship. Once I regained my breath, I replied that we wouldn't be seeing her again.

A brief period of routine settled in at Haverhill. Stores reduced by the winter began to be replenished, more new soldiers started their training and seasonal repairs to buildings commenced. An alarm was raised early one morning, the senior nun was found on the floor of her cell[60]. These cells, along with a small chapel, had been commissioned by me, prior to the nuns' arrival. I'd had them built as an extension to the White Room, specifying four cells; in case we had more nuns offered to us or visiting sisters appeared.

Senior nun was carried into the White Room; her eyes were closed, and she was very cold. Azizah was called, herded everyone out except the novice nun and spent some time coo-ing over the poorly sister. Much sniffing was done and then, to the puzzlement of all, she took the sick nun's under-garments out across the Bailey and over to the base of the North Wall, where she spread the clothes on the ground. In the early spring sunshine, she stood there for a long time, looking at the garments. Her guards stood stoically by her, anything Their Lady wanted to do was fine by them. After about an hour, Azizah dropped the clothes into the laundry, then requested an escort for a trip to the fields to our north and the forest to our south.

This produced a scramble of fifty soldiers wanting to go, but the Marshal counted out twenty-four, including five archers, and told the rest he could easily find other jobs for them. The off-duty men vanished in the blink of an eye.

Many hours later, she returned with several flowers and herbs. She worked through the afternoon to produce some potions and mixtures. Meanwhile, the nun had regained some of her senses in the warmth of the White Room and was able to sip some warm water. Azizah carefully sat her up and gently spooned some of her recipe into her mouth. After some protest at the bitterness, the nun swallowed all and was laid back to sleep some more.

I saw Azizah on the way to dinner and decided it was past time that she should eat with me at my high table. She sat with me, seemed concerned with the nun's condition and obviously felt very tired, as she had missed her breakfast and lunch.

---

[60] A very small room, just large enough for a small bed and writing table

"Is the sugar-water disease[61], my lord. Very hard make better."

"Lucky lady is... big" she said, miming a large stomach.

"No much feed her – help... much."

"So why the clothes on the ground, by the wall?" I asked, as this had been the talk of the castle.

"Ahhhh," she replied "you call them... ants, my lord. If man woman piss sweet water, ants walk on, take some."

Wonders would never cease I thought, and looked at her with admiration at her knowledge and in curiosity for the way she could eat so neatly and tidily with her veil in place, then sip up her lemonade through a hollow reed. I sighed to myself, at the price that fruit had been, all the way from southern Spain but smiled at how much she enjoyed the change from the barley or nettle teas.

When the senior nun felt strong enough, we wrapped her up well and put her on a carriage, and with a small escort, returned her to the convent. The whole castle turned out to wish her well. She had done much, for many and never earned a penny, so in spite of her very... firm manner, she was very much appreciated.

The following day, Blaedswith was walking across the Bailey to breakfast, when she stopped, swayed, put a hand to her head and promptly spewed on the ground. She was assisted to the White Room and Azizah arrived to see her. After some wrist-holding, brow-feeling and the gentlest of prodding and poking, Azizah looked thoughtful for a moment, then went to fetch from the kitchen: two shiny metal bowls, a big metal pie tray and a bottle of red wine. With no one else around, Azizah told her to piss in one of the bowls. The bowl was whisked under Blaedswith's skirts and she tinkled. Azizah put some wine in the empty bowl, mixed some wine into the piss-bowl and set them both in the pie tray. Azizah called for hot water then carefully poured some into the tray, to warm the bowls. After many minutes, Azizah took the bowls out into the daylight and compared the colours therein.

Azizah came back into the room, looked at Blaedswith, smiled with

---

[61] Diabetes to the modern world

her eyes and gently hugged her.

Blaedswith clasped her hands together, let out a shriek of joy and started laughing, crying, shaking, then more shrieking. All the kitchen maids came to hug her, and flutter round her. Blaedswith, at the age of thirty, and after more than a decade under her first husband with no offspring, had given up on her possibilities – but sometimes, you just need a change of rooster in the chicken coop! Azizah led Blaedswith along the corridors, across the Hall and sat her down in the parlour. The Marshal was fetched and, looking puzzled, was directed by Azizah to go into the parlour. Much happy sobbing was heard, and they stayed in there for a long time. Meanwhile, the men in the Hall were wondering what the holdup on breakfast was.

Next morning, I saw the Marshal coming out of his room. I gave him a hug of greetings and congratulations. Over his shoulder, as the door slowly closed behind him, I caught a glimpse of Blaedswith leaving their bed. She truly did have fine legs, and a nice arse, and breasts that stuck out much more than her modest dresses had implied. I thought to myself "No wonder this rooster crows so loud and so often!"

This also made me realise that Spring was in the air now and to feel it was time for another bath – or two...

The slightly improved weather allowed our hunting parties to go deeper into my southern forest. I doubled the manpower of these, always adding some mounted archers. After food-provision, our secondary aim was to make the forest untenable for bandits. These forays were also useful to give any new recruits some initial experience of some basic soldiering.

After a couple of days of the milder weather, I was trotting up the Keep before lunch, as I did most days. I'd found, over the winter, that not doing this led to me not being able to do it, so here I was. This also helped to maintain my guards' physical abilities.

I exchanged greetings with the lookouts, who pointed to the western horizon.

A thick, black, evil cloud extended there for miles and was clearly heading our way.

"Got your capes lads?" I asked, thinking they would soon need the leather garments to go over their woollen cloaks.

"Only three have turned up sir" one replied. I was annoyed with myself, that I'd again forgotten to obtain a leather-man for the castle, we'd been making do with odd purchases at markets.

"So, who hasn't got one?"

"Granger, sir" chortled the others as one.

I thought about my plans for the rest of the day and said

"It's your lucky day, Granger. I'll send mine up shortly. Just make bloody sure you return it."

"Yes sir, thank you sir" said Granger in some surprise.

I left them and went back down, smiling as I heard the other guards ragging on Granger for his good fortune. I grabbed my cape out of my room on my way to the Hall. Halfway across the Bailey I saw a young soldier, who stopped and bowed. I nodded back.

"Name?" I asked.

"S...S... Smith, sir" he stammered.

"You a fast runner, Smith?"

"Yes sir" he replied with enthusiasm.

"Excellent," I said, "run this up to Granger at the top of the Keep" and thrust the rolled-up cape into his hands.

"Yes sir" he said a little surprised, and just stood there.

"Now, you bow, turn away and run, Smith" I sighed as he did just that and I heard my guards try to suppress their chuckles.

I breezed into the Hall, saw Jeannot, slapped him on the back and as I'd finally remembered, tasked him to recruit a master craftsman in leather. I joined the Marshal as he stood to greet me at the high table. I tasked him to cancel the afternoon session of Manor Court, get the people back to town and tell them to spread word of an approaching storm – and sat down to enjoy my lunch. Instead of a court session that afternoon, I was able to join Gerald and catch up with some letter writing in his room. We could hear the wind beginning to moan past the arrow slits and whistle round the Keep. Then, after another hour or so, the rain started and went on and on increasing in intensity. Shortly after dark, we were just about to finish with the scrolls when there came a timid knock on the door.

"Enter" I shouted.

A very damp-looking gate-guard dripped into the room, looking nervous.

"Speak" I commanded.

"Errrr... A Lord and Lady K... K... Kanewella[62] request shelter with an escort of four, sir."

"Where are they now, soldier?"

"Under the gatehouse, sir."

I turned to Gerald and raised an eyebrow.

"A small manor and village, sire, about twenty miles to the east."

I turned back to the soldier and said

"Yes, let them in, tell the corporal to get their horses and men looked after and invite the Lord and Lady to the Keep.

"Yes sir", he bowed and left on his mission.

I walked down to the door of the Keep and looked out into the gloomy, torrential rain. Then I shouted for a chambermaid, told her to get the log-man to set a fire in what we still called 'the old sick-room', then she should do a quick dust and tidy in there.

I was also thinking that, firstly, we really must think of a better name for that room and secondly, I must find out where the log-man... goes... in between making up fires.

I watched as the six riders slowly rode their horses to the middle of the Bailey. The reedman had just finished his rounds, so we had lamps and torches going in the corridors of the Keep. I heard the corporal organise the disposition of all horses and the escort. He then accompanied the two remaining figures to the base of the Keep steps. All the new arrivals looked like drowned rats; their wool cloaks soaked through and they were walking slowly as if struggling with the cold.

I waved the couple up to the door and ushered them into the first room on the left. Somehow the log-man had been and gone, once again, totally unseen by me whilst leaving a cosy fire in the grate. Our visitors removed their sodden hats and bowed to me, introducing themselves as Lord Godwin and Lady Heloise Kanewella, both quite young, on the short side and rather plump of face and figure. I introduced myself as Lord Walter De Marren, of Haverhill

---

[62] Now known as Kentwell Hall

and Walden.

"So, this is… Haverhill?" asked Godwin. "It is," I smiled "were you lost?"

"Seems so," he replied, "it was such a bad storm and I think we got on the wrong road."

"No matter," I said, "warm yourselves, dry your clothes and come over to the Hall, opposite, when you're ready and dinner will be served." They looked impressed, spoke their thanks and I departed. I had the chambermaid ready to make up the bed in the room when they went to eat and, grabbing my cloak, I trotted over to the Hall.

A Haverhill dinner made its usual good impression. They were good company, though they asked to retire quite early, after much wine had been drunk, particularly by Godwin. Much later, I walked from the Hall and up the Keep stairs, thankfully the rain had now much abated. On passing through the Keep door, Heloise came out of her room as the sound of very loud snoring was heard from within. She looked at me shyly, as though she wanted to speak to me, so I waved my guards on up to my room and asked what was on her mind.

"I can never sleep until he stops that snoring" she said, somewhat wearily. "So, I usually read, or walk around a bit til later."

"Ah, I'm afraid we have few books here, bar those for accounts" I said. "No matter, I'll just walk for a… oh wait, do you have… dungeons here my lord?"

I nodded, thinking "It's a castle, of course it's got bloody dungeons."

"C… c… could I see them?" she asked in a small and breathless voice.

I was feeling somewhat amiable after a glass or two of wine, so I nodded again and offered her my arm. She took it and clung on nicely as we went down the first level to the storerooms. As we approached the beer store, wicked thoughts arose within me, driven no doubt by the season, or the moon, or just… nature. I motioned her to be quiet, opened the door and guided her to hide behind a pile of kegs.

"Our jailer is quite an… ogre," I said in a hushed tone "huge man, evil temper. I'd best get him out of the way, so he doesn't take to locking you up." Her eyes widened and stayed wide.

"Stay very quiet and I will come back when he's gone."

She nodded, still wide-eyed. I closed the door and went on down to the lower level, making sure to make loud footsteps and not make our gentle giant Milo startle too much. I pushed the dungeon door open and said, "Evening Milo. Any guests?"

"Good evening my lord, no guests" he said as he stood up and bowed. Our 'ogre' had clearly just started a new religious carving. I flipped him a very generous shilling and told him to have a night off and a drink or two with his cousin, the cook. "Thank you, my lord" he said, grabbed his cloak and set off for the kitchens.

I gave him time to leave the building then went to fetch Heloise. She was still wide-eyed and whispered, "I heard him go by, he sounded huge." I nodded grimly "Yes, but he's gone now, so don't worry."

I took her by the hand and led her down to the dungeons. The door creaked loudly and made her jump. She tiptoed in and saw the six prisoner cells, with grills and locking bars on the doors. The strong lamplight revealing her eyes wider still. She walked up to the nearest cell and peered past the door, seeing the fresh straw on the floor and the bucket in the far corner. Seizing the moment, I said in a serious voice, "Heloise Kanewella, I sentence you to three days for being drunk and disorderly in public." Before she could react, I pushed her in, slammed shut and barred the door, blew out the lamp light, stomped out and up the stairs to the next floor. Behind me, I could hear saying, "Wait my lord, there's been a mistake, my lord... my lord..."

I tiptoed back and listened at the door. She'd stopped calling and was now breathing rather fast, maybe too fast... I thought that I may have gone too far with the jest, so tiptoed in, relit the lamp and said in my best 'manor court' voice "Your fine has been paid, you are pardoned." On her 'release', she flew out of the cell and wrapped her arms around my waist.

"Ohhhhhhh, Lord Walter, I thought I was done for, that seemed so real – my god that was so mean of you, how could you be so mean" she said slapping my chest.

"I'm a feudal lord," I said, not joking, "it's a requirement of the position."

"Oh... I'm sure you're just saying that" she said and slapped my chest again. I was incredulous.

"I killed one Lord to win this castle and had another killed to win

Walden" I said.

"Ooooo, so how many men have you...?" she asked.

I shrugged, I had no idea, hadn't been counting.

"Just as many as I needed to..." I replied.

She gasped, then looked up at me with what I thought was a 'kiss me' face, so I did.

"Walter, I... Oh..." she murmured then kissed me back with a fury and we fell through a cell door onto the straw. After some long deep kissing, I placed a firm grip on the front of her dress and made ready to pull.

"Noooo," she gasped "I'll take it off, I've only got this with me" We locked eyes as we stood up and undid our clothing. She, light brown of hair, top and bottom, was short, pink and plump in body, sticking out in all the right places and I ached. Her eyes got wider again, at the sight of my instrument of intent. I took her by the hand and led her to the next cell, separating us from our clothes. It was just us, standing on the straw. She was panting hard now, chest flushed. We kissed passionately again. I felt it was time for me, so I threw her down on the straw, forcing her on all fours.

"Lord Walter" she said, in a prim voice "I'm a lady and I don't know if I do this like an animal." I rubbed the end of my cock up and down her slipperiness and she moaned.

"Don't you forget I'm a lady, Walter" she said and promptly forced herself onto my rigid knob. "So there" she said, "So there" repeating herself as she pushed herself back and back more to take me all inside her. I gripped her hair to pull her back down into my lap and squeezed her breasts. "You brute" she gasped, so I squeezed harder – she gasped more. I caressed a hand down her soft curving stomach, teased her furry parts and searched for her little spot. I played with her as she responded with more, or less volume, more, or less shaking until I found the just right speed and stroke. Her sound and shuddering then built and built... until she peaked with an incoherent cry. Then fell on her face on the straw, losing me on the way and lay still for many minutes, breathing fast but shallow. I lay beside her while she settled, resting a gentle hand on her luscious behind. After some time, her breathing slowed, she rolled to face to me and sighed.

"You are such an animal Walter, did you seed me?"

"I did not, but I will now" I said as I knelt in front of her, dragged her ankles up and apart and forced my plough, none to gently, into the soft furrow of her body. She was still saying what an animal I was, as I ploughed and ploughed her tiny field until I scattered all my seed with a triumphant shouting. We clung together for a long time, savouring the moments we'd had. Finally separating she gasped again at the sight between her legs and glistening on her thighs. "What am I going to with that?" she said.

"Take it with you," I said "when your husband wakes tomorrow, thank him for the wonderful time and show him what 'he did'…"

She looked at me, mouth agape "Are you mad? Or bad, Walter?"

"Does it matter?" I said as another idea occurred to me. I gripped her hand, led or dragged her naked, out of the dungeons and up the stairs to the beer store. She was frantically whispering to me that we couldn't do this, someone might see, and so on.

I sat her on top of an upended beer keg, all while she was still quietly saying I couldn't do this. Her protests stopped abruptly as I knelt before her and found her hidden gem again. Moaning started and she soon shuddered to another completion. I stood, held her swaying body, locked her legs around my waist and give her another planting to take back home with her. We held each other for a little while, gently kissing, then feeling much calmer, we suddenly realised just how cold it was and scurried back down to put our clothes on. We kissed farewell in the dungeon, and I slapped her backside hard enough to make her squeak, then she went back to her room. After a short wait, I slowly walked up the stairs to my room, nodded a goodnight to my guards and went to bed for a long and blissful sleep.

Next morning was bright and warm, the castle steaming gently from the previous days damp mixing with the sun. Heloise arrived just after me for breakfast and whispered to me that she had done what I suggested and… gone one better. She said she'd taken some of our… juices and spread them on him before he woke up. I looked at her and said "Heloise! Are you mad? Or bad?"

She blushed, replying with "Does it matter?"

"Just don't forget," she went on primly "that I am a lady."

"You are indeed a lady," I said, "one that likes to be ridden hard and put away wet." She blushed deeper and could only manage to whisper "Brute" at me as her reply. Godwin appeared, looking very pleased with himself and much jovial chatter ensued during the meal. They thanked me gracefully for the hospitality, then hesitantly and confusedly half-bowed to Azizah while thanking her for the meals. Our Stewardess gracefully curtseyed to them in reply and managed to charm them both.

I had Gerald draw them a map to take them on to Kanewella and waved them off from the door of the Keep. Heloise turned in her saddle to give a final wave and silently mouthed "Animal" at me.

A little later, I crossed paths with Azizah in the Bailey.
She silently shook her head and wagged a finger at me.
"I know, I know," I sighed, "bad lord, bad lord."

Come the middle of March, there arrived a letter, under Royal seal. The messenger looked exhausted, so I directed him to the kitchen for food and drink and had his horse taken to the stables. He mentioned that no reply was expected, and I went to my parlour to read. The content shook me to my core. The King required all lords of title to cause any persons of Persian birth, that resided in their domains, to attend his court at Berkhamsted Castle, two days before Easter Day. In my shock, I wondered how the King could have known about Azizah being Persian. We had enough trouble convincing our locals that she wasn't 'Arab'. We also knew that the tales that had spread, of our now legendary castle meals, all mentioned 'made from Arab recipes'...

I called for Jeannot, instructing him to go and casually acquire any more information from the messenger that he could. Jeannot returned with a little useful knowledge at least. Seemed that this was the same letter sent to all titled residences in England, with identical scrolls being delivered to Walden and one even thrown into the leaning Keep at Castle Camps. So, this was not about Azizah herself – but deeply concerning, nevertheless. After a reading the missive again more carefully, I could now see that it was not addressed to me by name, and that my presence was not actually required, merely that I should 'cause attendance' of any Persian folk. Also, at first glance, I had assumed this was the start of a purge, as happened to the Jews every so often. Whenever convenient scapegoats were needed by a higher power, they would get the blame and be shipped abroad, again. But then, if this was simply to be the latest eviction of a race, precious Royal time at court would not be needed, merely the despatch of armed gangs to effect the removals.

I sought out Gerald in his room and passed him the letter. After some thought, he said with a grave face "If they are not after all the Persians sire, it means they are after one or two." My head dropped, this was my conclusion too – but which ones and why? We discussed options, none of them seemed good. We couldn't say we hadn't received the letter, because of copies at my other fiefs meant too many witnesses, even if we 'lost' the messenger. Ignoring it accrued considerable risk, because we were well known to have a foreigner, of some sort, holding some position at the castle.

I reluctantly decided that I had to take her, and for once I would make a prayer, for her preservation.

After dinner that night, I sat with Azizah in the firelit parlour. She'd clearly known all day that something troubled me. I told her as gently as I could, but the news still clearly terrified her. She'd found safety here with us, appreciation, gentle adoration even, from all the castle-folk – and now this... chance event, threw her bodily into the boiling cauldron of international politics. She cried and her shoulders shook. I braced myself, resolved to try and help her better with this upset than her last, I knelt by the side of her chair, put an arm round her shoulders, brought her close and held her hand. She rested her head on my shoulder and her tears flowed for many minutes. Regaining her voice, she asked "Will you be with me, Lord Walter?"

"Of course I will Azizah," I said "we'll bring Luther and Jeannot – I'd rather take Gerald but I don't think he's able to travel that far yet."

"Is long way?"

"It will be at least three days, so we have to start tomorrow."

She raised her head, sniffed a little and nodded. "Best you dress like a kitchen maid and leave your khanjar in your saddle-bag." I said, "So... what name should we use for you?"

Azizah nodded and thought for some time, stroking her prized purple and white gown, as if in farewell. Eventually she replied "Nousha[63], my lord. "

Sensing she wished some privacy, I let her go with a final hand squeeze and she departed with a small curtsey, off to her room. I guessed her book would be much read that night.

I called for the Marshal and gave instructions for our escort of 24 and travel supplies to be prepared. Also, to notify Luther and Jeannot of the journey. Luther would just have to manage with his shaky arm and shaky leg, we would need his translation skills if Azizah lost her Saxon words under stress. We were to leave the next day at Terce.

After three days on the road and two very uncomfortable nights on straw mattresses in a couple of odious inns, we arrived at the mighty Berkhamsted Castle. I'd heard stories of this place, but you had to see it to fully appreciate the size. The white masonry nicely caught the light from the setting sun. I noted the double defensive ring, comprising two moats and two curtain walls, all to contain and protect a multitude of buildings, both great and small. Indeed, many towns were not as large as the sprawl within these fortifications. With last light fast approaching, I presented my letter at the outer gate to gain access but the senior lord supervising the gate denied entry for my escort. I checked that my sergeant and corporal had purses for subsistence and left them to find accommodation in the nearest village. A party of eight was to be at this castle gate every daylight prayer hour[64], in case we had finished – or needed to escape...

---

[63] Meaning: nice, kind-hearted

[64] So, every three hours

I took the last two rooms in a surprisingly pleasant inn and made sure the horses were being properly cared for in the stables at the back of the establishment. Jeannot had to do most of the saddle-carrying up the narrow stairs, not quite what he imagined was his job but all good experience for him. The dinner at the inn was very plain by our standards but edible. They didn't fuss when told to not serve pork for our 'servant'.

The florid-faced wife of the innkeeper was very intrigued with our party and made sure to look after our 'maid', in spite of her plain brown much-repaired dress, mismatching shawl and hurriedly made brown veil.

After the meal, we took turns in the midden, and adjourned upstairs to sleep. I pointed Luther and Jeannot to one room, beckoned Azizah to follow me to the other. The poor thing was clearly very tired from the journey and no doubt worried about events tomorrow. There may also have been additional concern from having to share a room with... me. The room had a pile of straw mattresses in a corner, like the road-house inns we'd just been through but at least here there was a bed. One bed.

With no hesitation, I threw two mattresses on this bed, took my sword belt off and laid the sheathed sword symbolically between the two mattresses. I smiled at her and nodded towards her saddlebags. Her eyes twinkled a little, as she fetched out her sheathed khanjar, tied the belt round her middle and sat on the edge of the bed. I sat on the far side of the bed, turned and smiled again to her, mostly at the... delicacy of our situation and said "Goodnight... Nousha."

"Goodnight, Lord Walter" she replied.

I swung myself onto my mattress, keeping on my chainmail and gambeson – we didn't know our standing here, so best be prepared. Considering the mail, daggers and purses secured about my person, the least bad sleeping position was flat on my back, arms folded across my chest. Seeing me settle, 'Nousha' wrapped her cloak around her and laid down on her side.

I awoke for the midden after midnight and saw our lovely Persian princess, fast asleep and snoring very quietly. She used the midden later and I counted the seconds until she was back then drifted off to sleep until dawn.

Over breakfast, we decided to go early to be near the Great Hall but not to enter until Luther had scouted and eavesdropped as much as possible. He wasn't able to gain access himself but, after some time, did find a couple of Persian people who could manage some Arabic, who'd been into the place and said they'd been asked about 'the Husayns' or 'family of Ala al-Din'... so Luther thought they said.

When he returned to us after a couple of hours and relayed the Arabic words he'd heard, I thought Azizah was going to faint. She clutched her head, shook in all her body and stumbled.

"They look my family, my lord," she whispered "Husayn is name all family, Ala al-Din is brother." I gripped her hand and held on.

"How many were there to go in?" I asked Luther.

"Several dozen, sir, far more than I expected to see… possibly fifty."

"Hmmmm, I see no advantage to going early, we'll join the end of the line, which is…?"

"About two hours long, my lord" confirmed Luther. I looked at him and asked him to linger near the door, to see if he could hear anything else. Jeannot was told to go with him and bring us news of… anything.

I sat on a low wall belonging to a nearby inn, Azizah sat next to me, her foot touching mine, just for reassurance. After about half an hour, Jeannot reported back.

"I got a look through the door, my lord, and Luther heard some things. The King is in the Hall," he said "and there are two men who ask questions. One could be a Mongol prince, huge chap, shaved head. The other is a Persian… ambassador person… short, pointed chin, white beard, grey eyes."

I thought Azizah was going to fall off the wall as she reacted and gasped "Shabani – I see him, he see me when I was girl…" then sobbed into her veil.

I caught her and supported her into the nearest inn. We sat at a table, I had some warm mead, with barley tea again for Azizah. Jeannot went back to Luther, as I sat and held her hand. Her breathing settled, she drew herself up and I saw our Princess come back to life.

"I not like him," she said calmly, firmly "he…." And she mimed something rodent-like.

"Always… play nice with my father but…" and she did the rodent again.

She sighed and went on "Today, I play maid Nousha – for my family… if he think I not Nousha – all will see Princess Azizah talk to this… thing." After that was said, and the way she said it, I knew I would fight the world for this woman.

Another half-hour and a midden visit went by, then Jeannot came back to say it was time to join the queue. As we got to the door of the Great Hall, the bells for Sext[65] were heard.

I was quite surprised King Stephen was keeping this going, there must have been a very large... consideration paid to both arrange and prolong the participation of His Highness[66].

I handed my sword belt and daggers to Jeannot and settled myself to wait. Azizah now seemed steady and calm. I saw her bend down and pop a small stone into her leather slipper. She now walked with a limp and had affected a drop in one shoulder. The supreme actress that had fooled everyone at Walden that fateful night was now 'on stage' once more. We reached the door and a young herald asked my name, ready to announce me into the Hall. The trumpeter, stood by him, clearly thought I did not merit any fanfare. Some lord's steward was called just before us and was quickly dismissed. The two very young Persian girl slaves with him looked scared and confused. I sighed at that picture in my head and then... my name was called out by the herald.

I walked as confidently as I could to the centre of the enormous room, turned left to face the King, who I had seen before, at the last London Parliament, walked to within twelve paces and bowed. I sensed Azizah following me at a, for once, respectful distance. I tried not to be distracted by the sights before me and all around the Hall. To my front was the King on a modest throne, with senior knights in full armour as his guards. All around the room were many hard-eyed lords, present to show their, current, loyalty to the King and to watch the show. All of these were clearly bored as fock with the proceedings and probably desperate for lunch or ale, or both. The two oddities were to the King's left – one, the largest man I had ever seen, he must have been the Mongol prince. He glowered, towering over all present, round of face and shaved of head, arms the size of tree-trunks.

---

[65] Noon

[66] Kings of England did not use the style of 'Majesty' until Henry VIII

The other oddity being the small figure of Ambassador Shabani. I had to suppress a smile at the rat-like features he presented, just as Azizah had described. I nodded to the Persian as a token sign of respect. Shabani assessed the figure of Azizah, who, as I glanced round, was kneeling and bent forward with hands pressed together as if in prayer. The Persian spoke to a plainly dressed, olive-skinned young man next to him, clearly a translator. The young man asked, in Saxon, "How and when did you acquire... this my Lord."

"Last year, sometime, in a slave market" I replied.

"What does she do, sir?"

"She works in the kitchen."

"What do you call her, sir?"

I hesitated a moment, then said "The cook."

As I'd hoped, this brought a round of chuckles from the watching lords in the Hall. The King still looked bored as fock. Shabani said something to the translator, who then asked, "What is her name and where is her hometown?"

I sighed loudly and shrugged, miming for the crowd as if to say, 'how the fock would I know that?' This produced a laugh from many assembled lords. I gestured to ask her directly and he repeated the question in Persian.

When Azizah didn't immediately answer, I gave the King a quick 'by your leave' bow, stepped back and gave Azizah a sharp kick in the ribs with the toe of my boot. This raised another grim chuckle from the audience, amused at a relatively young lord who was not intimidated by his surroundings. Azizah gasped from the impact and spoke a sentence in Persian. I heard the name 'Nousha' and something that sounded like a place name. Her voice, though, had changed... it was lower pitched and sounded thicker, differently accented from her usual sweet tones.

Shabani nodded at the answer, then appeared to see something that caught his interest. He addressed her directly with what sounded like a command. Azizah replied with a trembling voice, something that sounded like a negative, a refusal. Shabani spoke to the translator.

"Remove her veil please, my lord" he said.

"Bollocks," I thought to myself "well, at least this will entertain the crowd – and be spoken of for many a year..."

I leaned down to take her veil away, when...

A loud trumpet call sounded at the door.

The heralds voice was heard clearly "Earl Warwick - to see the King on urgent matters." In through the door swept Lord Roger and his two senior knights, cloaks trailing, boot heels sounding, spurs jangling. A magnificently impressive sight, all richly armoured and armed – but this, in the Kings presence – most, most unusual. This caused a huge stir and much reaching for sword hilts by the King's bodyguards.

Lord Roger stopped, well back from the king, as I pushed Azizah to the side with my foot. The Earl and his companions, themselves well back from their lord, all bowed deeply and dropped to one knee, helmets under their arms but still wearing their coifs.

Lord Roger spoke "Your Highness, my sincere apologies for appearing before you thus" and glanced up at the King who replied, "Say your piece, Warwick."

"I come bearing most urgent news, Your Highness – news that I believe should be acted on today."

The King gestured his advisers around him and a hum of conversation ensued and muttering around the Hall.

The Mongol and Shabani looked puzzled at this turn of events.

Lord Roger took a moment to survey the Hall from his kneeling position. I glanced across at him and our eyes met. He raised his eyebrows slightly, in recognition. He saw that I was now looking down on him, as I stood, a couple of yards to his left. I did my best to keep a straight face and gave him, merely, a formal nod of recognition, as if one peer to another! Realising the legitimate, if very temporary, advantage I held, he returned my nod, while narrowing his eyes very slightly to tell me "Just wait till next time, Walter!"

I believe the King caught this mutual acknowledgement between Lord Roger and myself, because, when the ambassador tried to protest the summary end of the session and hence his removal from the Hall, the King was firmly dismissive. Clearly not wanting to inconvenience further, any ally of his main ally, the great Earl of Warwick.

King Stephen stood, the Earl and his party stood, and all present bowed to the monarch.

He stepped away from the throne and left to go into a lavish side-room. A page walked to Lord Roger and whispered something to him. The Earl promptly handed his helmet, coif and sword-belt to one of his companion knights and walked away to join the King. The herald walked to the front of the hall, turned his back on the now empty throne and announced, "All guests of the King may take lunch in the refectory, all others to please leave the Hall."

I turned to Azizah, she was still on her knees, with her head bowed. I shoved her in the ribs with my boot again, but this time more gently, saying, "We go." She rose, and did the hobbling, crouched walk of 'Nousha' out of the Hall and into the sunlit fresh air. On spotting Luther and Jeannot, I tilted my head for them to follow us. With 'Nousha' hobbling behind me, we walked back to our inn, took a table and I clapped my hands for soup and bread to be served. Luther had been checking to ensure we were not followed and now we were no longer visible from the street.

'Nousha' then transformed in front of our eyes, back into Azizah – and her eyes blazed. Furious at me and more…

"You… kick… me, lord" she said, rubbing her side.

"Only because I had to" I replied with a big, and probably unwise, smile.

"And that… **little prick**, Shibani, play servant to Mongol, I want cut pieces, with words then…" I gently squeezed her arm, as it rested on the table and calmed her with soft words.

Meanwhile, Luther and Jeannot were looking stunned at Azizah's vitriolic delivery of Saxon kitchen slang. I don't think they'd ever seen her when her spirit was up. Jeannot was clearly looking most perplexed by recent events. I silently cursed myself for forgetting that he had no knowledge of Azizah's past and so had no inkling of the reason for our play today.

As lunch arrived, I ordered our horses to be made ready.

When our food was done, poor Jeannot had to stumble the saddles back downstairs and out to the yard. I caught a moment with him in the stables and told him that I would explain all this mystery to him, and Gerald, once we returned. He seemed relieved and reassured that he hadn't misunderstood anything so far. I considered that we had complied with the letter of the requested duty to the King. I thus felt free to leave and paid our inn-bill. Lacking knowledge of any agents of the Mongols or their Persian lackeys, I felt we should make a quiet but swift retreat.

We rode slowly out of the castle, easily making the Nones[67] rendezvous with my eight soldiers. They led us to the rest of my escort in the nearby village. With them quickly saddled up, we headed north through forest trails.

Of course, we took an indirect route, just in case, and I set a fair pace, reaching Toddington Castle, such as it was, by last light. The lord there was very accommodating but clearly poor as a church mouse, his wooden motte-and-baily fort being one of those left over from the time just after The Conquest. There was plenty of hay for the horses but no food to spare for us, particularly as our party doubled the population of this place. We had some of our bread and cheese from the saddlebags and squashed into the tiny wooden 'hall' for the night. I put Azizah to lay next to the slowly dying fire, on the best straw mattress we could find and settled next to her. As all neared sleep, I felt her foot gently swing back to find mine, just for comfort.

The northern route was longer by one day, but this journey did give us a cheerful evening and night in Cambridge. Sir Randall Brereton was again a very generous host. On reaching Haverhill, the sight of our castle brought a huge sense of relief. It felt a great deal longer than eight days that we'd been away. I think the strain on Azizah did not begin to reduce until after I'd helped her down from her horse and she headed off to have a bath. After dinner that night, we sat together on the firelit parlour. She reported that my new, larger, 'laundry' tub was a very good idea and with her dressed once more, in her favourite purple and white gown, I could see her eyes twinkling as she smiled for the first time in many days. She giggled as she tried to say, "Lord Walter bath day?" and her shoulders shook as I shook my head. Then her eyes clouded for a moment, "I think we... lucky, my lord."

"I think we were very lucky, Azizah" I replied, and said a silent prayer as thanks for the preservation of this wonderful lady.

---

[67] 3 p.m.

Next morning, I called Gerald and Jeannot to the parlour, dismissed the guards from the door, then barred it. I saw the two exchange a glance and a gulp, but I quickly reassured them that this meeting was not caused by any fault of theirs. I swore them to secrecy and revealed the full identity of our Lady Azizah, our Persian Princess. They'd guessed she'd become a slave only by circumstance and had always thought she was a lady of quality, but the news that she was a full-blood-royal was a profound shock to both; they sat back in their chairs at this, with 'Ohhh' expressions on their faces. I then watched them process the information and come to the same conclusion, as to how she could be at risk in our present times of Anarchy. They both confirmed a resolve to guard and protect our treasure, in any way they could. I shook their hands, sent them off to their duties, rousted my guards out of the kitchen and started my day.

First task for me was to review the boys that had appeared at the castle as artisan assistants or fetching/carrying lads. They wouldn't normally be paid but usually did get a meal. All lived in town and walked to the castle at dawn each morning to be best placed for any possible vacancy that would give them a chance of a paying job, anytime in the future. I was looking for potential squires, a role that was understandably close to my heart. We had no pool of noble offspring to pick from, so this was going to be a gamble.

There seemed to be four possible, of whom two were old enough at fourteen and big enough to have chance of mounting a full-size horse. They both passed a basic riding test with the corporals, so I took them on as squires-under-review to see how they fared. They were delighted with the pittance in pay, mostly because they also got access to our famous lunches. They started in the new-soldier training sessions that the sergeants ran out of the armoury. We could have done with some pages but none of the younger ones looked sharp enough to trust with even that.

That done, for the moment at least, I trotted up the Keep stairs, to the top; my guards breathing hard behind me, as I guess this pair had been on Lady Azizah's detail recently. I looked out across my domain and breathed in the freshest air.

I took in the views over each wall of the Keep, enjoying the early Spring sunshine.

I could see my eastern border, about three miles away, my southern border at five miles. Looking the other way though, my northern and western borders were far, far out of sight, lost in the haze.
My thoughts turned back to just over a year ago, as I smiled and shook my head to think I was a near penniless and completely landless squire back then.
I frowned now, as I thought ahead, to what the promise of this year might be.
My serfs saw this as a time of nature's renewal, but many of my peers and seniors had... other perspectives.
Were we to see the green shoots of Greed, the twin blossoms of Battle and Betrayal, the ripening of the fruit of Ruthless Ambition? Only time would tell.
I sighed from a sense of deep foreboding, then smiled at the thought of seeing Azizah again, very soon.

The Anarchy:
Slave To Fortune

Part 3

I reluctantly finished a long and wistful viewing of my domains, sighed and went to leave the battlements on the top of my Haverhill Keep; turning my back on the late-March morning sunshine. As I went through the door to the stairs, the chill and darkness within, ended my smile and blackened my mood. I could sense the tensions building within the realm as the strong tides of ambition surged one way and then back the other way. It was now a straight fight for the crown of England - between the Empress Matilda and King Stephen, other contenders having withdrawn, or died, last year.

Matilda's wave had certainly been surging a few short months ago but her high-water mark seemed to have been reached by this Spring of 1141. The tone of letters reaching me since the snows ended had been... cooler, if still... broadly in her favour. But, in our business, if you're not rising, then you are falling. With that in mind, I thought of my own position; I should look to be building my strength, usually done by increasing one's titles and lands through marriage, purchase or capture. I had been very fortunate the previous year, with a fight for the neighbouring fiefs falling my way, and the fruits of that enabling a land purchase.

Although still a minor lord, I was much better off than many – but complacency could lose you everything, so I would be looking for any opportunity. I stomped down the stairs of the Keep and across the Bailey to the Hall.

I half-noticed a minor panic among castle-staff as I made my way, with many sensing another black-mood-day in their Lord.

I sat at my high table on the dais and called for all senior staff to join me immediately. Azizah arrived first as she only had to walk from the kitchen, her guards in attendance as always. She smiled, curtseyed and gracefully sat at the table opposite me. Thinking ahead by quite a way, I motioned her to sit next to me, on my left. This surprised her a little as this implied a promotion of sorts, which was my aim. I foresaw a time this year when I would be away from my fiefs for an extended period. The Wardens of my castles were very effective administrators but not in any sense... commanders; whereas our lovely Lady Azizah, with her princess blood, was a natural, effortless and inspiring leader. The others soon arrived: The Warden, The Marshal, Gerald and Jeannot.

I gestured our two pairs of guards away to the Hall doors and began my instructions. The Warden and Jeannot would travel to as many of the region's larger towns as possible, for two weeks. Their aim would be to acquire quality horses of any sort, whether destrier[68], palfrey[69], broodmare or foal. I wanted to be first in the market, before prices increased, when the very likely calls-to-arms were issued. We could graze a couple of thousand at my recently purchased demesne of Great Thurlow, so there would be no problems with feed. Potential thieves stayed away from my holdings, following the fatal end that came to the previous such bandits.

The Marshal's task would be to spend a few days at Walden, looking for as many soldiers that could be spared and which of those were... effective. If Count Aubrey called for the 30 men that Walden owed him in war, then 30 he would be sent. However, if I was taking them, I only wanted competent soldiers that could ride.

The task for Lady Azizah was to look for more potential short-bow archers among our mounted soldiers – and any from the men sent from Walden. She would then train them to shoot from the saddle. This would follow her achievement in creating our initial force of ten men that could ride and shoot. These mounted archers had been highly effective against the forest bandits and in the short, sharp battle for my Haverhill castle.

I asked Gerald if he was well enough to visit Great Thurlow, just a couple of hours away. He firmly said he was, and so was tasked with checking on the new tenant farmers, recently arrived from Holland. He was to ensure they had not 'accidently' exceeded their allocated land and were up to date with rents. All at the table realised the meaning behind these preparations and I could see much brooding thought occurring. The next change required a little diplomacy, not always my strongest suit.

---

[68] A large, strong horse, bred and trained for war

[69] A type of horse that was highly valued in these times. A lighter-weight horse, usually a smooth gaited one that could amble, suitable for riding over long distances. Palfreys were not a specific breed.

"If I am away for a time, Manor Court will have to continue, both here and at Walden, it is vital to the good order and smooth running of my holdings. People have returned or moved here simply because we have a well-regulated domain. This means more of a market for our produce and more taxes to collect" I said and couldn't help smiling widely at that.

I went on "So, Warden, how would you like to sit in judgement at our Court? Gerald would accompany you…"

The poor Warden's eyes were wide open now, inwardly terrified at the prospect of having to decide legal matters, on the spot, in the moment, case after case. And… stunned at being given a choice – not a common offer from a Lord!

He stuttered "I… I… appreciate the importance and the honour, my lord – but if an alternative exists…?"

I pretended a small disappointment and said, "How about you, Marshal?"

It was his turn to stare wide-eyed and mumble his… limited enthusiasm.

"Very well," I said and turned to our Stewardess "Lady Azizah, will you preside at Manor Court?"

She looked momentarily puzzled and I realised I'd unwisely used 'preside' that she might not know as a word.

She whispered, "Sit in big chair?"

I smiled gently and gave a small nod.

It was her turn to briefly widen her eyes – but for very different reasons than the other two. She gently nodded back and said "I will, my lord" in a clear firm voice. The relief in the two men I'd already asked was visible, both clearly feeling like they had just dodged an arrow.

"That is good. I will make sure that Luther and Gerald are always with you. Jeannot may also be in attendance if available."

I had no doubt she would do an excellent job. She had sat in on several months of court sessions, always hidden behind the curtain. After each of the first few such events, I would explain anything she didn't understand and after a few weeks, we would be discussing anything she didn't agree with! She did 'tut' and finger-wag at me after I'd given a pretty lady a smaller fine than probably was deserved and seemed even harder than myself with punishments for theft and violent robbery.

I asked if anyone had any questions and then dismissed them all back to their duties. Azizah seemed hesitant to leave, so I gestured her to return to the chair beside me.

"Lord Walter, you think I good for Court?" she asked.

"I am very sure," I replied, "there is no one else I would rather have in that place."

I gave her arm a small squeeze of reassurance and we both stood. She departed after a graceful curtsey and an eye-twinkling smile behind her veil. I gave her a small bow in reply, and we went off to our respective duties.

Next day, I was on my rounds of the tradesmen and our blacksmith beamed with pride when he saw me and held up the newly completed battle-axe. He passed it to me with two hands. I hefted it, twirled it and complimented him on the excellent work. It was exactly as I had ordered, with no finery at all, just perfect balance and wicked potential.

I went on to see the leather-man and ordered a wide scabbard for the new weapon to be carried against my lower back.

We agreed that leather wasn't the ideal storage container for a steel item, but I rejected the idea of a wooden holder that would be heavy and forever banging my back when riding.

After a few moments of chin-rubbing, he suggested we ask the Marshals wife to make a linen-and-horsehair quilted pouch to go inside the leather, much like a little gambeson[70] for the axe.

"Excellent," I said as I clapped him on the shoulder, "make it like that."

The next few days were busy with sword, spear and bow training for the men, depending on their role. I also held full parades with the sergeants, to check that each man had all necessary equipment, from their new leather capes down to decent daggers.

---

[70] A thin but heavy, quilted long jacket, densely packed with horsehair - think medieval Kevlar

One man was found to have sold almost all his issued heorusceorp[71] for drink money. He'd escaped notice before by borrowing items for squad and guard inspections. He was stripped of anything left that I had provided for him, marched barefoot out of the castle in just his shirt and hose, then thrown in the moat. My remaining soldiers clearly expected nothing less to be the result of that offence.

Three days later, a letter arrived from Lord Roger, Earl of Warwick. The news was as I anticipated, a call to arms on behalf of King Stephen.

We were to muster at Burford Priory on Saint Georges Day[72].

I consulted with Gerald on the exact wording, because I held Haverhill from the Crown and not as a subject of Warwick.

He deemed it a legal document as the instruction was clearly on behalf of the King, the absence of the number of men expected was a trivial matter, likely due to some haste in issuing the summons. Haverhill owed merely 24 spears to the Crown in time of war, but as my usual escort was 24 and... I had some small ambition at least for the campaign, I decided to take 36 as lancer-swordsmen and 9 of the mounted archers. I had coin to spare for new recruits, to fill the gaps at home.

I wanted to leave on the 17th of April, three days hence, aiming to be there a day early and with more men than obliged.

The usual hum of activity at Haverhill increased to a furious buzzing, as all rushed to complete tasks before our departure; it could be breaking in new horses, food preparation, weapon drills, so many things.

From my time as squire, I had a deep aversion to nursing or guarding wagons during the ebb and flow of conflict during our time of Anarchy. The carts could often be so far behind the fighting troops as to be no function other than to provide supplies to a roving enemy.

---

[71] Saxon for 'war equipment'

[72] April 23rd

So, I ordered a palfrey as a spare horse for each man and a dozen more spares to carry supplies in the charge of my very new squires. New large leather supply-carriers had to be made along with suitable wooden frames to tie them to, so all trades were fully engaged with the enterprise.

The Lady Azizah had also clearly been thinking ahead. She ordered a very large, freshly killed forest pig to be shot a few more times by our longbowmen. Then she summoned all sergeants and corporals to a trestle table she had caused to be placed out in the Bailey. The soldiers gathered in front of the table, curiously looking at the animal lying there with multiple broadhead arrows embedded far into its body. Azizah, looked at them to make sure all were paying attention; hardly necessary, as our castle-folk hung on her every word. She picked one embedded arrow then tried and was unable to pull it out. She pointed to a young corporal and indicated he should try and was only able to pull the shaft off the buried arrowhead. She asked another corporal to pull a second arrow, which he managed to do but much meat and blood came out with the arrow. Now came her words for this demonstration.

"Pig is soldier, hit with arrow."

She pointed at the wound with the arrowhead still in there.

"Cut out steel, he may dead."

"Leave steel – he dead."

Pointing to the torn flesh where the second arrow had been pulled out, she said "He may dead." She then picked up a cloth that had been covering a few things at the end of the table. There was a small heap of quills[73], as used for writing, and a boning knife from the kitchen. She picked up two of the quills and used the knife to cut off the sharp ends. "Sergeant, please" she said and indicated that the senior sergeant came around the table to stand next to her. This large and swarthy thirty-year-old, veteran of many campaigns, turned into a blushing, bashful teenager when standing two feet from our Lady Stewardess.

---

[73] Writing tool made from a moulted flight feather (preferably a primary wing-feather) of a large bird

Under other circumstances, the other soldiers would have been falling about with laughter at this, but today, there was a respectful silence and intense curiosity. Azizah mimed to grip the arrow shaft with just two fingers, saying "Hold, please" to the sergeant. Then she held a blunted quill in each hand, gently spread the wound with her little fingers and probed for the arrowhead barbs with the hollows at the end of each quill. When both barbs were masked by the quill shafts, she said "Little pull, sergeant". He very gently pulled the shaft, and the arrow came slowly and smoothly out of the wound, with the head attached, the quills carefully held over the barbs – no blood, no tears to the flesh.

A collective gasp went up from the watching men and a spontaneous round of applause broke out. Azizah gave a small bow and indicated the sergeant should give a bow too.

To finish the explanations, she said, "Wash hands" continuing by indicating the wound, "Honey in there" and "Needle thread" as she mimed sewing up the wound. Copying me after my meetings with my staff, she said "Any kwe-chuns?" The men looked baffled until the senior sergeant leant over and whispered "Questions, my lady?" "Yes, thank you sergeant - kwest-chuns." A corporal raised his hand "My Lady, how do we wash our hands?"

"Soap and water or drink you can" she replied, there was a small groan at the thought of using beer or the like for hand washing. Azizah silenced this with a finger held up and wagged it firmly at them all. "Hand no clean – soldier you may dead." Another hand went up "We have no honey my lady, no needle, no thread"

"Have when you go" she replied and impressed nods were seen all round. She then stood to one side, presented the quills to the senior sergeant and waved the next man to assist with pulling the next arrow. The sergeant struggled a bit with his huge hands but succeeded when Azizah's small hands guided his little fingers to work separately from his fingers on the quill.

The sergeant had to be helped away afterwards, as he was overcome at being touched by the Lady Azizah. He said, much later that day, and after a couple of pints, that it had been "like being blessed by an angel".

In time, every man took his turn at removing arrows, with the poor old pig having to be shot a few more times by the very bored longbowmen.

With the meat well tenderised, the pig made a delicious dinner for all that night. Although Azizah, of course, had chicken pie.

We had a practise parade on the 16th, only a very few missing or ill-fitting items were discovered and easily remedied. While the men stood waiting by their horses, Azizah walked along the line and gave each man a pouch of herbs and spices, as used at Haverhill. The sergeants and corporals were additionally presented with small leather cylinders, with buckled lids at each end. These tubes had two straps, for wearing across their front or back or down the side. Inside the tubes was a jar of honey at one end, with quills, linen thread and needles in a cloth at the other end. All the gifts had an embroidered 'H' for Haverhill and were paid for by the Lady herself. Each man bent a knee to her on receiving his present or presents and heartfelt thanks expressed.

As I looked over the men on parade from the door of the Keep, I reflected that I was leaving the Marshal to look after military matters at both Walden and Haverhill, my Warden would keep an eye on administration and Azizah would run the Manor Courts. After much thought, I had reluctantly decided to leave my longbowmen behind. They were all excellent chaps, and I would miss the extra range they gave me over the short bows, however… they were all very large men, too heavy for our normal horses and their bows totally unsuited for use from horseback. Additionally, I planned no set-piece battle for our 'Haverhills', I wanted to present us to Lord Roger as a cavalry unit, for raiding, scouting and diversionary tactics.

Azizah joined me at the Keep, after completing her presentations. Something was clearly puzzling her, so I touched her arm and raised my eyebrows. "You take no maids, my lord?" she asked, in considerable surprise. "Who… look after you?" she went on.

"It is not one place, one battle we go to," I explained "we go many places, very fast, day and night, no castle, no house – I couldn't keep them safe and…" I waved at all the men still on parade "they have no maids…" "Ahhh," she said, "may you bath this night, my lord", continuing with "I tell them fill laundry after dinner" then curtseyed, before going up to her room.

"Good god," I thought "this is my last night here for what could be a very long time. I am going to miss Azizah most deeply..."

Little did I know that Azizah was in her room, sobbing and praying for my preservation and safe return.

Dinner was extra special that night, both in quality and quantity. All my senior staff joined me at my high table and much cider was drunk, with lemonade for Azizah of course. I retired to my parlour with Azizah and we chatted about the last few days, both avoiding the subject of separation the next day. After a little while, a soft knock on the door was heard. Azizah stood up as if to leave, I stood up as well. She curtseyed a 'good night' and I bowed in reply. As she stepped towards the door, I gently grasped her arm to stop her. "I will be very much thinking of you, on my travels, my lady" I said. "I think you much, my lord" she replied and, seeming flustered now, quickly left the room. Her guards left with her and on seeing the maid was the one who had knocked, I sent one of my guards to the Hall entrance and the other to the White Room door. I raised eyebrows at the maid, and she nodded and led the way to the laundry.

Deep in thought, I pushed open the laundry door and was met with gust of warmth from the new fireplace. The curtain was still dividing the room, so I walked around the end and saw... Three maids, stood in front of the fire, smiling ear-to-ear, as they chorused "Good evening, my lord!" I was stunned as they curtseyed, showing off that they had all adjusted their dresses to be very low at the top. For a moment I was almost bashful about undressing and stepping into the huge new tub – but that moment quickly passed, as I snapped my fingers for assistance to remove my sword belt and clothing. The girls competed with each other to see who could get the most from me the fastest, and in no time, I was ready to step into the steaming water. They then resumed their line in front of the fireplace as I sunk myself slowly into the tub. The girls tried to keep straight faces but failed, while blushing and giggling a great deal. I noticed the new red-haired girl was blushing the most. I held my arms out to her, and saw the faces fall on flaxen-hair and brun-hair, just momentarily, because I spread my arms wide to encompass all of them and said "Well? Get in then!".

With much excited squealing and more giggling, three dresses hit the floor and three pairs of slippers were left behind, as I held a hand out to guide each one in turn, into the tub with me.

I had flaxen-hair, sat tight along my right side, red-hair along my left and brun-hair knelt and sat, straddling my thighs. What a beautiful place to be I thought, and kissed them all in turn, making sure red-hair got a good look at my now-ready 'lance'. She blushed her creamy-white skin to a scarlet, all the way to her breasts and seemed to have lost the ability to speak. So, I kissed her again, then laid back to receive a good head-to-toes cleaning from all of them. I had no idea which hands were where, nor did I care, as my eyes closed at the bliss of it all.

A couple of hours later, I walked very slowly up the Keep stairs, into my room, fell face down on the bed and slept for a few hours. A midden-visit as the Vigil[74] bell rang in the town church was all I remembered until dawn.

Back in my room after breakfast that next morning, I slowly changed into my best gambeson, mail, coif, helmet and metal-backed gloves. This mode of dress would be mine for many weeks ahead. I could only pray that I would return here one day, to change out of it.

I secured four daggers and many purses about my person, strapped on my sword and slung the battle-axe onto my back. Sighing deeply, I recognised that this was the price I paid for the titles, the power, the coin. Would I have chosen differently; did I even choose this? No. I was born for this, though not into a high-ranked family, but spawned with a burning ambition.

This was... me, this is what I do.

My saddlebags had been packed and put ready in the stables the day before, so all I needed to start the fighting campaign of 1141, was to walk out of that door.

With one more sigh and a thought of Azizah's beautiful face, I stomped into the corridor, the spurs jangling on my boots. My guards fell in behind me and I went down to the Keep door.

---

[74] 2 a.m.

Waiting on the platform, just outside the door, was my Marshall, the Warden and Azizah. Drawn up on parade, facing the Keep, were the men, boys and horses I would be taking with me. All waiting, all silent. As was every other member of the castle-staff, watching from the walls or outside the Hall. The men looked first-class in their turnout and Haverhill colours. I shook hands with the Marshal and Warden as they wished me "Good luck" and "God speed".

I turned to Azizah and lost my words for a moment. I could see tears in her eyes and felt my eyes water too. I gripped her shoulders tight and she gripped my arms tightly too, both seeming to not want to let go – I could feel her shaking.

"Safe journeys, my lord" she said very quietly and a little huskily.

"Stay well, my lady" was all I could manage – but possibly, it was the first time I had called her 'my lady' in public. With one final squeeze of her shoulders, I forced a smile for her and turned away to go down the steps to the Bailey.

My horse was waiting at the bottom of the steps, held by a stable-boy.

I nodded to him, took the reins, mounted and walked the horse to the centre of the line and turned to face my staff at the Keep door.

I knew my Marshal was not a great public speaker but thought he would have a few words.

He wished us well on the campaign and told us to come back with some good stories. He finished with the old chestnut: "Soldiers... I command you, do *not* die for your lord - make the other man die for his." This brought a gasp and nervous laughs from the youngsters and wry smiles from the veterans, who had heard that once or twice before.

As a slight surprise, Azizah stepped to the rail and was clearly also going to say something; I noticed that Luther was now standing discretely behind her right shoulder, in case a word went missing. Somehow, she had recovered her poise from a couple of minutes ago, and after a few whispers exchanged with Luther she began. This was her 'hidden princess' speaking now, her voice surprisingly loud, clear and steady.

"Soldiers of Haverhill, fight well, fight hard, fight to win – that is best way come back to us"

As one, my men replied with a thunderous "We will My Lady."

She nodded, pleased at the response and with her now-famous finger-wagging gesture, continued "Remember, boil water before drink."

She saw just a few nods along the line.

"Promise me" she shouted with a volume that surprised even me. Then her voice broke to a sob, as she repeated "Promise me."

The men again roared as one, "We promise My Lady."

And we were to keep that promise – for a couple of months at least. Azizah crossed her hands over her heart, then threw her hands out to encompass the whole parade.

The First Sergeant called for "Three cheers for Our Lady" and if the castle had a roof, it would have been lifted by the resulting roars.

With the echoes receding, I waved to the Keep and everyone around the walls and Hall and turned to lead my force out of the gates and over the drawbridge. Heading always westward, first through Haverhill town, then the familiar route towards Cambridge. After that, Gerald's map showed me a route by way of Bedford and Buckingham – he had also marked the main manor houses along the way, in case we needed to overnight at any of them. I was not too concerned about overnight halts. I was riding to the Kings writ and would requisition inns or claim billets in village or town houses as I saw fit. At least under my usage, there would be fair recompense for the displaced occupants...

The journey was a steady five days, under bright but cloudy skies. We all rode our palfreys for long journeys, their stride pattern being much more comfortable at the gentle trotting pace we usually used. The larger, stronger military horses were thus kept fresh for the crucial times. I'd noticed we had a few more horses in train, more than my initial orders. They seemed to be carrying extra horse-feed and probably more arrows but no doubt I would be told the reasons for the change in due course. The extra horses were being looked after by what appeared to be boys from the castle, but again, I wasn't concerned with such detail.

We had only been gone a couple of days when change began back at Haverhill. It was a Wednesday, market day in town, and so a day for Manor Court at the castle.

After breakfast, the tables in the Hall were all pushed to the back wall, my dais table being replaced with my high-backed chair and the nominated longbowman in place behind the curtain. As an addition this time, three smaller chairs were placed to the left of the main one, seats for Luther, Gerald and Jeannot respectively. Luther's being set back from the others, to minimise his apparent involvement in the proceedings. There was a small buzz among the castle-folk, as word had spread that Lady Azizah would be taking the sessions, a very rare occasion for a woman to 'hold court' in England. Meanwhile, Azizah was in her room, thinking again about a recent decision. She had read her book, many times, about the matter and thought through the good and any possible bad effects of her choice. She was going to discard her veil when in the castles. This would remove the barrier that she felt was there, between those who were now, in effect, her subjects and the source of their justice. She felt safe to do this as castle people had made it clear they regarded her with near reverence, something she had never sought, asked for, or imagined - it just... happened.

So - it was time...

She reshaped her lace shawl, to allow her hair to show and frame her face, placed her veil on her table, smoothed her dress and turned for the door.

As she walked out into the corridor, both guards were a step late with falling in behind her. Both had been struck by something... different they thought they'd seen from the side of their eyes... "M...M... My Lady" stuttered one.

She stopped, turned back and said "Yes, Carter?"

His mouth gaped in shock and awe.

The shock that she knew his name and the awe from the vision of loveliness that was there before him. The surprise all the greater from 'common knowledge' being that her veil hid deformity, or at least, great ugliness and now visibly, clearly, blessedly, it was for no such thing. Both guards dropped to one knee and looked down at the floor, remembering the sergeant's description of 'an angels blessing' and realising his impression was close to truth.

"What trouble you men?" she asked, in a soft and gentle voice.
"Your m…m…mask, my lady – it is missing" said the other soldier,
also stuttering with the surprise of the moment.
"Veil not missing, Taylor. I not need here."
He gasped that she also knew his name.
She could see the men were curious to the point of nearly asking
"why" but were too wary of troubling a person of rank for reasons.
She smiled, though they missed that with their heads still lowered.
"Are you my guardians?" she asked gently.
"Yes, my lady" they said as one, with heartfelt expression.
"Are all people at castle, my guardians?"
"Yes, my lady" they said, again as one, but louder this time.
"Then all may see me, as I see them. Now, time for Court" she said
firmly, to end the conversation.
"Yes, my lady" they said, as they stood and followed her down the
stairs and across to the Hall.
As the three of them proceeded, a ripple of surprise spread
outwards. Chambermaids that gave way to them on the steps of the
Keep, pressed themselves back into the wall, their mouths gaping
silently. A squad of soldiers that were being marched around in the
Bailey, stumbled, tripped and fell all over each other. Their
sergeant's curse died on his lips as saw the reason for their
distraction. A mounted messenger leaving the stables, turned
around in his saddle so far and so fast that his horse went on
without him. As for Carter and Taylor, they were already proud as
peacocks, just to be on Their Lady's detail but now… now, they
marched like legendary warriors that had won a hundred battles!
As she entered the Hall, a series of gasps caused more and more
people to turn, look and add their gasps in turn to the collective
sound.
Azizah went up the small steps to the dais, nodded to the Marshal,
Luther, Gerald and Jeannot, to acknowledge their bows and took
her seat in 'the big chair'.
The four men were just as dumb-struck as the guards had been.
For the Marshal, as his mouth struggled to form any words,
managed to think "I was wrong". He had confided to his wife that he
didn't think Lord Walter's decision to allow Azizah to take Manor
Court would be a success. He just couldn't see a woman managing,

until... he saw her 'princess eyes' for the first time. He knew, there and then, that he was witness to something very special indeed. He'd heard tales of the Empress Matilda's ability to command a room full of lords with her mere presence but had dismissed that as myth, but... "Dear God, I believe it now" he thought, as he took in the beauty and serene confidence radiating from Lady Azizah. He blinked as he suddenly realised that Azizah was talking to him. "You may start Court, thank you Marshal" she said.

Still dumb, the Marshal bowed to her and left the stage. He then signalled to the guard on the Hall door, who in turn signalled the gate to allow the first three plaintiffs into the castle. Meanwhile, the number of soldiers 'on duty' in the Hall was going up and up. Some men, very obviously from the castle night-guard, were standing with their spears, looking very bleary eyed, from having been woken up by the stir that rippled through the whole place. They tried not to, but they all kept stealing glances towards the dais where Their Lady was sitting...

As soon as the third sergeant realised what was happening, he went around the Hall, ordering all the night-guards immediately back to bed. Not surprisingly, they all chose a leaving route that took them past the stage. To a man, they stopped in front of Their Lady, removed their helmet, dropped to one knee, with head bowed, then rose to resume their withdrawal. She acknowledged each with a smile and a gracious nod.

The first few plaintiffs had to be encouraged and helped to state their cases, as all became tongue-tied in Azizah's presence. After the first few had been through, received judgement and left the castle, the rest of the queuing people knew that I was away campaigning and 'the Lady' was running the castle in my absence. On hearing this, one would-be plaintiff immediately turned away, as he was unwilling to be looked down on by 'a darky' but quickly changed his mind and went back to the line when he heard what 'a lovely' she was.

The morning session concluded without problems and soup was served from the kitchens. Azizah asked her supporting staff of three to join her for lunch in the parlour. The chairs in there had been rearranged and small tables brought in, so this worked well enough. The meeting allowed them to talk about the cases heard and for

Jeannot to finish the record he was taking of the proceedings.

The only contentious hearing of the afternoon was a mother alleging rape of her daughter. The defendant was a local wool merchant's son, a young man of fifteen, the same age as the girl. The case had been called the previous week and then been postponed to summons the young man for today's hearing. The mother was furious at the insult to her poor but well-thought-of family and demanded imprisonment and a very hefty £10 in Wergild to compensate the loss of virtue. The father of the boy protested that this was all a teenage adventure, gone too far.

Seeing the blushing youth and the shy glances between the girl and he, Azizah leaned over to Gerald and held a whispered conversation. Azizah sat up straight again and motioned the youth to the bar.

"Will you marry this girl? Azizah asked him.

He blushed again and nodded, while stealing a glance back at the now-blushing girl.

"What?" said his father loudly "He's too young!"

"They are both of age and need no... permissions" said Azizah with a firmness that brooked no discussion[75].

She softened her gaze and spoke gently to the girl.

"Is your wish... also?"

The girl smiled wide and nodded emphatically. Azizah whispered to Luther for a word, then pointed the first finger of each hand at the young couple.

"No crime here; you two, see priest" and waved them away.

The new couple left hand-in-hand, oblivious to the sputtering protests of the parents as they departed the Hall. The court day ended when Azizah declared it so – the few plaintiffs remaining outside the castle gates would return the following week.

As she stood to leave, ten soldiers appeared, clustered and jostling in front of the dais, all claiming to be on the roster as her guards for the evening. Third Sergeant had to step in again to figure out the correct pair and scolded the rest away.

---

[75] Age of consent in this period was 14 for a boy, 12 for a girl

Azizah went up to her room for a rest before dinner and the castle-folk went about their day, content and somewhat relieved that things were working quite well without Lord Walter being around...

As for me, while this was happening at Haverhill, I had an uneventful journey to Burford Priory. We arrived a full day early and I reported to the largest tent I could see, leaving my First Sergeant to organise camp-space and feeding for the men.

I gave my name to the page standing well away from the front of the tall tent and waited while he disappeared inside. After a few minutes, he returned and asked me to go in.

Once inside, I was careful to bow very formally and was met with warm handshakes from Lord Roger and his usual two companion knights, all congratulating me on dealing with the devious Devereux and winning my additional titles. I could see the Earl was smiling at the memory we shared of our last encounter. When he was down on a knee, looking up at me.

"Walter," he said with booming voice, "what do you bring us in such a timely manner?"

"Forty-five on horse, my lord, including mounted archers, with pack-horses for all supplies" I replied.

The senior lords nodded in appreciation, knowing this was only a small force but a potent and useful one.

"Excellent, excellent," Lord Roger responded, "I will give orders at Prime[76], the day after tomorrow... but first I must speak with you alone."

He smiled his thanks to the guardian knights, as they nodded their understanding and left the tent.

"I'm sure you remember our last meeting, Walter" he began.

I thought "Good grief, he's surely not going to complain about my small jest?"

He went on "The Persian... woman, or was it... lady you were with at Berkhamsted; if that was your cook, then call me the Pope!" I could feel the shock on my face escape my control, this was so unexpected.

---

[76] 6 a.m.

"Ha!" he went on "So my... source was correct, those hands of hers belonged to no kitchen maid!" My shoulders sagged, I felt sick in my stomach – that is what Shabani, the Persian ambassador, must have seen – just before Lord Rogers highly fortuitous, if inadvertent, interruption to proceedings.

Lord Roger continued, "The Mongols have allied with His Holiness in Rome[77], in common cause against the Arabs. This means the Mongol interest in... eliminating the Husayn family and Ala al-Din in particular, is now the interest of... Christendom."

I gasped and sat as Lord Roger gestured to a chair. Speaking more slowly now, with careful thought, he went on "However... there are many of us who trust a Mongol no further than we could throw that giant bastard we saw at the castle..." "In particular, the Knights Templar[78] are convinced the alliance with The Pope is a temporary... façade, that will disappear when they have what they want." He dropped his voice to a whisper. "So... the Templars have granted protection to the Husayn family by allowing them to stay on Rhodes[79]. Well, all the family except... one" and he smiled widely as I wondered where 'Rhodes' was.

"I'm guessing yours is the Princess Azizah?" he asked in a whisper. Hearing her title and name from somewhere outside of my thoughts made me gasp at the heartache I suddenly felt - I even blushed a little as I nodded. He slapped me hard on the side of my shoulder. "Ohhhh Walter! We are supposed to choose our women with our heads, by hard calculation – you know that. I know you know that – because you declined the poor offering of the Lady Bigod."

I gave a rueful smile and a nod at all this.

---

[77] Aka, The Pope

[78] Templars became a favoured charity throughout Christendom and grew rapidly in membership and power. Templar knights, in their distinctive white mantles with a red cross, were among the most skilled fighting units of the Crusades

[79] A large island in the Eastern Mediterranean, strongly fortified and used as a base to raid Moslem-held port cities and shipping lanes

Then I saw his face collapse in sorrow, at some distant memory.
"I do understand, though" he said, now in a choked and hesitant voice.
"After my first wife died, my second... lady was my heart and soul – I lost her, and our child, at the birth."
We leaned in together, hugged and both wept for some minutes. He at his double loss, myself at the manner of his loss and the realisation of how much I loved Azizah and how close I had come to losing her. Then, with an unsteady voice, Lord Roger said
"Fock me, Walter, this won't do – we have a realm to preserve and protect." We stood and dabbed our eyes with the tails of our respective tabards.
When looking mostly recovered, he shouted for the page, who popped his head through the tent flap. "Fetch my clerk" said Lord Roger. The man appeared a couple of minutes later.
"Now Walter, thinking about the people far away that we just talked about... what... discrete message could we send to reassure them?"
I paused a moment then spoke slowly to the clerk, as his held his quill poised over paper.
"Arrows fly straight from a horse because the gemstone is safe in England." It was Lord Roger's turn to nod ruefully as the clerk departed.
"Good god Walter, even I don't understand the references there!"
I nodded, smiling and didn't elaborate. I knew the family would make sense of the archery and the meaning of Azizah's name[80], that Luther had explained to me once. With our business complete, Lord Roger said "So, Walter, prepare to move after my orders in two days."
"I will sire... and thank you" I responded, as I bowed formally again and turned away.

I returned to my men, who had set up 'home' in a copse of trees on the slope above the Priory – always better to hold the high ground.

---

[80] Sources vary but Azizah could be taken to mean: Precious, cherished, held in high regard or value

Some escaped chickens, living wild, had been found in the middle of the trees and were now doing their duty as lunch. A clean sheep-free stream had been found further up the hill, but we were mindful of our promise to Our Lady and the water boiled over a good fire. When all were fed and watered, our minds turned to looking after the horses, cleaning equipment and some instruction for our squires and boys. My men were always careful to be professional in their guidance of the juniors, I had made it very clear indeed how... displeased I would be if any bullying caused us to lose potential talent to another fief. On the other hand, the youngsters knew a moat or worse awaited any who failed to meet our standards. The mounted archers roamed over 'our' hill and into the forest beyond. They bagged a young but good-sized boar and brought it back for dinner. Small amounts of our precious spices from Lady Azizah were added and a good meal enjoyed by all.

The next day passed with mild weather and us watching the arrival of the bulk of our campaign army. It was quite obvious that the larger contingents were very light on mounted men and heavy on carts and wagons for supplies. We estimated more than 9,000 men had joined here as the Kings army.

I was up early the next day, eager to hear of our next move. All lords gathered in front of Lord Rogers tent and he quickly described our situation and our aims.
It seemed that Matilda's forces were taking a new approach, looking to sweep across southern England this time, with landings of Flemish mercenaries at Southampton and possibly other places to take place in support. Our first aim was to block her main land force that was converging on Stroud, prior to them moving on Salisbury. The cavalry of Rockingham would take the shorter route through the forest tracks to the Stroud area, then locate, track and report on Matilda's army.

The main force would take the open roads to Slad[81] via Shipton Oliffe and Ullenwood. Anyone getting lost to rendezvous at Slad. Main army to be preceded by Haverhill as vanguard[82]. Rear-guard to be the Norfolks. All to move off at Terce.

I was stunned but managed to keep my composure, as if I expected nothing less! There were some mutterings of "Haver-who...?" among the assembled lords but no one would quibble about Earl Warwick's clear instructions. After a short blessing by the local Prior, Lord Roger dismissed us to our duties.

My men were as pleased as I was with the honour of being the vanguard and began thinking of tales they'd tell back home, as they made final preparations. Meanwhile I was careful to check that Gerald's map extended far enough.

Just before we set off, a messenger from Haverhill found me with a routine letter from my staff. The correct words and signs were present to show it was not written under duress. It informed me that training of the new men was progressing well, a couple of new longbowmen had turned up and seemed promising. They told me that nothing had been heard from Count Aubrey about a call-up for Walden to him (and by implication for Matilda), which was good news; looked like Aubrey was back on the fence in terms of choosing a side this year. The taxes were coming in well from all three of my fiefs and Azizah's first Manor Court had been a success. I had full confidence in all of them, but it was good to have the confirmation that all was well. The messengers would leave Haverhill each Monday and Thursday, returning when I had a reply or message to send back. Their problem of finding us would increase as the campaign went on and we moved more often, because we wouldn't be telling the messenger or write where we were going next – just in case of interception...

---

[81] Slad is a village in Gloucestershire, in the Slad Valley about 2 miles from Stroud

[82] The advance party - to watch for ambushes and any enemy forces

I hurriedly scribbled my reply on the back of the original.
I thanked them all for their news and added a concealed message
for Luther; I asked him what the Arabic words were for *'Your family
is safe'*, knowing he would pass the meaning behind this on to
Azizah. The messenger then departed, and I got back to my business
of the day.

In truth, we were a little light for the vanguard role, so I pushed well
forward with three pairs of lookouts, well in advance of our other
men. Of each pair, one was a scout/tracker, the other an archer.
Only one pair moved at a time, while the others watched. This was
quite slow work, but we could still manage safe progress faster than
the damn carts and wagons – and of course the great number of
foot-soldiers. Luckily, we had distinct roads to follow for the whole
route and most junctions had signposts, which I always checked on
my map, in case some enemy or prankster had altered them.
Constantly on my mind was the first rule of a vanguard being "Don't
get focking lost", which would lead to a tiring and time-consuming
diversion for the whole army. I sighed with relief, when I heard my
scouts report "Slad quarter-mile ahead" at the end of the second
day. One of Lord Roger's senior knights cantered up to us, to choose
the camp-site and dispositions for the army; then we pushed on and
swept an arc beyond the village, as far as we could before last light
forced us back to camp. I left my men to pick a spot to camp and
reported to the other senior knight that no enemy had been seen
on our sweep ahead.

Next day, after many false alerts, the army moved two miles to the
River Stroud. A ford was located and all waded or rolled across
without mishap. Seems that Matilda's forces had been winding
through the country and were finally seen committing to forming up
on 'Rodborough Common Hill'. If they stayed there to give battle,
Lord Roger was very willing to take them on, despite their likely
advantage of numbers and apparent position on high ground. This
was because the Rockingham cavalry reported that the enemy were
very short of horsemen and so were open to flanking attacks[83] on
their hill-top. Around mid-afternoon, our army took up a position on
a very slight hill opposite that of our opponents. We had a stream
and bog that protected our rear and clumps of thorn-bush covering

much of our flanks. A fine place to launch an attack from and not a bad place for an over-night, as it was now too late in the day to start a full battle. Our army made a fine site, now nearly 10,000 men, with the right flank so far from us that the haze of the day partly obscured them.

A page delivered a message from our commanders to guard the left flank through until morning. No limit of exploitation was given, so I made my own decisions. First, I had the archer with the best eyesight and the corporal who was best at tally-sticks go along our front and count the enemy force to best possible. The counting made very tricky by the unexpected expanses of scarlet tunics, tabards and shields up that hill to our west. Then, I sent out four parties of four to ride a series of wide cloverleaf patterns to cover south-east of us, round to south west. They returned, as instructed, just before sunset and reported no enemy seen for up to three miles from us. I immediately sent out my three poachers-turned-soldiers to grab a prisoner or two, then wrote a note of our findings for Lord Roger and gave it my squire to "deliver to the big tent and ask if there was any reply".

He came back with eyes still wide at the experience of having to address men of such exalted ranks. I asked him if there was any reply and he frowned in concentration before quoting "Continue the good work, Lord Walter." I nodded and dismissed him to help with the cooking and water boiling.

Four hours later, well after full dark and I was beginning to be concerned for my poachers.

They had left their helmets and any bulky, jangly equipment behind; they were wearing their own 'hunting' capes of many shades of green, brown and grey and had quickly disappeared into the gloom of approaching last light – but they were overdue. Finally, after we had finished our meal, they all returned, with two prisoners gagged and trussed over the backs of the horses. The prisoners, both young lads, were separated and bounced around a bit by the First and Second Sergeants, with our larger men stood round them looking fierce.

---

[83] Going around one or both sides

I then intervened and 'rescued' the captives from their 'brutish' interrogation, in the hope they would spill all they knew in the relief of their 'saving'... They seemed somehow... ill-prepared for a night in the open, and totally unconcerned about the battle tomorrow! With gentle questioning from me, I fished through their memories, asking about families, their journeys here, things they'd heard – and began to form a strategic picture quite different from ours... The stories matched up near enough to confirm but did not seem rehearsed, they were just too relieved to be 'saved' that they held nothing back. I handed the lads off to the corporals to feed them and keep them secure, then set off for the big tent, with my squire following.

As I approached the command tent, I could hear a furious argument going on, in the Norman language. It seemed that Lord Roger and his senior knights all had different and firmly held opinions. I knocked loudly on the stout tent pole. Lord Roger glanced around and roared "Not now Walter!"

Something snapped in me, my ancestors slipped their leash again, unbidden again. I was indebted to Lord Roger, held him in the highest regard but was I subservient to him? No! I remembered his words when he confirmed my knighthood "think as a lord and act as one, without fear or hesitation".

So I said, loudly and firmly, "Yes, now sir."

The three senior lords whipped their heads round with a mixture of surprise and extreme annoyance. I cared not in this moment and stared firmly back into their gaze, particularly that of Lord Roger. These defenders of the kingdom, these hardened military veterans in front of me all folded their arms, but at least turned my way. The Earl pointed wordlessly to a spot three yards in front of him. I walked to that spot, bowed and began.

"My lords, there is no battle tomorrow, they are leaving after midnight, with a few remaining to keep the fires going and make noises."

I waved to the west to indicate the enemy-held hill.

"This is, sirs, a fly-trap, nothing more. We counted them twice and seems fewer than we thought, the use of scarlet seems deliberate to make counting difficult."

At this, one of the senior knights cuffed the other and said gruffly

"I told you the number was wrong..."
Unthinking of my company, I held up my hand for quiet, as I had not finished!
"A large number of horse and foot-soldiers were seen leaving Mathilda's army on the day before yesterday, along with crossbowmen with dark skins, big noses and a foreign tongue. There was much talk of a great many more of these, to be landing north of us at Longney, also many more foot soldiers are expected from the North." I nodded to indicate I had now finished.
"You know all this, how?" asked Lord Roger, though now with a more moderate tone.
"We made a careful count and we took two prisoners, my lord."
Lord Roger now looked concerned, rubbed a hand on his forehead and waved us all to take seats on the rough campaign chairs nearby. We formed a square of these chairs, facing in.
"This puzzle has more pieces than we thought," began the Earl, "when solved, it may look very different from our expectation... De Warenne, what of Wallingford?"
I was momentarily surprised at this formality of address, but then vaguely remembered that both the senior knights were called William. The companion answered "He is not just late sire; he has failed to send word. He either sits on the fence or comes against us."
"And what say you, FitzOsbern?" queried Lord Roger.
The other senior answered "With Count Aubrey clearly not mobilising, I'm afraid, my lord, we assumed that our rear to the east was secure... but if Brian of Wallingford has switched, then his forces from Pembroke are in play as well. Also, the Rockingham scouts did claim to see a knight with Chester's colours with them two days ago..."
"So with Wallingford and presumably Huntingdon active behind us, we have Chester, Hereford, Devon and now Pembroke in front of us... and now with Genoese crossbowmen – we are meat in the sandwich. What if..."
De Warenne finished the thought "Their real aim is to punch east for London, rather than south for Salisbury and Winchester...
"Indeed..." mused Lord Roger "which means... Gloucester will be their first target." The companions nodded in agreement.

Lord Roger abruptly stood up, so we did.

"Walter, how soon can you leave to scout Gloucester for us?

"Twenty minutes my lord" I replied.

"Very well, anything you need?"

"Four squires to act as messengers, sir."

"So be it, I think you know who to see for them" he said with a smile.

He went on, "We will march after the enemy departs, and leave some men to keep fires going and make noise as if we were still here... We will take the direct route, which is the..." he clicked his fingers for a place name.

"Tuffley, sir" said FitzOsbern.

"Yes, the Tuffley road, and we'll see you around mid-day, good luck Walter."

"Thank you, sir" I responded, as I bowed and left the tent.

I stopped a few yards away from the tent and shouted loudly into the night. I called for 'Squire Brooker', the young man who succeeded me as head squire at Warwick. He appeared out of the darkness and said "Yes, my lord" before he recognised me. We both grinned and shook hands warmly, but there was no time for reminiscence.

"I need four squires to act as messengers, to leave immediately, my squire will show them where we are" and indicated my Haverhill youngster, who had followed me away from the tent.

"Yes, sir" he said, bowed briefly and walked briskly away.

"Wait here for the four lads, then bring them to me" I told my squire. He nodded as I turned away and walked quickly back to my little force. On reaching my camp, I called for the First Sergeant.

"Leave the fires burning but... quietly, load up everything. We head north in fifteen minutes... quietly"

"Yes sir" he whispered with a grin and went about his tasks.

The four Warwick squires arrived and reported to me, just as we were ready to set off.

"Any of you know the Tuffley road?" I asked.

One raised his hand, so I said, "You will guide us, the others stay close to me."

All of my party stayed on foot, as we led our horses away from the main camp. Once we were far enough up the track, I signalled to mount, and we got on our palfreys for a swift trot for most of the twelve miles or so to Gloucester.

The further we travelled, the more frequently we stopped and scouted ahead.

I called a halt around Vigil[84], for water and food, as I had no idea when the next chance for this would come...

When we passed the sign to Abbeydale, we changed to our bigger, heavier war-horses, leaving the palfreys to be tied behind with the pack-animals. Then we proceeded cautiously until my scouts reached the edge of the forest overlooking Gloucester town.

First light had passed, and dawn was now breaking, giving them clear sight down the slope to the town.

A scout reported back "The town is under attack my lord, by a force of around a thousand, pressing at the west gate – but the defence is holding."

He looked grim as he went on "The south gate though... seems to be yielding, a few hundred enemy are fighting up to and under the gate-house." I glanced to see if the nearest Warwick squire had heard that, he nodded that he had. I slowly walked my horse to the edge of the trees and saw the critical situation at the south gate.

The bridge over the moat was lowered, and one-half of the gate was missing, or open. Both occurrences probably due to treachery.

The recently rebuilt castle was no help today. It was surrounded by the town and possession of the town would almost completely negate the effect of the castle.

The town thus relied on its outer walls, the river and moat for primary defence.

The place seemed to have given much attention to building endless churches and less importance to the fortifications...

I sighed, as I took in the sight, knowing what I, or rather we, must do next. I went back a little way to the squires.

Speaking to the one who'd heard the scouts report, I said "Ride to Lord Roger. Tell him of the enemy and that Haverhill will attack the enemy at the South Gate."

He nodded, said "Yes, my lord" and cantered away.

---

[84] 2 a.m.

I walked my horse a little further down the forest trail, until all my men could see me. I gave hand signals to form a single line following me, and to carry out a sweeping attack. My battle-axe in my hand, lances or bows held ready by my men. I led my small force to the east, staying in the trees, so as not to be visible to the larger force at the west gate, then trotted, cantered and then galloped towards the moat. I then curved our path to parallel the water and aimed for the rear rank of the attackers. We always aimed to keep our speed up. "Do not stop" was the message we had driven into them in training. If we stopped, we became vulnerable to any grouping of the enemy, however small. "Do not delay to ensure a kill, injure them as many as possible, to take them out of the fight" was another instruction from training.

Our first sweep past the rear of the enemy must have injured more than forty, our archers at the back of our column having done much damage.

I led them round in a loop and swept past the enemy's rear again, I changed my axe to my left hand, my lancers changed sides also. The archers also calmly swapped hands, as our Lady Azizah had taught them and between us, we all tagged at least another forty. By now there was great alarm in the enemy ranks, pressed in front by the defending soldiers at the gate and by us from behind. If they'd stayed as a formation, they could have resisted us better but as it was, they broke and ran along the side of the moat, trying to reach their main force at the west wall. What a desperate error this was for them. I curved my cavalry around again and chased them down. It was carnage. Their running in the direction we now rode meant that we had much more time in contact. I lost count of the number of axe strikes I got in, and each lancer and archer would have more than me.

I curved around for one last pass – there were no enemy standing between us and the gate. The survivors had either jumped in the moat or, more stupidly, were now running east, away from the gate, and us – as if they could out-run our horses... As we galloped past the gate, I glanced back to see my squire holding the staff with our Haverhill pennant stretched out by the breeze. The town walls erupted with a roaring cheer and the once vulnerable gate was now closing. None of the east-bound enemy escaped becoming a serious casualty or worse.

I led my force at a canter, back up the slope to the trees, to re-join our supply-horses. The men were buzzing like wasps, at the action and release from danger. I despatched two scouts on fresh palfreys to check the other walls of the town, then called my men to check for wounds, as sometimes they were not felt during a fight. We had some minor spear cuts to legs and arms and one very unfortunate lancer had what was obviously a Haverhill arrow sticking out the back of his right calf muscle. I noticed our archers all keeping their heads down, being very busy with their equipment and one or two whistling tunelessly...

We moved a hundred yards or so further into the forest and found a small clearing. I posted lookouts back to over-watch the town and we attended to the wounded. The man with the arrow in his leg had a queue of keen volunteers to take it out, just as Their Lady had shown them. The unfortunate casualty could only remonstrate that he "wasn't a focking pig" and eventually chose one of the corporals to do the business, starting with a beer hand-wash. This removal was done quite quickly, with the honey, stitching and binding being applied in short order. The onlookers 'helped', by quoting Azizah's disjointed Saxon words at each stage, and wagging an Azizah-like finger to emphasize the important parts – all in great good humour.

The scouts returned and reported the other walls were free of enemy, but many spear-points could be seen sparkling in the hazy sun, miles to the north-west of the town. "Bollocks," I thought to myself "that can't be the force moved from Stroud, this must be the forces from Chester or maybe Pembroke."

I wrote down all that we had seen and done, then gave the paper to the second Warwick squire, who departed to Lord Roger.

Thankfully, our army appeared just before mid-day, forced the enemy away from Gloucester and took up a strong position to the west of the town, daring the enemy to take them on. Such a prospect had clearly not been in the enemy's plans and they withdrew, even though they significantly outnumbered our Royal forces.

This tended to strengthen our thoughts that they had intended a more distant strategic target and not just another battle for Gloucester-town.

That night in camp, Lord Roger and the two Sir Williams sought us out. Our men were deeply impressed by their visit and the obvious sincerity in his words of praise to them. We had saved Gloucester from its fate, and the resulting festering sore that would be an important enemy-held town within the land normally held solidly for the Crown. We spoke afterwards and he told me to switch roles with Rockingham as the armies scouting cavalry. I asked for some more men and was given a dozen good 'Warwicks' and an assurance that I would always have six fresh messengers with me at the start of each day. The new men would normally have been a major problem with their ignorance of our methods, but I paired each of the 'new' Warwicks with one of my 'old' ones and all worked in well.

Our new role kept us well away from any of the pitched battles, but my god it was exhausting. Always first out and last back each day; that is, if we made it back. At least half the time we were too far away to return, usually because we had the sniff of an enemy headquarters in our noses. Many a night was spent wrapped in our woollen cloaks and leather capes. The clear sunny weather often bringing starlight and cold after sundown. We'd quickly learned that feints and diversions were not accompanied by the senior lords, so we watched the 'high ranked' like distant hawks. So, every genuine move the enemy made throughout May and June would be reported back to Lord Roger.

The high point for us happened on an unusually warm night in mid-July. My blessed poachers in their motley-hued cloth capes, had sneaked in very close to one important camp. The site was heavily manned but poorly organised...

Baldwin de Redvers, 1st Earl of Devon, went for a shit behind a large bush – and never returned to his tent. Our lads showed him steel to keep him silent and whisked him away through a series of bushes, long grass and moon-shadows, back to our waiting force.

The thirty-five-year-old, very senior lord, incredibly wealthy and the most influential supporter of Empress Matilda, was gagged and trussed over the back of a spare palfrey as we quietly withdrew, while trying not to laugh out loud, at our impertinence, and our success.

On approaching our camp around dawn, I took his pardon in my now rather practised manner, then had him untrussed and tidied up; before presenting him to our Earl. Lord Roger knew Earl Baldwin of course, from years before, even so, the astonishment on our leaders face and the misery on Baldwins visage when they met, will stay with me forever!

A very humble Lord Roger visited our part of the camp around that mid-day. He got down off his horse, shook every man's hand and finished by hugging me. I took him back along the line of men to introduce my poachers, now attired as soldiers. I made no mention of their... history but said that these were the men who had captured the Earl of Devon. He shook their hands once again, then got back on his horse to address us all.
"Haverhills, your actions throughout this campaign, have helped secure the realm. We have more fighting to do, but much will be on our terms now – in the Kings name, I thank you."
First Sergeant called for three cheers for Lord Roger, who then bowed low to us in his saddle, turning away as we bowed low to him.

As the Earl foretold, there were more weeks of riding and hiding to do; scouting for the main army. We were all by then beyond exhausted, feeling the effects of poor food, lack of clean water, lack of time to boil water and many injuries of various sorts.
Come the 1st of August, I was so tired that I misjudged a move across a valley one day at first light, I'd been too hasty and not put the scouts forward. So, I missed seeing a peaty bog that we had to divert around, and also missed a small camp of Pembrokes in a copse on the far slope. As dawn broke, we were still in the open when those bastards spotted us and loosed their Welsh longbow arrows at us, thankfully at extreme range. But one bodkin tip caught me in the side, just penetrating enough through mail and gambeson to make a small but painful injury. We were able to stop after a couple more hours and the wound was packed with honey and bound up round my chest, and I thought nothing more of it.

We returned to our main camp two days later, our horses walking slowly, our bodies slumped in our saddles. We were past the point of putting on our usual show and just looked like dirty grey ghosts. I think we even passed the Royal colours without salute that day and I'm sure we simply failed to notice at least one of the 'Sir Williams'.

For a final time, Lord Roger and both 'Williams' visited us. The Earl got down from his horse, waved the men to stay seated as they struggled to stand at his arrival. He looked searchingly into my face and hugged me. There were tears in his eyes as he turned and addressed us.
"You have done enough now Haverhills," he said "I hereby order Sir Walter to cease his campaign and take you back home. Thank you all. The King will be making his thanks known to you, in due course".
The 'Williams' both nodded gravely at his words. The three senior lords bowed low to us, and all we could manage was a small wave as they departed. It was two days before we were strong enough even to begin the journey back to Haverhill. We had ended up in sight of Saint Mary's Church, Fownhope; not far from Hereford and so very far from home. I guessed eight days, probably more in our present condition.
I felt so remote from all that was good, comfortable, routine.
I missed the sight and sound of Azizah so much, my heart ached.
I also had very little strength in me, about falling off the horse at the end of each day's ride.
I found out later that I was the deciding factor for how many miles we did on any given day – when I started to slide in the saddle, they looked for somewhere to camp. I vaguely remember the squires taking it in turns to feed me.

So it was, that twelve days later we slowly came upon Haverhil.
The townsfolk turned with eager faces, to see 'their boys' back from fighting for the King; but were all shocked into silence at the awful transformation they saw in us in just over three months.
Our tired horses scuffed their hooves on the road to the castle. Our shoulders slumped and we slowly clomped our way over the drawbridge and into our Bailey. The familiar sights, sounds and smells lifted my spirits enough to let me dismount with some style

at least; I did feel a little dizzy though.

The castle-folk surrounded us with welcome, someone gave me a bottle of cider that tasted so good! My Marshal and Warden shook my hand, but I couldn't really hear what they were saying, I just smiled and nodded. The crowd parted and I saw the lovely Azizah standing there, her beautiful face radiant with happiness as she saw me.

"Wait," I thought "your veil, where's your veil? People will see. What's happening?" This last was my thought as I saw Azizah's expression fall with sudden concern as she looked at me.

My concern at that moment was the apparent earthquake that was striking Haverhill. I looked to my right as the ground tilted towards me, then away, then towards me so fast it smacked me in the face. Blackness.

I lay in the White Room for four days, racked with a fever that they thought would end me. When Azizah and the nuns had peeled off my mail, gambeson, shirt and other clothing, they found the arrow wound in my side had turned poisonous. They bathed me when I was hot, wrapped me when I was cold. Endured incoherent cursing's and shoutings at any and all hours.

There was, by now, a new senior nun and another novice arrived, so between them and Azizah I was watched all day and all night. Many herbs and potions were made and somehow got down me. My memory is of terrifying dreams, of fighting demons and huge knights, always with my axe just out of reach.

On the morning of the fifth day, the worst of the fever had passed. Azizah and the senior nun were able to sit me up, so I could drink with assistance and be spooned a small but good amount of soup. Some more soup and lemonade was my lunch, then I slept until after dawn the next day.

Another two days saw me manage some chicken pie and I could feel now only a... normal, if rather extreme, tiredness in me.

Another few days of small meals and gradually more assisted walking saw me get to the laundry room. It took five ladies, or more, to get me into the tub, but I had no idea who they were and nothing... arose in me, even with the washing.

After a week of increasing strength, I was able to slowly walk across the Keep and up to my room. The castle-folk lined the route to cheer me but Azizah had clearly instructed them not to get too close in my delicate condition. My senior staff were gathered on the Keep steps and it was very good to see them.

Each day, I rose a little earlier and walked a little longer. I was soon taking regular meals in the Hall and enjoying a short lunchtime talk with senior staff in my parlour. Azizah was absolutely ruthless at controlling the time allowed for this. Heaven help anyone who wanted to tarry too long to discuss... anything!

I was soon able to make it to the laundry, on my own, for my next bath but promptly fell asleep in the warm water. I awoke to find brun-hair and flaxen-hair kneeling beside the tub, gently soaping me, my head resting on flaxen-hair's shoulder. Brun-hair had rolled up her the sleeves of her dress and was doing most of the washing. She soaped my bits and I gasped at the discomfort in my swollen balls. More gentle soaping saw my 'lance' raised in salute, for the first time in quite a while. She worked me to the point of a huge release that was almost painful in the quantity passed. I promptly fell asleep again on the other maid's shoulder.

We'd lost three dead on the campaign and had eleven carrying various injuries. I was sorry to lose any, but at least us casualties were now in the finest hands for treatment. There were two widows, who were each given all their men's back-pay that was owing and generous £10 to tide them over. The 'new' Warwicks had all requested to stay with us, so, most unusually, I came back with more men than at our departure.

When I held my first inspection after my return, you could clearly pick the 'campaign men' from the others. There was something about their eyes and the leanness of the faces...

I began to ride, short distances at first but soon was visiting my orchards in Great Thurlow, marvelling at their improved growth – and enjoying Azizah's attentiveness as she gently held my arm in case I stumbled. She took the opportunity to thank me for sending news of her family and their safety, her eyes shining as she smiled in gratitude. I told her that I had sent word to them in a coded message that their 'gemstone' was safe in England. She gasped and hugged me, saying words in her language, before stepping back and apologising in Saxon. I smiled and waved away her concern, then placed her hand back on my arm, so we could continue our walk.

Every day I went a little further up the Keep stairs, with my guards keeping a close eye on me. I could soon trot all the way to the top in just my shirt, hose and slippers; then added my repaired gambeson and boots, then the chainmail and finally my sword-belt.
Letters arrived each day throughout August, with news of the campaign and, later, of the negotiations.
Our capture of Baldwin De Redvers had taken the fight out of Matilda's forces. Many of them refused to believe his absence was unintended and assumed this was a play by the Earl of Devon to finesse a position with the King. With Baldwins consistent record of firm support for the Empress, this was preposterous, but in our times, the mere fact that it was a possibility was all that mattered. No major battles occurred from the morning he was found… absent. All factions moved here and there but with no real purpose and only skirmishes or minor battles occurred. Eventually a truce was offered by Brian of Wallingford, on behalf of all lords on Matilda's side – which, in any case, was a rapidly reducing number.
The Kings army massed at Cirencester, taking up an impressively strong defensive position on the slopes to the west of the town. The opposing lords were permitted to bring personal escorts but nothing more. Those proud Earls were required to walk the final hundred yards, up the slope to the Kings tent. No more inconvenience was put upon the renegades, as King Stephen was attempting to reunite his realm.
Lord Roger led the negotiations towards a lasting peace, which ultimately led to no loss of titles, some relatively small loss of lands but simply eye-watering amounts of compensation to the Crown. Earl Baldwins dues alone were said to total over £10,000 – in ransom and fines. The Empress Matilda was long gone by now, back to Normandy to re-join her husband. We all assumed she would try again; because she, herself, had lost nothing in this attempt.

A Kings messenger arrived on the 9th of September, late in the day. I bade him take a meal in the Hall and had the Warden find him a room in the Keep for the night.

I called for Azizah and Gerald to meet me in my parlour. We sat as I broke the heavy wax seals on each of the three scrolls. My heart raced in anticipation of the contents. This first referred to myself, I had to read the words twice out loud before they began to seem real. For my services to the Crown during the summer campaign, and my action to save Gloucester town at a critical time, I was to add the title of Lord Fulbourn to my rank and hold the honour of the 'The Five Manors of Fulbourn', owing taxes and 600 spears direct to the King.

At my first reading, Gerald's eyes opened wide as he pulled some paper from his leather bag of bits and pieces. Azizah found him a quill pen and he scratched us a map of the manors.

"This was carved out of Huntingdon's lands, my lord," he said, "part of his penance for riding for Matilda."

He finished his inking, blew on the paper and held it up for me and Azizah. We could see Haverhill and Walden right at the bottom of Gerald's map, and a huge triangle of land extending nearly to Cambridge in the northwest and then northeast to Novum Forum[85]. These lands butted on to my Walden and my Great Thirlmere and were more than twice the size of my existing holdings.

"Fulbourn has a small stone castle, "went on Gerald, "the land is rich for farming and sheep – and I've heard that Dunmowe Manor[86] alone produces a huge amount of coin each year for the owner..."

It was my turn to stand and hug Azizah.

The second scroll was another surprise.

I was almost dreading a large reward in coin for the men. They would then be likely to lose it or piss it up the wall, or both – and in any case, they would be lost to me as soldiers. However, I read out that Haverhill was to be extended about 10 miles eastwards, to the border of the Kanewella manor.

---

[85] The Roman name still in use in the 12th century, now known as Newmarket

[86] This is unrelated to Dunmow village, thirty miles away in Essex

So, I would be responsible for more taxes and spears from the enlarged fief but there would be some more income from this land, if no additional title. The meat of this message was that significant grants of land within this extension would go to all the men on the campaign.

The third scroll gave the three ex-poachers an additional and larger area of farmland.

I was much relieved. The soldiers couldn't lose this reward and I would have a chance to keep some of them at least. I doubted many would wish to be farmers, guessing they would prefer the modest annual income from the land.

After a private gathering with my campaign men, they did indeed all decline to be farmers and voted for the extra income, which would afford them good housing for life in Haverhill town and... a much better class of wife. We then held a public ceremony to hand out the several dozen individual grants of land that Gerald and Jeannot had taken several days to write and record. I took some time to take in just how wealthy this all made me. This would enable me to send larger amounts to my parents each quarter and I also celebrated by ordering myself a spare coif and an embroidered cloak.

Another idea of mine was a secret, a new purple and white gown for Azizah, this one with much gold threading and detailing.

I had the finished gown placed in her room, displayed upright on a wooden stand, while she was busy elsewhere. Then I sought her out and told her here was a new little thing in her room and could she put it on before meeting me in the Hall. Her guards had a word with me later and told me she had screamed in delight at the sight of the gown. Dinner that night proved to be a truly astonishing feast, even by our standards. Azizah came out from the kitchen, just before the meal was served, radiant in her stunning new gown. Everyone in the Hall gasped, stood, bowed then clapped. She acknowledged the greeting and walked gracefully to join the senior staff at our high table on the dais. We all bowed to her and she returned a full and graceful curtsey, then took her seat next to me. She gripped my arm and whispered her thanks, her eyes shining with happiness. Next day, with Azizah and Jeannot, I took a strong escort and made the easy one-day ride to Dunmowe Manor. We had overnight provisions in case the place was a ruin but found quite the absolute opposite. With no permit from the monarch to build a castle, the Huntingdons had created a stone-built, high-walled and moated... 'manor house'! The moat was wider, deeper and faster flowing than most established castles had, and the walls and house had battlements all round. It was about half the area of Haverhill castle, with a wide mound under the three-story house. This wide house took up much of the space within the walls, but leaving room for stables, barracks and workshops.

Inside the house was other-worldly. Wooden floors and ornate tapestries. There were many small windows, all with little sections of greenish glass. I noticed each window had a mighty wooden shutter available to protect it in time of conflict. The residence had the air of 'palace' rather than 'house'. Even Azizah was... surprised and she had no doubt been inside real palaces. The staff were all present, seemed organised and in good condition - certainly not drunk and were able to clearly introduce themselves.

I introduced our party and it seems we were expected.

Azizah curtseyed to me and left to inspect the ground-floor kitchens, with four guards keeping close to her. I had the Steward show me round the upstairs and up on to the battlements. I noticed the place was understrength for soldiers and resolved to improve that. I had Jeannot taking notes as we viewed the place.

On our way down from the defences, a couple of well-dressed and very comely young ladies appeared from one of the upstairs rooms. Seems Earl Huntingdon had thought of every... comfort to install here. They had just introduced themselves when Azizah appeared. She clearly took an instant disapproval of these two but said nothing – well not then anyway!

All our party were visibly impressed by the obvious wealth this place exuded. We had more than ample rooms upstairs for one each for the night, for me, Azizah and Jeannot. The men found plenty of room in the barracks and third sergeant sorted out the guard rota for the night. We had an excellent dinner, with some fine wine for us, and lemonade as always for Azizah. The very large but warm and cosy bedrooms gave us a restful night, well for some of us...

Next morning at breakfast, the two young ladies we'd found here, were closely and cosily sitting with a blushing Jeannot. Seems he'd had visitors in the night. Which did explain the smirks on the faces of my guards when I came out of my room earlier.

In a private moment, Azizah... suggested that 'the biccen'[87] should be moved on, as she didn't trust them. I found that strange as she seemed to have no problem with our maids... attending to me, but no matter, this pair were nothing to me. I instructed the Steward to have them leave and not return.

Shortly after breakfast, the Warden of Dunmowe appeared at the gate, and was allowed in by my men after a brief interrogation and checking with the Steward. He looked terrified at missing my arrival and grovelled his apologies while down on both knees in the hallway. Seems he had been out collecting taxes.

"Warden," I said to still his gushing of words "stand-up."

When he did, I introduced myself, shook his hand and said "Never apologise for collecting revenue. Have you eaten today?"

He looked dumb-founded and shook his head. I waved him off to the kitchen, telling him to find me after he'd had some food.

A little later, we saddled up to tour the lands of the manor. The Warden first showed us the lake, that was only 200 yards from the walls. It had many willows, casting their branches over the water. Many ducks and some swans were floating effortlessly with the light breeze. Around the far side of the lake, we walked our horses up to a long, dense hedge, then through a tall archway of flowers into an ornamental garden stretching away up a long slope. There must have been well over six acres of various plants, bushes and flowers. Some rustic peasants were toiling away on one side – they doffed their caps and bowed to us. At the top of the garden we stopped and looked back, to see the lake and its trees as a backdrop to the garden. Our soldiers seemed very puzzled as to the purpose of this place. Azizah was speechless with delight at the scenery. We left the garden, going on to see ranks of orchards, miles of fields in various

---

[87] Saxon for bitches

stages of crop rotation[88] with more peasants working away - and working harder when they saw us approach. Then many more miles of grassland with sheep, so many sheep and the occasional shepherd with a dog or two.

Our party stopped at an inn and all had a lunch of a very good stew. Half the escort ate first, then the other half.

The innkeeper seemed surprised when I instructed my Warden to pay for the food. Seems the previous owner of this demesne didn't bother with such detail...

We toured two more of the smaller manors within my domain of Fulbourn; the lands all seemed to be very well managed.

I was struck by the difference in the appearance of the fields - so different from the large areas in Warwickshire that we were used to. Even Haverhill had many large fields, divided into strips, that were lent to serfs as payment for their work for me.

Here in Suffolk, the land was used hedge-to-hedge, thus making better use of the acres, even though the fields were generally smaller. Indeed, with the high hedges, this patchwork of farmland reminded me of my father's tales of his native Normandy.

I turned us back towards Dunmowe as the sun began to lower in the sky and we reached there at sunset. An even better dinner was served that night and we enjoyed a quiet night - for all this time.

We viewed the final two manors on the following morning; again, all was in good order and both looked very productive. In arriving back at Dunmowe from a different direction this time, the Warden had a surprise to show us; a set of stables and breeding paddocks.

The headman of the stables was introduced to me and he explained that Earl Huntingdon liked to breed horses here and then race them at a track outside the village of Novum Forum. I just shook my head at the extravagance of some 'rich people'... The man went on to explain that the Earl made money by wagering on the races and the

---

[88] The practice of growing a series of different types of crops in the same area across a sequence of growing seasons. It allows the land to recover its nutrients, acidity, also reducing weeds and pests.

horses that came from this arrangement made excellent messenger steeds, that could outrun any pursuit. Now that last most definitely got my attention.

While we were talking, Azizah had walked her horse to a huge paddock where a single large and slightly unusual-looking horse was calmly eating grass, in the middle of the its enclosure. She dismounted, tied her horse to the fence, stooped to pluck some lush long grass, picked a couple of large carrots from a sack by the gate and proceeded to walk through the gate, towards the animal.

As she neared the beast, you could see just how large it was compared to her. It carried its head differently... lower than I was used to, more stretched out. The headman turned to see what I was looking at over his shoulder and gasped

"Oh no, my lord, the lady is in terrible danger... the stallion is so vicious" and clamped his hands over his mouth, clearly not knowing what to do.

When Azizah was about ten yards from the horse, it pawed the ground with a hoof. She stopped and bowed to it and damn me if the horse didn't bow back!

All the while, I could just hear her purring in what I thought was Arabic. She then walked slowly but smoothly up to the horse and fed it some grass. Then the horse raised its head and rested it on her shoulder, as she stroked it and played with its ear and mane. She fed it the carrots, then reached up to give it a hug round the neck, purr some more in its ear and finish with a kiss on its forehead.

She then backed away a few paces before they did their bowing thing again and she walked gracefully back to the gate. The headman and a gathered crowd of stable-boys were now standing transfixed at the scene as it unfolded in front of them. They stood rooted to the spot, until Azizah reached them and nodded a "Good Morning" to them; then they hurriedly bowed and replied to her. Seems the stallion had killed a lad a couple of months before...

Azizah walked over to me and gave a small curtsey.

"I like nice horse you have, Lord Walter, it has family from Arabia" she said smiling wide. Then nodded to the bowing and currently speechless headman.

Azizah took my offered arm and we toured the rest of the stables.

She discussed in detail with the headman, about the animals and the breeding methods. She was stuck for the right Saxon words at some points, but they clearly understood each other for the most part. Like many before him, the man was visibly stunned, not just by her looks but as much by her knowledge, directness and willingness to talk to someone as an equal.

After an adequate lunch at a different inn, we headed back, but this time with plenty of daylight remaining.

A thought occurred to me, and I led us back to the Dunmowe garden, had the Warden and our escort wait on guard outside and gestured to Azizah to follow me back to the top of the ornamental area. We tied our horses to a nearby small tree and sat next to each other on a long wicker chair.

"I have like this in Nishapor," Azizah sighed, "colour not like this, but I have water and flower, and tree, and bird."

We spent some time enjoying the view in the warmer-than-usual late September sunshine. I named all the things we could see that she didn't know in Saxon and finally got her to remember to put an 's' on words for 'more than one'.

With sunset approaching, we reluctantly returned to the manor house, for another good meal and restful night. We returned to Haverhill the next day, all was working well at my main castle – I had to smile at that, as I had a few now!

A couple of routine days followed. The last parts of the harvest were brought in and another batch of new men began training; I inspected the whole castle from top to bottom, finding several jobs that needed completing before the onset of winter.

Then, we had another 'all lords' message delivered by Kings messenger. I groaned inwardly, and my heart went faster, as I remembered the challenge that the last such missive brought to us. I offered the messenger a late lunch and called for Azizah, Gerald and Jeannot to meet me in my parlour. When we were all seated, I showed them the roll of paper, and clearly all shared my concern. I broke the seal and unrolled the message...

I read through it and gasped, read it again to be sure, then felt tears well up in my eyes. The others all looked at me with a mixture of curiosity and dread, but eager to know the cause of my emotion.

I found I couldn't speak and passed the paper to Gerald.

He read through it, gasped, and we shared a meaningful look.
He cleared his voice and said "The King informs all lords of England that the Pope has issued a 'Papal Bull'[89], to the effect that the Mongols have offended Christianity and are now regarded as the enemy of Holy Church. The Mongols have allied to the Arab countries. The noble nation of Persia is now our ally against the Arab hordes."

He repeated himself in simpler words for Azizah, who shrieked in delight. We leapt to our feet and hugged, then shook hands with Gerald and Jeannot. With much backslapping, for the men, we all realised and felt a weight, a shadow had been lifted from us. The unspoken but nevertheless real dread among us was a repeat of the summons that could imprison Persian people, or worse. I thought of Lord Rogers words from back in the Spring and nodded in appreciation of his foresight.

Azizah was suddenly unable to stand and I called for some nettle tea for her, as I knelt and held her hand. A beaming Gerald and Jeannot, bowed and left us, as the maid brought in the tea. As Azizah sipped her drink, I did ponder that this did not free her land from the grip of the Mongols but did at least ensure the safety of her family and any other Persians in exile. A truly momentous day.

After some time, it was now my turn to be supporting Azizah over to the Keep and up to her room, our combined guard details following. I tried to suggest that, just for once, she should leave responsibility for dinner to the kitchen staff that night, but she would hear none of it. I smiled, squeezed her hands in mine and left her to her rest, perhaps take a nap. As I closed the door behind me and walked down the corridor, I sighed, thinking "I so... much... wanted to kiss her..."

The next day, the Warden was due to leave for London to pay a very large sum of tax to the Crown, for my now much expanded holdings. Thinking ahead, I also asked him to find another... specialty item.

---

[89] An international decree issued by The Pope of the Catholic Church. It is named after the leaden seal (bulla) that was traditionally appended to the end in order to authenticate it.

Following the news of her and her family being safe and after much thought, I decided to grant Azizah a title of her own. I had more fiefs and demesnes now than I could manage with existing staff, and, if I was honest with myself, I wanted to give her more of a reason to stay with us – well, really, to stay with me. Also, for my honour, and my care for her, I would have no part in... trapping her here at Haverhill.

So, before the next Manor Court, I prepared all my castle-folk and swore them to secrecy. The morning of the court session, I asked Azizah to put on her new gown and attend the Hall, to "Watch a ceremony" I said.

She walked serenely into the Hall, looking radiant in the stunning gown. Unknown to her, everyone at the castle we could cram into the building was there and bowed, clapped and cheered her arrival. She curtseyed her thanks at the welcome but looked somewhat puzzled. My Marshal gently indicated she should join me on the dais. When she did so, I nodded to her and she curtseyed gracefully and deeply – still looking very puzzled.

I then presented her with a scroll of title, she was now owner of one of my five new manors; she was Lady Azizah of Dunmowe.

Her hands shook and she gasped as she received the paper.

"Is big house? Is garden? Is horses?" she asked breathlessly.

I smiled wide and nodded.

She squeaked in delight and flew into my arms for a brief hug while the crowd cheered. Then she realised where she was, quickly let go, stepped back and gave me a wonderful curtsey, saying, "Thank you, my lord."

I was proud to bow in reply to the new 'Lady Dunmowe'.

She in turn, curtseyed to the crowd, who just as proudly, bowed in reply.

I nodded to the Marshal to clear the Hall for the Court to begin and turned to Azizah, who was shaking with excitement.

"I live there? You want me live there?" she asked.

"You can live there," I replied, "but we would miss you very much, I would miss you."

I reached for her hands and squeezed them, saying "Let us visit your land tomorrow." She squeezed back and nodded happily.

We arrived at Dunmowe manor house the next day, late in the afternoon. I called all the staff together and announced that The Lady Azizah was the new owner of the demesne. She toured the house again, but with new eyes this time, weighing up changes and additions she might like to make.

The following morning, she appeared in a plain brown dress and newly-made boots, and wanted to go straight to the stables, to renew her acquaintance with the stallion.

On our arrival, I informed the head of stables and the boys of the change in owner and let Azizah step forward and request a saddle for the stallion. All bar one of the stable-lads recoiled in fright at the very thought. Azizah focused on the tall, thin lad who didn't seem as concerned and asked, "What is you name? You scare of horse?"

"I am Conrad my lady, and I am scared to ride it," he said, "but I watched you with the horse last time and if you are with me, I will saddle Diablo."

The stable-head spoke to me, "That's the name they gave the horse in Spain, my lord, when they captured him from the Moors. It means 'The Devil'…" I explained this to Azizah, and she smiled in amusement.

A saddle was fetched, then Azizah and a saddle-carrying Conrad walked into 'The Devils' paddock. The horse seemed to recognise Azizah and trotted over, to receive a couple of carrots and a lot of fuss. Azizah introduced Conrad to the horse and seemed to ask permission to put on the saddle and reins. Sensing acquiescence, Azizah gently said "Saddle now" and Conrad did just that. Azizah put the reins carefully and smoothly over Diablo's head, then with Conrad having fastened the girths, he turned and took a knee for Azizah to step up on, then boosted her by lifting her booted ankle, and keeping his eyes firmly to the ground.

The stable-people gasped and stared open-mouthed at the sight of Azizah on the horse – the previous attempt to do this had ended with the saddle being kicked over the paddock fence.

Conrad quickly adjusted the stirrups and ran out through the gate. Even in the plain dress, Azizah looked magnificent, completely in her element. She spoke to the horse and gently nudged it with her heels to walk. Then to a canter. Then, at the furthest corner of the large enclosure, she urged it to a full gallop across the pasture.

She stopped the horse in the corner nearest the watching crowd, spoke to the beast and gently tugged the reins. He stood on his hind legs, pawing the air and whinnying defiance at the gasping audience. With the horse back on four feet, she whirled it round and took off at a gallop again, straight towards the old wreck of a cart near the side fence. It had no wheels, just the flat-bed sitting on the ground, but the sides were quite high. Now this finally had me concerned, because up until now, I could see all this as natural to Azizah but this... this could end up badly and sadly for our little lady. I watched transfixed, as she urged the horse on, with her words and her heels, towards the cart. The horse took off, its neck coming up and back towards Azizah. They sailed over together, and the animal landed in perfect stride, going on to kick its rear hooves up with enjoyment of the feat. The crowd cheered and I gulped in relief. Azizah rode back to near the gate and beckoned Conrad back in. She swung herself out of the saddle, doing something with her dress to stop it rising and slid gracefully back down to the ground. While Azizah petted and coo'd at the horse, she slipped the reins off and Conrad took the saddle away.

With a final kiss on its forehead, Azizah dismissed the huge horse, which friskily romped away out into the middle of the paddock Azizah walked through the gate and over to me, her eyes shining with the excitement, enjoyment and satisfaction of the adventure. I was so proud of her and so relieved she was now safe, that I completely forgot myself and hugged her tightly and almost lifted her off the ground, before remembering we weren't alone and quickly letting her go. She smiled warmly at me and squeezed my hands; I think she understood that I was very pleased for her but also that I had been more than a little concerned.

We spent a delightful couple of days, touring her demesne and introducing the country-folk to their new Lady. With her purple and white gown back on, she was every inch the perfect, and fully justified, chatelaine of this manor. I had brought an extra-large escort with us, in case Azizah wanted to stay at Dunmowe but she quickly widened her eyes at the suggestion and shook her head, saying "All much fast, Lord Walter." So, we returned to Haverhill together and found the Warden was back from London.

He said the trip went well and then whispered that 'the item' was in my room and that it was a very fine example but had been a little... expensive.

The next day, the Warden and Azizah spent all day, going through the accounts relating to Dunmowe. She saw that even with the hefty amount of tax owing to the King and allowing for the 300 soldiers she would need for protection and war-time-liability, she would still be a very wealthy woman. The demesne had so many revenue activities, in fruit, vegetable, rye, barley and wheat farming, sheep, cattle and horse breeding, leatherwork and other things, it was unlikely that any one blight, disease or market collapse would cripple her economy. At dinner that night she was very quiet indeed. When the other senior staff had left my table, she squeezed my arm and requested a walk. I called for our cloaks and we took a turn around the castle. We were up on the gatehouse tower as the last light faded away and our guards drew back to give us some privacy.

She turned to me and seemed to be struggling for words.

"All much .." she whispered, "all much fast. I have nothing when come here, nothing but one dress. I speak thank you but is small word... words" she corrected herself.

I smiled at her and said, "I need someone to look after Dunmowe, you will be the best for the manor."

She gripped my hands then moved to my side and took my arm for the rest of our walk.

What Azizah didn't know was that while she had been busy with the Warden, I had been in consultation with the carpenter and Blaedswith, the Marshals wife. They were tasked with making something quite large, to go on the wall of the Hall opposite from the dais. The next day, a basic varnished framework was mounted on the wall. It seemed to be a very large but empty picture frame, about the size of a dining table. The following day, the frame had a pair of curtains covering it, with many cheeky castle-folk trying to see behind, only to find it was still empty. On the day after, it looked just the same, curtains drawn but two guards were now posted, to stop any peeking.

After lunch, I directed my senior staff to gather round the frame and dismissed the guards. With a dramatic flourish I pulled the cord to open the curtains.

It was a picture entitled 'All The Known World – A Fair Map'; it was very detailed in parts, basic in others.

It showed England, Wales, Scotland and Ireland at the top left, at the lower edge was the wide stretch of the lands of 'Africanus', and it went across to Persia and beyond at the right edge.

There was much thoughtful looking and chin-rubbing.

I think we were all dismayed how small 'we' appeared on this representation, especially when compared to France or Spain.

Azizah was very intrigued but then tutted, loudly when she saw the images representing the nations on the extreme right of the map.

"Are not 'Dog-head-people' there, and not People-One-Foot there' she said. But otherwise she seemed fascinated by it all.

I had a long wooden rod, ready to indicate the main countries for the non-readers. Then I pointed out Azizah's journey from Persia through the Holy Lands, then by sea to Spain and then by other boat to England. This done, I drew her attention back along that route, to point out the island of Rhodes that was in the sea a moderate distance from Acre, a port on the coast of the Holy Land.

I gently said, "That is where your family is, Azizah."

She nodded and was clearly holding back a tear, it did seem such a long way.

I left her alone with the implications shown by the map, giving her a couple of days to settle. Then I asked her into the parlour after dinner and sat her down. I explained that if she wanted to travel to Rhodes, then I would arrange and pay for a ship to take her in the next sailing season. She gasped, then gripped my hands and sobbed. I knelt by her side and held her tight round her shoulders until her crying reduced.

She nodded her thanks, stood up, curtseyed and rushed off to her room.

Azizah was very quiet all the next day, so I suggested a visit to Dunmowe. She smiled and nodded at this and we set off early the next morning. Soon after we arrived, I said I wanted to catch the sunset in the garden. This time we left our horses at the gate, with our escort spread wide to protect us.

Azizah took my arm as we strolled up the gently sloping path to the wicker chair. This time I made sure to sit close to her and took her hand as she sat down.

Seeing an eagle far above us, gave me an idea.

I pointed to Azizah, then up at the eagle and repeated the moves. "Me, bird?" she asked.

I nodded, then mimed catching the bird, pretending to look at it in my hand and stroke it, before 'releasing' the imaginary creature to fly away. Then I mimed two things, the bird coming back to land on my wrist and the bird flying away and away, to not return.

She gasped at the meanings behind all this play.

"Azizah," I said, as I reached for and kissed her hand, "I adore you, care for you very much, but I will not... trap you" and mimed the catching of the bird again, shaking my head, and then mimed the release.

"Thank you, Walter," she said, "I care you much also."

She mimed tapping her head, and tapping over her heart and stomach, as I had done in that cold forest many months ago.

"I have thinkings," she went on, "and I have... feelings. So much thinkings... so much feelings..."

She squeezed my hand and we settled back to watch the sunset. We both sighed, as a distant coughing from the Second Sergeant could be heard, reminding us we should be back before last light, if at all possible.

A couple of days later, once we returned to Haverhill, I found the castle-folk had developed an interest in the now-curtained map. Respectful groups quietly gathered in the Hall, after the evening meal, around the wall where it hung. So, if enough people showed interest, I would ask Gerald or Jeannot to act as 'guide'. The curtains were drawn, and maids held extra lamps and much interest was shown. In fact, many people came back for repeated tellings of the story of Azizah's journey to England, tales of the First Crusade or the Pilgrimage routes to Lourdes, Rome or Jerusalem. The castle rumour-mill never managed to miss a cause for speculation.

With the appearance of the map and Azizah's increasingly quiet and withdrawn manner, it was whispered that she was leaving Haverhill and going back to Persia, or The Holy Land, or to Rhodes...

The gossip spread to the town, and on the day of the next Manor Court there was a queue of many dozens, lined up from the castle gates to far back up the road. It quickly became clear that most of these were not plaintiffs, but town and country folk who wished to simply pay their respects to Lady Azizah. She had given them continuity and fairness of justice, helped many mothers and babies; also, she regularly sent her now famous pastry-parcels of meat and vegetables, by cart, to widows and the sick in outlying hamlets of our domain.

The people would enter the Hall when their turn came, stand in front of Their Lady, bend a knee, deeply bow or curtsey as appropriate and move away. This clearly caused surprise and a mixture of emotions for Azizah, to add to the swirl of her other feelings.

Azizah's guards came to me on more than a couple of mornings, showing signs of deep disquiet and conflicted loyalties. They whispered in private that Their Lady could be heard sobbing at length on several nights, in between her long prayers. All I could say was that I understood their concerns, but matters must be allowed to take their course.

As October drew on, the evening light ended earlier and earlier. The extra gloom each day matched my mood as winter approached.

I still saw Azizah on most days, and we talked much, about anything and everything - except her troubles. She would walk with me, arm-in-arm but the relaxed and joking banter we used to share, seemed to have gone – and I felt she was going too.

Later in the month, Azizah announced she was commissioning 'De Marren Hall'. This would be a very large wooden building, erected on an old disused motte she had located near the Fens, not far from her horse-breeding establishment.

The Hall would be used as a 'manor court' for the whole of my new lands. Its location was quite central to the region and access from far and wide via boat on the Fens was possible. Our initial monthly court sessions at Fulbourn Castle had not gone well, as that place was at the extreme western point of my lands. People just could not travel that far. This idea of this new court was obvious, with hindsight, but I had missed seeing the possibility due to my burden of other concerns. This was a perfect example of the reasons for appointing Azizah to assist with my domains – and added weight to how much I would miss her when she departed.

There was one small puzzle for me, she always took Luther with her on her visits to Dunmowe and seemed to be still taking the trouble to improve her Saxon.

Indeed, I heard one tale of a stable-hand mistreating a foal and then joking about it with the nearby lads when in earshot of Their Lady. Apparently, the volume and savagery of the dressing down she delivered, in the most direct and fluent Saxon was in instant legend in those parts. The man was sent to the dungeon in Haverhill for my judgement, as Azizah didn't trust herself to not execute him.

On one of the last days of October, a Kings messenger arrived.
I took a breath and exchanged glances with Gerald and Jeannot, as we sat in the parlour to open the sealed scroll. This was clearly a letter solely for me and not 'other lords' as well.

With some trepidation I read the contents and then passed it to Gerald.

He raised his eyebrows and passed the letter to Jeannot.

"Seems our domain is to have a visitor soon" I said.

"Indeed, sire," responded Gerald "there are only guidelines here, but the Kings stay is likely to be two or three nights, probable in the middle of the ten-day period mentioned."

We all nodded our shared understanding that Royal travel arrangements were never announced in any detail. It would be too easy for dark forces to plot against him if his whereabouts were known too exactly in advance.

"How large a retinue is there likely to be?" I asked Gerald, as he had witnessed several such visits at Chester over the years.

"The household staff will likely be around a dozen, my lord," he replied "this King is not extravagant in that way... but the escort could be two hundred or more..."

I sighed a bit at that, as the King had chosen to visit Dunmowe rather than Haverhill, this would all be quite a squeeze.

"I imagine he has visited there before and has good memories of the house" mused Gerald.

"Mmmmm," I said, my mind racing ahead, "we must begin preparations immediately, including tents and at least, defensive stakes for our men at Dunmowe, because the Kings escort will take every inch of barrack space inside the walls. Our men must have some protection to stay outside those walls..." I went on to ask "But... why us? Why now?" Jeannot ventured to suggest that the King was probably visiting Count Aubrey, to gauge his leanings for the following year and then travelling north to visit with his loyal Norfolks. Gerald concurred with this and we set to the planning and letter writing. Azizah was certainly going to have some new patrons for her wonderful menus.

As November began, Azizah advanced her preparations at Dunmowe, and we prepared for an obvious possible question that the King might ask... why hadn't he seen Azizah at Berkhamsted castle that day with the Persian ambassador?
Our final version of the story was that Azizah was waiting as next in line to see the King. With her Saxon, she could have appeared by herself and as a lady would not be appearing with Nousha. 'Nousha' had sadly 'expired with a fever'. As to her actual identity, if asked, Azizah would state she was a distant cousin, through marriage, to the slightly older Princess Azizah, and named for her out of respect.

As we so neatly 'disposed' of 'Nousha', the Grim Reaper must have been at our shoulders chuckling to himself, prior to resuming his never-ending work. A fire in Haverhill town caused the demise of eleven citizens when a burning row of cottages collapsed on some onlookers.
And then The Reaper's Scythe struck closer to home...
Our trusty Luther collapsed at Haverhill with a cramping of the stomach, some bleeding from his insides; then with agonizing pain in his side[90] and the need for much poppy-juice. Even with the nuns and Azizah doing their best, there was no saving him. The ladies concurred that it was a poison of the gut, but all potions failed this time.

---

[90] Acute appendicitis was usually a death-knell in these times

Azizah had called for a fresh wild pig to be hunted and brought to her as quickly as possible. Two hunting parties immediately raced to the forest. On the return of the fastest group, she swiftly gutted the animal and studied its insides. After some thought and prayer, she returned to the White Room to cut out the poison. More poppy juice was administered but Luther was fading in front of their eyes. He had a seizure, came out of it and lay back on the litter. He grasped Azizah's hand with his left hand, the senior nuns with his right, looked above him and the Sister began the last rites. The light went from his eyes and Azizah cried a river of tears at the realisation.

We were all saddened but Azizah was devastated at the loss of her loyal, discrete and steadfast companion. To my surprise, I attended his funeral at the town church and found the simple ceremony quite settling. Father Aldous allowed Azizah to visit on the following day. Her escort surrounded the cemetery, facing outwards, as she stood by the grave, chanting in what even I now recognised as Arabic – the language they shared. Luther was greatly missed. He had been promoted on merit to assistant warden at Dunmowe, had become engaged to the local mayor's daughter and was an important part of Azizah's court days. With him there, she felt she could take on and judge any case with competency but now, she felt lost.

Jeannot mentioned that, in reality, on most days Our Lady needed no help from anyone in Manor Court but Azizah confided to me that she was unsettled and cancelled the hearings for two weeks.

This gave her new trading connections time to travel far and wide. Merchants were eager to assist, as they valued her growing business and her fair and prompt payments.

The first Arabic-to-Saxon translator they found was an old soldier with years spent in the Holy Lands, but his attitude to Azizah nearly got himself killed by her guards, so was clearly not acceptable. No other prospects emerged at all, in spite of letters sent expensively as far afield as Spain.

Then I had an idea that could solve the problem – I asked Jeannot if he remembered the two Persian girls we had seen at Berkhamsted Castle, which he did. And after considerable thought, he remembered the domain that their steward was from. A quick word with Gerald revealed that the steward's castle was under the

ownership of William d'Aubigny, 2nd Earl of Arundel, one of
Mathilda's supporters in the previous campaigns.

Jeannot sighed at the anticipation of another long, cold journey, as I
chuckled at his obvious discomfort.

I gave him a significant sum in three purses, with instructions to buy
the slaves if they spoke adequate Saxon.

He left Haverhill with a small escort as I set out to briefly visit
Dunmowe, to encourage Azizah to hold her court as usual that week
and defer any cases she wasn't happy with. She wasn't delighted at
the prospect but recognised there was a duty to fulfil.

In the next few days she planned, and had the Dunmowe kitchen
staff practise, the menu that would be placed before the King.
The recipes were tried out on the local minor dignitaries, who were
very impressed to be invited as a reward for their efforts in making
the wider manor run smoothly.

The Kings messenger then arrived, announcing the Royal arrival at
Dunmowe for the following day. I rode at once for Dunmowe to
break the news and was amazed at the number and size of the
changes that Azizah had managed to commission. The West wall
had had a small gatehouse created through the solid masonry. This
led to a new wood-walled bailey that extended all the way to the
edge of the moat in that direction. Inside, the kitchens had been
extended back to the edge of the rise the building was set upon, and
upstairs, two guest rooms had been connected with a new doorway
to make an apartment with lavish furnishings everywhere and fine
paintings on the walls.

The King arrived the next afternoon, our roof guards having
reported distant scouting activity for the previous two hours. His
close escort extended out of the gate, over the drawbridge and
along the moat. All these were smart and alert, their heads turning
constantly while the King was in the open. As Gerald predicted, his
retinue was not large but consisted of visibly very wealthy and
senior lords as companions and personal bodyguard, together with
a couple of stewards and a few servants.

Their horses were all magnificent animals, with ornate leather saddles, caparisons[91] and bardings[92].

I welcomed him at the bottom of the steps to the house, along with the senior staff, so we were at no point looking down on His Highness.

I introduced him to the, now veiled, Lady Azizah - who was clearly an intriguing surprise to him, but he made no comment beyond returning our greetings most graciously.

Our other staff were acknowledged with dignity.

He seemed very tired and drawn and I decided to show him directly to his rooms, rather than attempt yet more introductions and drinks in the parlour.

Four very large Royal wolf-hounds followed him upstairs. The size of them caused me and Azizah to share a glance and a memory of one very cold night in a forest...

The Royal escort of 220 was soon taking up every inch of barrack space within the stone walls. My Haverhills and the Dunmowes, had moved into the wooden fort and made the best of the basic accommodation within. In any case, they were not going to be idle, as the senior lord in charge of the Kings escort agreed with my suggestion to send out strong roving patrols through the visit, both day and night. Some of his men and all my Haverhills would be the 'muscle', and the Dunmowes the 'brains' of these pre-emptive actions. Having delegated the defences for the moment, we adjourned for a taste of cider. We discussed the state of the realm and the lord confirmed the King had come from an extended visit with Count Aubrey – but declined any comment or speculation on where the Royal party might next be going, or not going. The Kings first steward came down to let us know that the King would take dinner after Vespers[93].

---

[91] A caparison is a cloth or other covering laid over a horse or other animal for protection and/or decoration

[92] Where a caparison is for armour it is known as barding.

[93] 6pm

The captain of the escort had inspected the whole house and all approaches, and stationed four men at each entrance, as well as those on the walls.

By now, the smells emerging from the kitchen were making our mouths water, and up in the tiny gallery to the dining room, four musicians began their final preparations.

The meal was a triumph for Azizah and her staff.

She'd been unimpressed by tales of the usual fare at large English banquets, which typically was a swan stuffed with a goose, stuffed with a duck, and so on, down to the smallest game bird available. Instead, she planned several small courses with each recipe from a different country.

The first was the English 'Sorcell Rosted, Wodekoke, & Snyte'[94], followed by a white flatfish from France, sheep-cheese and olives from Spain and finally a lamb dish with apricots and very novel rice from Morocco. All courses were served by maids in a costume representing the national dress of the source country, which required some rapid changes of clothes that entertained the guards on the door!

After a short pause to let all that settle, an enormous apple and blackberry pie with cream was the dessert.

Yet even this pie had extra entertainment value. The crust was fashioned as a castle, a very substantial one; one with an inner and outer bailey... No name or colours were showing but soon a chuckling spread around the top table as it was realised that this was a very fair representation of Chester Castle!

A maid bobbed a curtsey in front of the King presented him with a fine wooden box.

He opened it to find a pastry knife with the Royal standard engraved on the blade.

With a wicked smile on his face, Stephen proceeded to divide up the 'castle' of his frequent enemy with his 'royal knife'!

---

[94] All small game birds, wrapped in bacon or salted ham and then baked in an oven.

After the meal, I invited the King through to the comfort of the very large parlour. I suddenly realised that I hadn't checked on the... decoration in there and was somewhat concerned. However, the parlour at Dunmowe now had paintings of English kings, replacing those of young ladies in various... poses.

The King raised eyebrows in pleased surprise to find his portrait central to the room and next to one of Edward The Confessor. Edward had been notable for advancing the legal system in England and being a fair and effective ruler. The Confessor and his legacy were much admired by King Stephen. It seems Azizah had been listening to Gerald.

The King waved me over to thank me for the hospitality.

I bowed and thanked him but declined the credit, explaining that all at Dunmowe was under the Lady Azizah, and so the King requested her attendance.

I called for another chair to be found and placed to the King's left, then sent a page to invite Azizah to the parlour.

Our Lady had taken her meal in her room; we thought it more diplomatic to respect any possible sensitivities around the King dining with someone of another faith.

A still-veiled Azizah soon appeared in the parlour, her accompanying maids, also veiled, moved to stand in the corners of the room.

She gave the King such a gracious curtsey that he almost bowed in return, as he stood to greet her.

The senior lords of the Kings retinue seemed very sceptical of this meeting but kept their peace. Stephen however was good manners to a fault, seemed politely curious about her and gestured Azizah to take a seat next to him.

I could only catch scraps of the conversation between them as I engaged the other lords about military matters.

Seems their first topic was the paintings, and from there came a discussion of the history and current practice of English criminal law. As the talking went on, I watched Stephens face go through surprise, puzzlement and then to respect. I think they went on to discuss the practicalities of ruling a realm. After a while, Stephen looked in my direction and we exchanged a "who **is** this woman?" look, which I softened with a smile and a nod as if to convey, "you are not dreaming sire!"

Their cosy chat was interrupted by Stephen clearly being in some sudden discomfort. Azizah appeared to ask him what was wrong, and he indicated his stomach hurt, clutching his mid chest[95].

She asked to feel his wrist and forehead and the suddenly very pale Stephen nodded. She then gently held his wrist and rested the back of her hand briefly against his forehead. The senior lords stepped near to intervene, but the King waved them away.

After a couple of minutes, Azizah sat back a little and gently asked him some questions. Stephen then reached for his wine glass with his free right hand as Azizah continued to hold his left wrist. He stopped as Azizah tutted him. And then, dear god, Our Lady wagged a finger at the King of England! Very gently done it was to be sure, but even so!

The watching lords stepped forward once more and Stephen again waved them away, with more irritation this time. He turned back to Azizah, listened some more, nodding ruefully and appearing to whisper some words of agreement. She beckoned one of her maids to come near and issued some crisp instruction in Persian. The maid bobbed curtseys to her Lady and the King and left the room.

The maid returned from the kitchen with a cup of milky-looking drink. I stepped forward this time, to offer to be taster for the drink, but it was my turn to be regally waved away. After a few minutes of sipping the drink, the King looked more comfortable.

He listened as Azizah spoke a little more, with him nodding at intervals. Stephen then beckoned his senior lord and escort commander, informing them that he would be staying at Dunmowe for three nights. The senior began to protest but was silenced by a royal hand held up to end the conversation. Seems one or two nights here had been the plan.

After some more talking with Azizah, King Stephen stood and bade us a good night. We bowed or curtseyed as appropriate as he left to go up to his rooms, accompanied by his servants and his wolf-hounds; well, some of them.

---

[95] This likely being the start of a stomach ulcer, unsurprising for an English monarch during The Anarchy!

The two youngest of the four had taken to sitting either side of Azizah; one with his muzzle resting against her thigh to win some fussing from her. I thought to myself "You lucky dog!"

At Azizah's firm... suggestion, the King rested in the guest apartment all the next day. His meals were delivered upstairs and his prescribed choice of liquids were boiled water, lemonade made from boiled water or the milk, chalk and herb drink as tried the previous day.

Our Lady gently but effectively limited the time various lords had with the King and the various messengers and heralds that arrived were given clear instructions to not expect an immediate reply. Her commanding presence magically ensured compliance, but this was more than unpopular, for several reasons. Azizah's sex, race, religion and status of 'merely lady of a manor' were all held against her by would-be courtiers, but we heard later that all such protests had been quickly met with the Royal hand for silence.

Next morning, the King came down for breakfast in the dining-room. He looked very much improved, with colour in his cheeks and a jovial manner for all.

Afterwards, Azizah's plan for the day was some gentle sight-seeing. The horses were brought around by the extra stable-hands that Dunmowe had recruited for the occasion and we took the short ride to the garden and lake. I could see Azizah had commanded changes here too, there was much more colour on show than my last visit, no doubt from late-blooming flowers from... goodness knows where in the Western world. Azizah and Stephen walked together, followed at a distance by the Persian maids and Stephens two stewards. The titled pair went up the path to the wicker seat and rested for a while, deep in private conversation again; much to the consternation of the senior courtiers who had been left at the gate. They eventually returned to the horses and Azizah guided the Royal party and extensive escort towards where I thought was a rather tumbledown inn.

My stomach was ready for lunch, but I wasn't thrilled with that as a prospect, even without the King being there.

I should have known better; Azizah's ability to organise and delegate seemed to know no bounds!

The inn was transformed, as if a new building, with Royal flags flying. The usual keeper and old crones who worked here were not in evidence, but I did spot four Dunmowe carriages around the back and recognised many of the staff here as Dunmowe cooks and kitchen-maids. Inside was rustic to be sure but all bright and clean. We had a fabulous soup with chicken pie to follow, and lemonade of course. I guessed if the King was being... discouraged from alcohol, then we all were.

The escorting soldiers were fed, a dozen at a time, from one of the carriages being taken out to them and serving girls passing up cloth bundles of pastry-parcels and bottles of lemonade. At first, there were groans at the lack of ale or beer, but soon 'mmms' and 'ahhhs' were heard as they tucked into the pastries.

As the day had gone on, I could see the senior lord and the escort commander becoming more tense. They insisted on more and larger patrols, which would increase the strain on the available men quite unreasonably I felt, but we did our best to help.

After lunch, the assembled company leisurely rode the few miles to Azizah's stables. These too had been smartened up and enlarged; I saw many more horses of with the 'lower heads', which seemed to be mostly young mares. The King was taken to view Diablo and was astonished at his first sight of an Arab horse. He recognised it at once, from descriptions given by Templar knights. Stephen engaged in more eager talk with Azizah, about her breeding plans; and there was more grumbling from the distanced members of the retinue. I heard later that Azizah had promised to send Stephen some of her first Arab foals, with sires and dams arranged so that he could in turn breed from those foals. This naturally delighted the King and was further evidence of Our Lady's sure touch when it came to power and influence.

The seasonal failing of the light forced a reluctant Royal departure from the stables. We returned to Dunmowe Manor, had another sumptuous meal and a restful night was had by all.

The King made ready to depart after breakfast the next morning. The reluctance on his face and the relief on the faces of his escort made quite a contrast. His protecting staff were understandably nervous of the extended stay, in a place that was not a full castle.

All our senior staff gathered to see him off and he thanked us all most warmly; but his special thanks were reserved for Azizah. After her curtsey, he gave her an 'almost' bow and grasped her hands in his as he spoke his gratitude for everything.
As he stepped back to leave, he spotted his two younger wolf-hounds were stood between himself and Azizah, looking from him, to her and back again. He roared with laughter and said, "It looks like I have gained some horses and lost a couple of hounds!"
He pointed at the two, then at the spot where Azizah stood and said "Guard", at which they immediately took up positions, sat either side of Azizah, with their heads turning, ready for anything.
With another chuckle from the King and a nod to us all, he sighed and turned away to mount his horse, waved his party to move off and they all departed.
We looked at each other and remarked on how quiet and... spacious Dunmowe had suddenly become.
I had the gates closed, wall-guards set from the least-tired troops we had and sent the rest of my exhausted soldiery off for a meal and then to bed, in their own barracks once more. They walked their aching, saddle-sore selves away, complaining like only soldiers can.
The King and his troops departed westwards, but this meant nothing as I'm sure they changed direction once out of our sight.
We gathered our personal escorts and left Dunmowe to be rearranged, back to its usual state; the temporary fort was to be dismantled, and the wood given to nearby villagers to make the framework of some new housing. Thus, increasing Azizah's already high status in the area.
I rode with Azizah but not much was said after I thanked her for her tremendous efforts with the Kings visit. Her new dogs each seemed happy to lie across the back of any horse, while we were walking the horses; if we cantered for a while they would jump down, bounding along just behind Azizah's horse. Once we walked again, they would look to the nearest escort to help them back up, with a heave on their expensive leather and gold collars.
We reached Haverhill and had a late lunch, again mostly in silence.

Afterwards, I was crossing the Bailey, to see Gerald in the Keep when Jeannot and his party returned. What a sight they presented, all looking grey with fatigue, sagging in their saddles, with their horses too looking exhausted. They showed every sign of one or more nights spent in the open. My curiosity was engaged by three obviously female riders, the taller one of whom had an arm in a sling and seemed to be in significant distress. The two smaller females were sharing one horse.

Jeannot slide from his saddle, walked slowly towards me and bowed. "Good day, my lord," he began "I hope all is well with you?"

"It is thank-you Jeannot," I replied, "how went your journey?"

"We have the two Persian slaves as requested sir, and they have excellent Saxon... but... I did acquire another... item, for which I would crave your guidance, my lord."

"Very well," I said "see me in the parlour before dinner this evening – but first make sure the horses are looked after and the girl, or woman, is taken to the White Room.

"Certainly my lord, I will" he said as he bowed stiffly and wearily walked away.

After a discussion on the current political situation with Gerald, I sent a soldier to ask Azizah to meet me in the Hall.

Just as she arrived, the Persian slave-girls were brought from the kitchen after being given some soup and a quick bath by the maids. One of our maids led them by the hand into the Hall, as Azizah and I turned to meet them.

The girls saw Azizah and the look of profound astonishment on their faces was remarkable to see; their mouths gaped for a second before the threw themselves on the floor, kneeling and crouched down to her, as Azizah had been at Berkhamsted Castle, in front of the King; although I sincerely doubted that these girls were acting any role. The girls spoke in Persian, in a tone as if imploring, perhaps for mercy? Azizah's face broke and tears flooded down her cheeks, as she was able to use her own language, without duress, for the first time in years. Her tone sounded reassuring, in spite of the obvious shock to her as well.

I waved for a chair to be fetched for Azizah and she nodded her thanks as she sat. The slaves were persuaded to lift their heads, then with more words from Azizah, they stood most hesitantly, slowly approached her and all three hugged and sobbed together. After some time, Azizah dried her tears and looked at me with a question in her eyes.

"They speak Saxon very well, my lady" was all I said, as another wave of tears came from her and she mouthed "Thank you my lord, thank you".

When Azizah regained her composure, she whispered to the girls and they turned wide-eyed to me. Clearly the order of things here had just been explained.

Azizah stood and spoke some gentle but firm words in Persian. The girls took up position behind her and on either side. Azizah stepped towards me, smiling wide.

"Thank you, my lord, do you need me for more" she said.

"No, my lady, I will see you at dinner" I replied.

"Good afternoon my lord" she said and gave me a most gracious curtsey, as I bowed to her.

The girls did their fair curtseys to me as they said "Good afternoon, my lord" which I acknowledged with a nod.

The three turned and walked out of the Hall, followed by Azizah's guards, both smiling like doting uncles over their new charges. The hounds were also in close attendance. I caught my guards, momentarily grinning like village idiots, at the happiness they'd just seen in Their Lady...

The tranquility of the moment was suddenly interrupted by a blood-curdling scream from the corridor to the White Room. I was later told that the arm of the mysterious third female had been found to be broken, and without proper treatment, had started to heal out of line.

The nuns persuaded the blacksmith to break the bone again, so it could be set properly.

I guessed even poppy-juice had not been quite enough to make up for that.

Later that afternoon, I called for Jeannot to join me in the parlour and for a jug of warm mead for us to drink. The tale was tortuous indeed. His party had journeyed to Knepp Castle in Sussex, where the steward in charge of the Persian girls resided. Knepp was apparently a small, grim-looking castle, atop a wind-swept hill, one of those quickly built for The Bastard[96] during The Conquest. Its wooden Keep and palisade now partially replaced with stone.

No lord was in residence and the steward was unwilling to discuss the sale of the slaves; he seemed terrified of his overlord, William d'Aubigny. After testing the girls Saxon speech for himself, Jeannot then travelled on nearly twenty miles to Arundel Castle to attempt a meeting with the Earl.

It took a day of negotiation and bribery to gain admittance to the Outer Bailey and two more days to reach the Inner Bailey. All this time, his escort had to stay outside. Eventually he was granted an audience with the Earl, after dropping heavy hints of my connections to the King and the Earl of Warwick. This last was a calculated risk, as this branch of the d'Aubigny family, on both sides of The Channel, were known supporters of Matilda.

Jeannot found Earl William was full of his own Norman importance, scornful of all things 'English', his staff looked cowed by his every glance, the women in particular looked frightened all the time. Jeannot used a mixture of flattery and feigned poor haggling skills to seal a deal for the slaves and a very hefty twenty-four pounds were handed over to the Warden, in exchange for a receipt to be presented back at Knepp. The Warden then directed him to the kitchen for some very late lunch, as Jeannot had been living out of his saddlebag supplies for three days.

I yawned wide at this point, none of this was at all unusual in our times and I began to think about dinner.

"Forgive me, my lord" said Jeannot, "there is a little more…"

I gestured for him to continue and heard of his first sight of a pair of crystal blue eyes, looking at him from under a pile of cloth scraps, in the corner of a storeroom off the kitchen…

Unsettled but somehow curious, Jeannot went closer and saw a very young woman in very poor conditions, with matted hair and shaking limbs.

He'd asked the kitchen staff about the girl, and they'd hurriedly whispered the briefest information.

---

[96] William I

Seems this was a kitchen maid, named Trea, who had refused the Earls advances most vigorously and, in consequence, been thrown naked down the stairs of the Keep, thus badly injuring her arm. William had forbade anyone to clothe or feed her and instructed that she stayed in the storeroom as a reminder, visible to all.

The kitchen staff had thrown rags and sacks over her and were slipping her water and soup to drink during the middle of the night, and she clung to life.

Jeannot stumbled over his words as he told me her face was battered, bloody and swollen but something in her eyes and voice reached into his heart. I nodded in understanding of that... Azizah in her veil had had quite an effect on me, though in very different circumstances.

I now, more gently, urged him to carry on with his account.

After some thought, Jeannot had gone back to see the Warden.

An offer was made to purchase this girl as a slave, but the Warden was reluctant to even discuss this with his lord. Eventually, Jeannot was able to make a large bribe for the Warden to say the girl had died and allow Jeannot to 'dispose of the body'. Jeannot returned to the kitchen via the laundry, having 'borrowed' a couple of large linen sheets. At this point my eyebrows started to rise and Jeannot looked very bashful indeed. He stuttered along with his tale.

Telling the girl "If you wish to live, be silent, whatever happens", he used his dagger to cut head and armholes in the largest two sacks and got her to put them on, trying not to even glance at her thin and very pale nakedness. With the sacks as a short 'dress' he wrapped her in the sheets as carefully as possible and knelt to put her over her shoulder. She gasped at the pain in her arm but that was the only sound she made. With his hands shaking while pretending a calm and superior manner, Jeannot took his unusual bundle out his horse, with no one raising interest, let alone a challenge. With even more care, he draped the roll of sheets and their contents over the back of his horse behind the saddle.

He led the horse from the inner to the outer bailey and then out of the castle, nodding along the way to guards he'd bribed to gain access in the first place.

He went across the drawbridge and down into the town.

Luckily for him, my loyal Haverhill escort had taken turns on watch, day and night, in the hope of his return. The watcher this hour, took him to the stables where they were staying.

With due care, his bundle was unhorsed and Trea revealed.

To my soldiers, she looked to be in a bad way.

To Trea, this looked to be escape from one nightmare and arrival in another, surrounded by rough soldiery, even though these were better turned out than most. The look of terror in her eyes revealed her thoughts but the corporal quickly moved the men back from her and Jeannot reassured her on her safety. They gave her some water to drink, then some bread and cheese from their meagre supplies, all of which was gratefully received by Trea. She began to look less wary but still concerned as to her situation.

Jeannot had a brief discussion with the corporal, to let him know the purchase of the slaves was complete but... the girl's absence might cause a local disturbance!

They both sighed at the necessity of an immediate withdrawal from the town, in spite of the daylight now failing.

For the moment, Trea would be wrapped in the sheets and could use one of the ponies that had been brought for the slave-girls. Naturally they went west, the opposite way to their next destination, and camped for the night in a small forest that was well off the road.

At first light, they went north and then struck directly east for Knepp Castle by way of small lanes and tracks. By then, Trea's arm had been crudely splinted with a tree branch and some strips of linen cut from a sheet. The party pressed on as quickly as possible to Knepp, collected the Persian girls and made an initially slow departure as if next going to London. Once fully out of sight, they altered course once more and pressed on for Haverhill.

The corporal had two scouts go well out ahead and a one-man rear-guard, just in case.

Jeannot's now much depleted coin and a need for concealment meant nightly camping out was necessary, in some bitter weather, until they arrived at Haverhill.

Jeannot apologised deeply for, in effect, buying something I didn't need; we were never short of girls wanting to be maids at the castle. He requested me to treat the significant sum of ten pounds, spent on freeing Trea, as a loan to himself. As he said, there was the issue of 'ownership', the girl was no slave and so we couldn't, legally, compel her to work off the debt incurred to save her life. I thought for a moment or two; Jeannot had exceeded his authority but the circumstances of that and his prior loyal service were all considered. I agreed to the loan and he seemed much relieved. I dismissed him to see Gerald, to write up the terms of his commitment.

Next day, we held a simple ceremony to release the Persian girls from slavery and they were appointed as maids to Azizah.
A few days after the Jeannot's return, I noticed Azizah becoming even quieter and more remote in more ways than one. She and her maids began to stay at Dunmowe Manor for three or four days at a time.
Her absence caused a small but noticeable drop in morale at Haverhill. The place still hummed with activity but somehow with less intensity. My soldiers were still as professional in their duties but not smiling as much!
I don't know if they were sensing my bad temper or just missing our Lady; I suspected a bit of both were in play.

After returning, and then just a couple of days at my castle, Azizah departed for Dunmowe once more and the busy, bustling castle felt lifeless to me - my misery increased.
Two days later was a Wednesday and so market-day in Haverhill town and 'Manor Court' at the castle.
Any guilty parties that day felt the full force of my foul mood, to an extent that Gerald felt it necessary to have a quiet word with me at lunch. I took a breath, sighed, and admitted to my harshness. I also agreed to his suggestions to lighten the punishment in two particular cases.
I managed to maintain more patience and impartiality for the afternoon session, well, until just before Nones[97] at least, when a tankard of cider called loudly to me and I closed the court for the day.

---

[97] 3p.m.

After that very welcome drink, I stomped up to my room in the Keep, hurled cloak, hat and gloves onto the table and used the small hoist on the wall to help myself out of my chainmail. I growled at the sight of the bed drapes being closed all round; I hated that, and the damn chambermaids should know that by now. It lit up pictures in my mind, of my first arrival in this room, with things hidden, and the serpent like movement of the bedclothes – which turned out to be just the two orphan girls but the experience brought up all the superstitions of our time…

Now, come deepest winter, when *I* was *in* the bloody bed, the drapes were fine for staying warm but now, they irritated me greatly. I walked towards the bed to correct this situation, but then felt a more urgent calling to the midden for a very extensive piss. After that relief, I stomped to the bed and hurled back the drapes. What I saw caused my mouth to drop open and my eyes to bulge out of my head. I thought I'd left my body for a moment and was looking down at the sight, so astonishing it was.

Azizah was sat up in the bed, sheets pulled up to her neck but clearly bare of arms and shoulders. A shy smile played on her lips and a mixture of greeting and shyness showed in her eyes.

I gasped for breath, almost started to apologise for barging into her room, then thought…
"Wait, what? Her drapes are purple, mine, here, are blue – this *is* my room!"
She extended a hand, which I took and kissed.
Her face softened more, and sympathy appeared in her eyes for the shaking my body was visibly going through.
I kissed her hand again spoke the blithering obvious.
"You're here my lady. How are you not at Dunmowe?
"I sorry my lord, I not mean alarm you" she began.
"No alarm my lady, but a big, big surprise!" I replied.
"It's a wonderful surprise" I went on quickly "all of Haverhill has missed you; I have missed you" and kissed her hand once more, as I felt my breathing steady and the shaking reduce a little.
Our eyes locked together, hers now showing something else, something new, something for me… I knelt on the bed, leant down

and kissed her gently, our first kiss!

She returned the kiss a little more than gently and the experience for me, transcended the kisses of all previous ladies put together! We smiled into each other's eyes and kissed again, longer this time. Unthinking, I stroked her arm and felt goosebumps on her skin.

"You are cold my lady…" I said and, trying and failing to keep a straight face, smiled wide as I went on "shall I call for a fire to be made, or…" She smiled again, drew me in for another kiss and my hand stroked her arm, then her shoulder and down her back, as our kiss went on for some time. She was definitely without clothing under those bedclothes.

"Let **me** warm you" I said eagerly, as I used the foot of the bed post to drag off my boots, then tore off my gambeson, two thick winter shirts and my hose.

At this very moment, as the hose hit the floor, I saw with profound shock that my 'lance' was not… ready for action.

I realised I'd spent a year hiding and inwardly denying my lust for Azizah, although clearly those desires were welcome now.

I willed it to rise.

Nothing stirred.

I mentally commanded it to stand to.

Nothing happened.

For the first time in my life I felt panic.

I was immediately furious with myself for this, furious at this weakness in my body. I'd heard that excess drink could do this, but here I was, sober… I was devasted with shame at this feebleness and more furious still at that. With an angry snarl at myself, I swept clothes and boots into my arms and turned to go. I couldn't look at Azizah but caught a glimpse of shock and worry on her face from the side of my eye.

"Walter!"

Her cry caught me, just as I laid hand on the door to leave. I glanced back, she looked distraught – no scorn, no pity, no ridicule. Simple agony in her face at seeming separation. Her hands stretching out to me, palms up, an imploring in her eyes and words in her language tumbling out – she had lost all her Saxon speech. It almost killed me to see my wonderful, my precious Azizah in such distress.

Certainly, my fury and my foolish pride died right there. I dropped my clothes, ran to her, took her hands and knelt by the bed. We gripped our fingers tightly and sobbed with each other at our near catastrophe. My bloody, stubborn, Norman pride – had purpose on occasion but held no merit here and now. Through her tears, she managed to say "Trunk-tree, warm you" as she lifted the covers to make them like the tree-trunk in which we had spent that cold and stormy night together. I got into bed with her and she immediately put her head on my shoulder, with her hands together between our chests – just as we'd been that night.

"Walter" she whispered through her reducing tears.

"Azizah" I managed to say in return, while I kissed her hair.

"I watch you long time" she said.

"I watch you care for me... protect me... protect me from all" she went on.

"Protect me from you..." she said very quietly.

"That is true," I replied, also quietly "after your first night here, I was always most caring for you."

"Today... want... care you, care me" she said, still struggling for words.

"Now, we care for each other" I said, as I waved a finger to point back and forth to both of us and then put both arms round her to hold her as close as possible.

"Yes... please" she sighed with relief as she pushed one arm under me and one arm across my chest and squeezed me tight.

This also squashed her firm breasts against my skin and wonder of wonders, my cock reared into life and poked her lower stomach.

"Oh!" she gasped, as she looked me boldly in the eyes and slipped a small soft hand down my stomach.

"Ohhhh Walter!" she cried, as she wrapped her feminine fingers round my now very firm shaft. We kissed with a fury and we're both panting now. She lay back and guided me over her, wrapping her arms around me and her legs around my lower back. She stroked her smooth calves up and down the backs of my rough legs, then placed her tiny soft feet on my backside, rubbed my buttocks with those feet and then pressed firmly down. I needed no further invitation! With as much patience and tenderness as I could manage, which was not much of either, I fumbled my way to her hot little entrance, and we rocked our way to our joining with much loud gasping and shouting in several languages.

She looked up at me as I looked down at her, both now elated at our union. We kissed again, long kisses, with great passion – then I felt her feet rest on my backside again and her loins push into mine, and again she pushed against me, and again.

Now she'd uncaged the beast within me.

I forced my arms under her back, gripped her shoulders firmly enough to bruise her and rode her hard, until I triumphed with a roar that must have been heard in town. I collapsed to the bed, just managed to miss her with most of my weight and drew her close. I kissed her gently and told her incoherently how much she meant to me, all as she stroked my hair and soothed me with her voice. I slept for a while, maybe she did too.

On waking, I kissed her, rushed to the midden and quickly back, for this late November day had turned chilly – well outdoors anyway! She too visited the midden, and, on her return, I watched her, with my mouth and eyes wide. Lit by the last of the afternoon sun coming through the archeres[98], she was so beautiful, with her dusky skin, smooth and curvaceous in every part, long shiny black hair, far down her back. Dark brown nipples jutting from her proud breasts, small waist, a perfect triangle of black hair at her groin and long tapering legs to her small feet. She saw me looking and stopped. She drew herself up to full height, lifted her chin in a confident pose with hands on her hips, while looking me right in the eyes. Then she moved her hands up to gather and hold her hair above her head, making her breasts rise even higher and showing off her graceful neck. Then she stood on tiptoe and very slowly turned around, paused and then completed the turn.

I thought my eyes would fall out, they stared so hard.

I forgot to breathe until I felt dizzy.

And my cock thought he was in heaven.

If she wanted attention, she was certainly going to get it.

So, I pulled back the covers to invite her back in.

---

[98] Arrow slits aka archers' loopholes

She bit her lip and shook her head! Then scurried beyond the end of the bed where I couldn't see her, because the bed drapes at the end were still closed. Unthinking, I dived out of bed and shot round the end of the bed, and she's not there. I heard the bed creak a little and darted back that way, only to see her pert backside disappear round the end of the bed again. I double-bluffed her, flushed her away from the bed and she ran squealing to the end of the room. I pursued her and finally cornered her. I checked her carefully for anywhere she could possibly have hidden her khanjar about her naked person, then feinted high and dived low for her legs, putting her over my shoulder and slapping her arse for impertinence.

She's shrieking through all of this and manages to bite my ear along the way. She tries to bite my back and I give her another, much harder, cracking bottom-slap to behave.

I carry her to the bed, throw her down and ruthlessly use my size and weight advantage to spread and pin her arms and legs – making it perfectly clear I could have my way with her from this position. She struggled hard and well, for some time more before conceding, with very bad grace. Her eyes blazed, "I Princess, I have you..." and then many furious words in her language. I forced a kiss as she tried to keep her mouth away. Then I got off her, rolled on my back and asked what was for dinner that night. She sat bolt upright, looked at me with utter astonishment on her face.

I sat up, trying to keep an innocently questioning expression, like I really wanted to know what the hell was to eat that night. But I failed and smiled broadly at her wide-open eyes and mouth.

I was ready for her when she came at me, which was just as well, because she has provenly fast hands. At the third or fourth attempt, I managed to catch both her wrists and had to admit I was 'joking' her. She tried to keep looking furious but failed and we both collapsed, laughing in a heap on the bed. I think I now have learned the Persian word for 'bastard'.

I got my breath back, sat up and gently reached for her hands and sat her up too. She saw something in my face and willingly joined me, eye to eye. I guided her hand over my heart, pressed it down with my hand and said

"Azizah, I... love you."

With tears again in her eyes, she replied

"Walter... I love you" and pressed my hand between her breasts. I'm sure a cloud of concern must have crossed my face, as I now wondered, was this a passionate farewell, or new and wonderful beginning...? I believe she saw that moment, guessed the question in my eyes and gently smiled.

"You wish me, I stay" she said.

"I wish... I wish with all my heart and soul" I replied, and we held each other and sobbed together with our joy and relief from doubts.

We swived all the rest of that day and on into the night. I used all that dear Eede had taught me, took subtle hints from Azizah for guidance and, I believe, surprised and delighted her to exhaustion. I had thought that some of my previous ladies had been quite... vocal in their appreciation but they had nothing on Azizah. She could be gentle, or passionate, quietly murmuring or echoing off the castle walls, as the moment took her, in any of three languages. What a woman!

Sometime after dark, I sent down for some food and drink.

The kitchen sent meals, tactfully supplying both warm mead and warm lemonade, when I had ordered, unthinking, just the alcoholic brew.

After we had eaten, the log-man was summonsed and made up a glowing fire for us as we hid in the bed, with the drapes drawn tight all round. With him gone, as usual, totally unseen, I gently led Azizah by the hand, out of bed and onto the bearskin rug in front of the fire. We both knew the significance of this, from her first day in the castle – this rug being the one the 'slave Azizah' had suggested that I should spend the night upon! Lit by the glow of the fire, the contrast in the nature of our bodies was truly astonishing. My large, rough muscled bulk against her elegant and dainty smoothness – her dusky yet lustrous skin against my paleness. We drank this all in and my resolve stiffened once more. I looked in her beautiful face, lost in her beautiful eyes, cupped a perfect breast gently in one hand, my other hand on the peach of her behind and softly kissed her. She smiled at the sight of my strength, gently indicated that I should sit on the mat, which I did. She reached for my hands and slowly sat down in my lap. I grasped her under her arms and lifted, while she shifted my cock to her satisfaction.

Both sighed deeply and kissed when we were fully joined once more.

Much later, we were feeling somewhat tired, then heard the distant church bell ring for Vigil[99] and we giggled as one. I picked Azizah up in my arms and took her to bed, to sleep entwined together.
We woke very late the next morning and celebrated our love one more time.
Reluctantly deciding that we had duties to begin, we finally thought about getting dressed. Azizah was sitting on the side of the bed, still gorgeously naked, when she looked down at herself.
"I need bath," she said, "you pour me with seed Walter."
I peeked between her thighs and saw her point.
"Would you like some more, Azizah?" I said, as I moved my loins towards her face. She stood, looked boldly up at me and said, "Yes Walter - tonight," as she gently squeezed my balls, saying "make much for me!" We kissed and with shared wistful sighs, started dressing, ready to begin our workday.

Of course, we were the talk of the castle. Our mutual, coincidental and very extended absence from view would have set tongues wagging but that, combined with our noises in the Keep and the whispers spread from the kitchen, had all caused much merriment. Once we were dressed, I unbarred our door, offered Azizah my arm and we swept proudly out into our world.
Our soldiers had never bowed lower and our maids never curtseyed deeper. It was touching how pleased everyone seemed to be for us. When we had to separate for a while, to be able to hug and kiss Azizah on parting, and again on meeting, made my heart sing.
When in private once again, our swiving took many forms, with much that was new to me. We could be gentle and slow, quietly whispering and coo-ing words of caring and love.

---

[99] 2 a.m.

At other times, she flaunted herself outrageously and gleefully suffered the consequences, of being thrown across bed, floor or table – to then be ravished with a fury that I'm surprised she survived, let alone to finish breathless, flushed and smiling. I'm sure she was relieved that by this time, we had the great luxury of polished oak boards put down in our personal rooms!

For some of our swivings, she would give herself completely, then the next time, take me for a ride, with me feeling her firm thighs, knees and heels guiding me like I was one of her ponies.

Sometimes, when we were alone, anywhere around the castle, she would lift her gown, front or back and show me a promise of things to come. She would then giggle at my consequent inability to walk very much for the next several minutes.

On occasion, when in my room, she would don a simple white maids dress that contrasted her dark skin and was very short and very tight on her, showing off her slim waist, curving hips, her legs below the hem and much of her bust at the top. The 'maid' would then do her 'Emperors' bidding – well, some of the time. This dress needed frequent repairs and once, complete replacement, after 'the maid' refused 'her Emperor'.

In contrast, she could 'play the princess' – certainly not a big leap for her! In doing so, she would command certain... services from her 'manservant'. One of her favourite orders was to have her pretty feet massaged, her toes sucked, nibbled and firmly licked between. This would make her lady parts weep with desire, until she could take no more, and then would spread her arms and legs to welcome me again.

In between our passions, we would talk for hours about many things. Azizah would rest her head on my chest and sigh contentedly, as she listened to my voice 'rumble in you body', as she described it. She shared her first memories of Haverhill, her inward terror of being at the slave market. The not knowing where she would next be captive. The Templars had treated her well, using her knowledge of food and medicine to good purpose - both on the voyage from Acre and her time in Spain.

The elderly Templar who had brought her to England treated her more as a daughter than slave. Then, at the market, this harsh-looking Norman lord started bidding on her - and a fat merchant, who was leering at her with clearly bad intentions...

I buried my head on her shoulder at that point, slightly embarrassed at my main reason for buying her!

She stroked my hair and said "There, there, Walter – you not know trouble I am."

"That is true" I said, smiling.

She gently cuffed me round the head and went on "I fast see you care for me", little tears appearing in her eyes. We kissed with the joy of finding each other and we slept, with her snuggled in my arms.

That following week, we had some time together in the garden at Dunmowe.

Azizah pressed against me as we walked arm-in-arm, our warmth and shared humour was again all that it used to be. We had a simple joy in each other's company.

We looked up, saw an eagle flying high above us and both smiled gently in recognition of this symbol of the choice she'd had to make. She held my arm even more tightly.

"I love my family..." she began "I believe they... care for me" she began, then paused for thought.

I led her to the wicker seat and sat her down, close against me with my arm around her slender body and her head resting on my shoulder.

"But..." she slowly continued "they see me as girl, a girl to take for wife and do as husband say, for all things..." and stopped for more thought.

"Here I see woman have land, with law protect... and Matilda nearly was Queen! Here *I* have land and *I* say what is the law!"

I nodded and waited for more feelings that I thought were in her.

"I have see that..." she struggled for the Saxon, "people think me well and what I do for them good" she finished.

"We treasure you Azizah, you are special and precious to all in our lands. The people love you – I love you" I said.

She beamed a happy smile and rested her head back against me.

"I not leave you Walter…" she said "I not leave… my horses!" and giggled. I playfully grabbed her hair and jostled her around, briefly playing the 'bad husband'; then we kissed deeply and longingly, our tongues tussling together. We both were breathing harder now, and both instinctively looked around for some hideaway spot, somewhere in the bushes or behind trees. We caught each other's eye and burst out laughing at the ridiculousness of our amorous ambitions. Even if we could both keep quiet, which given the history of our togetherness so far was highly unlikely, there were still 100 or more soldiers dispersed around the garden, with the Warden and First Sergeant waiting at the gate - discreet this would not be!

We used the energy built up in us to walk briskly out of the garden and thence ride back to Dunmowe Manor.
On our arrival, I briefly discussed guard rotas with the sergeant, while Azizah quickly checked the progress in the kitchen for the evening meal and on supplies for the following days.
We met up together at the bottom of the stairs and did our very best not to run up them to the top floor.
To spare our guards blushes at both Haverhill and here, we now had them stationed at the stairs rather than our doors, so we had a little privacy.
We scampered into our room and raced to see who would get rid of their clothes first. Azizah won of course, even with her winter clothing, as both my mail and gambeson snagged up in my haste. But it mattered not, when I saw her naked in the candlelight. We ran the few steps towards each other and smashed together, fell on the bed and made one body from our two.
Dinner was served a little late that night, when we eventually appeared, but luckily nothing had spoilt, and it was as tasty as always.

On our return to our room, we found it nicely warmed by a roaring fire. We stood in front of this and I slowly undressed Azizah and she undressed me. I kissed every part of her, from head to toe, stroking everywhere I could reach along the way. She was breathing very hard now, panting like one of her racehorses, with her legs shaking. I picked her up and gently laid her on the bed.

I kissed her again, then kissed down her body once more, to her most sensitive spot. I tongued her gently and slowly, picking up pace and pressure until her whole body started to shake and kept my efforts going steadily there until she shuddered and bucked, while a loud, incoherent moan escaped from her.

I held her as she settled, then carefully put her on her side and spooned against her while throwing some bedclothes over us.

She appeared to sleep for a little while, then I felt her delicious behind moving against my loins. Needing no further encouragement, I threw her on her front, lifted her hips and joined with her. Her movements and sounds drove me wild and I quite brutally ploughed her very moist little furrow to my exquisite satisfaction. It was then her turn to hold me and cover us, before we slept most deeply.

It was early in the December that we received a message from Lord Godwin and Lady Heloise Kanewella.

We were gathered with our senior staff in the parlour after dinner at Haverhill and Gerald read out the letter.

It announced that after many years of prayer, they now had their first-born, a boy. My immediate thought was that "sometimes prayer isn't enough – maybe a different rooster had also been needed!". I could see Azizah's eyes twinkling in the light of the wick-lamps, but she said nothing except "Ahhhh! I please for them, they very nice man and woman."

There was no reproach, jealousy or anger from Azizah, just amusement.

When we were alone in our room that night, she tutted at me while smiling and said, "The poor, gentle people – think when little Walter turn and look at them when he have ten years or more!"

"I don't know it's mine, it does seem a long time since she... er... they were here" I said quickly, but she just giggled and came to hug and reassure me that the matter was of no consequence.

I thought to myself "When your father has children out of four wives and probably many other ladies too, it must give you a very relaxed view of these things."

The winter celebration of Christes Maesse was soon upon us, with church services packed throughout my domains and much fine food and drink consumed by all my staff.

Azizah funded grand celebrations at Dunmowe and the villages of her manor but she and her maids were hardly seen at all during the time until after the Epiphany had been passed.

On her visits to Haverhill, we had many shared baths, where we very much spoiled each other; we would be in the warm back room of the laundry for quite some time...

One of many more surprises was one morning, when she was just out of bed to get dressed, she bent over to pick up some clothing and I playfully flicked her beautiful backside with my heavy leather belt. I admit it landed a bit harder than I intended and made a real cracking noise against her firm posterior. She gasped, jerked her head around, eyes blazing and furiously shouted "Not do more Walter!" but somehow left her gorgeous rear pointed at me...

My own instinct shocked me, as it led me to crack the belt on the other side of her bum! I held my breath, as she closed her eyes and breathed in through her clenched teeth, with a loud 'sssss' noise. Then she turned her head slowly away from me, rested her hands on the bed, hollowed her back and sighed. Now, driven to continue what I'd started, I give her several strikes with my belt on each of the offered cheeks, every crack causing a gasp or a hiss to escape from her mouth.

After these, I began to be concerned, as now some obvious marks were left on her skin; but again, instinct drove me to firmly grab her hair at the back of her neck, stand her up and twist her round to face me. She was clearly very, very pleased to see me; her eyes wide, face glowing, lips pouting and nipples standing out like bodkin-tips. Without a word, I threw her on the bed, forced her legs apart and took her savagely. For the first time, we peaked our passions at the same time; a very vocal and truly tumultuous experience.

We lay stunned for some time, before she contentedly snuggled into my chest and purred "Mmmmm Walter... I kill other man do that to me..." and giggled softly before falling asleep. I napped too, after thinking that I should keep my spare belt well hidden from my lady! Breakfast was served very late that day.

By mid-January, it became clear that the young woman we rescued from Arundel had become a significant problem. Her arm was healing well, and her face was much recovered; she had then proved to be quite attractive to the young men of the castle. The clearly besotted Jeannot had been visiting her in the White Room, several times a day. This seemed to have given Trea ideas above her station, as she feigned 'weakness' to avoid moving from her sick-bed and declining to start even light duties in the kitchen. After a visit from Azizah, she immediately started work in the kitchen but soon became a disruptive influence, with poor work and blaming other maids for many imagined faults.

This continued for a short while but culminated the day one of Azizah's maids requested some nettle tea for her Lady, to be provided in the parlour. Trea responded with a fury, saying she wasn't born to 'wait on any darky harlot'. The maid stood her ground and insisted on the instruction, at which Trea slapped her across the face, produced a dagger from somewhere and raised it to strike.

One of Azizah's guards levelled her to the floor with the butt of his spear. Fortunately, Azizah and her two guards had been in the Hall when the altercation started, and no real harm befell the maid.

Trea though had sealed her fate. When she recovered her senses a few hours later, she found herself tied to a litter in the White Room, then was put before me in the Hall the next morning.

Freed from the ropes, she was stood at the bar as I looked down on her from my chair on the dais. Azizah kept well away, as we knew her feelings were too strong to judge this matter.

I called witnesses, who described the event of the previous day, as she stood, showing neither remorse nor regret.

I asked if she had anything to say and she changed into this gentle, soft-spoken, eye-lash-fluttering creature who wished me to believe that everyone was lying about her, and she couldn't possibly have done such a thing.

When I challenged her concerning ownership of the dagger, which we now knew had been 'earned for favours' from one of the night-guards, she said that was a lie and she had no such weapon.

Seems that knife was not her only weapon, as she used her piercing blue eyes, soft light-brown hair and feminine wiles, in an attempt to woo me to her cause.

Unfortunately for her, she willfully failed to recognise my rank, in spite of many whispered prompts from the First Sergeant.

The sergeant finally reached the end of his patience, took off his riding gloves, nodded to me, and slapped her full in the face with them; followed by a shouted instructions to recognise whose fief this was and who held her life in his hands. After a blinking moment of shock and fury, she recovered her 'soft' demeanour and apologised with plenty of 'my lords' thrown in.

I found her guilty of bodily harm with intent to kill and ordered her to the dungeons to await sentencing. Trea shrieked and howled as she was tied back to the litter and delivered to the Keep and Milo's tender but professional care.

I consulted with Gerald, to confirm that this offence was not considered worthy of execution, unless the attacked was of high rank. Other cases had resulted in any combination of imprisonment, fines or compensation; but none of these outcomes seemed suitable or even practical.

For the first time in my life, I contemplated a casual murder to resolve a situation...

After a week in the dungeon, she was little changed, now claiming we had 'kidnapped' her and Jeannot was to blame for 'everything'. I smiled wolf-ishly, stroked my chin and offered to return her to Arundel.

In an instant, she turned white and also contrite, maybe finally realising her 'game' was up. She hung her head as she was taken back to the dungeon.

Two weeks later, she was presented again, this time during Manor Court.

My final judgement was that she was to be banished from any domain of mine, and from Cambridge, Rockingham, Norfolk, Suffolk, Essex and Warwick – on pain of death if she returned.

All she said was "Thank you my lord" as she was led back to her cell. The next day I sent her with a small escort, to drop her off on the outskirts of St Neots, with just the clothes she stood in. This was the place that the renegades from Walden had ended up and was a hotbed of chicanery and treachery against the King.

It amused me greatly to throw this scorpion into that nest of vipers. Jeannot was mortified at the whole saga but came to me to confirm his commitment to paying off the loan and apologise for his 'weakness'. I waved away his apology saying, "our instincts cannot always be right... and good intentions can be... betrayed"
He soon found that a few of the castle maids sought to talk to him, eager to console him; he completely cheered up after a few days of this attention.

As the year progressed, more and more letters arrived from Earl Warwick and our allies; these indicated a likely peace and rebuilding in the realm this year. Matilda's supporters had been bled white, financially, the previous year and were clearly unwilling to attempt anything this approaching summer.

My Marshall had been overseeing recruitment and training at both Haverhill and Walden; he now offered to take Manor Court at Walden if that would be of service. He said he would have Warden Nash there assisting.
I believed his pride had been somewhat dented by the success of Lady Azizah in presiding over Manor Court at Haverhill and then at Dunmowe.
He was still reluctant to spend overmuch time at Walden but did his duty very well on my behalf. His keenness to be at Haverhill no doubt had something to do with his younger wife, who herself was said to be keen on adding a second child to their family. Thankfully they had moved to a newly purchased house in town, and we were spared their loud swiving sounds that used to echo round the Keep on many nights.

For my part, I developed fond hopes of visiting my parents; perhaps with Azizah. We could also make a formal visit to Lord Roger on the same trip.
I was standing on the Haverhill gate-tower one morning in early February, thinking these contented thoughts, when 'single rider approaching from east' was announced by a Keep guard.
In a short while, the horse trotted into view, its rider slumped forwards, hanging on to the animal's neck.

I directed the corporal to call for a report from all towers. They replied, 'no forces seen' and I ordered a couple of men to sally over the drawbridge and catch the horse that would otherwise have probably passed us by.

On closer approach we could now see arrows sticking out of the rider's body and saddle. He had on broadhead in his right thigh and another in his lower right back. There was blood all over his lower half and the horses caparison. Closer still and we could make out the embroidered 'K' of Kanewella on the cloth.

The horse was led into the Bailey and the rider gently eased down from the saddle. He was laid on the ground, on his left side and still appeared to be breathing. A litter was called for and he was rushed to the nuns in the White Room.

The arrows were removed, and his wounds dressed; many prayers were said, as his loss of blood seemed likely to end him.

He woke for a while, whispered to the senior Sister, as the new junior nun scribbled on some parchment. He then lapsed back into sleep.

The elder nun visited me in my parlour, we nodded to acknowledge each other, and she sat where I indicated.

"How is the wounded man?" I asked.

"He breathes, Lord Walter, but maybe not for much longer. He did give us a message..."

I gestured her to continue.

She glanced at the paper she held and went on "He says he escaped Kanewella, which is under siege by the Duke of Ipswich. The Duke demands repossession of their lands as their lease has expired, claiming ownership to his line going back 200 years. He has given the Lord and Lady three days to leave, and none of their subjects can leave until they do."

I nodded respectfully, stood up, thanked her and she returned to the White Room.

I passed orders for the arrows to be brought to me, for Gwilym the fletcher to be brought forthwith and Gerald to attend me at his earliest convenience. Gwilym arrived very quickly, cast his eyes over the arrows and was clearly unimpressed.

"Crudely made they are, my lord. Rough casting of the heads, duck feathers and crude binding for the flights.

Something made in a village perhaps, but not in a castle of any status." I nodded and dismissed him back to his work.

Gerald listened as I relayed the message and laughed heartily at what he immediately knew was the fraudulent title 'Duke of Ipswich', as no dukedoms had yet been granted in England, unlike the significant number in France and beyond.

He also chuckled at the eviction demands, recalling correspondence with the 'clerk of rolls' at Norwich Castle, during the previous year. Gerald had been curious on the origins of Kanewella, simply due to the unusual and very old-sounding name. He had been assured that the manor had been bought by the Lord of Norfolk, from a Saxon noble, in the decades before The Conquest. It was then sold to Frodo, brother of Abbot Baldwin, passed to Frodo's sons, who had sold it to parties unknown, presumably the current Lord and Lady. What was certain was that some imposter was making a play for a good piece of land, falsely based on outdated records from before the reign of The Confessor, never mind The Conqueror. I nodded and smiled in recognition and relief that my significant expenditure on letters could reap such benefits from around the realm.

"I will take action of course, but what is my... standing?" I said.

"You may ride to simply end this Breach of the Kings Peace, my lord" Gerald replied. He went on "There is also a matter of a treasonous claim to land that is, by birth-right, the property of the King; the false claim to such a high rank is a capital offense." I raised my eyebrows and nodded.

"With Haverhill owing spears direct to the Crown, you may act on behalf of, and in the name of, King Stephen" Gerald concluded.

"So... who... owns Ipswich?" I asked.

"Well... no one my lord. It was a small, prosperous burgh[100] and port at the time of The Conquest but... sixty-five years ago, the Saxon Earl of East Anglia made rebellion and The Bastard[101] seems to have taken this very personally, because the retribution was absolute.

---

[100] A walled and fortified market town of significant size. Most date from the time of King Alfred

[101] William I, aka 'The Conqueror' among other things!

Death and destruction, mass burnings of villages and towns. That corner of Suffolk was laid waste and barren. No trade was possible, no survivors were left, it has become a dark part, almost separate from the realm."

After a pause, Gerald continued "There are rumours that the Celtic Church clings to some of its buildings at least, but no … administration exists." I nodded, gave him my thanks and he walked stiffly back to his room in the Keep.

I sent my squire to instruct the kitchen to begin lunch early and sent messengers to Walden and Dunmowe. My orders were for any and all armed and trained men who could be spared, should ride to Haverhill immediately, with spare horses, pack animals, food, water-containers, arrows, winter clothing, bedrolls; everything to be ready for a campaign of three weeks. Any shortage of horses should be made up from stocks held at Great Thurlow.

Each fief was to assume defensive measures, so gates would be closed, and drawbridges raised unless expected visitors appeared. I also instructed my Marshal to remain in-charge at Walden and made a request for Lady Azizah to arrive at Haverhill by noon the next day.

Other despatches went to Cambridge, Rockingham and Warwick to advise them of the situation and my initial actions. As an afterthought, I sent a message to Fulbourn Castle to send 50 men to Dunmowe as reinforcements.

After lunch, I called my best 12 scouts from the last campaign and 12 mounted archers, to gather around the stairs to the Keep. Speaking from the top of the stairs, I ordered them to scout the road towards Kanewella village and the manor itself.

Their aim was to locate and assess the force or forces besieging Kanewella.

I warned them that we had no idea of the number, type or disposition of the enemy. I told them all that was known was they were brigands but had at least one leader. They were to remove identifying marks from their equipment and be the sneakiest and most careful they have ever been. Their priority was to remain undetected themselves while learning what they could.

The men looked steady, if a little wary of the scant information I had given them. I stated that, if lost, they should head west to the River Glem and then south to the junction with the Stour. This was also where I would meet them once they had seen enough of the opposition. I told them their action if attacked, was to "Run like fock" which brought a grim chuckle from them all.

I told the corporals to collect campaign purses from the Warden and left them to gather their equipment and depart when ready, no need to oversee that group of men.

The Walden contingent of 90 under the young Sergeant Jacot arrived by Vespers[102] and the 110 Dunmowes did well to arrive a couple of hours later.

At first all raw recruits were lumped together but this proved to be like herding cats; so, each veteran soldier was given three or four of the new soldiers to check their equipment and draw from stores as required.

By calling all recently retired and some disabled soldiers back for duty as castle guards, I was able to scrape together 130 men of Haverhill. Not counting the scouting troop, this total of 330 was much less than the number I was expecting but had no time to reason why; merely resolve to do a muster[103] as a quarterly exercise in future. I added my longbowman this time, 24 of them with a good supply of arrows in weather-protected carriers on pack horses. The surrounding farms had all their plough-horses requisitioned to act as mounts for my very large bowmen.

Each longbowman had a castle-boy allocated, to lead two packhorses each, with spare arrows and protective stakes lashed to the animals.

The kitchen fed everyone in relays of one Hall-full at a time and I commanded all combatants to be resting by midnight.

---

[102] Church bells for prayer time at 6pm

[103] To assemble (troops), especially for inspection or in preparation for battle

Everyone squeezed indoors where they could, we had the 'Waldens' shoulder to shoulder in the dungeons and storerooms, the beer-room being locked of course. The 'Dunmowes' squeezed into the Hall once the last dinners were served.

Rollcall was to be at Prime the next morning.

The tradesmen's work however continued through the night; there were many supply packs to make for the horses, we could never have too many arrows and the leather-man and his apprentice worked their hands bloody to turn tanned hides into capes for those still without.

St Agatha's Day[104] dawned bright and cold

We took a rollcall in the Bailey to confirm numbers and allocated men to one of ten companies of around 30 each[105].

After a hasty breakfast we reconvened in the yard and walked through the various maneuvers that would be called, by hand signal or trumpet call. This was much to ask of the men, as we had done no attacks with more than one company at any point in my tenure; something else that I was going to add to the quarterly musters...

After two hours of practice and a full equipment check, we held a full parade.

This made an impressive sight and, with perfect timing, Azizah arrived with her escort. I waved to her and indicated that she should ride in review of the parade. She slowly rode her horse along the formation, nodding at each man in turn. Each man bowing his head as she went by.

Almost none of the Waldens had seen her at all, let alone on a large Arab horse, with an ornate saddle, embroidered caparison, wearing a very high-status gown and head-dress, and no veil.

The ripple of stunned surprise was evident to see, with some of the newest men nearly departing their saddles through a combination of awe and enthusiastic bowing.

---

[104] 5th February

[105] At this size, they were clearly not equivalent to 20th Century companies of 90-150

She rode back to me by the Keep, followed by her maids on ponies and her hounds. On reaching me, she bowed her head and I responded with a bow to her.

"Wonderful to see you my lady" I said, with my eyes saying, 'I've missed you'.

"Much... very good to see you my lord" she replied, a mixture of happiness in her face but concern in her eyes.

"This very... new for us" she went on, with a nod at the parade taking up much of the Bailey. I agreed and invited her to lunch with me.

I called the First Sergeant to begin the relays of men for lunch, handed my horse off to my squire and waited for Azizah to dismount and take my arm as we walked to the Hall.

Over the meal with my senior staff, I divided the responsibilities of the domains amongst them. Azizah was to stay at Haverhill in my absence, the others knew their roles from the previous summer.

After all had eaten, the men were gathered round the base of the Keep. Standing looking up at the platform by the door. I addressed them from there.

"Soldiers, men of my domains. Today we ride to defeat renegade forces that threaten attack on Kanewella Manor to our east and so breech the Kings Peace.

They are led by a brigand who acts in treason by claiming a false title."

There were growls from some men who had relatives 'out east' and then louder more general gasps of surprise at the mention of treason. The veterans in particular now knew the stakes here were life and death, no half measures.

I concluded with "We act in the name of the King, good luck and god speed to all".

As I stepped back, I was pleased this time that I got three cheers, as I was damn sure Azizah would get that accolade if she chose to speak; which of course she did.

She announced that all men would have a pouch of herbs and spices; sergeants and corporals would have their treatment items, as had been supplied in the summer.

After she wished the men well and a safe return, she got a very rousing three cheers.

The men were then directed to a packhorse at the back of the Bailey to collect their gifts provided by Their Lady; the Dunmowe kitchen-staff and tradesmen must have been up all night making those.

We mounted up in formation and departed the castle on the only road to the east. This in itself made me wary, so I pushed one experienced company well ahead as vanguard.

Our route generally followed the wide river valley of the Stour. Gentle hills on either side. We passed silent hamlets and quiet small villages until the daylight began to fade.

I directed my force across the river at a ford and called a halt at a handful of cottages and shacks that proved to be Pentlow.

I sent two companies out as a hunting party, I saw my First Sergeant draw breath to query the size of this detachment, but he saw my expression and held his peace. With nothing of substance known about the opposition, we had to keep our strength together as much as possible.

The residents emerged from their hovels, totally bewildered by the huge mass of humanity now surrounding them.

I think they understood me when I took possession of everything in sight, in the name of the King of course. Their replies to me almost incomprehensible, in some local version of Saxon. The common factor, as ever, was coin; I pressed a few pennies into their grubby hands and promised more when we left. We instantly became as welcome as long-lost members of their families.

My main interest was the many barns I had seen from the road. These were large and built fairly close together. My men used carts, bits of broken cart and some newly felled trees to fill the gaps between the barns, creating a crude fort.

Rough it was but we needed the space, over 300 men and almost 400 horses take up a lot of room. We paid generously for the hay our horses needed and paid something for the straw the men were to use for bedding. The hunting party did well, returning with seven wild pigs. These were quickly butchered and cooked in pieces in quickly dug oven pits lined with stones.

No time to slow roast whole carcasses. Vegetables from the nearby farms were added to the pits and men served themselves onto their plates carried in their saddlebags. Water from a nearby well proved to be safe to drink. We were found to be short on cooking pots, which was a grave oversight but the better cooks amongst us made a stew of leftovers, with tiny amounts of Azizah's spices and offered the product to the residents. They shot out of their doors and gobbled up the stew with their hands and wooden spoons.

Seems they were so moved by our various generosities that the elder of this hamlet approached me with a young female in tow. Apparently, this was a sincere expression of appreciation and I was clearly expected to take the offering, in all senses.

Thinking quickly, I bowed my head in acceptance and took the girl by the hand and into a barn. This caused much tittering by the men from Walden, who clearly didn't yet know me.

Once in the barn, I made sure the girl was fed and watered, then put her under guard for the rest of the night.

Later, what made me shake my head more, was the fact that even through my undying love for Azizah, the embedded grime on this girls face and hands, her dirty black dress, the matted black hair and obvious lice infestation, she could make my loins stir... there was something in her deep blue eyes, her sensuous mouth and her movements...

I put the men on one-third alert, so each third of our force would get a total of eight hours sleep in the next twelve hours. I couldn't see such a cosy arrangement lasting much longer though.

I quickly adjusted to military hours, attaching myself to the middle watch, so I was up between midnight and roughly four of the morning.

Come the dawn, and after paying a few more pennies prior to making our farewells, I endeavored to return the girl. However, it seemed she was a gift and great offence was nearly taken when they thought I didn't want her. In the interest of preserving the Kings Peace, I explained that I did want her but thought I should pay a dowry, which of course was acceptable. I gave them forty silver shillings and they promptly viewed me as their King in my generosity. They bowed and doffed their grimy caps to me as I led the girl away, pointed to a spare horse and told her to get on it and mightily slapped her arse to get a move on. Apparently, this was the right thing to do in these parts because the locals clapped and cheered my firmness. My men tried not to look puzzled by the whole play; for my part, I wished that arse hadn't felt quite so good.

We travelled the few miles to the junction of the Rivers Glem and Stour and waited in a protective circle while we put out parties to find a suitable place to stay, perhaps for several nights. They returned quite quickly, having located an abandoned hill fort only a quarter mile away at a place a nearby peasant said was 'Cranfield'. This place was ancient in origin, a very wide if not very high mound, atop a gentle hill. The two rings of ditches and earth walls had some Norman improvements consisting of wooden palisade, large stables and a hall. There was also a small stone watchtower with steps on the outside and room for three men standing together on top.
I directed the men to begin repairs to the sixty years of neglect and clear the long grass and bushes back to the forest edge. Meanwhile, I had realised that I had missed ordering breakfast to be taken that morning and was wondering how I was going to feed my seeming horde out here; this was so different from managing a few dozen men...
Fortune came for me when the last search party returned, with news of an inn just three furlongs[106] to the north-east. The owner had said that if we kept paying, he would keep feeding us, day and night. The corporal in charge of the party had already paid for a purchase of grain to make a very large amount of bread.
The First Sergeant was directed to send two companies at a time to the inn; each visit was to be by a different route, and they should always return other than the way they had gone. This would give us two meals a day during daylight and would have to suffice.

---

[106] A very old English measurement. A furlong is an eighth of a mile, so 220 yards.

I put sentries on the tower, to watch for anything but mainly the hoped-for return of my scouts from Kanewella; the river junction was just visible from our adopted fort. The girl had disappeared but was then spotted, helping to clear our field of fire with a borrowed sickle[107] and mucking in with the best of the men.

The renovations were completed by last light and we settled down to rest, by three watches again. The girl seemed resigned to living in enforced isolation, as we had no way of cleaning her up or fixing her lice problem. I had passed the word that she was my property, so there would be no improper approaches, even though there might well have been improper thoughts.

The first night passed without alarm. Next day we patrolled far and wide during available daylight, always with strong parties. Another quiet night followed and as the day after began to pass, I was increasingly concerned for my scouts.
However, as last light approached, movement was seen by the river and a small smoke signal put up.
They appeared at our new gate in short order, blessedly all were present, but they looked exhausted and... scared shit-less. These were my bravest and boldest and a small doubt now began to grow in me...
Some basic chicken soup was made up for them and we had plenty of bread and rustic butter. The scout corporals then requested a quiet word with me...
We adjourned to a quiet corner of the fort, well wrapped up in our cloaks, with mugs of still hot boiled water.
"Your report?" I asked, "What did you see?"
"What we saw, my lord, was irregular cavalry besieging Kanewella. They number about 150 and sit in companies around the village, making occasional small patrols. There is no fixed cordon, but they seem to have intimidated the locals to a curfew during darkness.

---

[107] A single-handed agricultural tool designed with variously curved blades and typically used for harvesting, or reaping, grain crops or cutting succulent forage chiefly for feeding livestock, either freshly cut or dried as hay.

We also saw... evidence of a large force or forces of foot soldiers. Numbers and dispositions unknown because they only seem to move at night and hide up during the day... somewhere. They use a very low-pitch horn to message at night, between groups, and a point a long way to the east, my lord. There are strange chantings in the night and occasional... screams..." he faltered to a finish, but I saw nods of agreement all round and took this as a fair summary. I looked at the strain they showed and had noted the emphasis on the word 'saw' and asked, "And what did you... feel?"

He took a deep breath and said "Scared my lord, we often felt watched, even when we were at our most careful to not leave sign. If we galloped a while, we had a sense of... freedom, but if we rested anywhere within three miles of Kanewella, for any length of time, we felt... watched again..." once more there was nodded assent from all the corporals.

"Good work men," I said, "rest well tonight, you will not be on watch these next two nights."

"Thank you, my lord" they replied as they bowed and turned away towards the hall and a well-earned sleep on the straw we had scrounged.

After a few minutes in consideration, I called for the First Sergeant and gave orders for the night. Half our force to be stood-to at a time, on two-hour watches. I emphasised most clearly that handovers to be **silent**. There was the usual grumbling from rank and file about the short sleeps, but this was not my problem.

I bumped into Sergeant Jacot and enquired on the state of his three Walden companies. He replied, "Well my lord, this is all very new to us, so we just watch what the 'Haverhills' do and do the same."

I smiled at this frankness and knew this was no attempt to flatter me; I didn't think that was in his young Norman nature.

"Very well sergeant," I said, "carry on and practice silent watch handovers, with no talking or jingly-jangly equipment."

"Certainly my lord" he replied as he bowed and turned away to his duty. First Sergeant returned and reported that the first watch was set.

"What moon tonight?" I asked.

"Errr... half-moon sir, should clear up as the night goes on and likely to be fock... er... sorry sir, very cold by morning."

"Thank you, sergeant, I'll be with first watch, pass the word for quiet in the camp and no lights."

"Yes, my lord" he replied and bowed away to his task.

Much later that night, I was up with my watch, standing in the moon-shadow of the stables, keeping an eye on the yard in case of a ladder assault or other breach of the palisade. I tried to keep my steaming breath inside my cloak because, as the sergeant had predicted, it was 'fockin cold'.

A very hard frost had set in during the last half hour and the ground, roofs and our cloaks all had a dusting of that dense white coldness. The chimes of Vigil from a very distant church bell were long since passed, and as I wriggled my toes in my cold boots, I very much hoped we were near the 4 o'clock changeover.

Then... I saw movement, either side of the gate.

I looked slightly to one side of the movement, to let my night eyes see better and saw... six of my archers were at full draw.

I knew the palisade stakes were offset, alternating one forward, one back, which created gaps through which the archers could shoot out on the diagonal but it was not possible for an enemy to shoot in, as the palisade appeared to be solid from the front.

Their actions implied there were hostiles to our front and very close at that.

I glanced to the other side of the fort, in case this was a diversion, but no unease was apparent there, so I looked back to the gate just as the archers loosed and loosed again and again. The lad with the trumpet sounded a decent 'Stand To' and there was much fury and yelling from my men. Some of our spearmen got some thrusts in as a few of the attackers attempted to come over the palisade but my archers were continuously pouring arrows out through the fence. The lads too young to fight were carrying more arrows out to the shortbowmen and topping up the quivers.

I heard a longbow loose from the lookout tower but had no idea of the target. After a couple of minutes, the archers' rate of loosing slowed, and the First Sergeant shouted "Stop! Watch and shoot. Search the fort."

The archers stayed at their posts, arrows nocked and ready.

Spearman lit torches and every nook of the area was searched in case we'd let some in. Nothing was found but there was much groaning from outside the fence. In case this was merely a probe before a full attack, everyone was on watch until after dawn. I then saw that even the girl had been on alert, guarding the horses with her sickle and a determined look in her eyes.

First Sergeant reported no serious injuries, all were ready to fight. I then ordered strong patrols out, to cloverleaf and dominate the area around the camp. Nothing was found, bar the casualties to our front, but these were enough to fully engage our curiosity.

The initial count was twenty-nine, which seemed odd; until Rolfe coughed for attention and pointed towards the forest, at the thirtieth body, the one he had skewered to a tree with a bodkin tipped arrow. God knows how he saw the target at that distance from the tower, let alone hit it...

Five of them still drew breath, though disabled by multiple arrow strikes and chilled to the bone from the frost.

I gave the sergeants and corporals a grim nod and as one, we set to extract the usual information.

We wanted numbers, locations, leadership and intentions. Violence and pain were inflicted, to no immediate effect; indeed, one laughed at my soldiers' efforts and proceeded to swallow his own tongue and ended himself...

We immediately forced sticks between the teeth of the remainder and used twine round their heads to keep the wood in place and so prevent a repeat occurrence. Then we staked out the four survivors, with arms and legs spread, removed the 'armour' they wore front and back, made from thin, curved hard-wood staves; made as if a copy of a rib cage but worn over a leather surcoat. They had foliage tied to this armour. Underneath they had patchwork clothing with greens, greys and blues predominating and simple leather boots with more foliage tied to them. Strangest of all were their eyes... their pupils were so wide, wider than I have seen in dead men. With their view now enforced up at the sky, the rising sun was making them shut their eyes in between trying to see what we were up to... I stepped away and drew my seniors in to confer.

Second Sergeant started with "Tough bastards eh sir?

I think they understood our questions, but they just didn't seem to… care about the pain…"

"I agree…" I said, then turned to watch as the girl walked to the nearest live one, her sickle still in hand. She looked down at him with a hostile stare. He made some insult by the sound of it and she promptly turned her back to us, put one foot either side of his head, lifted the front of her dress and from the sound of it gave him a stream of piss in the face. She finished with her own insult and walked towards us. Stopping a couple of yards away, she nodded a sort of bow to me and said, "Sea devils lord."

I made a gesture for her to go on.

"I have not seen before, but we hear bad things from the east and our relatives to the north. They steal children and horses, kill men and… hurt women… These stories I hear all my life…"

Her accent made it difficult to understand her fully, but we got the gist of it! I nodded in thanks and asked, "Where do the stories say these things come from?"

"The marshes lord, in Dedham Vale, where the Stour reaches the sea. No one is safe if you are near a waterway, they can run on water and have many boats…"

"Shit!" exclaimed one of the scout corporals.

"Sorry my lord," he went on "that's how they could vanish so quietly from under our noses and appear behind us next morning… and they must have rowed down the Glem to catch up with us last night…"

I held up my hand to stop him for a moment as I watched the girl inspect the next of the enemy. She fixed him with a stare and slapped the handle of her scythe with seeming intent, and for the first time a saw a moment of fear flit across the face of one of these foes.

"Come here girl" I commanded.

She walked back to us, "Yes lord?"

"Are you prepared to kill one of these?"

She calmly nodded assent saying, "Yes lord, I put down wounded animals…"

I heard small gasps and low whistles from my men behind me… clearly now revaluating this young woman!

I indicated myself and said, "Lord Walter" then pointed to her and she said "Linza, lord" and gave a little bow as I nodded back.

I had the four survivors blindfolded and tied to vertical stakes; their armour was passed to the archers to inspect. Then, out of earshot, I instructed all on their play to perform.
I cut away the blindfolds and stepped a few yards away to their front, as I was backed by my seniors standing with arms folded, looking stern.
I began "Sea devils, today you die, for insurrection against the Kings Peace."
They did their very best to spit at me and mouth insults past the sticks forcing their teeth apart.
"Now, I wish to know how many there are of you, where are your forces, who leads you and why do you take Kanewella."
They laughed at me and followed with more incoherent insults.
I went on "I only need one of you to tell me..."
More loud but mumbled jeering.
"Then I will kill you quickly, or...."
Silence now, I had their attention.
"She... will kill you slowly..."
Linza stepped through the ranks of my men and stared at them with unblinking gaze. There was some attempt at more bravado from 'the devils' but it wasn't convincing anymore. She stood about six yards from the line of stakes and looked down at her scythe.
She dropped it and held her hand out for a spear.
She was given a throwing spear, and immediately grasped it confidently, quickly finding the point of balance on the corded grip. With no warning she threw the spear into the loins of the devil to her left. The force delivered was most impressive, considering her small frame; clearly not her first strike with such a weapon...
The resulting scream was surprisingly loud considering the gagging effect of the stick.

We adjourned for a simple breakfast and reconvened a half-hour later. The speared-one was still breathing but sobbing quietly as he bled out. Linza appeared again, with another spear, extending her left arm at first one, then the others of the remaining three...

This really seemed to scare them now, as I stood at her side and meaningfully tapped my sword and then her shoulder, saying "The choice is yours..."

Second on the left cracked first, mumbling past his stick "I tell lord, I tell."

This immediately earned scorn from the two on the right, particularly from the far right one. I locked eyes with Linza and inclined my head towards the right-most 'devil'.

"Well damn me," I thought, as she struck the exact same spot with this spear, "I thought she'd just dropped low the first time!"

This ended any resistance from the middle two, they were cut down, ungagged and sung like larks for an hour, telling us everything; including saying that they thought only our scouts were at the fort, hence the bold attack the previous night. A short time later, I cleaved their heads from their bodies when they weren't expecting it; Lord Williams sword proving its quality once more.

I ordered urgent preparation to leave and noticed some good-natured teasing of Linza as word had spread of her skills; "Be nice to Linza!" and "Don't lend her your spear!" was heard. Later, when some detail of the interrogation had been passed round, my men learned that the sea-devils believed that women sucked power from a man, and if they were killed by a woman, they would wander in the void for eternity and never reach Valhalla[108]. Now the sly joke was, "Hey Linza, want'a suck my power!"; to which she would respond with a firm middle finger, before going back to hand-combing her hair and cracking lice between her fingernails.

Time was short now, so together with the scout corporals, we formed a hasty plan. I needed their party to act as bait and draw the enemy cavalry to my ambush. They thought of a suitable location for the action and by mid-day my whole force was well on the way towards Kanewella. The scouts left us at the near end of a large oval clearing in an otherwise dense wood. The trail to Kanewella led north, up the middle of this open space.

---

[108] In Old Norse and German/Saxon, this is 'warrior heaven'

I placed my main force of lancers on the left flank, waiting back in the trees, my mounted shortbow archers would wait on the right flank and our longbowmen would be dismounted in the trees at the south end of the clearing. Our scouts were to flee after initial contact with the enemy cavalry and draw them south into our 'bag'. The bag would be closed behind our scouts by the squires and boys raising ropes from the pack horses across the path and quickly making fast around tree trunks.

The light breeze brought us sounds of conflict and a trumpeted 'retreat' sounded by the scouts. After a couple of minutes, the scouts burst into view at the far end of the clearing, galloping south as hard as they could go. The enemy had a half dozen riders well ahead of the rest, I just prayed my squires would think to let these through before 'bagging' the great mass that were following. Thankfully they did, the ropes suddenly rising across the trail caused a shocking sight of horses rearing, falling, others piling into them, more horses swerving the first pile and running straight into trees. By then, I'd ridden out from our left flank with my lancers in line abreast as we charged into the side of the massed but now mostly stationary cavalry.

Chaos and panic ensued, they could see they were dying from the front as arrows appeared from the trees to their front and punched clear through bodies. More than one was pinned to his horse by a bodkin that joined his leg to the chest of the dying animal. Survivors drew away to our right flank and were met by a hail of arrows from our mounted archers, all proud to show the skills taught by Their Lady. A few wayward longbow arrows passed close across my front and some short bow arrows flicked passed our heads, but I just sighed to myself at this penalty for a hasty plan. A few enemy late-comers managed to escape and were initially pursued by some mounted archers, but I quickly ordered the trumpeter to sound 'Recall'. We had to maintain our strength together for the foreseeable. The scouts had wheeled around and taken care of the leading group, mostly by arrow strikes.

We hacked our way through any survivors, all looking much like their foot-soldier brethren but equipped with small shields and larger spears; no prisoners were sought or taken.

We had a small number dead, including, sadly, two of the castle lads who had thought to tie their rope around themselves... The force of a galloping stallion had jerked them off their feet and slammed them into a tree. One or two others had arm or leg wounds but nothing that would stop them riding.

The least bad compromise I chose to make now, was to leave the enemy weapons and horses where they were. Time was more precious now than anything. We were south of Kanewella, and had been seen there, so that was the last direction we would attack from. The scouts conferred and agreed the widest approaches were from the north-east, so we skirted right and then around the village, silently formed a series of lance-led 'V' formations and punched through very light resistance by a few foot-soldiers and took the remaining devil-cavalry in the rear as they watched to the south.

I gambled and despatched three companies to fetch in the bodies of our fallen from the clearing. They fortunately returned later and without incident.

Meanwhile, I advanced back through the village, past the church, up the main street, and towards the manor house at the other end. It was deathly quiet, not a soul stirred, just a couple of cats came out and hissed at us. I had other companies riding in parallel with mine but through the back gardens of the cottages on either side. We were still exhilarated from the earlier fight, furious at our losses and ready to take on anything. We reached the manor house and my companies encircled it, half facing outwards. I walked my horse nearer to the massive wood door and shouted "Hello in the house. Lord Walter of Haverhill attends..."

A window upstairs swung open and a dozen archers drew back and aimed.

"Walter? Is that you?" said a woman's voice that I vaguely remembered sounded like Lady Heloise.

"It is Madame[109], your messenger reached us" I replied.

"Oooooo, wait and we will come down!", squeaked the voice that was definitely Heloise.

---

[109] This Norman/French term is correct in period, the short form "ma'am" was not in use for another few centuries

We could hear footsteps resounding down some stairs, and much thumping, grunting and unbarring of the door. The door creaked open and three manservants holding daggers stepped warily out to 'confront' two companies of chain-mailed lancers, flanked by many mounted archers!

"At ease men" I commanded, to them and to mine.

Lord Godwin walked out timidly, followed by Lady Heloise.

He looked plumper than before, she looked slimmer, more... mature; I guessed that having your body invaded by an infant and your manor by sea-devils would change you.

I dismounted, shook their hands and they expressed their thanks a multitude of times, to me and my men.

I noticed my First Sergeant trying to make eye contact and I grinned and nodded back.

I managed to stop the Kanewellas' gabbling and brought up some necessities.

"Can you feed my men?" I asked.

"Of course, Walter," Heloise replied "we have carts packed with food ready for us to leave with, but... I suppose we won't be needing to do that now?"

"Indeed my lady, you may stay... but we will be preparing for... trouble tonight."

Godwin looked scared at that, Heloise looked resigned but resolute.

"How many are there to feed, Walter?"

"Say 300, Heloise, we lost some on the journey..."

"I'm so sorry," she said "have your men come round the back when they're ready, we will provide bread, cheese and ale from the carts. We have good wells at each end of the main street, hay, oats and stream-fed water will be found in the barns" she finished, indicating substantial buildings behind some trees a hundred yards away.

I bowed my thanks, looked at the First Sergeant to check if he'd got all that.

"Yes, my lord" he said and proceeded to organise food and water for horses and men by company.

After a quickly taken lunch for all, the men prepared the village against likely attack that night, the villagers being commanded to assist. There were too many buildings and too widely spaced to fortify the whole place, so other measures were taken.

The people and soldiers blocked all ground floor doors and windows, makeshift ladders to roof or second floor were made, that could be pulled up behind the occupants. My men 'mouse-holed' through roof spaces of terraced properties, and arrow slits were made in all roofs. Tubs of water were made ready against fire. Also, after initial resistance from the priest, the church[110] was manned with longbows at one end of main street and the roof of the manor house at the other end. In the church tower, the bell-ropes were dropped and the stairs to the roof weakened in the middle, so you could only use the very edges of each step to ascend. Spears were used to scrape gutters down the middle of each street and on the approaching paths. A mixture of pitch and saltpetre[111] from the manor stores was trickled into these gutters. We needed illumination to level the odds if they came in the dark. Perches up trees were made for shortbow archers, each with a squire or boy beneath them, with a spear for defence.

The barns themselves were fortified as best we could, with two Walden companies under Sergeant Jacot guarding them, in case the enemy went out that way. Just before dusk, some inquisitive deer nibbled at the vegetation in the back gardens near the church and ended up in the manor kitchens for the hot stew that would be served later with fresh bread.

While these preparations were in hand, I took barley tea in the manor parlour with the Kanewellas, to delicately enquire... why they were still alive? "We were greatly concerned, Walter," replied Heloise "we had heard all the stories of these... devils and feared the worst. They seemed somewhat divided amongst themselves, at least two claimed to be 'The Duke of Ipswich', which was obvious nonsense but... all seemed very wary of Haverhill and wished to hold Kanewella 'by right'. They treated us better when we said we were related to you, Walter. Hope that was all right?"

"Of course," I replied, "did you hear anything else about them?"

---

[110] Norman church towers were all flat-topped. Spires are later additions.

[111] Potassium or sodium nitrate, used as a food preservative or fertiliser and, in later times, for gunpowder.

"Our maids heard talk of plans to take Dunmowe next year…" said Godwin. A cold hard fury settled deep within me. With those few words, these creatures had sealed their fate. This was the tipping point, the start of the loss of my lands or the strengthening thereof. If I had been wondering how to leave this, there was only certainty now. This poison must be cut out, the cult exterminated.

Heloise and Godwin must have seen a change in me, because they went very quiet. I steadied my breathing and spoke.

"We believe they will come tonight, probably after midnight. They don't know for certain who we are, or our numbers, but they can't advance further without dealing with us…"

I paused, with them still staring wide-eyed.

"We know they are Satan-worshippers, presided over by one they call 'The Black Bishop of Dedham'…" more gasps from the couple. "But is Dedham a valley as I've been told, or…?" I asked.

"It is both a shallow valley and a village Walter," said Heloise "the village is at the far end of the valley, next the River Stour and not far from the sea." She closed her eyes to remember more…

"The whole land was razed by The Conqueror, in revenge for the rebellion of a Saxon Earl. Our local legend has it that William stayed in Kanewella for a couple of days and he is oft'quoted as saying he wanted to 'burn that valley back to the Stone Age'… He then gave our village enough money for a church."

"That place has been without governance ever since," added Godwin, "a nearly empty expanse but with lush land and grazing. We hear the few people who live in there complain about taxes, and boats have to pay tolls each way to navigate the Stour… but no one knows where the money goes…"

"I think we can guess…" I said. The First Sergeant knocked and was called in to give his report.

He bowed to the Godwin and Heloise and slightly deeper to me, and I gestured him to begin.

"All men fed again and half on watch my lord. Flint and steel[112] are ready on all roofs. Your er… property is in the biggest barn, helping with the horses. We've heard those horns going a lot already sir, so looks like it's on tonight."

"Thank you, First Sergeant, keep the watches going until Vigil[113] then all stand to. Keep in mind the bells here will not be ringing, as Rolfe took the ropes down. You'll have to keep your ears open for churches nearby. I will be on the roof here."

"Very good sir, I'll be in the big black and white house in the middle of the village, you'll hear me from there."

I nodded and he bowed his way back out of the room.

"Property..?" enquired Heloise, "Helping with the horses?"

"A long story" I replied with a finality that discouraged further discussion of that matter.

"Where should we be?" asked Godwin nervously.

"Do your cellars have... secret tunnels? To the forest?" I asked.

They exchanged a glance and Heloise answered, "Yes Walter."

"Then be down there, and make sure all females are armed, the devils only fear is to be killed by a woman..."

"Well, bless me!" said Heloise, as I nodded a farewell and headed up to the roof.

I spoke in whispers to the corporal on the roof, found out First Watch had just gone for a sleep and joined them in a corridor. I rolled into my cloak, enjoying not being cold or wet... and slept. Two hours later, a gentle shaking from my corporal woke me.

I drew some deep breaths, eased some numb parts of me and headed quietly up to the roof. Like many manor houses, this had a walkway behind a wooden parapet that was better than nothing. The sloping thatch roof was behind us as we looked out over the blackness of the village. We had all taken our white tabards off for the night action; everyone kept well back from the edge and kept movement to a minimum.

The moon slowly eased its way across the sky but with much more cloud than the previous night, we had less light, although not nearly so goddam cold as before.

---

[112] Use of flint and steel was a common method of firelighting

[113] 2a.m.

The faint chimes of the distant churches rang for Vigil and the other watch joined us. Silently, carefully, methodically. I was really pleased with the men. We had thrown them all together and they had done us proud. I knew we had spearmen downstairs in case of a break-in there but our killing power this night was planned to be the archers, on and in the many roofs and trees.

After just about an hour later, a couple of village dogs began to bark, and we all strained eyes and ears to find out why. It must have been a full twenty minutes later that an archer, at the south-west corner of the manor, gave a thumbs down signal - meaning 'Enemy Seen'. The boy next to him quietly took his gloves off so we could see his hands better and held up ten fingers, three times. The first company of thirty devils had arrived, silently padding down main street, looking for any sign at all that we were still in the place. There were no sentries of ours to see, no horses, no sign that we were here.

I saw tiny movements on the roof of the First Sergeant's house and realised it was a pair of hands twisting towards me, then away, towards, then away, repeated once more. He was silently signalling that they had another company in sight on our western flank. Judging the moment from his central position I saw First Sergeant strike a light to ignite a torch, that was then thrown into the street, at the junction of the nearest 'gutters' containing pitch. This was the signal for all the other gutters to be lit up, from the church up to our manor house. The devils were now perfectly silhouetted for our archers and their night-eyes negated.

Some of them tried to crash the nearest doors, but failed; others dashed for side alleys, only to be dropped by our tree-archers aiming for head, neck or shoulders. Many on main street were already impaled by longbow arrows thudding or thwacking into their lower bodies, below their protective 'armour'.

In the light of the pitch flames and the brighter flares of the saltpetre, we could see we had bagged three companies of the enemy. Only a very few of these had small round shields, and when they sought to back away behind these, it was only a few yards before the next cottage-roof or tree would have an angle to take a head, leg or arse with an arrow. The arrow slits in the thatched roofs being very difficult to see, until it was too late for the observer.

A great proportion of the devils were now injured at least and were crawling of hobbling away along any wall or fence they could find, mostly seeking shelter from the dreaded longbows.

Inexplicably, the weight of fire from the trees and most roofs now slowed down. To my consternation, we weren't killing off these creatures. No 'stop' command had been given…

Worse news soon arrived…

"Lord Walter!" hissed an archer.

I looked his way as he gave me a thumbs down and was pointing to the east. I peered into the night in that direction. Just at that moment, a nearby cottage took light and its flickerings revealed a sizeable force between us and the barns.

"Shit!" I thought to myself.

Based on earlier contacts, I'd proceeded to underestimate their ability to plan and organise, let alone keep a strong force in reserve. What I said was, "Thank you…?"

"Randall my lord."

"Thank you, Randall, watch and shoot."

Nothing to be gained by flapping in front of the men…

As the cottage burnt brighter, I could make out probably three companies of devils, all better equipped than their battered brethren on main street; these all had shields and long spears. The mass of them held their round shields over their heads as if protecting against rain, or arrows. The front and side ranks had the tall curved shields that I'd seen at Warwick, in pictures of the Roman Legions.

They were coming our way with slow but purposeful strides, keeping good formation, blast them. With these shielded numbers, they could crash into each of our strongpoints in turn. My options were few, but to nobly stand and die was not going to be one of them. There'd not been enough pitch to supply roof tops, and bar the church, there was no stonework to breakup and hurl down, so offensively we were pretty well focked.

I checked to see my trumpeter was near and gave myself one minute more to think of something, before sounding the "Withdraw"; this was set to cause everyone to run like blazes to the barns and then ride like furies to regroup at the Cranfield fort.

Nothing came to me and I drew breath to give the command, when... A pair of short trumpet toots were heard to the east, followed by a single drawn out note. Two toots meant Walden; the long single meant they were attacking. A drumming of hooves was heard, and a company of my lancers bore down the wide lane towards the rear of the devils. The Walden 'V' formation split the rear devil-company asunder, impaling some, bowling over many. This lost the Waldens some momentum, but they correctly broke off before meeting the next company and veered away right, through the sparse trees there.

More trumpeting and more hoof thundering announced a second 'V' that tore through the tatters of the last devils and smashed into the mass of the middle ones. This time breaking off left, through unfenced gardens and away into the dark. After a few moments of growing confusion in front of us, a third set of trumpet calls was heard.

"Fock me Jacot," I thought, "that'll be a neat trick if you can pull that off, you have no more men until you regroup!"

Consternation ensued in the devils. The rear ranks of the last complete company called for the tall shields to move to the back; other voices shouted to stand fast.

Enough dithering occurred to expose their leaders, as the shields turned one way then the other.

The three commanders were revealed and stood out, wearing some sort of burnished plate armour instead of the wicker type of their rank and file. The twats!

My archers had been straining for unshielded targets and they were thus rewarded with brilliant aiming marks, reflecting the flames of the now fully alight cottage. Turned out that metal was no match for a bodkin-tip from a war-bow. Some very satisfying thuds were heard as the devil-leaders went to their Valhalla.

Now, with no warning at all, a company of lancers came out of the darkness into the unprotected rear of the last company of the enemy. Any remaining morale in the devils collapsed and they scattered to the sides and ran for apparent safety, many to then meet a shaft from above. This time, my lancers ploughed straight on to near the manor house, before turning around, forming up, charging again, thus sweeping away any stragglers before disappearing in the direction of the barns. Their quiet progress now explained by sight of tabards double-wrapped around their horses' hooves and secured with twine.

A relative quiet now fell across the conflict.

I sensed the moment, took another chance and ordered "Sally"[114] to be trumpeted. My spearmen and swordsmen now raced down their ladders onto their main street and set upon the small groups of devils still trying to withdraw in good order. Wounded were dispatched with no quarter given.

I allowed only a few minutes of this; in case the bastards had any more surprises for us. I ordered "Rally" to sound and hoped it wouldn't be taken as a call to a general reassembly. For avoidance of doubt, First Sergeant's voice thundered over the village "Back in your boxes biccen!" Within seconds, the streets and alleys were clear and only sporadic wizzes and thwacks could be heard as the longbows claimed the last of their victims. The cottage had burnt out and now quietly smoked; silence fell as we watched and waited until dawn. The only interruption was a distant double scream and a shout from the direction of the barns, but with no continuation or sounds of fighting, I just prayed that all was well with the Waldens and our precious horses.

The sun rose and we waited another half-hour before I ordered "Rally" to be sounded twice. The Waldens appeared from the barns leading all our horses onto mainstreet. Three companies of Dunmowes mounted up to patrol the approaches to the village. I put the Waldens past the manor kitchens to grab some fresh-baked bread and cheese, then the Haverhills went for food and so on as we alternated companies to push out and dominate the area. I caught a moment with First Sergeant as we chewed our delicious bread.

"How are they Sergeant?" I asked.

"They've done really well sir," he replied, "but they're well knackered now, and they're starting to make mistakes, sir."

---

[114] Sally as in "rush or attack suddenly" from the Old Norman/French "saillie"

"Agreed sergeant" I nodded, "I can't even remember what bloody day it is!" After some thought and finger counting, we agreed it was Wednesday. That made me sigh, my darling Azizah would be taking Manor Court at Haverhill.

"Dear God, how I missed her" I thought, with my eyes closed.

"Alright sir?" enquired the sergeant.

"Just thoughts of home, sergeant" I replied.

"I'm with you there sir... but seems it'll be a while yet..."

I looked at him with slightly raised eyebrows, so he went on.

"These fockers have to be dealt with sir, else they'll be back and knocking on our door pretty soon..."

I nodded again and asked, "Do the men realise that?"

"It's clear as day to the veterans sir, and they'll keep the young'uns going as needed."

"Thank you, sergeant, there will be no move before Terce on Friday. Rest the scout troop as much as possible. Keep patrols going out. Have the boys help with the horses and let the men catch what sleep they can. Three watches will do tonight unless our... visitors return. Also send out strong hunting parties, it's not a Royal forest so any deer or pigs will do."

"Very good sir, thank you sir" he said as he bowed and began to move away to implement my instructions when something occurred to me.

"How are we for shortbow arrows, sergeant?"

"Good sir, but... there was a cockup yesterday, only a quarter of the spares came off the carriers, so the archers were expecting a resupply... that never came. Longbows were stocked well, thank god!"

"Indeed First Sergeant, I think we need a corporal or sergeant-of-archers, to watch for things like that."

"Yes sir, I will look for any suitable men to suggest."

He bowed again and walked briskly away. Next, I requested Sergeant Jacot to report to me. He appeared looking very tired, strained and uncertain of himself.

"You called my lord" he said as he bowed.

"Indeed Jacot," I replied, "how are your men today?"

"Tired and hungry sir, but I hear we will have time to recover, God willing. I think they did well last night..."

"Sergeant Jacot," I interrupted, "you and your men did an excellent job last night, the three actual charges and the feinted one on the enemy reserve force were exceptional in concept and execution!"

"Th... Thank you sir," he said as his face lit up, looking most relieved, "I will pass your words to the men."

"Is my... property still alive?"

"She is sir, in fact, it was she who suggested the muffling of the hooves for that last attack..." he confirmed, while looking slightly puzzled at something, then went on "She also... intercepted two devils who had snuck into the main barn, getting them in one thrust with a large pitchfork while shouting 'That hurt fockers?'. Some other devils ran away when they heard her voice. The men seem to really like her sir..." he finished with a very confused look on his face. I believed his organised Norman mind had women in the kitchen with the children and men doing the farming and fighting. Clearly, he had not been around our Lady Azizah very much, and so missed seeing her many abilities.

"Ahhh..." I said, "we wondered what those screams were, late in the night..." He nodded then asked, "Orders sir?"

"Rest the men as much as possible, see the First Sergeant for patrol and watch duties, and Jacot..."

"Yes, my lord?"

"Delegate more, find at least a couple of men per company to try out as corporals. You won't be right every time, but some men... grow into responsibility, once they have it. If you approve them at that rank, my Marshal or I will confirm it."

He nodded, somewhat ruefully, in recognition of that need.

"I will sir and thank you sir" he said.

"Carry on with your duties sergeant and send Linza to join me at the front of the manor."

"Yes, my lord" he said, as he bowed and turned away.

I'd just seen a tired-looking Lady Heloise approaching and needed to ask a favour.

"Good morning Walter, very pleased to see you safe and well."

"Same to you Heloise" I replied.

"It all sounded terrifying last night. Did you win? Did you lose many?"

"We won the battle, Heloise, but the campaign has to go on until

they are... exterminated. There'll be no peace til they are gone..."
"Indeed Walter, thank you again for everything. Anything the village can do for your men, will be done."
"Ah..." I said, "there is one extra thing I'd request madame."
"Name it Walter."
I nodded in the direction of the approaching girl "Can you... take care of Linza for me, she was a... gift, from somewhere we stayed a few days ago."
"Oh the 'property'?" said Heloise
"Yes" I smiled.
Linza stopped a couple of yards away and gave us both a small bow. She was still begrimed and trailing a slight dusty haze behind her. It was Heloise's turn to say "Ah... hello Linza, let's get you cleaned up a bit."
Heloise clapped her hands and three maids came out of the manor house.
"This is Linza," said Heloise, "make her welcome, take her round to the kitchen back door and get the big tub out. Tell cook you're to have lots of hot water, soap, apple vinegar, ginger... mmm... and beeswax and the... special comb."
"Yes, my lady" they chorused as they curtseyed to her and myself, then beckoned to Linza to follow them.
They departed and Heloise turned back to me, raised an eyebrow and said," As you're not infested too Walter, I guess you didn't scratch that particular itch eh?"
"Heloise!" I said, genuinely surprised at the suggestion.
She laughed and said gently, "Walk with me Walter."
We went around the back of the manor, hearing girlish squealing and some splashing coming from somewhere nearby. A maid appeared in sight, holding a long pole with a tattered and dusty black dress hanging from the end; she dropped the garment onto a small bonfire that was burning at the back of the yard, well away from the house. Then she turned round and appeared to gasp as she resumed her breathing.
Heloise led the way along a path, through the tree-line at the back of the manor yard, and we stepped out into a huge vegetable garden, extending away from us, up a gradual south-facing slope.
"Nothing much in season at present I'm afraid Walter, but later in

the year, this is a lovely place..." she said, then changed the subject rather. "We hear great things of your Lady Azizah, Walter..."

"Yes, she is truly wonderful" I agreed.

"Mmmm, indeed, the echoes of your... happiness have reached even here" she said through some giggles. I had no reply to that!

"But to be true, her influence has spread far further than your swiving sounds!" she went on. My eyebrows shot up but again, I had no riposte.

"Your Lady's standards for commercial and legal matters have improved the lives of **all** folk in the eastern lands. They no longer tolerate poor goods or services from merchants or tradesmen. Anyone cheating or short-changing is threatened with 'Azizah's Law', even when clearly not in her jurisdiction. When a miscreant claims immunity by that fact, a crowd gathers and chants 'Ah-Zee-zah, Ah-Zee-zah' until the perpetrator gives in!"

I was deeply moved, and my face showed it, "I will be sure to tell her, thank you Heloise" I said.

She went on "Her stables and horse-breeding are well-known too. That Diablo of hers has quite a reputation with the mares and... many husbands round here tell their wives that their man is 'feeling like Diablo tonight'!"

She paused and sighed... "I wish Godwin was a little... sprightlier... I'm very fond of him and he does try but he likes his food and especially his wine, quite a bit too much... And... talking of such matters, our son is thriving thank you Walter"

I gasped, "Is he really... ours!"

"Ohhhh yes," said Heloise "no doubt at all Walter! I felt... odd... different... the day after I got back from Haverhill and the other changes... blossomed from then on. Of course, Godwin thinks it's his, but he had his chances... and... talking of chances, I'd like another sometime. So... if I'm not with child by next year, perhaps I could... visit Haverhill again?"

"Heloise!" I gasped again, but louder this time, "What are you thinking?"

"What I'm wondering is... how much will your dear Lady charge me... to put **you** to stud?" and she laughed until tears came. Laughing at my face I think, because she seemed goddam serious about the 'stud fee'!

She regained her breath and said "In fact, I may just write to her and ask her if she can spare any... seed. Because rumour has it that the poor woman is in receipt of a goodly quantity, and I'm sure she could leave... a planting or two for me!" and promptly dissolved into peals of new laughter. I slapped my forehead in confusion, said "Enough Heloise!" and stomped off back to the manor, my men and a more familiar, if harsher, world.

As the day went on, the village became a nest of support for my men and horses; we were a large enough group of customers to cause an informal market to spring up as farmers and traders got wind of a sales opportunity. And any oven of any size in the village was baking bread day and night.
The patrols reported no contact with the enemy, and nothing seen of them; this continued through the night.
A funeral was held at noon that next day, with all the villagers attending with my soldiers, although the Waldens were, of necessity, out on watch. Lord Godwin spoke well at the service and promised headstones with battle honours for all the new graves. We had lost eighteen dead from the two skirmishes, our only consolation being the vastly greater losses inflicted on the enemy. We didn't bother counting but I estimated it was more than 100 of the possibly 200 committed by the enemy. They would have wounded to contend with as well. The villagers needed many cartloads to take away the corpses. They were dumped in a common pit, with lime spread over them, and there was no service or prayers said for Satan's followers. Anything of value was stripped from the corpses and shared among the manor-folk. I did order twenty sets of devils' clothing, wicker armour and some shields to be loaded on our packhorses, just in case.

By the end of the Thursday afternoon, everyone was looking in much better condition, as I walked the length of the main street, checking the state and morale of all the companies.
Arriving at the manor once more, I saw Heloise walking towards me, looking somewhat contrite; I nodded and started the conversation on a safe topic... "The damage to the village and church, madame, we will certainly pay for all that and for the food provided by

yourself, just name your price?"

"Oh goodness Walter," she replied, "think nothing of it, we are very thankful to you and your men, and we are fully mindful of the sad losses you have suffered." She thought for a moment and continued "I must apologise if you thought I was disrespecting your feelings for your lady yesterday; she clearly means much to you..."

"She is truly my heart and my soul" I replied.

"I fully understand" she said with all seriousness. Then a twinkle came into her eye and a smile flickered on her lips.

"But I don't need your soul Walter, and I don't seek your heart..." Then she curtseyed as if to leave and I gave her a small bow in response. As she passed me, she lilted quietly...

"Just your cock would nicely do, only for a minute or two!"

She walked on towards the little market, humming her new little ditty to herself and giggling.

Shaking my head, I walked on to the manor, hoping to find some cider there. At the front door I saw a girl playing with or perhaps teaching a pair of young Alaunts[115], one a light tan, the other black as the jet gemstone. The girl had her dark fair hair cut unusually short and wore a man's tunic, hose and some maid's slippers.

"You girl," I said, "what job do you do here?"

She stood and bowed a little awkwardly, replying

"No job at all, lord" she replied with a lovely smile.

It took a moment or two to remember where and when I'd heard that accent before; then I looked in her deep blue eyes, saw the full and luscious mouth.

"Linza?" I asked.

"The same lord, but not the same."

"Good God!" I thought, "She has cleaned up well, the black hair must have been from years of soot and dirt in that cottage but great goodness... she can't be more than fifteen! She looked like a pixie with that short hair but the way those clothes fitted her..."

---

[115] An extinct Mastiff-type dog breed that lived in Europe, Central Asia, and Northern Caucasus till the 17th Century. They were large-sized dogs bred for fighting and hunting, having muscular bodies with thick thighs and wide chests.

Blinking myself back to sanity, I forced myself to ask a sensible and vaguely lordly question.

"So, do you like dogs Linza?"

"I love dogs sir! I trains them for shepherds sir, and for guarding. Was some money in it too, which helped the farm…"

"Excellent" I said, thinking quickly. There had been dozens of dogs at Warwick during my time there, for several purposes but there were none at Haverhill when I arrived, I guess the impoverished garrison must have eaten them. Then, in the scramble to make the place functional, I had failed to see something that… wasn't there. This dire lack had suddenly dawned on me two nights ago, when the two village mutts got wind of the devils, long before we saw them.

"When this fighting is done, will you come with us to Haverhill?" I asked. Her eyes widened in surprise. "I have to come lord; you paid a whole two pounds for me…" I didn't have the time nor the inclination to debate the matter, whether with myself or her! So, I nodded and said, "Very well, stay with the maids tonight but be ready to leave with us at Terce tomorrow, with those dogs. From now on, you are the head dog trainer for Haverhill Castle."

Her eyes got wider still, as I pressed a shilling of advance pay into her shaking hand, and her mouth opened and closed in surprise.

"Thank you lord, thank you" she stuttered as she bowed to me as I went through the door, still in search of cider.

I left the manor as the daylight faded, feeling much more mellow after a couple of pints. Linza and the dogs had gone but my First Sergeant was waiting and seemed… unsure about something.

"Evening my lord, may I have a word?" he asked.

"Certainly First Sergeant" I replied.

"It's the men sir, they've been asking about the girl. Seems they see her as a good luck charm, a mascot almost… and they were hoping, err… she would be with us for the next err… push, sir?"

"Well sergeant," I said, rubbing my chin as if in consideration "would she be a weight for us to carry and look after?"

I was mischievously enjoying this, knowing full well that Linza was already ordered to come with us!

"I'd say she was mostly a threat to the enemy, sir, given her record so far and... I'd take it as a personal favour, on behalf of the men, my lord..." I didn't want to make this honourable man beg, so I immediately replied

"Well First Sergeant, you and the men have certainly earned your mascot, I will make it so."

"Thank you very much sir!"

"Do we have a set of Haverhill equipment spare, in a small size?" I asked.

"Sadly, we do sir..." he replied, "young Smith caught a spear late on, in the night battle..."

"The fast-runner-Smith?"

"Yes sir, a good young chap, a grievous loss to us all."

I was very saddened by that news and we paused for a moment, lost in our thoughts. I took a deep breath and went on "Have his equipment cleaned up, repaired and delivered to Linza in the manor at Prime. We'll need a horse ready for her too. All men not on watch to be at the front of the manor for my orders at Terce. Carry on Sergeant."

"Yes sir, thank you sir" he said as he bowed away into the gloom.

Heloise now returned from the village, so I opened with another safe topic!

"Madame, I am requisitioning the two Alaunts for our campaign, could you let the owner know?

"Oh, excellent Walter, thanks," she replied, "they were just strays from another village and were shitting all over my garden!"

I kept moving away as she went on through the manor door, humming to herself again!

After another quiet night, I rose from a corridor floor at Prime to find another bright, breezy and very cold day. Not a time of year I would have chosen to campaign but needs must.

I pondered how much to say to the men; some lords would keep every part of every plan in their heads, but if they went down or were separated, you ended up with an army of headless chickens... Having been at the receiving end of things as a squire, I knew there was a balance between that nothing and too much information for the simpler soldiers, who just needed 'Enemy over there, go kill'.

So, I stood on the walkway of the manor house roof and looked down at the upturned faces.

"You men of my domains, are also soldiers of the King." Nods from the men.

"We go on with our fight against the God-less ones…" I paused for growls to subside…

"To help preserve the realm, and to protect our families and loved-ones back home…" a longer pause for louder growling…

"We **pretend** to go north because we **pretend** we are scared of the devils…" silence from the men.

"Then we go south and east… to their home… and kill every last one of the evil bastards!"

Huge cheers ensued.

I shook hands with Godwin and Heloise at the manor house door.

"Good speech Walter!" said Godwin enthusiastically, "Almost made me want to join you!"

"Thanks Godwin," I replied, "but we need you here, to watch the land and be the foundation we can return to!"

They both looked thrilled with that dollop of steaming bullshit… such is life…

I saw Linza waiting in a doorway at the rear of the house and waved her to follow me to the horses. I had seen that she now wore Smith's leather undercoat, chainmail tunic, Haverhill tabard, helmet, sheathed daggers, riding gloves and boots. The helmet sat a little low, but that would be fixed at our next stop.

As I reached my horse and she walked past me to where a lancer held a horse ready for her to mount. I could then see that, although the mail hid most of her curves, it did nothing to hide the swing in her hips! The appearance of this smartly attired soldier-woman getting on a horse, caused a ripple of mutterings up and down the column as she mounted.

The clearest comment was "Who's that? Where's Linza?" On hearing this, she twisted around and with great agility and balance, leapt up and stood on her saddle, facing the rear of the long column.

Putting her hands on her hips, she let rip in her unmistakable accent
"T'IS I, LINZA OF PENTLOW! WHO WILL LEND ME A SPEAR?"
A ribald cheer went up, and cries of "Lin-za, Lin-za" were now
heard! She then took her helmet off, glanced down at the repairs on
the lower left stomach area of the tabard she wore. She placed her
hand over the patch and bowed her head. Instant silence followed,
as the men bowed their heads too and remembered Smith.
After some moments, she raised her head, put her helmet back on
and placed her right hand on the Haverhill emblem, raised her
clenched left fist and shouted
"SEA-DEVILS, LET'S KILL'EM ALL!" Cue loud cheers from the men as
she spun round and slipped down into the stirrups. For a girl that
couldn't read or write, she had just shown incredible skill with
communication. And she wasn't finished yet, with a shrill "Ayyyyy-
yip" she summoned the two Alaunts from round the back of the
manor house. They came on at great speed and leapt up, unaided,
onto the back of Linza's horse. One laid across the saddle-roll, the
other across the horse's rump. I exchanged a meaningful look and
raised eyebrows with First Sergeant.
A look that said, "Thank god she's on our side!"

The locals all turned out to cheer and wave us off.
I waved a farewell to Godwin and Heloise, trying not to see what
she was mouthing at me!
Scout troop appeared 100 yards ahead, indicating that the route
was safe to begin, and we trotted out of Kanewella, heading north.
On the edge of the village, a messenger from Haverhill galloped up
to reach me. He passed me a letter from my Azizah, which said all
was well with the domains and that we were in all their thoughts
and prayers; a very precious moment for me. I gave the good news
to First Sergeant to pass on to the men. I pointedly looked at the
messengers back, and he smirked as he handed over my battle-axe
in its soft sheath. "Sorry my lord, nearly forgot!" he said.
"Cheeky focker!" I thought.
This item had been left behind in my haste to start the campaign.
Now, with William's sword on my hip and my axe on my back, I felt
like 'The Conqueror' on a good day!
I gave the messenger a short verbal reply to the effect that:

Kanewella had been saved, we had some losses and we now headed north. I couldn't say more, in case of interception.

The chap was instructed to switch his horse for a spare and stop at the manor house for food and rest. He seemed relieved to escape any consequences of his small jest, as he bowed in the saddle and trotted away; we resumed our journey.

Within half an hour, the wind got up and sleet started hitting us sideways. All took their woollen cloaks and leather capes out of their saddle rolls and we pressed on. Third Sergeant got Linza organised into her weather protection. I then glanced back at her and saw a very pensive look on her face... she was now wearing and riding on, the worth of many decades of profit from her family farm, and I guessed that realisation had shaken her...

The dogs were given two layers of cloth scraps to shelter under and they seemed happy enough.

We kept a steady pace on the track towards Bury St Edmunds. We didn't want to go too fast, because we needed their watchers to be able to keep up! I also needed to keep to the directions I had memorised from the large painted map that hung in the manor house parlour.

I kept the scouts on a very tight leash, just far enough out to detect any large ambushes but not enough to risk tripping over the enemy observers, who I was sure were around.

I had wanted to leave a three-day trail to the north but the turn in the weather changed my mind. I needed to get us to Hadleigh by the end of the next day. This would leave us about a quarter day's ride from Dedham, our ultimate destination. The scouts had spotted some movement and were sure the watchers were on our left flank, following some waterways.

As the light began to fade, I had the last two companies, of Dunmowe lancers and archers, halt in a small but dense wood that we passed through, where they would spend the night on cold food and half-watches. We then stopped in the next copse we came to and had a party, with plenty of fires, singing and pretend drinking. We also pretended not to hear the enemy message horns in the distance.

Yes, they were quite a way from us, but they had definitely moved north with us.

I didn't have a complete plan for the next morning but a chat with Linza fixed that. I asked her how she had trained the dogs so quickly, she said she hadn't... someone else had trained them, the dogs had 'simply' taught her what they could do! I was astonished and asked her if they could do what I now had in mind...

I knew that, sometime before dawn, my 'stay behind' companies were to lead their horses on foot, head south for a mile, brave the stream to the west and come north again up the far side of the bank. Then at first light, they would charge up the riverbank to a point near us and see what they could flush out.

Our response had to be chosen in the moment. A large enemy force there would take on my men across the river and we would then leap from our 'sleep' and take them on by charging with lances. If nothing happened, I would send the dogs in to flush out the hiding watchers. If no one was there, I was going to look like a right tosspot.

We left the horses saddled all night, not ideal but necessary this time. After the 'party', we put the fires out, took our tabards off and went on half watches, so two-hours sleep at a time.

Before first light, the duty sergeant woke me and we silently mounted our horses, while staying in the trees. With the arrival of the pre-dawn light, we could see there was quite a mist around us but clearer to the west.

On the far bank of the stream, the Dunmowes thundered out of the gloom; lancers leading in a perfect 'V', a double column of archers behind, arrows nocked and pointing out to the flanks. They looked very warry indeed. Nothing stirred, so they carried on another half mile or so, lost in the mist, then came pounding back.

They slowed opposite us and at a single hand signal from the corporal, went smoothly into a defensive circle, alternating lancers and archers, facing out. All very impressive.

This earned them applause and whistles from the soldiers with me, and even at this distance we could see the pride in their bearing. If one could swagger while sitting on a horse, they managed it.

But... we had no results for our efforts so far.

I nodded to Linza and she dismounted with her dogs and trotted back to the packhorses.

Her progress being marked by a series of loudly blown kisses from the men, shouts of 'Hey Linza, I love you' and so on; to which her usual response was a stiff middle finger.

She undid the lashings on one carrier and fished out a couple of sea-devil tunics and leggings; she then knelt and let the dogs have a good sniff. She then gave them a single word command, in impossibly accented Saxon and the dogs shot out of our copse but... in opposite directions.

They were trotting fast on diagonals to the bitter east wind that was picking up with the dawn now breaking behind us. The dogs worked their way across the meadow and back, moving gradually westwards. After crossing the stream, and making their first quartering of the far side, they stopped, appeared to confer and then raced to the top of the stream bank, barking non-stop at the bank on our side. The Dunmowes moved to investigate, lancers on the flank now, archers ready in the centre. After a few moments of puzzled looking, they gave a thumbs up, for 'no enemy seen'.

Linza was now back on her horse and had moved up to beside me. "Dogs say they are there lord" she said.

I moved to the edge of the copse, stood in my stirrups and gave an exaggerated chopping movement with my gloved hand.

I could see the uncertain glances between the archers but their new corporal gave a shoot order and 30 arrows promptly landed in the long grass and weeds, near the top of 'our' bank, roughly where the dogs were pointing their muzzles; and still barking.

Another volley followed a yard down, then another, a further yard down.

This last drew a gasp of pain from under a bunch of reeds and, as if from out of the ground, eight sea-devils emerged, hands held high.

I sent two companies out to check our flanks and moved our column to the stream, keeping out of the line of fire of our archers, as the devils waited at the top of our bank.

I paused the column near the enemy and turned to First Sergeant to issue instructions. Unseen by us, Linza had hopped down from her horse and moved to fuss her tan dog. The nearest devil produced a hidden dagger and lunged for her back.

I turned around in time to see a black blur clamp its teeth on the raised knife-arm and drag the man off to the side, then a tan blur leapt at his throat and tore it out. Linza stood frozen in shock, her hands to her mouth. First Sergeant reached her and led her gently away, an arm round her shoulders. Clearly, she had not herself seen this happen before, with any of her dogs.

The seven devils remaining looked as if their world had ended; which indeed it had. I offered them a choice; talk to me or talk to the wolves tonight. They blabbed all they could; they were meant to follow us and report our location by horn. All their comrades were to muster back at Dedham to rest and celebrate a feast on St Odrans Day[116]. As the talking finally slowed and stopped, I exchanged a grim nod with the Second Sergeant, then we worked our way from opposite ends of the line of the now kneeling captives. He used his dagger on the throats, I used my axe on the necks, aiming between the bones as blacksmith had suggested that would better preserve the edge. A quicker end than they would have given us.

I then directed the scouts to carefully inspect the lair on the riverbank. They found it was made of four of their dubroons[117], turned upside down, in a large natural hollow in the streambank. Turves of reeds and grass had been cut from under the boats and placed on top, resulting in a slightly raised appearance, but nothing that would attract any attention at all. Very sneaky and very effective; without the dogs, I would have been stuffed and mounted. A long horn was found, made up of six sections that pushed together; these parts were stashed on First Sergeant's pack horse, with a 'pain of death' order to forbid anyone tempted to play with it and thus reveal our possession of it. No maps or letters turned up, just their usual shields and weaponry.

I ordered all troops to ride by this lair, to view the ingenuity and remember it.

---

[116] 19th February

[117] Local name for a small, light-weight, two-man boat, like a coracle, with a wicker frame and hide stretched over that.

A cold breakfast was ordered, the usual bread and cheese, but at least very good Kanewella bread and cheese. We then pressed on to the southeast, my concern over the weather increasing as the day went on.

The scouts were now given their head, probing well forward of my flank companies. By late morning, the trackers came across the reason the sea-devils were able to 'walk on water'; seemed the enemy had another use for his boats... On several rivers and the deeper streams, the devils had sunk lines of boats, upside down again but this time weighed down in place by rocks and stones from the riverbed. This gave them a form of bridge, just under the surface, that they could flit across but yet give no advantage to us for crossing or knowing where they crossed, well, until now.

The trackers also found that spare boats would often be stored 100 yards upstream of these 'bridges'. All very ingenious and useful to oppress a defenseless rural population but against my forces in a straight fight, not so effective. Still, I must remember to not underestimate them, well, not again anyway.

The bridge-boats and spare boats were all holed with hand-axes. A brief stop for lunch followed, which was bread and ham, for a change.

As a watery sun showed through the clouds after noon, the wind picked up and the temperature dropped.

We were now a little behind schedule and with snow on the way, it would not be advisable to be caught in the open as darkness fell. So, I sent word to the scouts to forget Hadleigh as our overnight, and to look for a village starting with 'S' just to the north of our original route. That was all I could remember from the Kanewella map.

After an hour of lost sun and worsening cold, the scouts reported back that Semer was the likely village of interest, but that it was burnt to the ground. They had found a big stone and brick building, just beyond the village that would do for our stay. I immediately sent out hunting parties, one with Linza and the dogs. With a mile to go, I put out firewood gathering parties, to drag fallen trees, branches and wood bundles behind their horses. We reached the huge building with twilight approaching fast.

You could see It had once been white-walled with red-tiled roofs, but grass now grew on the roof, ivy climbed the sides and small trees pushed against the once-proud walls. But the size of it... I'd seen smaller castles than this place[118]. There was much damage, but that looked to be older than the recent sea-devil troubles. I imagined this was the sort of place that the rebellious Saxon earl had used, back in '75 or thereabouts. It was square in form, with a courtyard as large as my Bailey at Haverhill. Stables took up two sides. Living quarters, the other two. We fitted in easily, all of us, and the horses.

In no time the firewood and hunting parties were back, the combination of dogs and archers was very successful, with six large deer dragged in behind the horses. The other archers were in the high lofts, making more irregular holes to shoot from if required. Two huge rooms were found to be undamaged and could easily be shielded for light, so cooking fires and makeshift spits were quickly made.

As the last patrol came in, the snow had started to fall and settle. A very good meal of roasted venison, Kanewella vegetables and Haverhill seasonings was enjoyed by all. The dogs got plenty of leftovers and some bones to gnaw on.

I'd been feeling a fever coming on all day and took myself off the watches for the night; I settled down to rest, not far from the small fire that was just enough to keep this whole room off the chill.

A few yards away was the unmistakable shape of Linza, lying on her side; her head like mine, resting on a rolled-up leather cape as she gently snored. Her large cloak was draped over her but failed to hide the curves of her arse, hips and waist. I sighed as I remembered the curves of Azizah, and I yearned for her so much. I then smiled at how safe Linza was, even amid nearly 300 rough soldiery. Safe once as my 'property', safe twice with the two killer dogs asleep beside her. Just as I drifted off to sleep, I noticed how the dogs would lift their heads, every few minutes, to check the room...

---

[118] This would be what was left of a high-status Roman villa from around 450 AD

Azizah was gently kissing me as I stroked her hair and neck...

Then I awoke to find the tan Alaunt disgustingly licking my face; I spat out any dog spit and wiped myself as Linza silently giggled.

"Good morning lord," she said, "are you rested well?"

"I am, thank you Linza" I replied.

We had a breakfast of Kanewella porridge, then held a rollcall and count of supplies.

I found I had lost a tenth of my force, through deaths, wounds, illness and a couple had 'got lost'. For one night battle, two firm skirmishes and a week and a half on the road, this wasn't bad at all. My biggest concern was feed for the horses, I hadn't realised just how many horses you needed to carry... feed for the horses. This also explained why cavalry was not often seen at these numbers outside the summer months, and why Earls with many hundreds of spears to provide to the monarch, always came with foot-soldiers and wagons. Added to that, the plough-horses, carrying our longbowmen, were showing signs of wilting; they being bred for strength not stamina.

As for the 'lost' men, I fully expected to find their horses and equipment at Kanewella; they would know that to keep it or sell it wasn't worth the risk of a vengeful Lord Walter. I would guess their motivation would be found amongst the comely farmers daughters that had been at the little market...

As we prepared to move out, I was asked to look at some items the men had found under mounds of straw in the stables.

I tried not to groan as the men proudly showed me their 'trophies'. I had come to realise that soldiers on campaign were like bloody magpies, wanting to take away anything that wasn't firmly nailed down. They had two very long lengths of superbly made rope that was very dusty, a large grappling hook with one prong missing and the pieces of a lightweight cart of some sort. I forced a grin, a nod and some vaguely approving noises, then ordered that they had ten minutes to assemble the cart, hitch it somehow between a couple of horses and load their bits onto it. They joyfully set to the challenge and we left shortly, following the scouts and the flank guards.

The winter sun was stronger today and the snow from the night was already melting away.

Our horses splashed and slid their way down the track; my intention today was to reach Hadleigh and advance to the devils' village when the scouts had spent the night sneaking around. I estimated we had three, maybe four days of being an effective force. If there was no way to end this in that time, I would need to pull back to find horse-feed and rest everyone; especially the poor over-worked scout troop.

The look of the land as we continued southeast was bleaker with each passing mile. Anything 'The Conqueror' hadn't smashed or burnt was robbed out by the devils. We hadn't seen anyone working the land since three miles out from Kanewella.

Hadleigh turned out to be less than four miles away, completely deserted and burnt out. Some barns and cattle sheds still stood some way from the ruins, a home from home for us.

I ordered a rest for the scouts all afternoon and everyone else on half watches with patrols out. One hunting party was sent north with the dogs and again were very successful, thank god.

Following a late evening meal, the scouts were tasked with searching the area of Dedham village. They sought the enemy home, any outposts, their numbers and activities. They were to take no risks of discovery; I would accept less knowledge rather than tip our hand. Once in sight of the devils' lair, the close observation would be led by two of my ex-poachers from the campaign the previous summer. The third one had been left at Kanewella with a cough that would not stop.

The scouts returned an hour after dawn; they looked tired and very concerned. I sent them to have breakfast and we convened in the large barnyard afterwards. To one side, there was a large cart, without wheels; I stepped on to the creaking platform and looked down on the emerging map the scouts were drawing in the mud with sticks, then adding stones for buildings and walls, with little sticks and straw for trees. They started with the River Stour and worked outwards. Turned out that Dedham was south of the river, where it had been shown to the north on Lord Godwin's map. I smiled grimly at this. As a very new squire, I had Lord Roger slap the back of my head with his riding gloves; I had asked another squire "Why don't we attack now?". The Earl was behind me and heard my 'opinion'; after the smack he said, "Time spent scouting is seldom wasted young man". Of course, he was right, we spent the time and thus saved a lot of casualties in taking our victory. He had at least called me 'young man' instead of 'shithead' which was my usual form of address back then.

With the large map in the mud complete, the corporal found a long stick to reach with and point out various points of interest. No outposts had been found, and it seemed they had abandoned the use of horses after our routing of their 'cavalry'. The sea-devils had one location for their headquarters and garrison. An extensive south-facing manor house, well outside Dedham village, had been walled around to enclose a very large yard, with many wooden outbuildings to the sides and rear. The wall was high in most parts but thin and roughly constructed, with a narrow wooden wall-walk in some places. There was one gate, to the south, that was high but narrow and looked flimsy by our standards.

The whole site was poorly chosen, with rising ground and trees not far from the walls. From those trees, the scouts had watched a midnight procession that seemed to involve all the devils. The scouts then looked at each other and I asked, "How many?"

"Around 400 my lord," answered one of the 'poachers', "they were moving all the time under torchlight so we can't be sure..."

I nodded my thanks, realising just what a problem this was. To attack a fixed position, we would normally wish to have a significant superiority in numbers. I got down from the cart, walked around the map many times, asked questions about some details.

"How did you find their location?"

"The tracks all run one way sir and... the smell my lord, it is truly sickening. You can even get a whiff upwind!" They all nodded hard at this.

"Where does the enemy sleep?"

"In the outbuildings of the big yard sir, we saw very little movement in the house. The discipline is very poor sir, we saw the gate and wall-guards were all asleep by Vigil."

"Can the wall be climbed?"

"Yes, my lord," was the reply," but only in places, and with no more than a dagger with you..."

"Any dogs?"

"None seen or heard, sir. Might be some pigs in the sheds at the back, couldn't be sure"

"Will the short-bows reach everything from the trees?"

"No, my lord, the yard is too long and wide."

"Very well," I said "excellent work, thank you all. Have a rest and be out here after lunch to hear my plan; whatever it may be." They chuckled at this and went off to find warm corners to nap for a while.

There were several possibilities, none of them completely convincing. I would certainly follow one of Lord Rogers other famous sayings: "Always tickle their necks before stabbing them in the heart.". So, I needed one or more diversions to reduce the imbalance of numbers... but not so complicated a plan that it could easily come unglued...

With lunch done, all sergeants, corporals and scouts gathered round the map in the mud. It was now my turn to use the long stick to point out the key points and the stages in my final plan. I took a few questions afterwards, mostly from the Norman or part-Norman soldiers. Then I dismissed them all to prepare their men and organise the making of some simple additional equipment. Our biggest challenge was that we would be fighting in groups of similar weaponry, mostly, so not in our usual companies, and with no time to try that out...

We departed after a large evening meal; it was going to be a long and very significant night. I made sure we rode through the layout of the 'mud map', no sense leaving that for a late-returning sea-devil to come across...

We made good time riding south from Hadleigh, by the light of an almost full moon, scudding between the clouds. Then our progress slowed as the scouts brought us on a furlong at a time, and then 100 yards at a time.

On reaching Flatford Mill on the Stour river, the scouts turned to us, reached up and made an arch above their heads. The point formed by their hands meant this was the 'Withdraw to point' if that was sounded by trumpet. The signal being repeated down the line. Three scouts then went on foot into the darkness.

They began to swim the river upstream and finished crossing roughly opposite us. Given the coldness of the water, these were some really tough individuals. The rope they had pulled with them was tied off at each end, to act as a guide for the rest of us. We waited for the scouts to give us an all-clear, then the horses waded the firm gravel-bedded river without problems, the precious carriers being mounted high up the pack-animals by careful design; the small cart was partially raised by more rope attached to its sides, to control its crossing.

We left the guide rope in place for a speedy withdrawal. The possibility of one of the shallow-draft trading boats coming down at night was very unlikely. We were also praying the bloody devils were all at home for their party, the one we planned to spoil.

The trackers led us another half-mile, to a small but densely wooded hill. The horses were tied there, with just Linza, the dogs and one company guarding; this being another risk I was taking...

The exception being six plough-horses that were unsaddled and then hitched up as an improvised team, using lengths of rope. These horses then had their hooves each swaddled with a couple of mill sacks that had been discovered the previous night.

The scouts led us on the last half-mile on foot; we had been getting a whiff of the destination for a while now, it truly stank, with a burnt pork kind of taint to it.

Everyone, whether archer or not, carried arrows, lots of arrows, I carried arrows; we were not going to run short this night.

With the full moon now due south of us, I estimated the time to be around midnight. We waited well back in the trees, looking down on the walls, the huge yard and the big manor house, just as the 'mud map' had shown us. Many devils, some with torches flickering, were milling about in the yard. The celebrations seemed to be quieting down, with some singing that sounded well sozzled.

We waited nearly two more hours, until a little after the faint ringing of a church-bell for Vigil was heard, many miles away. Then the scouts began to move. They split up and each one silently began to lead a group of archers to the correct trees to climb, or longbowman or spearmen to bushes to hide behind, and the longest job of all, escorting the plough horses and the soldiers of that group to near the track that led from the gate.

At last, one poacher-soldier returned from the area of the gate to the bushes halfway down the side of the wall. Careless of the devils to leave this vegetation there. His mate, the other poacher, had taken up position way over the other side of the huge walled property. Both had checked the positions and readiness of our forces, moving like ghosts with the shifting moon-shadows.

The archers in the trees, that could see the walkways on the wall and the gate-guards, mimed 'sleeping' down to the scouts.

All was ready.

The older poacher gave a perfect barn-owl cry, his pal gave a perfect tawny-owl reply from the far side. The 'barn-owl' gave one final cry and the dice were cast. On each side, a longbowman's helper-boy slowly stood and spread his cloak as wide as he could. Behind it, the archer struck flint and steel to light a fire-arrow. This was then nocked, drawn and sent in a perfect arc onto the respective end of the manor's huge thatched roof. The two fire-arrows landed almost at the same time. The arcing flight of these harbingers of doom for the garrison started more bad things happening for them.

Longbowmen in bushes facing the gate wall sent several fire-arrows up, over and down onto the devils' outbuildings.

A few drunken shouts could now be heard, with doors banging open and footsteps echoing in the yard.

The shortbows now joined the fray, from their awkward positions, shooting down into the yards from between tree branches. They weren't very accurate, but we were still 'tickling' at this point.

Meanwhile, a party of spearmen had gone forward to the gate, lifted the large grappling hook by means of a long stout branch and quietly placed it on the top inner edge of the gate, near the hinge. Scampering away on tiptoe, like naughty village children, they dived clear of the track and the plough-team took the strain on the long rope that joined the hook to their harness.

With a muffled word from the team's driver, the noble beasts leaned into their work and with a surprisingly loud crack the top beam came away with some of the hinge and half of the gate fell flat to the ground.

The waiting two companies of Dunmowe spearmen, the only ones of us with shields, charged the gap, killing a few devils who were in the way. Our men took up a half circle, based on the gate, crouched down behind their shields and stayed down.

Close on their heels was our cutting edge for this night. Twenty-four longbowmen, with boys behind them to keep the quivers topped up followed in and took stance behind the Dunmowes.

I took up a position just behind these archers, admiring the chaos and confusion high-lighted by the furiously burning roofs of the manor and the outbuildings on both sides. I watched as the killing started, the culling of a dangerous breed.

With each volley from these magnificent archers, at least 24 of the enemy went down. An arrow could claim two if one stood too close behind the other. Massed longbowmen were not common in our times, due to the costs and time it took to train them but, my god, it was awesome to see them at work.

Our crouching spearmen were frozen with concern, as they sensed the sheer power that lashed over them, every few seconds.

As the long bows scythed down the ranks of enemy in front of us, an empty lane appeared all the way to the manor house.

A few devil archers emerged from the main door and twanged a few arrows against our men shooting from the trees, but with no effect, the distance was too far for shortbows. In case these men noticed us, right down the other end of the yard, I called six of the longbowmen with a shoot order to take them on. The light broadhead arrows sped in a flat arc and punched through the hips and legs of the enemy archers. Clearly, I'd underestimated the range a little, but no matter, they were out of the fight.

Meanwhile there was some resistance forming among the enemy, a commanding voice was heard and we at the gate were threatened from both sides by large groups of shield-and spear-holding sea-devils. The corporal of the longbowmen called for the assisting boys to 'push wax'.

The boys excitedly juggled the small wax balls from pouches on their waists.

As bodkin arrows were nocked, the boys knelt by their bowmen, and steadied their shaking fingers long enough to push the wax balls over the sharp tips of the arrows.

With this bit of Welsh magic, the needle-sharp arrows punched through the shields; I had no idea why this worked, I was just glad that it did!

Unnerved by this raw power, the devils began to waver and fall back.

I sensed a critical moment and called the reserve companies of spearmen from the bushes south of the gate. I ordered the archers to pause, the Dunmowes to form a 'V' and press right.

As the mixed companies of Haverhill and Walden spearmen poured through the gate, I shouted to them to "Form 'V', attack left". They made a perfect formation first time, tightly packed shoulder to shoulder; I could have hugged them.

The Dunmowes pushed right and our reserves pushed left, both groups moving at a regular stamping pace, all chanting a haunting Saxon war-poem that emphasised the steady movement, adding a relentless feel to our actions.

The devils wavered, started to step back and then turned and ran, trapped by the very walls they thought would protect them.

An unexpected storm of arrows now greeted them, unexpected by me as well!

Our daring shortbow archers had sensed the battle shifting towards the gates, so they had taken it upon themselves to slither down from their trees, rush the wall, send the smallest man to climb it with a rope. That was made secure and men, bows and packs of arrows were soon on the walkways near the top of the wall.

With no enemy archers left to contest them, our shortbows now dominated most of the yard. The few enemy who tried a thrown spear or two were turned into pincushions by the shortbows higher rate of fire compared to the longbows.

With all walkways now manned by us, and the scout troop joining us at the gate, I called in the rear-guard companies from south of the gate. We then outnumbered the remaining uninjured enemy by a good amount.

The devils crowded together and began kneeling down in the middle of the yard. A loud and stern voice commanded them to "Rise and attack", but more men knelt and revealed the shouter as wearing one of those polished plate armour sets, this one also reflecting the light from the fires, as his late colleagues had demonstrated at Kanewella.

To avoid the wasting of arrows, the corporal called "Rolfe, shiny bastud, bodkin, shoot."

Our young giant archer smoothly drew, loosed and got the 'bastud' in the side as he turned and pointed an arm out towards us.

That single event sent a wave of despair over the remaining enemy. The yard was already littered with dead and dying devils. They were lying in heaps in many places. There was much moaning and groaning in front of us as we surveyed the scene; though the loudest sounds were the crackling of flames from the outbuildings and the beginnings of a roar from the growing conflagration that was the manor house.

The devils suddenly dropped all their weapons. My men herded them together, into a large mass in the middle of the yard.

These once-arrogant, abusers and murderers of the innocent and helpless, knelt and raised their hands in pleas for mercy.

"My lord!" cried many voices.

I looked the way the men pointed and saw an enormous man walk slowly out of the burning manor, just as the first flames licked round the edges of the main door.

He was dressed in the style of a senior churchman but with black as the colour of his cloth. Another difference was the mitre[119] he wore had rams horns curling out and up from the sides.

"One guess as to this one's identity!" I thought to myself.

He stopped his walk and looked around calmly, almost regally.

It appeared he wished me to approach.

---

[119] a tall headdress worn by bishops and senior abbots as a symbol of office, tapering to a point at front and back with a deep cleft between.

I appeared to go along with his play, after checking his hands for any weapon. I stopped three paces from him, looked in his eyes, which were very black indeed and seemed more than a little mad...

"Kneel wlth your misbegotten crew!" I roared.

"I kneel for no mortal man," he replied and, daring to look down his nose at me, went on "I wish to negotiate..." and fell backwards, suddenly unconscious as the metal end of my axe-handle swung into his face, just below his nose.

"Wal-ter, Wal-ter, Lo-ord Wal-ter!" chanted my men.

I ordered the trumpet sounded to bring the horses and their guards to us. This was another gamble but a necessary one. Once they were in, we would be ready to patrol and dominate the area around this awful place. To our relief, the long strings of horses appeared a few minutes later. The first scouts then went out straight away.

Leaving most of our force to guard the enemy, I took some men to check and clear behind the manor. We eased our way along the walls, keeping as far away from the heat of the manor as we could. Some Haverhill spearmen were first to the 'pig sheds' at the rear of the house; however, no pigs were in residence.

To our shock, several dozen women were chained up in those sheds. All in dreadful condition, dirty, looking starved and in tattered clothing. The smell of this place seemed even worse now.

A sergeant and some corporals went around to the large area behind the sheds, swords at the ready.

After a sudden silence I heard some scuffling, coughing and retching sounds. Some strangled gaspings of "My lord" reached us.

Together with my four personal guards, I ran around the rear corner of the shed.

And went straight into Hell.

A huge metal box stood on short legs above a firepit.

Visible above the rim of the box were... pieces of people.

Littered around and about, thick on the ground were more pieces of people, and many skulls, so many skulls.

As I looked more closely, I could see, with a mounting horror, that the size of the skulls indicated many had been children and that most of the rest had remnants of scalp and female hair attached. Just as I formed the thought that truth could sometimes be worse than myth or legend, my stomach threw my last meal past my teeth as I bent over, retching without end.

My guards too were throwing up and when the worst seemed to have passed for them, I gently but firmly pushed them back round to the front of the sheds.

I went back to my more senior men, saying "Nothing we can do here" and ushered them away.

I could see.
I could hear.
I could speak.
I could walk.
But I could... not... think.

I walked steadily back towards the main yard, oblivious now to the flames nearby. Trailing behind me were the sergeant and corporals, leading, helping, carrying the now-freed women.

I burst through a thick pall of black smoke and into the yard; my men turned in my direction.

I do not know what they saw, but they looked shocked at something... in my manner, in my face... something.

I stopped after a few more paces, waited a few seconds until I had all their attention and... slowly but firmly drew the edge of my gloved hand across my throat.

The killing of the surrendered sea-devils took quite a while, there were a lot of them. Many tried running to escape, through the open gate, but you do not outpace an arrow, however scared and fleet of foot you are.

After some time, the yard seemed much quieter, even the manor seemed to honour this relative calm by starting to burn itself out. Dawn broke and helped us take in the measure of our success. Though there did seem to be one survivor; the Black Bishop himself, was waking up and groaning.

I glanced around, as if open to suggestions.

My ever-ingenious soldiers came up with an idea, and the small cart was brought in from the bushes outside the gate.

A rope was hung from the walkway above and a noose fashioned. The 'bishops' hands were tied behind his back, the noose put over his head and the larger bowmen were able to stand him precariously on the small cart, as the archers on the walkway took all the slack and tied off firmly.

This evil man was now alert to his situation and tried wriggling and spluttering, to then realise that any struggling seemed to make his position worse on the wobbly cart.

"Black Bishop," I began, "you are condemned to death for rape, murder and... child murder."

My men roared their dismay at the crimes and their approval at of the sentence but the convicted one seemed unmoved.

I held up my hand for silence, then went on,

"You are condemned to wander in the void for eternity."

This finally produced a reaction, of incredulity and then terror, as I looked towards the group of abused women and inclined my head towards the cart.

A dozen of them howled and ran forward, gripping the cart.

To begin, some were pulling one way, others the opposite, then one became leader and told the others to all grasp the draw bar and wait...

They all looked at me and I gave them a 'proceed' gesture with my hand and they shrieked various oaths at the 'bishop'; then with a triumphant flourish, pulled the cart from under him, to leave him dangling. His bowels and bladder emptied, and he kicked and gurgled for some time before finally succumbing.

The women stood and watched his departure, shouting their final messages to the source of their oppression; my men turned away and out of habit, began to collect the enemy weapons into piles.

Word had spread of our discoveries behind the manor. Two of the corporals that had been with me had seen human teeth-marks on the body parts in the burning-bin...

No one could manage to even think of breakfast, and some retched at just the telling of the awful things.
We treated our wounded and covered up our thankfully few that had been killed.

With my four guards, I walked out of the gate and sat on a log just off the trail. They faced outwards, as I sat with my head in my hands, trying to think. We were short on food, both for men and horses, were very tired and now had the women to consider.
Of necessity, we'd destroyed almost all shelter here, so I dragged my mind to consider going back by Semer; I certainly felt an urgent need to leave this awful place...
I sighed and tried to think of the simplest plan. I'd seen a faint line on the Kanewella map called 'The Old Road', that ran the shortest route to the west through the Vale, but... was it still there, would it support carts or wagons? Transport would be needed for food supplies and to carry the women away to a safety.
So, now I could take the choice of lowest risk and swing back the way we came, on a northern arc. To go south around the river valley, with a force of our size, would be too... provocative to Count Aubrey. Although I was quite pissed at him for not cleaning this mess on his doorstep himself.

Forcing myself to act, I stood and walked briskly back through the gates. My men, bless them, spontaneously formed a corridor for me and applauded me.
I could only modestly nod my thanks and in my turn applaud them.
On reaching the remains of the house, I called Second Sergeant and instructed him to take one company of lancers and one of archers, to Colchester and acquire food for the horses, dry food for us and carts or wagons to carry it.
I gave him two of my purses, quite a lot of money, as I guessed we would be creating a 'sellers market'.
I said we would be moving to Dedham Church that was just visible through the trees, and to return to us with all due haste.
He departed with two companies of Dunmowes, heading off at a steady canter heading south; they would be doing well to be back before dark.

I was about to start organising and delegating for the move when First Sergeant whispered in my ear "Something for you to see, Lord Walter."

He led me into the still smoking ruin of the house, now reduced to piles of ash, some blackened timbers leaning at odd angles and the remains of hearths and kitchen brickwork. The still warm tiles of the entrance hall led to some stone steps, that went down to the cellars. The one to the right held some burnt bodies of unfortunate prisoners. The one to the left, was a very different matter.

With some daylight coming through the remnants of floorboards above, you could see four money chests, the same size as those I'd seen at Walden…

There was some charring to the lids, and I used the pommel of my axe to smash the blackened wood and free the shackle of the lock. I prised open the lid, and saw it was full of shillings.

We exchanged a glance, "I'll put a guard round the place, my lord" he said, as he left to go back out to the yard.

I just nodded and carried on to the next one, which was half full of pennies.

"Oh well, too bad" I thought.

But… the other two were also full to the brim with shillings! Seems that was the unit of coin in which the river tolls were collected. I had no concept of the value, or how to count this. In my tired and strange condition, I was more irritated by the practical problem of shifting all this weight, to then have to legally send it to the King, as the product of tax, tithe or tolls…

"Bollocks!" I thought, "more shit to shovel."

Then I saw something, in the gloom at the back of the cellar room. A pair of much smaller wooden chests, merely smoke blackened. I pushed the top one, which easily fell off and thudded emptily to the floor. I idly kicked the bottom one and hurt my toe.

Using a piece of broken lock from one of the big boxes, I prised open the lid of the second chest.

"Good god!" I thought.

This was full of very crudely formed gold bars; long and thin and very knobbly they were to be sure but sod the appearance I thought!

And all this… this belonged to me.

One could speculate as to origin, but with nothing approaching proof, this was going home with me now.

I looked around for witnesses and on seeing none, I spread the heavy bars between the two chests, for ease of carrying and left them in the dark corner.

On heading back up to the yard, I saw there were guards already posted round the ruined building.

I scanned my soldiers for Corporal Gregory, the one who was good with 'tally sticks', caught his eye and waved him over.

He followed me back down to the boxes.

"How long to count this coin?" I asked, having shown him the contents.

"Days, my lord, days…" he replied with his eyes wide.

"We could… weigh it sir? Would be close to the sum?"

I considered that for a few moments and said "That may have to do, I don't suppose the King will mind if we send a bit more than we say…"

"Ahhh" said Gregory, clearly a little disappointed that this wasn't for Haverhill. I nodded in that shared emotion and ordered "Not a word to a soul, be here at Prime tomorrow."

"Of course sir, yes sir" he responded, and he bowed and went back to his duties.

I wearily made my way up to the yard and waved First Sergeant back to me.

"Orders for the day, sergeant. Send a company of lancers with six packhorses back to Flatford and get them to bring back any sacks from the Mill or the village. We must have all they can find. A hunting party to go out with Linza and the dogs. Move everyone else up to the church and make good the building for the night. A half-company of lancers and the same of archers to keep guard on the manor here. Make sure they have a trumpet boy with them."

I looked at him to see if that all made sense, I was too tired to be sure of myself.

He smiled, saying "Understood my lord, by the way we found a well in one of the outbuildings by the gate, water seems good, but we'll boil it if we can…"

We shared a wry smile at that and wagged an Azizah-like finger at each other.

I looked round for my horse and my squire appeared at my side, with the saddle in place and ready to go. The lad was learning.
I nodded to him, mounted up and left with an escort of 12 that one of the corporals had been keeping ready.
I really needed to leave this deathly strange place and thus took a tour round Dedham village that ended at the very large and once-fine church.
Leaving my horse to be looked after, I went up to the bell-loft, rolled into my cloak and slept for a few hours.

I woke in the mid-afternoon, to the smell of roasting pig wafting up the tower.
As I went down the stairs, I smiled to see Linza and her dogs, cosily asleep in a small alcove.
At ground level, I could see the battered remains of the pews had all been removed and rows of sleeping soldiers packed the floor; the rescued women were all at the raised alter end, huddled near each other, some asleep, some whispering together, a couple sitting, staring around them and rocking back and forth.
I walked down the narrow aisle that was free of bodies, and out into the churchyard, following my nose.
Third Sergeant passed me a goatskin of water and it tasted really good.
"The men found a well at the bottom of the padres garden, my lord," he said, "seems to be straight over spring water". I nodded my thanks and drank more.
"There's food round the back, sir..." he finished, but I sensed a question.
"Speak sergeant" I said.
"Well sir, the men have asked, just curious like..." he tailed off, suddenly uncertain of his position.
"What's next?" I suggested.
"Errr... yes sir."

"If the supplies come in tonight, we leave Dedham after Terce tomorrow... heading for home, at a steady pace, as we will have carts with us. So, sergeant, let First Sergeant know, then, you can both pass the word."

"Thank you, sir." he said while bowing, as I made my way in search of food.

At the back of the church, a couple of large and elaborate wrought iron gates had been laid flat, each held up by four piles of headstones, with a good fire of old pew pieces going underneath. Some grand servings of forest pig were in various stages of cooking. The soldier running the 'kitchen' passed me a decent helping, along with a small piece of bread; I guessed we were now very low on supplies.

After my meal, I came across First Sergeant again and he confirmed my concerns over supplies; we were out of feed for the horses and there was now nothing for us, bar what we could catch in the forest. We both agreed this brief campaign had given us several very important lessons and we would be preparing much better in future.

With the last of the daylight, I forced myself to return to the manor and show my face to the men on guard, to let them know by my visit that they were doing a useful duty, even if they didn't know exactly what that was.

Back at the church, as darkness fell, my concern began to rise; then the Second Sergeant and his men arrived with seven wagons heavy with foodstuffs, and my purses much lighter.

We had oats, bran and horse-bread[120] for the animals, heaps of dried vegetables and bread for us.

They'd had to fight off an ambush by a large band of would-be robbers, who'd guessed their return route, but our archers had stayed out of the town and were thus able to surprise the thieves to the point of extinction. None of ours had more than a scratch.

A quiet night followed, for me at least.

---

[120] Made from pressed peas, beans, vetches and sometimes lentils

Sadly, sometime during the dark early morning hours, one of the most disturbed women had taken a dagger from a sleeping soldier and killed herself, almost... ceremonially.

Holding the knife to her chest, she had stood at the crossing, where the nave joins the transept, and fallen flat onto the floor, the force enough to pierce through her small young body.

All the men were deeply affected, young or old, veteran or otherwise. The corporal whose blade had been taken was distraught, and to be led away by First Sergeant and consoled.

We all wondered at the power of the forces at work in her mind, the power that had driven her to this mortal sin... in time, some of us would come to know more of these matters.

She was buried next to and along with our soldiers, the ones who had died in the action that had saved her, if only for a while. Many tears were shed over that significance.

I was able to steel myself just long enough to manage the 'Lords Prayer' in Saxon, which the men seemed to appreciate[121].

After a bread-and-water breakfast, we loaded as much onto the pack animals as we could, throwing the good pile of 'Flatford sacks' onto one of the now four empty wagons and the remaining women placed on the others.

We all rode down to the manor yard and I then made my way down to the cellar; ignoring the sprawling mounds of stiffened sea-devil corpses.

As instructed, Corporal Gregory had just finished counting shillings into a single sack. His work the previous evening had been to make simple wooden see-saw-like 'scales'.

I called for the sacks to be brought down to the cellar and six men to assist. I had two men scramble on top of each box of shillings, scoop shillings into the empty sacks by using their helmets.

---

[121] Walter would have first learned this in Norman/French

Early on, they were squashed into kneeling by the floorboards above, but the work got easier as sacks were filled and passed down, with grunts at the load, to Gregory for the weighing and trimming against the known bag of coin and keeping tally.

The weighed sacks were then loaded by other men, on to the empty carts, with more grunting.

I kept the pace up by changing the 'scoopers' at frequent intervals.

I had the lancer who had once been a fisherman come down and tie my gold-chests most securely. He then added more rope as a net, with handles, to enable better lifting.

There was to be no hiding the importance of these, the weight on its own *could* indicate lead, but what lord would trouble himself with that.

So, I called First and Second Sergeants down, ordered the chests placed on the best wagon and two corporals or above to be on watch of them day and night.

First Sergeant called down four men for each box and, with the rope handles, they managed without too much grunting.

After much effort from the men, it was less than three hours to complete the loading of the sacks.

Quite a few looked a bit winded, until... I instructed the men to form a line, and half-fill their helmets from the chest of pennies.

They all seemed to perk up quite well at this, especially after one of our cheekier soldiers asked, "Is this pay, my lord?"

When I answered, "Spoils of war, soldier, spoils of war", a muttered "Yuss!" went down the line of waiting men.

Of course, First Sergeant was observing the scooping of the coin, and there was enough left to give corporals and sergeants a little more than half a helmet each.

I'd no idea where the pennies had come from and I really didn't think our fair-minded King would quibble over this.

I noticed Corporal Gregory looking down at his bundle of tally sticks, rather perplexed; I was desperately hoping he hadn't lost count...
I walked over to him and raised my eyebrows.

"It's more than I thought, my lord," he said quietly, "just over... sixteen thousand pounds..."

"Good god!" I thought, but what I said was, "I think that's about right, corporal", as if I saw this much on a regular basis.

That seemed to make Gregory content, so he bowed and trotted off to get some water.

We had some sacks left, and these were slit at the bottom and lower sides to then upturn and make rough smocks for the females, to give them some more warmth for the journey.

With the money making up the maximum load on three carts, about half the women could ride on the last empty cart, the remaining ones were put on horses, behind our lighter riders, the squires and boys.

Some of the squires were visibly having mixed feelings over this arrangement.

I know I should have said a few words before we finally left this god-forsaken place. I tried to think of something, but I didn't have it in me this day. So, I simply rode out of the gate and the rest followed me.

A scouting troop preceded us as ever, and in the daylight and with minimal threat in play, were able to locate the shallowest crossing for our food-carts.

Our guide rope had been cut by some river boatman, but we collected the two halves for some future use.

Finally, we had some kindness from the weather and our two-day journey back to Kanewella was mostly uneventful. We only needed the one-night stop near Semer, even with the wagons and failing plough-horses slowing our progress.

A handful of sea-devils had been discovered along the way, all heading north. I guessed this was the least-bad direction for them; away from me, they thought, and away from Count Aubrey's lands.

Linza's dogs had found most of these, the rest were turned up by the scouts or flank-companies; though the end was the same in every case.

We arrived as darkness fell. Godwin and Heloise came out to greet us but then looked concerned, as if they sensed something amiss with us, though I thought we looked much the same...
They said that they thought we had succeeded, when no more horns were heard. That being the first completely silent night for some years.
Our wounded had as much treatment as could be provided, and all had a good meal that evening.

Five of the women had been taken from nearby villages, so we left them behind the next morning, but only after they had thanked and touched every single one of our men.
Their final act was to fall at my feet and kiss my boots...
I tried to acknowledge their gesture appropriately but again, my words were not flowing well.
Thankfully, Heloise was all business this day; a relief because I was in no mood for jesting. I'd had two nights of bad dreams and was starting to see pictures in my head. Pictures of the night-battle at Dedham; even in the daytime, whenever reminded by something, like a smell, or sound...
We were now free to take the most direct route to Haverhill and arrived at nightfall.
They had been forewarned by a messenger and the Keep lookouts saw us, even in the fading light. They lit a beacon to welcome us, and many torches were lit around the castle.
I suppose I was glad to be back, but somehow didn't feel... anything, except some strange need to keep moving... moving away, always away...

I noticed Linza staring up at the Keep, she said it made her feel dizzy, just trying to think how high it was up there.
Scout-troop waited outside, for me to lead our force in, under the Gatehouse and into the Bailey. I rode to the Keep, dismounted and handed my horse off to a stable-boy.

Azizah flew out of the Keep door, squealed with delight, hitched up her gown, ran down the stairs and flew into my arms.

I could not believe such a beautiful person existed, let alone was holding me.

I doubted my eyes at this vision of loveliness, I doubted my hands that could be actually touching anything so wonderful. But... I felt... not connected to her, even though she was squashed against me.

A doubt, a small fear arose in me... what sorcery was afoot...

Almost without thinking, I waved the carts and horses with the rescued women to be taken to the White Room, no doubt someone would look after them from thereon.

The carts with the coin were directed to the Keep, the horses unhitched and taken with the others for a brush down, food and water.

I put the garrison soldiers to the work of carrying the sacks of money up to an empty room on the third floor, there being not enough floor space in my original strong-room. Although my two smaller gold-chests were locked away in that first room.

Meanwhile, I sent my campaign men off for a well-deserved dinner. After the meal, I sat with Azizah in my parlour, but I still found difficulty in talking.

Her initial gushing happiness at my safe return gradually quietened down, as all I could produce was short answers; just variations on "Yes", "No" and "Maybe".

To avoid the concern in her eyes, I excused myself and went out into the Hall and joined my veteran corporals and sergeants for what turned out to be a long drinking session, celebrating our success, and survival.

This became the pattern of the next few days, or was it weeks? I lost track of time.

It slowly dawned on me that I could not begin to relate our experiences in any detail to our garrison colleagues, or our friends here. If you hadn't been there, how would I even begin to explain? If you had been there, you just knew. We knew, and we consoled, or maybe just... distracted ourselves.

I imagine the time I spent with these men and the amounts we drank both increased.

I was vaguely aware that some of us were behaving a little strangely but that was often just an excuse to call for another round...

One corporal could be very quiet one night but then could be garrulous and boastful the next; relating tales of achievement, even we didn't recognise... Never mind, have another drink my man...

After a few more evenings and nights of this, the corporal was found one morning on the ground of the Bailey, having fallen from the Keep battlements. The lookouts on duty reported that they saw him arrive with them but didn't see him leave. They just assumed it was a surprise inspection and thought nothing more of it. It was just that, to me, the body was a long way from the base of the Keep for a 'fall'. Anyway, I sent a note to the church about the 'accidental death'. I paid for a full burial service but didn't attend. This was very poor of me, but I just couldn't be arsed, too busy feeling sorry for myself.

Days later, we lost another corporal, who was found dead in his bed one morning. The senior nun said it looked like he'd choked on his own vomit.

"What a way to go..." we all thought, as we looked forward to the next evenings loud drinking party.

My time spent with Azizah became less, but somehow my treatment of her became worse. I would drink more, arrive back in our room in an increasingly worsened condition, shout down her gently worded concerns and use her body to briefly escape the literal demons that pursued me, whether awake or asleep.

Come the next morning, or more likely the afternoon, I would try to diminish my behavior, but as the darkness blocked my words, this made me frustrated and infuriated once again. Thus leading to more shouting and the blaming of her for 'not understanding'.

At some point, maybe two or three weeks after I returned from the campaign, Azizah, her maids and her escort left for Dunmowe. Of course, I had no awareness that she had stayed with me all that time, which caused her to miss three court days in her manor, as well as many other administrative duties gone begging.

I barely missed her, merely being briefly puzzled at the quietness in my room and the amount of space in my bed, before falling unconscious.

On her return to Dunmowe, Azizah found that one of her sergeants and two of her corporals had been drinking to excess in the village, getting into fights, with... anyone; also, they were remiss in their duties and standard of turnout.
She knew they had been on the campaign with me and this shocked her even more; the realisation that it wasn't just her Walter, or the Haverhills that were caught in this... evil storm.

The next morning, she requested the other two of her sergeants who had been with Walter in The Vale, to meet with her in the parlour. She had her maids fetch teas or lemonades as requested, then the maids and Azizah's guards were directed to wait outside. Both men were truly overcome by being in her presence, and in the quiet and dignified room that had recently hosted the King and his courtiers; but with her gentle encouragement, the whole story gradually came to light.
Each man had seen different parts of the actions and each had some gaps in their memory but after a couple of hours, and more refreshments, Azizah now had the horrifying truth.
She recognised that some parts of the account were hearsay[122] but were consistent between them, and these were men whom she trusted with her life.
She stood up, thanked them with all her heart; the men stood, and bowed deeply before leaving for a well-earned lunchtime soup.
Azizah sank back in her chair and considered her discoveries.

---

[122] the report of another person's words by a witness, which is usually disallowed as evidence in a court of law

By carefully leading the two 'witnesses', which was not something she would normally do, and asking a few quiet questions, she had established that the men who had gone behind the building of Dedham Manor, freed the women and witnessed the unspeakable horrors there, these were the ones that were now… apart from all others.

She cried for them for quite a while, mourning their loss of their peace, then went to her room and prayed for guidance.

The next morning, she called for her escort and travelled to Haverhill Town, hoping that Father Aldous was not out and about somewhere in his parish.

She found him in his church garden, left her maids at the gate and, after exchanging polite greetings, asked him for help, as she described the plight of the men who seemed intent on… destroying themselves, in mind and body. During their talk, Azizah noticed the priest was much less reserved with her on this visit, even though the reason escaped her, she was just relieved to be heard.

Father Aldous felt the care and concern of Azizah as his own, gently gripped her shoulders and promised to visit the castle as his next call.

Azizah bobbed a small curtsey in thanks and walked back to her horse, tears still in her eyes. She then led her escort back to Dunmowe, went to her room and was not seen again that day.

While this was going on, all unbeknownst to me, I was 'presiding' over Manor Court.

Well, to be honest, I was merely trying to stay awake during a morning session.

I got bored, then thirsty, so I closed that session early, cancelled the afternoon one and had the Hall cleared.

I was having a peaceful nap after a nice liquid lunch.

Then came a knocking at my door, by someone who had obviously passed the guards...

"Is that the... Earl of Warwick?" I slurred.

"No" said the voice.

"Are you... the King of England?"

"I am not" said the voice.

"Well, fock off then!" I roared, hurting my head with my loudness.

The door opened and Father Aldous came in, held up a hand to still my next outburst and pulled up a chair, a little way from the bed.

"I represent a Higher Kingdom," he said, "and a Lord above all others."

"Ha! That's a fine claim Father," I said with all the self-righteousness of the moderately drunken, adding "but could there be more than one contender for that throne?"

As this also reflected our time of Anarchy, I thought that retort was so witty, I chuckled grimly.

To my surprise, Father Aldous nodded his head.

"I know there is more than one contender..." he said, holding my gaze.

In some confusion, I sat up on the edge of the bed, too fast, and as my head spun, I threw up.

"Maid!" I shouted, and quite quickly the girl trotted in, ready with a bucket of water and little mop.

"Good grief," I thought, "have I become that predictable?"

I looked around and Father Aldous passed me a jug of water off the table. I swilled my mouth clean and spat into the bucket, just as the maid finished with the floor.

"Will that be all, my lord?" she asked.

I smirked and drew breath to say something very inappropriate to this innocent young girl.

Father Aldous was quicker, saying "Run along now, my child"

"Yes Father" she replied, as she bobbed a curtsey to each of us and left.

"My staff, Father!" I protested.

"My flock, Lord Walter!" he riposted.

"Ha!" I said, adding volume but no constructive value.

Father Aldous steepled his hands, as if to start a prayer and spoke calmly.

"Walter," he began "I have watched you rebuild this domain and others nearby. Your Lady has also been deeply impressive with her work for the people. I am...", he paused for the right word, "ashamed... that I had judged her harshly, based only on her faith..."

I listened in stunned and slightly dizzy confusion.

"She has requested my help; she has concern for your body and your soul..."

For the first time in a very long time, I felt an emotion, a good emotion, stir within me, and tears flowed.

He stood and came to me, resting a comforting hand on my shoulder.

"Come and see me tomorrow, Walter. I regret it cannot be today... I have a christening, a wedding and a funeral to do this afternoon. That is the best ecclesiastical jest there is... what we call a 'Hatch, Match and Despatch'!"

I laughed heartily, for the first time in quite a while and again tears rolled. I stood, hugged him, said I'd think about tomorrow and saw him out the door.

I took a deep breath and wondered what I should do next...

Before I had left for the east, I'd ordered the two archeres in my room be opened out and joined to become a window, with small greenish glass panes. This gave enough afternoon light to read again some letters from various lords. As my head slowly cleared, I realised there was more in these than I'd first grasped, and I resolved to read more carefully in future, well... maybe...

As evening approached, I felt a small appetite for solid food and ambled over to the Hall for dinner.

It was a fair roast chicken and vegetable meal, but I couldn't manage much; what I could manage though, was a pint of pear cider.

I was contemplating a second, when I caught a whiff of myself; I looked round for Azizah, but realised she was at Dunmowe.
I sighed and contemplated a bath on my own... 'or maybe not', said my darkness...
Catching the eye of a serving wench, I told her to pass the word for my tub to be filled.
"Yes, my lord" she replied, and trotted away.
After a leisurely second cider, I strolled to the laundry, my guards taking up position at the kitchen door and the White Room door.
I found my tub full of steaming water, and some more warming up over the fire. There was soap, brushes, cloths and towels, but no one to... apply these to me.
I shouted for attention, but no one came.
I was just about to go to the kitchens and lose my temper when a new addition to the room caught my eye. Azizah must have bought the mirror, shaped like an arch and with a wooden frame, decorated with elaborately painted flowers.
It was mounted at her eye level, so I guessed she used it to fix her hair or some other lady's purpose.
Idly curious, I walked over, stooped slightly, and leapt back.
I jerked my head around, as my right hand went for my dagger; because some evil bastard had snuck into the room behind me.
But... with another shock, I realised there was no one there.
I very slowly went back to the mirror.
That evil bastard... was me...
Not so much the 'young Lord Walter' now, because I looked like the misbegotten son of that reprobate Ranulf of Chester, or I could be a terrible twin to the description of wicked William d'Aubigny.
To my consternation, I'd become the very image of the supercilious Norman lords that I'd seen so many of, at Parliament or Berkhamsted. My black hair, long and unkempt, an untidy grown beard, pale puffy skin, red-rimmed and slightly mad eyes.

Numbed by this realisation, I slowly undressed, separating daggers and purses from the clothing. I then eased myself into the tub and began soaping.

After a few minutes, I heard whispering outside in the corridor, followed by footsteps.

Quite the largest and oldest maid I had ever seen entered the room. "You called, my lord" she said, in a very matter-of-fact way.

"I did," I replied "pour me some more warm water..?"

"Cecily, my lord."

I nodded and gestured her to get on with it.

After she had poured the small bucket, while looking fixedly at my feet in the soapy tub, I said "and two more."

With that done, I nodded to the pile of clothes and my boots, saying "Have those cleaned and a change of clothes fetched from my room – with boots."

"Yes, my lord, will there be anything else?" and I think she was holding her breath at this point.

Still shaken by my experience with the mirror, I decided not to tease her.

"That will be all, thank you Cecily, carry on."

"At once my lord" she said, looking somewhat relieved, and she scooped up the clothes, bobbed a kind of curtsey and left the room.

I washed my hair and lay back, resting my head on the rim of the tub. On closing my eyes, a whirlwind of pictures suddenly ripped through my mind.

For once, not the pictures of the dreadful things from the last campaign, but all from here at the castle.

With a growing horror, I remembered now... how I'd shouted down Gerald over a point of law, on which I knew I was wrong, but couldn't be arsed to deal with the fixing of it. So, I'd shouted more until he hung his head, saying "Yes, my lord" before leaving; and I'd made him come back to bow before leaving again.

I'd shouted at the Warden because he couldn't remember a particular number from way back in Hugo's time.

I remembered that I'd shouted and scowled my way round the fief, since I'd returned.

Looking back, I realised how empty the place had seemed recently; staff were either hiding or had already left. Was I turning into another drink-sozzled Hugo?

As a final heart-stopping memory, a picture of the hurt in Azizah's eyes when I'd made fun of her pronunciation of a new Saxon word. Was that me? How could I have done that? I slid down under the water and blew childish bubbles to distract myself from the pain I felt, and the pain I'd caused.

On surfacing again, I saw a very nervous looking young maid, standing there, with my fresh clothes and boots.

"Just put them on the chair" I said.

"Yes, my lord" she said and having done that, curtseyed and scurried away.

I dried myself slowly with the linen towel and got dressed.

Just as slowly and reflectively, I walked through the kitchens to the Hall. I nodded to the staff as they bowed or curtseyed and waved away the offered cider jug.

Fortunately, I suppose, my usual drinking partners were not in tonight, either on duty or drunk in town somewhere.

The only person in the Hall was Linza, having a late meal after returning from her latest search for more dogs. Her own dogs sat obediently either side of her.

I sat down opposite her and waved her back down when she went to stand.

"Hello Linza," I said, "how are you managing with life at the castle?"

"Very well, thank you sir." she replied, then asked "How are you though Lord Walter?"

"Fine thanks Linza", slightly taken aback with her familiarity.

She looked at me calmly, with her deep blue eyes, for a long moment; then went on in her distinctive accent,

"If sir be fine now, I'd hate to see him when he be rough."

And she followed that with "I owe you everything lord, but by my faith, you look like a shit pie without the pastry!"

Too stunned to take offence, I was amazed how that sounded almost... poetic in her dialect.

I merely nodded ruefully, and said "Harsh times Linza, harsh times..."

Grasping for a change of subject, I asked how my newly-built kennels were for stock.

"Coming on sir," she said, "we have seven strays of odd sorts that will do for guarding and eight puppies from the Alaunt breeder, who's tenant of yours at Great Thirlmere sir... the young'uns come from different litters, so we'll be able to breed from them in time... there's a couple of castle boys liking the dogs and the looking after..."

"Very well," I said "they can work for you for their lunches. If you decide to put them on our strength, let the Warden know their names so we can pay them a little."

"Yes, my lord, thank you my lord" she said brightly, visibly pleased at my reaction.

I nodded and said "Keep going with the search Linza, for more tracking dogs. We could use a couple of dozen..."

"I will my lord" she replied as she bowed and left to go to her quarters, with the dogs bounding along beside her.

During our talk, my throat had been getting more and more parched. I shouted for the cider, to have just the one prior to bedding down.

I woke an hour after dawn, with the mother of all splitting headaches.

I found myself face down, over the edge of my bed, with a fresh pool of vomit on the floor.

If I'd been lying on my back, that could have ended me like that corporal...

Sighing deeply, I painfully recalled that the dreams had been worse than ever, despite the extraordinary amount of cider consumed the previous evening.

Nothing seemed to be stopping the growing darkness and turmoil my mind, or was it in my soul..?

It seemed that whenever I closed my eyes, I would still be fighting red demons, and green devils. They would stop me rescuing the children and I was always too late to save the women, always too late. And skulls, so many skulls, piles of them, burning...

I groaned, crawled off the bed and stumbled to the midden for a monumental piss.

Memories of Azizah's concern for me gradually came over me.

I found a feeling, that deep inside me, there was love, love for her; but some... spell was pushing me back from that caring.

With a huge effort, I formed another thought, that maybe the drink wasn't helping; and promptly threw up again.

I walked unsteadily to my door and opened it, while hanging on to it.

"Maid!" I called, though not too loudly.

The duty chambermaid arrived quite quickly; a different girl from yesterday, but similarly equipped.

"Good morning my lord, what should I do?" she asked.

I just waved at the two places to clean up.

As she stood to leave, I said "Have the kitchen send up nettle tea and lemonade."

"Nettle tea and lemonade, my lord?" she asked in considerable surprise.

"Yes, now go" I said, and she did, taking her shapely behind with her, which caused me to sigh with a fervour...

I stayed in my room all morning, drinking teas and lemonades; wanting to feel a little nearer to Azizah by having her favourite drinks.

Not yet able to face lunch yet, and remembering something else that might reassure Azizah, I opened my door and said firmly, "Escort of 24 in half an hour, Lord Walter to Haverhill."

I heard the order passed down the Keep and shouted across the Bailey to the duty sergeant.

At my required time, I stomped down the stairs to the Bailey and mounted my horse. My escort followed, as I trotted out of the castle and the short distance to Haverhill Church.

On arrival, a very elderly gardener directed me to the priest's cottage, where I would find Father Aldous. I walked my horse the 100 yards to the large but plain building, dismounted and knocked at the door. An elderly housekeeper opened the door and invited me in. Father Aldous had clearly just finished lunch, but this was being tidied up by another very aged lady.

I removed my helmet, as he welcomed me and guided me through to a room like a parlour with a nice fire going in the hearth. He indicated a comfy-looking armchair for me to take and as I sat and looked around, I began to feel a little... overdressed in these cosy surroundings, with my chainmail, sword and coif. I pulled off my coif, undid my sword-belt and slid the sheathed weapon under the chair.

"Very glad you could find the time to visit me Walter," he began, as he sat down in his chair, "although I would wish for happier circumstances..."

"How's your head?" he went on.

"Painful" I said.

"Hmmm, I imagine it is..." he nodded, "the quantity of drink consumed at the castle has become legendary... again..."

I rubbed my forehead and inwardly groaned at that, not in surprise but with a strengthened recognition that I was emulating the decline of the unlamented Hugo; clearly both of us now knew and accepted this as fact.

Driven by thinking this, I blurted out another thought "I feel cursed Father.".

He nodded calmly, asking "What is that feeling?"

I paused, now breathing hard, my heart racing; this was **not** how I thought things would proceed. I just wanted some character-building Bible verses read out to me, a few 'Hail Marys' to say and be done...

I Did Not Want to Talk About... This Thing.
Just to Have It... Go Away.

Father Aldous, clearly seeing my struggle, got up, stepped forward and squeezed my hand on his way to the door.
He stepped out for a minute and I heard him request something from one of the housekeepers.
He came back in, sat down, saying "We'll take a minute and have some barley tea."
"What, no mead Father?" I joked, somewhat grimly.
"I appear to be temporarily lacking any of that." he said with an utterly innocent expression on his face.

The barley tea proved to be very pleasant indeed, the honey in it being very welcome, as I'd had no lunch.
Now slightly revived, I took a breath, saying "I'd rather face a cavalry charge Father."
"Of course," he replied, "that's your vocation Walter, your experience, your knowledge. Where you are now is new, strange and... very, very difficult."
My breathing picked up again, my stomach turned over, but I managed to say through clenched teeth
"It's... a weight... a darkness, it presses on me, pushes me back from... my voice, my senses, everything..."

Father Aldous nodded slowly, saying quietly "In naming the forces, you have taken the first step to defeating them... this may seem like sorcery... but I assure you, as a friend and as your priest, this is not a spell. It is a wound..."
He held his hand up as I interrupted to point out I had no scratches this campaign.
"No scrapes to your body Walter, but... I'm sure you'll accept that your body could bleed to death from a dozen cuts... or one severe thrust."
I nodded, as he paused for thought, before continuing...

"There is another battle that goes on, in the spiritual realm of mankind. The endless struggle between our Lord of Hosts and Satan himself, between good and evil, both outside and inside ourselves... In this battle, you can see evil, or have evil done to you, maybe many times, maybe once but... when it's bad enough, it can wound your very soul."

I rocked back in my chair, looking unblinking at the priest, a recognition dawning within me as I listened more.

"Will you accept that we see in our lives, examples of complete love and goodness?" he asked.

I nodded slowly.

"And also, the **absolute** opposite."

I nodded again as he spoke more quietly now.

"For any one man, the balance point between their... potential for good or evil can be shifted by their journey through life... none of us, priest or not, knows how to tell... if what we are is due to spiritual wounds accumulated or a change in our scales of goodness... all I can say to you Walter, is that time is a great healer, as is love.. if you can be open to accepting that..." that last was just a statement, not a question, and it led me to close my eyes and just nod my head, ever so slightly, back and forth, back and forth.

Father Aldous arranged for some more barley tea, as we began to talk gently and at length, about the day-to-day matters in our respective domains. Apparently, the gold I'd donated was enough to fix the church roof and found a home for parish orphans in the town. This small surprise was enough to completely undo me, and I broke into a sobbing that would not stop. I was crying in grief for the children I couldn't save, in relief at ones I would go on to save and for the loss... of... part of me.

Father Aldous moved his chair next to mine, put an arm around my shoulders and calmly passed me fresh linen handkerchiefs as I reduced each one to a damp mess.

When I eventually settled, a question occurred to me

"So, Father, was Hugo injured in this way?"

"Ohhhh dear me no," replied Aldous, "that one was born lazy and selfish... his evil increased through his miserable life, as he became more and more a user and abuser of all around him. I... must confess to praying for his... replacement."

"And you got me Father!" I laughed as best I could with my nose full of snot.

"A feudal lord would make an unlikely saint, Walter." he chuckled back.

"Your qualities were immediately apparent from your first arrival." he went on, "Your people respect you and, I for one, do not fear your dark side... and nor, in time, should you, young De Marren."

A gentle knock was heard on the parlour door.

"Ahhh, time for the next service" said Father Aldous, with a small sigh.

We stood, hugged, slapped each other's backs and I took my leave, thanking the ladies for the tea as I passed.

With coif, helmet and sword-belt back on my person, I got on my horse, turned and trotted for the castle. I was so lost in thought that I barely noticed my escort taking position near me.

My next conscious thought was in my room in the Keep, when I suddenly realised how hungry I was. I called the maid and shook my head when she held up her bucket. I then told her to pass the word that dinner should begin early, and to let me know when they could serve mine.

After enjoying small helpings of my first proper meal for, well, some weeks, I also enjoyed some hot lemonade; this helped to slightly dull the tingle in my throat that called for cider, or ale...

To avoid being further tempted by such things, I went up to the top of the Keep, to watch the last light fade away and the stars come out.

The lookouts had exchanged a few odd glances when I first appeared, it must have been a long time since I was last up here.

I did have some dreams that night but not as bad as before. I still had a headache on waking, but again, not as bad.

I had no real stomach for breakfast but just nibbled some warm bread with honey and had some barley tea.

I cancelled all the mornings requests for meetings with me, whether on castle or town matters; I was avoiding close contact with anyone, because my hands had begun to shake.

After much thought, I went to the White Room to ask the senior nun about this.

No one was there, in fact I had to wait a while for the sister to finish a prayer in the little chapel next door. It was unexpectedly quiet but that helped me, as I thus felt less bad about sharing this weakness.

After a brief and formal greeting, she sat me down, held my wrist for a while, had me take my chainmail and gambeson off, then put an ear to my back as I breathed deeply for a while. She looked at my tongue, pulled down my lower eyelids and looked puzzled.

"So, Lord Walter," she began, "how much ale are you drinking these days? Or cider...?"

"Nothing yesterday" I replied.

"Ahhh!" she exclaimed "This shaking is one penance your body is making for the excesses gone before... There are usually other penalties to pay?"

"I do have a headache and feel somewhat warm" I replied.

"All to be expected" she said crisply, as I glanced around the room, which seemed... unusually empty somehow. Seeing my look, the nun spoke "I sent the novice nuns back to the convent." before going on more sternly "I didn't feel it was safe for them here..."

I was appalled, and I'm sure it showed on my face; the final realisation at the proof of how far things had declined here in a few short weeks.

"Did they have an escort?" was all I could stutter.

"They did, Sir Walter, the Marshal arranged that while you were... resting."

I could only nod, thank her for her advice and walk slowly away with my garments.

I'd left my guards in the Hall, and they helped me throw my gambeson and mail back on, before I returned to the Keep.

The following days were kept busy with... not drinking, well nothing intoxicating anyway. I caught up with my letters, using the new clerk Jeffery, who was another recommended by the Warden of Rockingham. I thought I would give Gerald some peace from me, as I wondered how to make my peace with him...

With each passing day, I hoped to see Azizah ride through my gates, but time went on with no sign of her. This caused me to wonder just how much hurt I had caused...

I tried to distract myself with rides out, a few hunts and by causing much amusement for my bowmen as I tried to improve my archery. After dinner one evening, I talked informally with my First Sergeant, who was now the 'leader' of the enthusiastic drinking group – all veterans of the recent campaign.
He clearly didn't think there was a problem with the large amounts consumed, every night, and worse, he wasn't listening to me like he used to...
I resolved to keep them very busy with work over the next few weeks, keep them out and about with patrols against possible forest bandits, training and so on.

As another week passed, with no sight of Azizah, I resolved to go and see her; to at least find out the worst of things.
I planned to visit Dunmowe on my way back from Cambridge, where I had some significant purchases to make.
In preparation for these, I had used my father's teachings as a blacksmith to make many coin-like disks in the castle forge, from one half of a Dedham gold bar. Naturally I ensured my blacksmith was away at the time. The only small disappointment from the process was the silver content, that being slightly higher than I expected from the colour of the bars, but nothing to cry over.
I made an early start the next day, heading for Cambridge with an escort of 30. That town had the best and largest armourers' establishment in this part of England.

Once there, I chose a new silver-sheened coat of chainmail and a new gambeson. Both of these were higher in the collar than my trusty Warwick items.

For my garrison, I ordered 200 new Haverhill and 150 Walden tabards with better-quality embroidered coat of arms on them; also 200 round shields of the same type as the Dunmowes were using. These being faced with thin steel over many very thin layers of wood that were glued and pressed together; this kept them light but impressively strong. I also added some more personal items intended for my men.

The items for my soldiers would be delivered when completed, whereas mine would be adjusted for me overnight. I made payment in gold, after some good-natured haggling and some more shields and tabards thrown in.

The premises next door had a superb saddle with finely tooled forest scenes upon it; that was expensive too, but I had plenty of gold. My old saddle was just beginning to fail, so I had the new one put on straight away.

After a lazy lunch at a riverside inn, I found a barbershop, run by a couple of ladies; a little uncommon but not at all strange. They gave me a very nice shave, made a fringe from my, now shoulder-length, hair and tidied up the rest. A difficult moment occurred when they asked whether they could do 'anything else' for me, but it quickly became clear they were offering fingernail and toenail trimming. This was also a new and good experience.

We arrived at Cambridge castle well before sunset, this time. Lord Brereton was a generous host, as ever, but did seem rather subdued and, like me, was only sipping a glass of wine with dinner. I was able to give him the short story of my latest campaign and I think he understood not to ask for more detail.

He did chuckle as he told how my Lady of Dunmowe had changed his domain; seems a regular court session has become expected in Cambridge now. But he did concede that there were some considerable benefits from the extra time incurred. Trade had increased, more people had moved in and there was less fighting over disputes. All of this made good sense to his coffers.

Another matter he had noticed, it seemed ladies of any quality were now dressing more modestly, at least in public. "Well, well," I thought to myself, "Amira Azizah, arbiter of justice and now fashion!"

We left after breakfast the next morning and headed east. I should have shown my face at my Fulbourn Castle that was nearby, but I felt the need to press on to Dunmowe. Yet... the nearer I got to Azizah, the slower I went, with a concern, almost a fear, of what I might find, wondering if the trust between us was broken...

After an adequate lunch at a roadside inn, I ordered a rest for horses by the banks of a canal and sat around with half the men at a time, talking soldier-shit in the warm spring sunshine. We all agreed that I had royally cocked-up by not having dogs with us from the start of the last campaign and... Linza was the best thing to happen to Haverhill since the Lady Azizah!

Another reason not to rush was my thinking that this was a court day at Dunmowe, and so I would not wish to pompously ride up in the middle of a session.

We arrived at De Marren Hall in the late afternoon.

I sent one man on ahead to announce our arrival to the guards, but with instruction not to interrupt proceedings if they were still working.

I saw that the place now had a decent palisade around the large wooden building and its mound. I stopped my escort a few yards from the entrance, then removed my spurs, helmet and coif and had my two guards also leave spurs, spears and helmets behind. We donned cloaks with the hoods up to minimise any possible distraction.

The gate was manned by one of the best Dunmowe corporals, who promptly pretended not to recognise me. But he did laugh when he recognised my middle finger.

The court session appeared to be nearing the end, there was no queue of plaintiffs at the gate or the door of the main building. The two guards at that door were clearly trying not to grin at the sight of their overlord arriving in such a modest manner; not my usual style at all.

I gestured my two guards to wait outside and walked quietly into the huge main room of the building.

It was like entering a great cathedral at prayer-time.

There was a large number of spectators, all standing silent and motionless behind an ornate red rope, supported by small gold-coloured columns.

I walked softly around the end of the rope to join the throng and used my height to see the stage. You could have heard a pin drop. On the stage at the front centre of the room, Azizah was conferring with Jeannot; as a plaintiff and defendant waited at the bar before the steps to the stage.

She looked stunning, wearing clothes I hadn't seen before; a wispy black shawl that draped over the gold and black of the dress. She had gold jewellery across her forehead and gold bracelets at her wrists; this all suited her perfectly.

Azizah turned to the plaintiff and her beautifully accented voice filled the room and made my heart surge.

I cannot remember the words or the judgement, but the defendant hung his head in resignation and acceptance, while the audience nodded sagely.

That was clearly the last case for the day, because Azizah gestured to the sergeant and he began to usher out the crowd. I started to move towards the door, then turned around the end of the rope as if to go towards the stage. The sergeant was quickly in my face, but I lifted my hood a little, winked at him and put a finger to my lips. This veteran of all my campaigns simply winked back, ignored me and carried on herding out the other folk. I could see Azizah talking to Jeannot about some paper or other.

Unsure how to proceed, I took a few more steps towards the stage and pushed my hood back; then took my cloak off and handed it to a nearby guard.

The gasps from the last of the audience, at my sudden appearance in shiny new mail, with my colours and sword on show, caused Jeannot to glance up once, and then again in surprise.

His distraction distracted Azizah and she turned to see what the fuss was about. I heard her gasp as she picked up her skirts, ran down the stairs and towards me, her face radiant with smiles.

As she neared me, she suddenly realised our setting and she slid to a stop on the polished wooden floor and curtseyed low, and I bowed low to her.

"Good afternoon Lord Walter, I very happy and good to see you" she said.

"Good afternoon Lady Azizah, wonderful to see you too" I replied.

She trotted the last few steps to me and grasped my hands with hers.

I could see her.

I could feel her.

I was with her.

Our eyes sought each other's, and we looked deep into our very beings. She saw my emotion, took my arm and guided me to the stage.

"Are you well Walter?" she whispered.

"I am... better thank you Azizah. How are you?"

"I much good now" she said smiling brightly up at me while squeezing my arm.

The final court details were completed quickly, and we called for the horses to depart for the manor house.

The dinner that night at Dunmowe was excellent, as usual.

I sat next to Azizah as we ate with her senior staff and their wives. Much was asked about my new armour and saddle, but nothing at all was said about my last campaign or my subsequent and extended absence from view.

All through the meal, Azizah had a slipper that was pressed against a boot of mine, and as we handed plates or jugs to each other, our hands would stay where they had reached. Her hand on my thigh, my hand stroking her lower back.

She seemed to notice that I was sipping from the same wine serving all evening and drinking mostly lemonade.

Towards the end of the meal, I asked Azizah if I could say a few words.

"Oh, yes, Walter" she said, looking slightly surprised and little curious.

I stood up, which caused a quick reduction in the babble of conversation in the dining room, then I tinged my glass with a spoon and achieved total silence. Even the work in the kitchen stopped and maids popped their heads around the door.

Feeling now that I could reach for my words, I took the opportunity to thank Lady Azizah and all her staff at Dunmowe for the superb meal and hospitality; then went on to tell them how the legend of Our Lady's standards of justice and governance had spread as far as the coast to the east, and as far as Cambridge in the west; mentioning how her very name was used as a battle-cry against criminal behaviour in those far off places.

Azizah looked stunned and thrilled at the same time, when I bowed to her, as everyone else present stood, clapped, cheered and whistled.

Azizah stood herself and shyly bowed to everyone, as they did to her, and, I finally discovered, for a fact, that Azizah does blush!

Afterwards, I waited in the parlour while she completed her chatelaine tasks of organising and delegating the staff for the next few days, then she joined me in the room, having closed the door and slid the bolt across.

I had stood up as she entered and waited by the fire as she walked to me. Taking her gently in my arms, I kissed her also gently, but deeply. I then held her to me, stroked her hair and whispered how much I had missed her, how much I cared for her. She responded with sweet and caring words then lifted her face to be kissed again. She then looked in my eyes and lifted her shawl and hair, so I could kiss her neck and throat. She lifted more of her glossy hair, so I would go behind her and kiss the back of her neck and nibble her ears.

We were both breathing hard now, with pulses quickened.

She put a hand on my chest to let me know to give her a minute to settle. Then she took a deep breath, walked to the door and unbolted it. Walking back to me she stood on tiptoe and whispered, "Is you bath night, Lord Walter?"

"Why yes, it is, Lady Azizah," I quickly whispered, "which maid will help me tonight?"

She flashed her eyes at me and replied, "The dusky one!"

"Mmmmm," I said, "she is very much the best!"

As we went out the door and up the stairs, we began discussing… horses… and dogs.

To my surprise, she went into the guest suite that had been occupied by the King that time, seeming now so long ago.

There were good fires going in the sitting room and the bedroom. Also, in the bedroom was a wooden screen, painted with images from her garden and lake. Behind this was a proper bathtub. Something I had heard of but never seen, shaped like a crib, although very much larger, and half full of steaming water, with more in kettles warming on the hearth.

We raced to get undressed, and as usual, she won – but then came and helped me with my new and rather stiff gambeson.

Her eyes widened at the evidence of another stiff item, as she eased down my hose and all of me sprang into view.

We stepped into the tub and slowly lowered ourselves in as we became accustomed to the heat. Then we took turns to soap each other, twice over. Azizah was very gentle and coo-ing over the obvious state of my bulging 'purses'.

"Oooo Walter!" she exclaimed, "you look like Diablo this night!"

I just raised my eyebrows and lifted her to kneel astride me. She guided my rigid sword into her hot and luscious sheath. Then leaned to kiss me and caress my chest with her breasts, as she very gently rode me, making the water lap against the sides of the bath. She next sat back a little, to watch my face as she played with depth and pace to find the most exquisite of all the blissful moves she had.

I was beyond thought at this time, entranced with her beauty and obvious love for me. She smiled with just a hint of triumph, as she found that perfect rhythm and very soon, I growled as I spent everything I had inside her wondrous little body.

She giggled and nestled on my chest as I held her close.

"Oh Walter," she sighed, "have you no maids at Haverhill?" and giggled some more.

"No, I think I scared them all away…" I said without thinking.

She gasped and shushed me with a finger to my lips.

"You safe now Walter, and you good man... for all peoples."

We soaped again, rinsed off and dried off. Wrapping our linen towels round us we stood, looking out of the windowpanes; I nestled into her back and put my arms round her to crush her to me.

It wasn't long before the towels were on the floor and I had grabbed her hair and forced her head round for a passionate kiss. I had been thinking to be very gentle if we did join this night, because I had been so rough with her in my drunken states.

However, my instincts now told me that 'gentle' was not what my lady wanted in this moment. With my left hand gripping her hair at her neck, I pulled her to walk on tiptoes across the floor and pushed her onto the bed. I forced her to kneel and slapped her gorgeous arse, very hard, several times, she hissed, gasped and struggled a bit but my grip remained firm – as was my now recovered 'weapon' and I 'put her to the sword' again.

I gripped her upper arms and pinned them to her sides, so she was completely in my power, and now it was my turn to judge... the thrust and angle while listening for her noises. I took her near once and slowed down. I took her very near again... and slowed down. This brought a short burst of Persian from her, including the word I thought meant 'bastard', as she still panted in her breathing. I started my sword-strokes again, and this time we finished together, as we shouted, moaned, quivered and collapsed in a breathless heap on the bed.

After a while, we slowly crawled under the covers, where she snuggled into my arms and we slept. My first dreamless night in a very long time...

A few days later we were at Haverhill and the place had begun a revival. The kitchen seemed to be back to strength and even the nuns had returned to us.

I now had twelve tracker dogs, bought from a breeder all the way down in Thaxted. I checked with First Sergeant if Linza had had an escort for that trip. He roared with laughter, before apologising for the outburst when he got his breath back.

"Excuse me, my lord, "he said, "it's just that every man in the castle wanted to join that detail, just like for Our Lady sir!"

"I had to beat them off with a stick, sir, and sent 12."

Linza had started to train the dogs and train any men who showed interest and aptitude to work with them. This, unsurprisingly, was initially a very large group, but she was a hard taskmistress and soon whittled the numbers down to a manageable level.

I soon introduced Linza to Azizah. I think Azizah struggled somewhat with the girl's accent, but they seemed to mutually recognise a kindred spirit, both fighting females. Linza was awestruck at Azizah's status and exotic appearance but once they got used to each other, they got on very well indeed.

I promoted Linza to a tiny room of her own in the Keep, instead of sharing the maids' quarters beyond the stables.

It so happened that I was with Azizah at the door of the Keep, looking out over the Bailey; when Linza left the kennels to come our way, and Jeannot left the stables to also come to the Keep. Jeannot was reading a letter while walking and naturally glanced at the person who was on a converging course. Linza glanced at the person who was glancing at her and... it was as if a lightning bolt came out of the sky, then divided and struck them both. I saw Linza go shy and bashful and Jeannot's mouth was struggling to form a greeting. I groaned and said to Azizah, "Jeannot has such a weakness for blue eyes!" and then realised that their separate duties must have prevented any prior meeting.

I shouted "Jeannot" and he looked my way, "Meet Linza" I went on. They gave each other awkward nods and tiny bows and walked awkwardly together to the Keep steps.

Jeannot let her ascend ahead and I suppressed a smile at the lovely view he must have, of her in her tight hose, climbing those steps! They both bowed to us in turn and went on into the Keep.

I looked at Azizah and she looked at me and we both smiled at our shared thought.

Later that afternoon, Azizah had visited the Marshalls wife in Haverhill town. Her hope was to borrow a dress, as a surprise for Linza.

On returning successful to the castle, Azizah called Linza to her room to let her know she was invited to have dinner with us that evening, as she was castle staff now.

Linza was stunned but said she only had the clothes she wore, including the chainmail. Azizah revealed the royal blue dress on loan from Blaedswith and Linza was speechless.

When the maids had done a little adjustment, the dress fitted very well, and I heard that Linza's entrance to the Hall was a surprise for all. She had a natural grace about her, in spite of her shyness about her humble origins. The dress suited her colouring, her hair had grown out a bit and been lightened to a glossy gold by the strengthening Spring sunshine. She was now the very image of a Saxon beauty and brought back memories of my dear mother, who must have been very like her when she first met my father.

The men at that sitting for their meal were themselves rendered speechless, quite an achievement with that lot. They just followed her progress with their heads, their mouths agape.

The Warden welcomed her warmly to the high table and sat her next to Jeannot as we had instructed.

Lastly of course, we made quite an entrance ourselves, myself in my new silver mail and the first of the new finer Haverhill tabards that had just arrived. Azizah was in a new gown, in purple, cream and gold.

I went into the Hall with Azizah on my arm and all present stood and bowed to us. We smiled and nodded in recognition to all and took our places at the high table.

The meal was wonderfully back to our best standard and Jeannot and Linza seemed to have found a mutual interest in visiting all parts of the realm, as well as a strong interest in each other.

As my world continued to look brighter, I still visited Father Aldous on occasion. We talked of many things; the temporal and spiritual, the public and the private. On one such visit, the dear old ladies served a plate of home-made honey-oat cakes with the barley tea; these were delicious. Then on leaving, I partially repaid my moral debt to the priest, by leaving five of my home-made gold disks on the empty plate, strictly for good works in the parish.

A crucial remaining task, or obligation, was to make my peace with Gerald. He had been rarely seen round the castle, since my appalling treatment of him that fateful day of Manor Court. He even took many meals in his room in the Keep. So, early one afternoon, I changed out of my mail and other 'lordly' apparel, dressing in a simple shirt, long tunic, warm hose and short boots. With some uncertainty, I went down a floor to his room and knocked.

"Enter" said a quiet voice.

I went into the nicely fire-warmed room; Gerald stood and began to bow. I stopped him by a wave of my hand, saying, "Gerald, I have broken your trust and your respect. I must apologise and ask forgiveness, in time if needs be... However, if you feel this may not be possible, you are free to leave my service with a suitable pension." And I hung my head.

"Please sit, Lord Walter" he said, still in a quiet voice but sounding surprised.

We both sat, either side of the glowing fire, surrounded by piles of papers and some books; I noticed one titled 'Annals of St Neots'.

He coughed nervously, but began with, "It was a shock that day, my lord, but also a shock to later find out the... details of the campaign in The Vale..."

"I felt as if I had turned into the image of Ranulf..." I blurted out.

"Indeed, you had sir," Gerald replied, "but that image was his natural state, and so unnatural for you." I nodded at his very generous summary.

"I thank you for the choice you offer, Lord Walter," he continued, "but I would find it difficult to retire, I would miss my letters so very much... Through them, I feel I have the pulse of the realm at my fingertips, the combined knowledge of the reeves and stewards of all England is fascinating to consult with..."

We both nodded some more, as we looked into the fire, before he began again.

"I would wish to stay, my lord, once I have confessed..."

I simply raised my eyebrows in considerable surprise.

"That day of our... disagreement..." he went on slowly, "I... left the Hall... and... told the defendant... that we had discovered a point of law that exonerated him after all..." and it was his turn to hang his head.

"After I found him guilty, well, wrongly found him guilty" I said.
Gerald nodded silently.
"So, you have been... waiting for me to find out?"
More nodding as he said, "Waiting and dreading, my lord."
I chuckled.
"So the keeping out of my way was not **just** because I had turned into a drunken bastard?"
"No, my lord."
I chuckled some more.
"Ahhh, Gerald, my domains would be vastly the poorer without you... will you stay?" I asked.
"If I may, my lord" he said
"You certainly may!" I exclaimed, as I stood, reached for and shook his hand.
We then bowed to each other and I took my leave.

Unknown to me, my reconciliation with Gerald had come not a moment too soon; because the very next day brought a Kings messenger, with a couple of scrolls, just for me.
It had been weeks ago that I had instructed the Warden to write to King Stephen, summarising our campaign in the Vale of Dedham and revealing the huge sum of money that had been taken in his name, from the river tolls and other impositions on the people.

The eventual reply was lengthy, very detailed and simply staggering in its importance for me. I settled in my parlour, read the first few lines and promptly called for Gerald and Jeannot. Azizah was, unfortunately, back in Dunmowe for a few days
As they arrived, I called a maid for barley tea and honey-oat cakes to be made for us, I just had a feeling this would be long discussion.
Jeannot arrived first and seemed preoccupied; then Gerald came in, looking eagerly at the size of the scrolls.
I winked at Gerald and quietly said to Jeannot, as he looked off to some far horizon, "So, how is Linza today?"
"She's wonderful!" Jeannot blurted out before he realised where he was and who he was with. "Err... sorry, my lord, I was a bit..."
"Distracted!" we both said together.
"Yes, my lord." he said looking a little dismayed at his lapse.

"Understandable" I said, "she's a fine young lady, but for now…" and I tapped the hefty rolls on the little table.

I read out the first scroll, which was a very fulsome congratulation from the King to myself and my men, for the elimination of a lawless region. It went on to say, in general terms, just how important the area could be for trade, and hence taxation. It also gave thanks for the recovery of such a significant sum and stated that both church and state would be further recognising our efforts. We had, it seemed, removed the need for a Royal Army to be raised and sent for that task, thus saving the cost to the Treasury and risk to elsewhere in the realm, which were both important factors in our current times.

We looked at each other with slightly wide eyes.

Now though, bored with the sound of my voice, I had Jeannot begin the reading of the second, much heavier scroll. This turned out to be a long list of instructions and actions.

The main items were that, firstly, I was to assume the new title of 'Lord of the Vale', which was defined so as to include Dedham Vale and a significant strip of land along its north edge, to include Lavenham and Ipswich; thus joining my Five Manors to the sea.

We sat back utterly speechless, this alone was stunning and unexpected, and this just the first few inches of paper!

Next was the disposition of the £16,000 I still held in my guarded room in the Keep. An escort would be sent from London under Lord Waleran de Beaumont, 1st Earl of Worcester. He would take half of the money to the Tower Treasury in London and I was to use the balance for a long list of tasks.

First among those were the rebuilding of the Saxon forts at both Walton[123] **and** Ipswich into full scale castles, along with recruiting suitable garrisons. The burgh of Ipswich was also to be made good in all respects, for fortification and commerce.

Next, there was to be a chain of watchtowers along the coast and estuaries of my new domain, to give beacon-warning of raids by 'Northmen' or invasions from Flanders or France.

---

[123] Now just a district of the adjacent and more recently enlarged Felixstowe

I was also to oversee a recovery of the merchant class of Ipswich and repopulate the rural areas of my new domain. The people to seek for this were to be Saxon-speaking from abroad, and **not** to be enticed or even welcomed from neighbouring lands.

If any historic sites belonging to Holy Church had been taken over by others, those others would be required to vacate.

No more tolls were to be levied on river traffic.

No taxation was to be forwarded to the Treasury for a period of three years, although accounts of income and expenditure on stated tasks were to be provided.

No spears would be owed to the Crown for four years, and then numbers would be discussed.

Thankfully at this point, the maids appeared with the tea and cakes. We were sat back in our chairs, looking frog-eyed at each other, incapable of finding one word to say at this point.

I thanked the maids and asked them to fetch the log-man to revive our fire. He appeared a few minutes later and I finally saw what he looked like.

"God, he's an ugly bugger." I thought, "Just as well he's good at something!"

When he finished, he bowed and said, I think, "Good day, my lord" in a nearly incomprehensible accent, far harder to understand than Linza's. I thanked him, saying "Good job, my man" and waved him on his way, before tucking into the oatcakes.

After the tea had gone down, I called for a new round and looked at my trusty assistants. Gerald was first to find his voice.

"This is amazing news for you, my lord!" he began, I could only nod and sip more tea.

"The revenue potential is simply huge..." said Jeannot, and we all nodded.

Gerald went on "If my recent sources are correct, this is also a snub for Count Aubrey, as he should have resolved the problems in The Vale long ago."

"Pray tell" I said.

"In the last few weeks, there has been much... speculation that The Black Bishop was taking bribes from the weaker lords to his north; payments to leave them alone, and in turn, he was paying Count Aubrey to not intervene in the ravaged lands..."

"Well, well, well," I mused out loud, "it never ceases to amaze me... how the high and mighty will stoop so low, for a relatively small amount of coin..."

Gerald nodded, saying "Of course, if I have heard this, from well-placed persons, then the King will certainly have also heard all too..."

Gerald reached into his satchel and pulled out some paper, quills and a bottle of ink.

I sat back while the other two did some scratchings and mumbling calculations.

This went on for some time as I read through the rest of the scroll; this was mostly the detail of the borders of my new domain, the parts of Vale Forest that were now to be considered as Royal, and a very long list of historical fishing rights, river crossing rights and property leaseholds that were now null and void by this Royal decree. All these assets were now to be mine!

Gerald and Jeannot finished their scribblings and rocked back in their chairs looking surprised, yet again.

I looked inquisitively at them and gestured for someone to part with the new thoughts.

Jeannot took his turn, clearing his throat before starting.

"The new domain is roughly one and half times the size of your present holdings, my lord..." he began

"We estimate that within five years, the profit from the **new** land will be... three to four times more than your **current** domains..."

Gerald explained that the amount of goods passing through a port was so high, compared to a single market town, that even low import tariffs could raise huge amounts for the Royal Treasury - and the private purse!"

"We think Ipswich, Walton and Harwich can all be grown to be bustling trading ports, especially if your land includes the south of the Stour Estuary?"

I smiled wide and said, "It does!" and tapped the lower part of the scroll; then I gasped at one new thought; I would be getting yew staves for new longbows[124] at bulk prices with no import tax, well, not for me anyway.

It was time to pause and give our poor heads a chance to stop spinning, so I dismissed them with my heartfelt thanks and said we would reconvene in the morning. They bowed, smiling and left me alone to consider much.

I wandered out to the Hall and sat in my big chair on the dais.
To try and settle, or maybe just distract myself from the enormity of the news, I called for my carpenter and blacksmith. I instructed them both to seek an additional apprentice each as my expanding responsibilities would require much more of their work. As immediate tasks, I ordered a door to be put on the corridor from the kitchen to the Hall, this would keep distracting noises and smells to a minimum on my court days. I also directed that Gerald's room should be improved with the addition of bookshelves, drapes for round his bed and over the archeres. Jeannot should also have drapes for his bed. I tried not to think of his chances of having a very special... visitor to share that with.

Blacksmith was commissioned to make some brass stanchions[125] for the Hall. These were to support the guide rope that I wanted to copy from Azizah's court.

---

[124] Contrary to the myth, 'English Yew' was mostly not of adequate quality for longbows. Our shorter, often rain interrupted summers meant that the straight lengths needed were usually not formed in the trunks. Although not a common tree in the countries across the Channel, the proportion with enough 'straightness' was much higher. Indeed, the strategic importance of this foreign raw material was marked by Henry V, when he made import taxes compulsorily payable in good yew staves and coin was not accepted as an alternative.

[125] An upright bar or post for a support or barrier

The rope would be made from that we recovered from the Stour after our battle. The two parts would have been dried out and I now wanted the halves stitched together and dyed red. The result would be place over the top of the stanchions. I had no idea who would do the rope work, I just told them to make it so.

Over the next day or so, the rest of my ordered items came in from Cambridge. The new shields went to the armoury stores, and the various campaign badges were now completed for awarding to the men. My old 'Warwick' mail and gambeson had been repaired and improved.

The next Haverhill court day arrived, and I was surprised how much difference was made by the small changes. The extra distancing of the plaintiff and defendant from the spectators seemed to increase the discomfort of the liars and the guilty. The audience was much quieter, more respectful of the proceedings behind the new and very stately-looking rope and metal barrier. The red of that now happily matching the curtains at the sides of the dais. The closed door to the kitchen corridor was a big improvement too.

On my next visit to Dunmowe, I had a glorious day out with Azizah and her latest acquisitions. She had taken on a couple of falconers from a Northern shire and was showing a keen interest their trade. A new house had been built for the men, in Dunmowe village. Also new, was an extensive mews[126] for the birds and a huge barn-like structure for part of the training of young birds and new handlers.

Azizah was delighted at her progress with a young kestrel, and she successfully cast off the bird to bring down pigeons.
For my part, I was astonished to see the gyrfalcons[127] put up by the falconers against herons. These men were some of the most sun-browned and weather-beaten I had ever seen.

---

[126] A wooden building, usually consisting of partitioned spaces with perches, designed to keep tethered birds separated

Even their faces resembled their charges, with curved noses and small bright eyes.

My lady was wearing very practical brown leather tunic, breeches, boots and hat but still managed to look incredibly attractive.

Typical of her, she had won over these dour countrymen, with her keenness to listen and learn. Her guards, however, were not so easily won over to these incomers and kept a very close eye on Their Lady.

We had a very special day out; the flight of the birds high above causing me and Azizah to share meaningful glances at the reminder of the choice she'd had to make.

Also, significantly, the taken prey helped feed the manor and some of the village.

---

[127] The largest of the falcon species, is a bird of prey. The abbreviation gyr is also used.

Tuesday 5th May 1142, Haverhill Castle

This Spring day dawned bright and mild, putting a smile on my face as I viewed *some* of my lands from the top of the Keep. I sighed in a contented way, when I thought back to a time when I could see *all* that I owned from here.

I also reflected that I knew my darkness was still in me, somewhere, but was… smaller and now pushed back by new strength. I accepted its presence and at least partly understood it, but no longer feared it.

I breathed in some more fresh air and thought,

"Such a lovely day, a perfect one for surprise inspections of all parts of my castle."

As I left the Keep to begin a review of the stables, I saw Azizah walking towards me from the White Room and felt a wide smile appear on my face; I felt such joy at the sight of her! She was eagerly smiling too but with some uncertainty in her eyes, most unusual for my princess…

Off to my left a solitary horseman entered the Bailey from the Gatehouse and was announced loudly by the tower-guard: "One rider, a Kings Messenger".

He saw me and made as if to approach, but I waved him away to the Hall. The Kings wishes could wait, I wanted to talk to My Lady.

She came to me, took both my hands in hers, looked up into my eyes, and drew breath to tell me her news.

Thanks for buying this book, I very much hope you enjoyed it. Please leave a rating and review if you can.

My contact details for feed-back are:

Follow Rod Banks on Twitter: **@rod_banks_auth**
Email: **rod_banks_writes@yahoo.com**

For a change of pace, have a look at my collection of short Steamy Romance stories, search for 'Flights of Fantasy' and 'Rod Banks'.

Printed in Great Britain
by Amazon